-a Finder's Keepers mystery-

WICKED
DISREGARD

Prologue

The black fog enveloped her mind but soon evaporated like a mist lifting. She tried to move. Her arms ached. Scratches and cuts covered the hands bound in front of her. The confining space closed in around her. The fear in her heart escalated. Beads of sweat dripped into her eyes. The odor of fuel and oil surrounded her. Her legs cramped, her muscles hurt as if she'd been beaten.

The child lay still for a moment. *What did I do wrong?* She thought about her daily trek to school. She never suspected. She and her friends had not been warned. A predator hunted nearby. Usually, she walked with Nancy but yesterday she'd been late and made the journey alone.

The roar of the engine ceased. Forward momentum stopped. Hope invaded her thinking. A car door slammed. The sound of footsteps infiltrated the darkness inside the trunk. She held her breath. Fearful anticipation filled her as the lid began to lift.

Tears flowed freely down the girl's face. "Let me go! Please. I won't tell."

"Shut up." He grabbed her. The brute set her on her feet. Her legs buckled. The man circled her arm with one hand. He dragged her around the back of the car and untied her hands. She managed to force her limbs to cooperate. Her slender legs kicked at his shins. He shook her so hard, her head snapped back.

The girl tugged her arm. His hold never slackened. She kicked again. She tried to scratch the hand that took her. Her scream hurt even her ears. Her captor slapped her, his open palm leaving a hot stinging sensation across her lower jaw. "Let me go!"

He laughed. They moved toward a circular stone-walled structure. The girl dared to fight harder. She yanked her body every which way, slipping on damp, broken pavement. Her gaze flew to his face. He pushed her against the wall. The cold from the stone wall seeped through her jeans. *What is this?*

The man's grip tightened on her arm as he swung her to face the deep, black hole. *It's a well!* His other hand reached for a rope. The scratchy hemp hung from a round log bracketed between upright posts standing on two sides of the well. She twisted away from him using her feet to leverage her- self against the stone. His grip released but he used his body to imprison her. Escape was futile.

She glanced down into the depths before her. "No. Don't drop me in." She checked out her surroundings. She yelled for help, taking a deep breath to fill her lungs again. She remem- bered the instruction her voice coach taught her. She screamed again, a little louder. He didn't care. He wrapped a rope around her torso. The knot at her waist bit into her spine.

The kidnapper released her. He grabbed the handle for the winch used to lower the rope. She tried to reach behind to untie herself. The corded strands were strong, course, and scratched her skin. Her arms weren't long enough.

The brute turned the handle. Her body was pulled closer to the well, then up. He set her on the edge of the wall and the struggling stopped. She didn't want to fall. He pushed. She dan- gled in mid-air. Her screams escalated but they seemed to be in the middle of a large vacant field. She screamed louder. "Let me go! Let me go!"

Her body began its descent into blackness. She was falling. The darkness grabbed at her, wrapping tenta- cles around her body and her head. It pulled her into the abyss, enveloping her like the coils of a snake. Her screams echoed from the dank walls. Her eyes adjusted slowly as the ground below seemed to advance toward her. She gazed up but now a round piece of sky was the extent of any light source. His face leaned over the edge. "Untie the rope."

"I can't." Her feet slipped out from under her. She fought for balance. "Don't leave me here." Tears cascaded down her cheeks.

"Do it." He yanked on the braided fibers swinging her in the air again. "I'll shoot you."

She struggled, her hands managed to move the rope a few inches around her torso. She tugged again. Her fingers grabbed the knot. She worked the twisted hemp un-til the knot released. She wanted to grab the life line as it disap-peared over the rim of the wall above her. *He's going to leave me here. All alone.* Her tears turned into a bawl. "No! You can't do this!"

Silence. She screamed, "Get me out of here!" The sound echoed around her but seemed to go nowhere. "Help me! Someone!" She raised her screams a decibel higher.

"Shud up." Someone sniffed and then sneezed. The girl jumped, her trembling body took a step backwards.

The person sniffed again. The girl blinked. "Who are you? Where ...?"

"Don't do no good screaming. I know."

The girl's eyes followed the sound. She spotted a body, scrunched against the earthen wall. She swiped at the moisture clinging to her eyelashes. "How long you been here?"

"Four days." Her voice contained little emotion. "What're you? Twelve?"

The preteen hiccoughed. She cleared her throat and took a step toward the other girl. "Yeah. Why is he doing this?"

The other one laughed. The sound held more contempt than joy. "Can't you guess?" She altered her position a little. "Might as well sit down. You're gonna be here a while."

This time the tears flowed freely down the girl's face. She stepped to the opposite wall. As she looked for a dry spot, she spotted its beady eyes shining from the darkness before she caught sight of the rodent. She screeched. The sound could tumble walls if they'd been made of something other than the earth itself.

"You'll come to think of him as a friend soon. Sit over

here. He won't come any closer as long as you don't fall asleep." The older girl pointed to the bite marks on her arms and legs. "We can help each other now."

Chapter One

Christine roamed through her compact yard. Leaves littered the ground in profusion making it difficult to see the green hue of the grass underneath. Wriggling her nose, the crisp, cold air circulated around her and Chief. "Pretty soon, we'll bundle in lots of layers for these long walks we're used to." She reached her hand out to pat the animal, her constant companion, but quickly returned them to the pockets of her short jacket. The dog glanced at her for direction, his tail wagging. "Yeah, I hear ya. You wear layers all the time." She giggled when Chief appeared to nod his head in response.

The walk that morning gave Christine, an investigator by trade, a chance to think about the phone call she'd received yesterday. The woman seemed frantic to the point of hysteria so she'd arranged a time and a place to meet. Since she'd been stalked by a killer for a few months, she met potential clients away from her office. The only way they could contact her was by phone.

"Chief, we need to get ready for our appointment with Sylvia Anderson." The dog looked at her. "Yeah, I know. I'm the one who has to hurry." The animal, her search and rescue companion, moved toward the back door. Her little home, situated near a major park in one of the city's more established residential areas, was a sanctuary most of the time. Christine chuckled.

"You're smarter than a dog should be." She followed behind the 125 pound German shepherd.

Christine took a second remote from her pocket and disarmed her security system. She unlocked her back door and stepped inside. Chief wove his body around hers to gain access to the kitchen area. He lifted his head, sniffed and took a step toward his water bowl. Christine monitored his body language closely to determine if her home stayed safe. She relied on her canine for more than search and rescue. He was her protector and a partner in many ways. The dog broke the ice when she encountered a scared child who'd been mistreated by the adults in his life. Kids loved Chief and he was gentle with them.

She opened the door to her refrigerator and grabbed a container of water. She snapped off the seal on the top, twisted the cap off and gulped a long swallow. "We're going to start carrying a water bottle with us when we hike. The distance is getting longer each time." Christine swallowed another mouthful. Chief looked up from the water bowl he'd quickly emptied. Water dripped from his chin but his eyes gleamed with understanding. His tail waged back and forth. He dipped his head for another slurp, a whine indicating he was still thirsty.

Christine used her bottle to fill his dish again. A glance at the clock told her she needed to move if she wanted to arrive for the appointment on time. She walked swiftly toward her living room and the hall to her bedroom.

Samantha was the name of the girl Mrs. Anderson spoke about. *Sounds like a runaway to me but the mother refused to accept that explanation for her daughter's disappearance two, now three days ago.* Christine stripped out of her running clothes and stepped into the shower.

She let her mind wander as the hot water pummeled her shoulders and neck. Jeremy Goodman's face filled her subconscious. Dimples erupted every time he laughed. His eyes sparkled some of the time. However they became dark and cloudy if he thought she made a bad decision or risked her life.

She used her bath sponge to swipe the thought from her brain. He doesn't have the right to control the steps I take to find a missing child. I rent space from him. Nothing more. She made quick work of the shampoo in her hair, rinsed off and stepped onto the bathmat. Grabbing a towel, the image of Jeremy's tall form encased in jeans and leather jacket surfaced. She dried herself vigorously, an attempt to erase the disconcerting ideas that seemed to surface more frequently of late. Christine shook her head. "Okay so he was hired by Uncle Conrad to keep me safe but the killer is dead. I don't need his protection anymore."

She glanced in the mirror over her bathroom counter. The grimace on her face expressed what she thought about getting caught talking to herself. Chief inched his way past the door frame to her bedroom as she stepped in front of her closet. "Where were you when I needed you?" *At least I can pretend I'm talking to someone when he's in the room. Harumpff!*

Christine Smith took very little time with her appearance as a rule but lately, she'd begun wearing some blush and a little lipstick. After drying her hair and adding some moisturizer to her face, she grabbed the brush to reduce the tangles left after drying. Chief whined from his cozy position on her bed. She completed the work of enhancing her sallow complexion and headed toward the front door. Her companion soundlessly followed on her heels.

Chapter Two

Starbucks, at the corner of Graham and Kennedy, was located in the center of downtown Winnipeg. Christine parked in the first empty space she encountered along the sidewalk, grabbed Chief's leash and led him through the doorway of the coffee shop.

A tall woman, her light brown hair streaked with blond highlights, crossed the room toward them. She held her hand for Christine to shake. "I'm assuming you're Christine Smith because of the dog."

"You assume right. Hi, Mrs. Anderson. I'll grab some coffee and join you." She walked to the order desk.

"Miss, you can't bring that animal in here." The barista behind the counter smiled tentatively at her but his smile did not reach his eyes.

"Chief is a service canine. His harness is clearly visible." Christine glanced around the restaurant assessing the inconvenience her dog would be to the other patrons. Only two other coffee connoisseurs took up space and seemed engrossed in personal conversation, not paying attention to anyone or anything else. She returned her gaze to the man wearing a Starbuck's shirt. "I'd like a 'Mocha', please."

A frown covered his face as the young man handed Christine her beverage, but he didn't utter another word of protest. She dropped Chief's leash across his back and reached for the hot mug of frothy liquid. Both investigators moved toward the distraught woman in the far corner of the shop. Sylvia Anderson sipped her smoothie through a straw but her eyes glistened with unshed tears when she glanced up as Christine approached.

She settled Chief at her feet and grabbed the woman's hand. "Mrs. Anderson ... Sylvia. Tell me about your daughter."

"She's twelve years old; slim, with long blond hair. Here's a picture." She searched her purse to find the three by five photo.

Christine glanced at the snapshot. "Tell me about her. What does she like to do and who are her friends?" The photo revealed a petite young girl, pretty, with thick flowing gold tresses halfway down her back. Cute dimples and sparkling, dark blue eyes framed her smile.

Sylvia waited a few seconds while Christine scrutinized the picture. Then she began. "Samantha is a good student. She loves school and has lots of friends. She gets good grades but hardly studies. The teachers all love her; say she is respectful of others including the teaching staff. About a year ago, some of the girls started having sleepovers but before that Samantha had never been away from home." She sniffed and snatched a tissue from her handbag. "My daughter did not run away."

Christine nodded. "Preteen girls can be difficult. I gave my guardians a lot to worry about, wanting to be independent and such."

"Not my Samantha. She obeyed our rules without question and her friends had strict parents." Sylvia took another sip of her pink coloured smoothie. "I'd begun allowing her to take the bus to and from school by herself. Before, we ... I drove her to school and picked her up every day."

Christine reached her hand toward Chief and patted his head. "What does your husband do?"

"He's an electrical engineer, works for Manitoba Hydro. But he and I are divorced." The woman stared into Christine's eyes.

"You look as if you're fairly well off."

"I do okay. My ex-husband is generous. We live in a good neighborhood. Our neighbors come from all walks of life. Some are lawyers. Some doctors. Professional people." Her eyes reflected a thought. "You don't think someone took her, kidnapped her!"

"No use speculating, Sylvia. I won't be able to figure things out until I've a chance to talk to her friends. I'll need a complete list." Her eyes roamed around the room. Did anyone give them undue attention? One man, sitting by himself, worked on his computer. He'd arrived after she found her seat, but he seemed harmless. The other couple appeared self-absorbed, with no regard for the people next to them.

Christine studied Sylvia Anderson as the distraught woman wrote some names on a piece of paper. She suspected the mother had probably aged since her daughter went missing. "Add their phone numbers and the number for the school. That environment will work better and faster than going to their individual homes."

Sylvia scribbled a few more notes and handed the paper to Christine. "If I remember any more names, I'll call you. The cell number you gave me would reach you anytime, anyplace. Right?"

"It does." Christine stood to leave. "I can't promise you anything, but I will do my best to find your little girl. I won't use Chief to track her yet. Did you file a missing person's report?"

"I did but they didn't seem too hopeful. They told me over 100,000 kids disappear every year here and in the US. Hard to believe." She shook her head. "They figure most are runaways but said because she's only twelve, they'd send out an amber alert and start the wheels rolling. That's when I called you."

"Well, I worked with a sergeant at the station so I'll check in with him too. He might steer me in the right direction." Christine grabbed Chief's leash again. She glanced toward the floor and then back at Sylvia. "I'll be in touch. Try to leave the worrying to me." She made the comment but understood sleep would elude the mother until her daughter was found. *I wonder if she has a faith base - like Jeremy and his dad.* She shook her head again as she exited the coffee shop. *I'm beginning to think like him, too.*

Chapter Three

Her Jeep Grand Cherokee pulled up in front of the middle school where Sylvia Anderson said her daughter attended. Christine stepped out and stood beside the open door for a second pondering the validity of taking Chief with her. The image of the last frightened boy clasping the dog around his neck surfaced. "Come on, Boy. The kids seem to trust you faster than they do me." She fastened his leash to his harness. "You might help them relax a little and tell me more than they would otherwise."

Canine and handler walked briskly toward the front entrance to the one story brick structure. Christine opened the door and allowed Chief to enter ahead of her. The duo strode to the door marked 'Office'. A clerical type, with gray streaks scattered randomly through her hair, approached the counter separating the staff from the visitors. "May I help you?" She peeked over the glasses perched on her nose, a look of disapproval erupting when she spotted Chief.

She cleared her throat to bring the woman's focus back to her and introduced herself. "I'm Christine Smith." She handed the woman her credentials. "Sylvia Anderson hired me to find her daughter."

Sympathy erased the disdain as the woman gazed at Chris-

tine's card. "Poor woman. Poor Samantha. We are beside ourselves with worry. I can't imagine whatever happened to
her. Such a good girl." She shook her head and sighed, "How
can we help?"

"I'd like to speak with Samantha's friends and her teachers. I'll need a place to conduct those interviews and would you
arrange for these girls ..." She handed the list from Mrs. Anderson to the clerk. "... to meet me in that room?"

"Oh, I don't ... I mean ... I'll check with the principal. The
rules, you see, about who speaks to our kids." The woman
wrapped one hand around the other in a wringing manner, her
disapproval showing again. She turned toward a closed
door. "I'll be right back."

"Just tell her this is important if we're going to find Samantha." Christine spoke to the woman's back. *Rules. Darn
rules. But I suppose in this day and age there's a need for caution.* She turned toward the empty chair situated behind her.

Before she settled down to wait, the woman returned. "Come with me. Mrs. Gleason wants to talk with you
first."

Christine followed the woman around the counter after
making sure Chief would obey her command to stay. She entered the smaller room and made eye contact with a tall, slim
woman of indeterminable age. Her gray eyes sparkled but not
from merriment. A tear escaped and slid down her
cheek. Christine took the chair in front of her desk. She reached
her hand toward the distraught administrator. "I'm ..."

"I know who you are. Sylvia Anderson phoned me and
told me you would be coming. She described you to a tee. I am
so upset about Samantha." She dabbed at the trail of dampness
marring her make-up. "I wanted to tell you about the child before we set you up with her friends. Samantha has attended here
since kindergarten."

Christine leaned back in the chair. Her brain reminded her
that Chief had a short attention span when kids were around. *If
one of them ...* "Would you mind if I bring my dog in here?"

"No, of course not. Sylvia said you used a service animal."

Christine rose to her feet and slipped her head out the
door. "Come." The dog poked his head around the corner of the
counter and walked with purpose to her side. The duet moved
back into the room and Christine closed the door. "Go ahead,

Mrs. Gleason. What did you want to tell me?"

The older woman waited while Christine got settled. "As I said, I'm well acquainted with the Anderson family. Samantha is a bright child, well behaved, and respectful. No report has ever been submitted of her teasing another kid or acting in any way other than helpful and encouraging. Her grades are in the top percentile, always. She gets her assignments done on time and the kids all like her. She has a lot of friends here. Do you want to talk to all of them?"

"The ones closest to her. They may know something that, pieced together, could give us a line on where the child is. Would all your teachers tell me the same thing you did, do you think?" Christine glanced at the extensive list in front of her.

"They would but as you said, you'd need to ask the right questions. The adults aren't a problem but one of us will sit in on your interviews with the children."

Christine frowned. "That may cause them to clam up. Can you think of another way?"

"School policy prohibits strangers from talking to our students. Mrs. Anderson vouched for you, but ..." The principal furrowed her brow. "There is a room with a small second room attached. In there, I'd be out of sight. I'd leave the door open a crack, you understand."

"That'll work. Chief breaks the ice for the kids so it's important he comes with me." Christine reached down to pat her friend.

The administrator stood behind her desk. "Good. Let's get started. I'll tell Mrs. Paige to call each student out of class, one at a time. You can talk to the teachers afterwards since the three o'clock bell will soon ring."

Christine rose from her seat and allowed Mrs. Gleason to go ahead of her through the door. Instructions were issued to the woman she'd first met. She followed the administrator out the main door and down the hall. They entered a room set up with a couple of unoccupied cots. "This is the nurse's office. She has her desk back here." She opened a second door. "I'll wait in here and you can arrange a chair in the room next door to talk to the kids. The first one should be here in a few minutes."

Christine nodded her head and moved a chair near one of

the cots. She sat and waited for the first child to meet with
them.

Chapter Four

Chief raced around in circles chasing his tail. The flag pole in the center of the school lawn became the perfect spot for his attempt to work out the kinks from sitting so long. Christine chuckled. *I wish I had as much energy.* She rolled her shoulders from side to side as she walked toward her vehicle. Two hours had dragged along like four but at least she gained a glimpse of the child she'd been hired to locate. The teachers parroted the principal's statements about the young girl although they told of more spunk than the administrator or her mother described. The girl had an inquisitive mind. *I wonder if she acted on her curiosity.*

The kids told some interesting stories about Samantha, once they felt comfortable in front of her. Chief aided in that regard. They all went to him as soon as they entered the room. Except for one little boy. His cautious demeanor lasted longer than the other students but he, too, relaxed with Chief's head on his knee. Her friends shed a few tears when they expressed their fear for Samantha. No one, even her best friend, said the girl wanted a more liberal upbringing or more freedom. They all insisted she loved her mom and would not run away. Extra time on the computer was not approved by their parents or teachers. "Mrs. Anderson assessed the situation wisely. These kids are under strict rules but don't seem to mind." She held the door for Chief to jump into her Jeep. The dog settled on the passenger seat and Christine stepped inside.

"Now where?"

Chief barked. She grinned and put the vehicle in gear to pull off the school property. "I agree. Let's go visit Sergeant Irving."

****

Christine led her canine by his leash through the double glass doors into the noise and confusion of the main police station in Winnipeg. Its central location allowed all the substations access, if needed. This building housed the lab, the morgue, and several offices for people who oversaw the entire force. Drawers slammed as computers signaled incoming messages or a website found. A couple of criminal types sat handcuffed in chairs beside desks occupied by policeman who asked pertinent questions.

After the officer on desk duty phoned Sergeant Irving to give him a heads-up about Christine's visit, the woman and dog duet wove their way past the goings-on in front of them. She focused on gaining whatever leads the police uncovered, if anything, about Samantha Anderson's disappearance. She wrapped her knuckles on the dark wood frame of the open door.

Sergeant Irving lifted his head from the stack of paperwork lying on his desk and signaled her to come in as he pointed to a chair nearby. "What brings you down here on such a nice day?" The large man smiled. "I thought I'd gotten rid of you for a few days anyway."

"Yeah, well. I got this phone call."

"Always another one eh?" The Canadian vernacular popped out of the Sergeant's mouth. "Who ya lookin' for this time?"

"A missing child ... Samantha Anderson. Her mom phoned and ..."

"Wait a minute. Let me check the computer files for the name." The sergeant pressed this key and another until he'd found what he was looking for. "Here's the file. Only twelve, eh?"

Christine leaned forward hoping to catch a glimpse of the screen. Irving acted a little protective, however. "Her mother called yesterday. That poor woman is beside herself. I talked to her friends and the teachers from her school and this doesn't sound like a kid running away. What can you tell me about ... well anything would be a help." She reached a hand toward Chief to pat his head.

Irving scrolled through the little information he found and glanced in Christine's direction. "Not much to tell. Not a trace of the girl and no leads. We also did interviews with friends and family but that's a dead end. She's disappeared like so many kids do these days."

"What do you mean? How many children are we talking about?" Christine's forehead creased when the sergeant's mouth turned down at the corners.

He shook his head. "We're not supposed to get personally involved but this is an epidemic. I talked to a friend the other day, a former CIA Director. He said the number of kids who go missing in Canada and the United States reached 100,000 this year. Most of them are never found." He shook his head again, the frown lines etched deeply across his face. "I almost fell over. We had no idea it was this bad but apparently his job entailed compiling the data and connecting the dots. Some are runaways but all end up as contraband for human traffickers."

Christine gasped. "Is this guy for real? How could so many kids disappear without a trace?" She hit the desk with her fist a little harder than she intended. "You cops don't collect information about this?"

Irving appeared a little sheepish. "The people he suspects are rich and influential. They control the media and many government offices, including police officers. According to him, the tentacles reach into almost every profession. They've prosecuted lawyers, doctors, personalities ... you name it. Samantha Anderson is the one we know about in this area but I'll bet many others are in the same boat."

Christine's shoulders slumped. "Locating her may be too late if what you're saying is actual fact. They've probably moved her out of the city by now."

"Could be. Although, a large culture of prostitution exists here. With Samantha's looks ... she's a beauty, isn't she?" He placed his forearms on his desk. "I'm not suggesting your search is a waste of time but ... well you may not be any more successful than we've been."

Christine rubbed her hand over Chief's boney head and scratched between his ears. "I have to try. Are you acquainted with some of the working girls?"

"Or guys. Boys are on the streets, too."

"Somehow that seems worse. I suppose things like this were going on when my parents died. I could have become a statistic." Christine shrugged her shoulders. "Instead I was protected."

Sergeant Irving chose to ignore what appeared to be introspection on Christine's part. "I know someone you need to talk to, a person who'd be able to hand you the info you need ... maybe. Shonney prostituted herself for 14 years, from the age of eleven when she ran away from an abusive stepdad. She'll tell you the how and why as well as the what and when of this criminal activity. With any luck you'll obtain the information to find the girl before time runs out for her. Our hands are tied with jurisdiction and the law when it comes to working girls. Besides, they won't talk to us."

Christine stood to leave. She glanced around the room as the police officer penned a name on a sheet of paper. He added the woman's telephone number. "Shonney is busy so if you can't reach her the first time, try again. She's raising two boys and studying for a Bachelor's degree of some sort." He handed the contact information to Christine.

"I thought you said she was a prostitute."

"She got out about ten years ago. Got religion or something. Anyhow she kicked her drug habit and began getting her life in order. Her oldest son was adopted by then so she visits him regularly." The sergeant maneuvered around his desk in the tiny office. "Let me know how you make out. If I hear anything, I'll contact you."

"That's all I need. Another religious fanatic. Jeremy drives me nuts."

"Preaches at you, does he?"

"Not so much. But he seems to always know something ... like he has a direct line to the big guy." She pointed toward the ceiling. "Just bugs me. He thinks he's right all the time. I don't think I'm going to involve him in this case." She cruised back the way she'd come toward the front door, allowing Chief to drag his leash as he followed.

A few waves and a short conversation here
and there slowed her exit but soon she stood out on the sidewalk. She checked the sky and noticed some dark clouds closing in. "I think the meteorologist might be right about snow
coming today." She spoke to no one in particular but Chief
woofed beside her. "You got that right," She answered him.
"Let's go home."

Chapter Five

Jeremy Goodman ran a cloth over the shining chrome on his 2012 Harley Sportster. He looked around the interior of the shed-turned-garage. "I've got to purchase a house." He turned toward the bike again. *I'm tired of renting. Need my own digs.* He worked his way past the lawnmower, and a wheelbarrow to the door. His large frame barely fit through the opening. He snagged his phone from the holster on his belt. After dialing a number from memory, he waited, listening to the familiar dial tone. "Hi Dad. Got time for dinner somewhere?"

Jeremy's father, a lawyer with a select list of clients including Christine Smith, was a wonderful mentor. "What do you think about me buying a home?" He grimaced over the comments about settling down. His father began, again, suggesting a family was a good thing. "Dad. It's just a house. I need more room for my stuff and a garage so I can store my bike for the winter properly." He listened as he Father ended the call.

He sauntered to the back door and his tiny kitchen. Other tenants occupied the upstairs. He poured another cup of coffee, sipped the bitter concoction, and threw the contents down the sink. *I should purchase one of those one-cup-at-a-time jobbies.* He twisted his lips in compliance with the bitterness on his tongue.

The walk to his bedroom took only a couple of seconds. *Even Christine's house is bigger than this. I wonder what she's up to today.* He thought about the last time he talked to her. They'd delivered a young boy to his parents when Christine received a phone call. She'd left shortly afterwards but all she'd told him was she had another case. *It'll be interesting to see where this one will take her. I wish she was in another line of work.* He stopped flipping through the shirts hanging in his closet. *Wow. That woman is getting to me.*

Jeremy slipped a black Van Heusen shirt over his torso. He was familiar with the restaurant his lawyer buddies frequented. *I might find some new clients.* Conrad Finder hired him to protect Christine but now that the killer was dead, his job ended. *I'm happy I'm not needed anymore but I liked the excuse to be around her. I wonder if she needs me for this case. We might team up again.*

He fastened the last button on the shirt and tucked the hem into his black jeans. A glance in the mirror over his chest of drawers reminded him his hair could use some attention. He grabbed the brush and ran it casually through his medium length hair. *Need a haircut.* His blue eyes twinkled as he remembered Christine's comments about hair curling around his ears. *She never said she liked longer hair on men but she never said she didn't either.*

He passed a hand over his tresses. *Gotta stop thinking along those lines. She's not a believer. Sharing office space is one thing. Anything more is forbidden.* "Lord, keep my thoughts away from her until or if she accepts you as her Saviour." He slid his hand down the crease in his right pant leg as he walked toward his front door. *Stay focused, Goodman. Stay focused.*

Chapter Six

Barkley Goodman leaned back in the large leather chair that complimented his antique desk. *Finally! Rompart Industry executives agreed to meet with Christine. This initial meeting won't last long. She's only considering the possibility of running her father's company. This was a place to start.* As her lawyer, his advice to sell everything was also a consideration. She enjoyed other interests and, well, he hoped she would become Jeremy's partner. *They work so well together.*

He smirked, picturing Christine in a more personal context for Jeremy. *For now, I'll settle for partners.* He slipped past his desk, grabbed his top coat from the clothes tree near his private office door and stepped into the hall. He heard Clare bustling about in the reception area. "Hi Honey." He sidled toward the side of her work station.

The slightly gray haired woman stood. She wrapped her arms around his waist and leaned her head on his chest. She gazed at his twinkling eyes. "The reservation for you and Jeremy is made. Hope you have a pleasant father/son time."

"He wants to discuss a house. He's thinking of buying one." Barkley enveloped her in a bear hug. This woman was an indispensable part of his life now. "We need to go out again. How about the theater this time?"

"I'd like that. Name the date." Clare stepped back. "Does Jeremy know about us?"

"He suspects, I think. Especially after the time he found us with our arms wrapped around each other at my place. There's never been a conversation about our relationship, though, so ... maybe tonight would be a good time. We've wasted enough time, don't you think? When are you going to say yes?" Barkley slipped his arms into the sleeves of his coat.

Clare's face took on a slightly pink hue. "I want you to be absolutely sure. Talk to Jeremy. Find out what he thinks. I'll give you my answer tomorrow. Promise."

Barkley grinned. "Can you give me a hint? The suspense is killing me. The night I proposed to Jeremy's mother, she said yes right away. I want my son to approve too but ultimately it's not about him. Our wedding is about us."

"I like him. I want his approval, that's all." She turned back to her desk. "Your friends might think I'm a gold digger, just after your money."

"Oh, like there's a whole lot of that. What they think doesn't matter either. I believe you love me and I love you. We need to be married." He walked toward the door to the world outside. His hand on his forehead, he recited, "I'll wait till to-morrow with bated breath. Parting is such sweet sorrow."

Clare laughed. "Oh you. Get going. I'll lock up."

Chapter Seven

Jeremy perused the menu in front of him. The restaurant provided the perfect place to conduct a meaningful discussion with his dad. He glanced up as the older Goodman walked through the door. He stopped, spoke to the hostess, and pointed in Jeremy's direction. The woman smiled as Barkley advanced toward the table where Jeremy sat. "Hi Son. Been waiting long?"

"Naw. Just got here. Busy day?" He kept his eyes on Barkley as his father took the chair on the opposite side.

Barkley settled his frame for a leisurely visit. "No, not too busy. But I finally got Rompart executives to agree to a date and time to meet Christine. I'll call her after we order." He studied the menu. "Anything appetizing?"

"All the food is first rate here. My mouth is watering over prime rib so that's what I want." He ran his tongue over his lips.

Barkley nodded his head. "Sounds good to me. I'm starved." He searched around for their waiter. A tall man in a pristine white shirt and black pants approached. The two men ordered and waited while he poured frosty, cold glasses of water.

Barkley took a sip and then wiped his face with one of the crisp napkins beside his plate. "I need to make this call and then we can talk about your house plans. Excuse me." He pressed the speed dial for Christine Smith. "Hi Christine. Rompart wants a meeting tomorrow at eleven. I think they hope, with lunch only an hour away, you won't take too much of their time." He gazed across the table.

Jeremy's eyebrows lifted as he listened to his father's side of the conversation. *What is their problem?* His dad ended the call promising to meet Christine at Rompart at 10:45 in the morning.

"What are your instincts telling you about the board?" he asked Barkley.

"I think they're scared Christine will make some changes they aren't prepared for. Now tell me about the house you're thinking about."

Jeremy took a long sip of his water. He cleared his throat and paused before answering his father. "I gave this a lot of thought. I used to think when I bought my first house, I'd be married. That's not happening and I need some place for my bike and truck. I want more space."

"Are you working with a realtor?"

"I am. They want me to check out a house not far from Christine's neighborhood. The price sounds a little high but ...." Jeremy stopped when the waiter brought their soup course.

Barkley bowed his head to pray as soon as the young man left. "Father, bless this food to our nourishment and may this conversation honor You. Amen." He studied his son's face across the table. "Are you looking at a home as an investment or as a more permanent place to live?"

Jeremy swallowed his first spoon of hot mine- strone. "Both, I think. I want something comfortable with room for growth if I ever should find a wife. And, if she doesn't like the place, I want to be able to recoup my money or even add to the value a little. Something that needs a few modern touches, I think."

"You have given this a lot of thought. I think you're on the right track." He spooned some of the steaming broth into his mouth. "M-m-m. This is good." He enjoyed the hot liquid mak- ing its way down his throat. "Keep an open mind. Don't stop at one house. Visit three or four at least and decide what you like about each of them. Weigh the pros and cons." He chuckled. "You know all this. Why did you want to talk to me about your plans?"

Jeremy returned his father's smile. "I like talking things over with you and we've not visited for a long time. I value your opinion." He pushed his empty bowl aside. "How are things with you and Clare?" He wiggled his eyebrows suggestively.

Barkley's face grew serious. "I asked Clare to marry me and ..."

"Woot. Woot" Jeremy raised his arm in a circular fashion. "Way to go, Dad." He clamped his hand over his mouth. "Sorry." He glanced around the room and continued in a quieter tone of voice. "I think that's wonderful. When?"

Barkley grimaced. "She hasn't said 'yes' yet. She's waiting till I told you. She wants your approval first."

"It's not like she'll need to mother me ... at least not any more than she already does. Tell her I approve." He grinned. "She'll make you happy. You're both believers so that's not an issue and you like the same things."

"I love her, son. When your mother died, I thought no one would ever interest me again. But, this relationship is different. We're established and won't be raising a family. The idea of sharing my life with someone again is appealing. God got my attention and I believe He approves, too."

Jeremy grinned. He winked at his father but waited to respond until the waiter finished removing bowls in place of their entrée. The man walked discretely away. "It isn't good for man to be alone. Isn't that what God said to Adam before He created Eve? I'm happy for you, Dad."

"I plan to go over to her place after we leave here. No more excuses." He chuckled as he dug into the delectable prime rib on his plate. The au jus added flavor to the baked potato. Barkley's grin made eating an adventure. "We're both moving up in the world."

Jeremy's eyes stared back at his father with a more sober countenance. "I dream of heading in the same direction. I guess I need to begin praying in that regard. Sometimes ..."

"Life gets lonely. God's way of getting our attention. He places the desire for a mate in our heart and it's up to us to open our eyes to the possibilities He brings us." He chewed a little and then asked the question on his mind. "Are you sure God hasn't already brought someone into your life whom He might want you to think about?"

"Life is busy. I've thought about a life mate but not a lot."

"Oh, I think you have. I saw you the last time you and Christine sat in my office. Sparks were happening." Barkley grinned. "She perturbs you and she challenges you. That's a start."

"You're crazy. We're comparative strangers and ... besides, she's not a believer. She's not interested."

"Didn't you say she started asking questions?" Barkley took another bite.

Jeremy frowned. "Yes, but that's still a long way from ..."

"That's a beginning." Barkley wolfed down a mouthful. "Let's eat. I want to arrive at Clare's before she goes to bed." He swallowed and then asked, "How's Jenna?"

Jeremy's face released its cloud of doubt. "Changing the subject, eh?" He cleared his throat. "This course of chemo is taking its toll but only one more and she's finished. I hope the medicine does the trick. The doctors are hopeful."

"Is she back at work?"

"She is but she tires easily. Christine suggested we place a twin sized bed in her office for Jenna to use. Christine works mostly out of the office anyway." Jeremy's voice trailed off as he studied his father's expression. "Never mind."

"What?" The exaggerated innocence on Barkley's face was not lost on Jeremy.

"You're analyzing me again. Christine investigates her cases and I work mine except when they overlap. The kids she searches for are so different from the cases I usually cover. Now she's looking into a missing twelve year old girl. These kids take such a toll on her emotions. I ..."

Barkley chuckled. "We were talking about Jenna, not Christine." He threw his head back and laughed. "I know the signs."

Jeremy sent his father a grumpy scowl. "Leave it alone, Dad. She's an office mate, nothing more." He filled his mouth with the last bite from his plate. "You guys are all alike. You fall in love and everyone else must join you. Let's get outta here. Go see your fiancée."

Barkley stood and beckoned the waiter over with the check. "My treat. Should you check on Christine?"

"Dad." Jeremy shook his head and stalked toward the door. "Tell me when you set a date."

"Let me know when you decide on a house." He patted his son's shoulder. "See ya later."

"Thanks for dinner, dad. Say Hi to Clare for me." Jeremy walked toward his truck and waved over his head in his father's direction. *I wonder if Christine is having a tough time with this case. Maybe I should ...*

Chapter Eight

Christine sat hunched over her desk. Her shoulders curled forward as her stomach muscles clenched, the slight nausea threatening to erupt. She raised a hand to her left temple, closing her eyes in an attempt to erase the images. Her computer screen provided the only light in the room.

She glanced at Chief. "How can adults do those things to a child?" Chief's brows rose a little as if contemplating an answer. Her question created a memory of her own childhood. *I felt protected, loved, and cared for before my parents died. They made sure nothing about my father's dealings touched me.* Things changed but even when she lived with the Finders, she'd felt safe. *They loved me, too.*

Christine used her cursor to scan the data uncovered about human trafficking. "These kids didn't stand a chance. Boy, am I naive." Chief walked over to lay his head on her lap. She set her hand on his fur, feeling comfort in the touch. *I know nothing of this world where boys and girls are abused and used for the pleasure of adults. No one seems to care about the damage it does to the children. Total disregard.*

She tried to speak but her voice choked up as tears slid down her cheeks. She pounded the desk top causing her computer to jump. *I guess I do understand a little after meeting Matthew and Jimmy Trimble.* She swiped at the wetness. *Those kids won't ever be the way they were meant to be. Now ...*

She manipulated her mouse to the page found on prostitution and runaways. Several former prostitutes submitted their stories to the website. She cringed as she read some of the details of their lives, circumstances that caused them to run away in the first place. Her arm swept the air surrounding the computer screen. Chief raised his head. "Some people should never become parents in the first place."

She shook her fist at the imagery painted by one of the girls who wrote about a relative who'd sexually molested her when she was only five years old. *The same age I was when I went to live with the Finders. Uncle Conrad would never ... and there're the ranch hands, all rough-around-the-edges kind of guys. Not one of them made me uncomfortable and certainly not that way.*

"Chief, I need to delve into Samantha's home life. Each of these girls say no one guessed what was going on in their life but how could the adults not see the signs?" She leaned over her keyboard and grabbed a pen from the desk beside her mouse pad. She scribbled a note to ask Sergeant Irving about complaints by anyone regarding Samantha's home. "I need to talk to the neighbors, too." Chief whined as if he understood.

Just as she placed the pen down again, a faint knock disturbed the peace and quiet of her home. Her partner, from his position on the floor beside her desk, woofed but his tail wagged. *Can't be an intruder.* She slid her chair back from the desk and stood, walking the few feet toward her entrance.

Christine checked the identity of the person standing on her doorstep through the peephole in her front door. Jeremy grinned back at her. His self-assured posture forced the anger of the information she'd uncovered to the surface. She swung the door open. "What. Do. You. Want?" She glared into the evening shadows and targeted Jeremy with her most pronounced stare.

Jeremy lifted his hands in self-defense. "Whoa. Is that any way to greet a colleague? What's got your shorts in a knot?"

Christine ran a hand across her brow. She turned away from the door, muttering an apology. She stepped aside to allow Jeremy access to her private domain. Chief nosed his pant leg in welcome.

"I figured you'd be up to your ears in comfort zone issues. What did you discover about the Anderson girl?" Jeremy took his leather jacket off and laid it across the back of the sofa. He looked in Christine's direction.

Unwelcome tears escaped her lowered lids. "I'm fine. Don't worry about me." She tossed her head away from his scrutiny. "Quit looking at me."

Jeremy chuckled. "For someone who's fine, those are a lot of tears racing down your face. What's got you so upset? You find out Samantha's mom is not who she claims to be?"

Christine's shoulders folded in on themselves as she dropped down on the sofa. "How much do you know about human trafficking? This research ..."

"Why human trafficking? You think that's what happened to this girl?"

"Sergeant Irving told me a little about what goes on with working girls. He says a real possibility exists Samantha was abducted for that purpose. He thinks she's what the pimps look for when they want to build their stable." She made quote marks with her fingers. "So I ..."

"You decided you needed to find out if he was right." Jeremy sat down gently beside her. He placed an arm around her rigid shoulders but she eased away from his touch.

"Want some coffee or something?"

"Sure. If you can stand the intrusion." He followed her to the kitchen. "Christine, I've had some dealings with the prostitutes in this city. People think their profession should be criminalized but these girls are the victims. The Johns who frequent them should be prosecuted. Crime is higher and drugs are more rampant where these women are but not because they bring it with them. Their handlers do. Addiction keeps the girls working."

"I found a story about a former hooker who said her pimp got her hooked on Crack Cocaine and put her out on the street to pay for her habit." Christine busied herself with coffee preparations.

Jeremy sat down at the table. "I have the name of someone who has exited the trade and earned a degree in social work since. She'd be a good one to talk to."

"I don't think I can handle any more information. This whole scene is disturbing. I found a site where a former CIA

agent discloses all kinds of sordid details about how extensive this is. He collected documented proof that many more kids than any of us realize are trafficked every year. The perpetrators own newspapers, are doctors, and lawyers ... professionals. They keep the information from the public so we hide our heads in the sand and pretend this business is happening in other countries but not ours." She placed two cups of steaming liquid on the table and sat across from Jeremy.

He took a tiny sip and replaced his mug on the table top. "This is news to me but the fact that trafficking occurs within our borders doesn't surprise me. Evil ..."

"Don't start with your religious hypothesis. This has nothing to do with your Christianity." Christine took a longer gulp than she intended and dropped her cup before placing a hand over her mouth. "See what you made me do."

Jeremy decided to ignore her last comment. "Don't you think of all this as evil? I mean prostitution and drugs are certainly not good."

Christine glared in his direction but shifted her gaze quickly toward the wall behind him. "I just don't think your religion is the answer to everything the way you do. As a matter of fact, what about all those priests who've molested little boys? They're Christian right?"

"And that's why the enemy capitalized on their weaknesses. If he can demoralize believers by using our weaker brothers, he will. That way the rest of the world has an excuse for walking away from their faith." He took a long drink from the now-cooled beverage. "Anyone who terrorizes little children, Christian or not, is evil."

"There I agree with you. The whole idea is so far from how I lived. And my guardians didn't need a book to tell them about right or wrong." She shook her head. "Castration is too good for what these men do. At least that's my opinion."

"Yeah, and the civil rights lawyers would camp on the courthouse doorstep if it became law." He rested his elbows on the table. "I don't know what the answer is but it seems more people are talking about this than ever before. I wonder what God's plans are. Only He knows."

"Stop. He hasn't done anything up till now and human trafficking is a world-wide problem. Talk is cheap. Something needs to stop this." Christine placed her empty cup in the sink. "Samantha's mom, her friends, and her teachers all tell about a great kid but she's missing. Her mother hired me to find her and ..." Tears slid from beneath her lowered lids. "I don't think I can."

Jeremy leaned toward her as she took her seat at the table again. He placed his hands over her trembling fingers. "I'm busy this week with another case but after that I have some time. You've got the meeting with Rompart ..."

"How do you know that?"

"Dad and I were having dinner when he called you. I guess he didn't think the information was privileged." He drew his hands back and leaned back in his chair. "Does it bother you? That Dad discussed this with me, I mean."

Christine swiped at the tears and stood to grab a paper towel. She blotted her face and used her fingers to dab at her eyes. "No, I guess not. I ... It's just ... I don't want everyone in my business or my father's business. The board's been so reluctant to sit down with me, I can't help but wonder why and what I'll find out when we do meet. They may have picked up where my father left, if he was laundering money and stuff. Man. Life is never simple, is it?"

"How are the renovations to your house going? You hope to move in before the weather gets too cold, right?" He took the last sip of coffee and shoved his cup a few inches away from him.

The gesture appeared to Christine as stalling. "It's getting cold faster than I anticipated, though. Why do you want to know about my house?"

"Just making small talk. Oh, and I'm looking for my own place, too. That's why Dad and I met earlier this evening. Wanted to get his opinion."

Christine relaxed against the chair. "I'm kind of excited about the project at my house. The contractors should be finished in a week or two. I'll have more than enough space to live in and even invite guests over. The other suite will have a separate entrance and we'll share the parking garage. That structure housed four vehicles at one time. I'll keep two of them and partition off the other two to make a secure situation for all concerned. You looking forward to having your own place?"

"I am. Need room for my bike and truck and ..."

"Men and their toys. Where are you looking?" Christine smirked but returned to her serious expression again.

Jeremy tapped his fingers on the table. "I'm looking around here actually. I like the older residential areas. Bigger yards, more space. Besides, being close to the park is enticing. But you won't be here by then."

"No, I guess not." She hung her head. "I need to rest if I'm to meet with your father tomorrow morning before going to Rompart. Thanks for coming over even if I seemed upset in the beginning."

"You darn near bit my head off but who's keeping track. I knew you'd be up to your ears in research. I also understand how this stuff bothers you." Jeremy stood, pushed his chair back toward the table and stepped into the hallway leading to the front door.

Christine followed with Chief right on her heels. She reached for the dog's furry coat and ruffled his neck. The dog gave a big yawn. "He's tired too."

Jeremy chuckled. "Chief's life is hard." He grabbed the door knob. "Try to separate yourself from the missing kid this time, okay? You'll make yourself sick if you keep your emotions on your sleeve."

"I'm not a hardened investigator like you. But I'll try." She closed the door behind him and leaned toward the peephole as he strode to the black truck parked along the curb. "He's not as tough as some people think he is. Eh, Chief." The dog barked as he looked up at her. He yawned again. "Okay. I get the picture. Let's go to bed."

Chapter Nine

Christine stretched her lithe figure as she stood beside her bed looking out the window. Her dog extended his legs and slowly opened his eyes, one at a time. "Chief. The skies are clear and very blue. We have another sunny day to enjoy. I hope the sun shines on the offices of Rompart Industries as well." She walked gingerly toward her bathroom, grabbing the clothes selected the night before from the bench at the foot of the bed. "Time to make myself presentable."

Chief settled down on the carpet to wait for her return. She chuckled but then grew serious. *I don't have time for a meeting at Rompart today. I need to talk to the Anderson's neighbours and phone Irving about complaints. Mrs. Anderson should be willing to give me the name of their family doctor.* She stripped her night clothes off and threw them in the hamper. Reaching past the shower curtain, she turned on the hot water, adjusting the temperature subconsciously.

Christine sighed. Learning the details of the business left to her by her Dad was intriguing but so many other commitments stole her time. I wonder if I'll be able to run the company as efficiently as my father obviously did. I certainly don't intend to deal with any criminal types as he did though. Scrubbing her body with a bath sponge, she made quick work of her morning shower and stepped onto the fluffy carpet that appeared more decorative than useful.

She wrapped the towel turban style around her head and proceeded to apply lotion to the rest of her body. *I'm sure the board of directors is as uncomfortable with me coming into the business as I am in meeting men who worked with my father. But they will be able to tell me a lot about the man behind the company.* She continued her routine by brushing her teeth and applying moisturizer to her face.

Christine glanced toward the bathroom door as Chief stepped across the threshold. "Hungry, boy? I won't be long." The dog wagged his tail thumping the vanity. He turned back to the door and walked a few paces ahead as she followed to her bedroom. She tossed the covers over her bed in a haphazard attempt toward neatness and strode down the hall leading to her living room.

She purchased her home when she first moved to the city and yet, the house would never truly belong to her. The rooms were cozy enough but lacked any special touches to make the place hers. *When I take over my parent's house, even though the structure is divided into two residences now, the atmosphere will be different. I'll take some time and personalize that apartment. I probably should have done the same here too. I guess a move into Mom and Dad's was imminent though.*

Tipping the bag of dog food, she filled Chief's dish. She glanced out the window in the door, her eyes following as the animal traipsed across her backyard looking for the right tree or blade of grass. *The weather must be a little warmer today than yesterday morning. He's taking his time.* Christine flipped the on switch for her coffee maker.

Chief's bark erupted outside the back door at the same time as the phone jangled on the counter top. She picked the device up and walked toward the door. "Hello." Chief brushed against her legs as he made a beeline toward his water bowl.

"Good morning, Barkley. I was about to have some coffee and head into the office." Christine listened to the lawyer who'd handled her affairs since her parents' demise. "I'll meet you at Rompart. Should I bring anything with me? Birth certificate or some such ID?"

Christine's eyes widened as Barkley relayed some new information. "Why did the police phone you and not me? I'm the one he stalked." Her mouth turned down in a frown. "Well, you need to tell them they need to call me as well and besides, someone hired him so this case is not closed. Whoever killed him wanted his silence."

She balled her hand into a fist. "I intend to follow up. He murdered my Mom and Dad and I will find out why." She listened to the calm voice on the other end of the line. "That's crazy. I believe they unintentionally got involved with the wrong people but my parents are not ... were not criminals. You know that. You acted as their lawyer."

Christine focused on Barkley's response but expressed her frustration by hitting the counter, albeit gently, with her fist. "We'll meet in an hour but somehow, I think Rompart Industries are part of this mystery. The sooner this face to face happens, the better." She took a deep breath as Barkley reminded her Rompart was her heritage. "Yeah, well, we'll talk later." She hung up.

Chief lifted his head as soon as she placed the cell phone back on the counter. He walked to her side and nudged her with his nose. "You're a good boy. You understand, don't you? Mom and Dad's reputation is at stake and mine, as well. Barkley advises caution and I agree but I won't let this go until I figure out why they were killed. I want to live my life without this cloud, that's hung over my head for as long as I can remember." She ran her fingers over the dog's coat and scratched behind his ears. Sitting in a nearby chair, she took a sip of coffee and leaned forward to wrap her arms around her canine's neck. "I love you Chief."

Christine lifted the steaming mug to her lips but before she took a drink the doorbell broke the silence in the little house. Chief's ears perked up and his usual woof told her the bell caught his attention, too. The click of his toenails on the tiles as he raced across the kitchen disappeared as he gained access to the carpeted hallway.

By the time she arrived at the door, her visitor rang the bell again. Christine peeked through the tiny hole in her door. *Jeremy. What's he doing here? Again.* She released the lock. Sunlight streamed across the threshold creating a shadow from the man she shared office space with. "I thought you were working on a case today?"

Jeremy stepped inside. "Good morning to you too." He hesitated before answering. "I did. I do. I just thought I'd touch base before you met with Dad. We've both researched

Rompart's executives and nothing popped out at me. How about you? Any red flags?"

Christine frowned but, since her first cup of coffee hadn't done any good yet, she ignored his question. The man certainly brought out the ugly side of her sometimes. *It's a crime to look so good this early in the day?* She cleared her throat. *Enough of that.* "I made coffee. Want some?"

"Sure. You're dressed for bear." Jeremy's scrutiny sent a shiver up her spine as he critiqued her clothing choices.

"What does that mean? I'm just trying to appear professional. After all, I have a board of directors to impress. And, no, nothing gives us a clue for the reason why they seem so reluctant to meet with me. I intend to think positively when we do get together, though."

Jeremy walked to her cupboard and helped himself to a clean mug. He poured the fresh brew as he took a long sniff. "Is this some of the flavoured stuff?"

"Yeah. I made Kahlua today."

"I thought so. I love the aroma of this one." He took a sip. "M-m-m-m-m." He peeked over the rim of his mug. "Any ideas where you might find the Anderson kid?"

"That depends. So far I found nothing to indicate she was the type of girl to run away, from what her friends and teachers say. Anyway I do want to talk to her family doctor, though. If any abuse existed, he'd have the information in his files."

"He might not be able to tell you anything. Patient confidentiality and all that." Jeremy took another sip from his mug as he sat down at the table looking for all intents and purposes as if he planned to spend the morning.

Christine rinsed her cup in the sink and placed her hands on her hips. She glared in his direction. "Jeremy. My schedule is full today. I need to hustle. Did you want anything specific?"

Jeremy glanced at the table top. He raised his head and seemed to study her body language. "This stuff is uncomfortable for you, dealing with pedophiles and now this kid. I just thought ..."

"I'll handle it. In my research last night, I found out there is no end to the number of children I could be searching for. That former CIA director says 100,000 kids go missing every year. I don't know if that's just the US or around the world."

Jeremy finished his coffee and added his mug to the sink. He followed her to the front door. "I'd probably take some of the information with a grain of salt but there're a lot of runaways, that's for sure. Do you think your kid was abducted?"

"I haven't any idea." Christine grabbed her handbag. "I need to get something from my file cabinet. Are you going to the office now?"

"No. I need to check in with my client. Afterwards I'll swing by to get some paperwork done."

Christine, with Chief right behind, followed him out the door. She turned back to engage the lock and arm her alarm. "I can't wait for the reconstruction of my parent's house to be finished. I'm having them install a state of the art security system to include each apartment and the entire yard. The current one is twenty years old. Improvements have been made since my parents were alive."

"Won't the memories make you uncomfortable?"

"The place will have a different appearance than when my Mom and Dad lived in the house. But,

I suppose the outside will still be somewhat the same. I may get them to paint over the stone or do something with the landscaping to make a few changes." She walked toward her Jeep, opened the back door, and guided Chief inside.

"I'll probably see you later. Will you come back to the office after your visit to Rompart?" Jeremy took a couple of steps toward his truck.

She shrugged her shoulders. "A lot depends on how long the meeting is and what Mrs. Anderson says about me seeing their doctor. I want to do that ASAP if I can." She stopped in her tracks as she rounded the back of her vehicle. Christine dropped her head to her chest. "Jeremy. Thanks for asking. I don't intend to be so ..."

"I know. Take it easy. Remember. God cares too ... about the girl, I mean." He walked around the hood of his Dodge Ram and waved nonchalantly before stepping inside. The engine roared to life and, as Christine stared at the truck, Jeremy maneuvered toward the street.

She carefully settled herself on her own front seat, smoothing her slacks and jacket against the cushions. Chief's tongue hung out the left side of his mouth with a tiny drop of moisture he quickly drew back in. To Christine, he appeared to grin. "Anxious to go? We'll see what the Rompart executives think of us when we arrive together at their offices, eh fella?"

She eased her vehicle into traffic before turning the radio to her favourite station. The announcer for a local news channel caught her attention. "A man, whose body was found day before yesterday in one of our gated communities, is allegedly connected to the murder of Teresa and Brian Rompart, which happened over twenty years ago. The police linked him to the case by DNA evidence collected during the time of the shooting. How his body ended up on the same property is anybody's guess. Now for the local weather."

Christine shook her head. She glanced at Chief. "If the cops think that's the end of my parents' investigation, they can think again. I won't stop until I find out who killed that creep and why." Chief cocked his head to one side. The radio station began to play some music as Christine planned, determination written across her face. *I need to clear their name. Mine too.*

Chapter Ten

Rompart Holdings CEO, Richard Belcher, stared across
the table at Brian Carruthers, the board chairman. "How are we
going to handle this meeting today?" Both men had turned
prematurely gray but Richard's face still displayed a youthful
appearance while Brian's contained a few wrinkles.

Jason Mitchell, the firm's attorney and the youngest man in
the room, answered before his senior partner had the opportunity. "We'll deal with Melissa Rompart as we dealt with her
Dad. She legally owns the firm and if we want to keep our jobs,
we need to be as helpful as we can." He gazed pointedly at the
two men who made most of the decisions.

Board member Jerry Dingham, his blond hair and blue
eyes a magnet for the women who worked in the building, folded his hands on the table in front of him. "I understand Brian
Rompart was an easy man to work for. Do we have information
about the girl?"

"She's hardly a girl. But whether or not she comprehends
the slightest thing about operating a company this size is anyone's guess." Bert Mason, the dark haired pessimist in the
group, always sported a five o'clock shadow "She's been herd-
ing cattle from what I've uncovered."

Tom Golden, the newest member, adjusted his bright red
tie. His fluttering fingers smoothed the lapels of his gray suit.

He was reticent about making any comment concerning Melissa's introduction to the company her father bequeathed to her.

Dean Mathews, the man the board hired before Tom, remained silent also. He absorbed the body language of the other members.

Richard Belcher didn't plan on letting those two off the hook, however. "Come on, guys. I need your input. All we've been able to find out about Ms. Rompart is she grew up on a ranch and returned to this country about a year ago. What she's been doing, aside from remodeling her parents' house, is what I want to know. We ..."

"... don't handle her. Did you forget about Barkley Goodman? Her lawyer will be with her and he's been involved in the overall operation since the murders." Jason, ever the attorney, leaned forward, resting his elbows on the table. "He'll pick up right away if we aren't up front with the woman."

Tom and Dean spoke at the same time. "Why are we ..." Dean relaxed his back and nodded for Tom to continue. "Yes, why are we so concerned about this visit? I mean, this is her company and we work for her even if she's been absent, right?"

Brian Carruthers cleared his throat. He glanced toward Jason and dropped his gaze to the hard surface in front of him. "We're worried with her inexperience, that's all. We'll do as our lawyer suggests and treat her with the graciousness due her Dad. Open our company books if she wants." He coughed into his closed fist.

Richard stood, placing his hands on the edge of the large conference table. "Tom and Dean, would you excuse us for a few moments. Bert and Jerry, you guys too. Some details have to be clarified with Jason and Brian that don't concern Rompart. We'll tell you when she gets here. Thanks for your input."

The four stood simultaneously, used to being excluded from certain aspects of their relationship as members. None of them ever served on a board before so assumed this was customary.

Once Jerry closed the door behind them, Richard returned to his seat. He glanced at Brian and then toward Jason. "How's the case against Fine going?"

"The kid's nowhere to be found. His mother or someone is

in hiding with him. The aunt's house is unoccupied and no one is telling where they went." He shrugged his shoulders.

The CEO jumped to his feet sending his chair skittering backwards on its wheels. "The man needs to be acquitted. His threats will destroy us. He has too much information."

"Yeah, well, why don't you try to do better?" Jason crossed his arms over his chest, his close cropped hair accenting his military background. "There's another way to shut the guy up."

Richard coughed as if clearing a lump from his throat. "What are you going to do?"

"That's on a need to know basis. You don't. Need to know, that is." Jason's trim moustache seemed to wriggle as he spoke. "The less you are privileged to the better. Plausible deniability."

Brian dropped his head into his hands, his elbows taking the weight as they rested on the table. "This is getting out of hand. Why can't we pay him off?"

"Maybe that's what I planned? Leave the whole thing to me. The problem will go a..." A knock on the door interrupted the intense conversation between the three men. "Yes?" Jason chose to speak first.

A young woman poked her head around the edge of the door. "Ms. Rompart is here with her lawyer."

"She can wait for another ten minutes and then bring them in." Richard walked over toward the door and closed the open portal after his secretary turned to leave. He twisted his body around to face his cohorts. "Jason, deal with the man as you determine necessary. He's your problem. In the meantime, we need to offer a united front for the Rompart woman. Brian, call the others to join us. Let's proceed with this meeting."

Chapter Eleven

The rope descended into the dark pit. The two captives stood waiting. Their arms remained at their sides, however. They feared the man who dropped them in the well. They bowed their heads as soon as a head appeared over the rim.

They waited. The rumbling in their stomachs echoed off the dank walls. The older girl ran her tongue over cracked lips. They continued to hold their breath.

Finally a voice. "The tall one. Grab the rope. It's time."

Time for what? The short one didn't care. Her older companion reached toward the scratchy cord but smaller hands got to it first. She yanked the twisted strands from grasping fingers. "Back."

"Don't leave me here. You can't forget me. Please." Sobs punctuated the words.

"Shut up. The man says I go. So I go. I been here longer than you anyway." She tethered the lifeline around her waist. She whispered, "I'll try to come back for you." An empty promise.

"Please." The pleading stopped with the one word. Quiet reigned. The taller girl rose to the surface. Her legs dangled. The child counted the bite marks that seemed raw and infected. She scratched the spot on her own leg where it itched uncontrollably. Sticky fluid filled the space between nail and finger. She wiped her hand on her uniform skirt.

The older girl stepped over the rim of the well. She disappeared from view. Quiet suffocated the one remaining. The little one waited for her turn. Tears slid unbidden down dusty cheeks. Her vision blurred. She held her breathe. Then she screamed. "Wait." Her scream grew louder. "Don't leave me."

Chapter Twelve

Christine sat on the edge of her seat. Barkley Goodman reclined next to her. He leaned toward her and used his quiet voice. "Remember, you're Melissa Rompart. Some information, like what you're working on in Winnipeg, is none of their business."

"Mom and Dad were the last ones to call me Melissa. I hope I respond when they use my legal name. Has this board been in control since my Father died?" Christine leaned back, placing her spine against the seat back and sitting as straight as she thought a professional should. She crossed her legs at the ankle.

"Richard Belcher and Brian Carruthers are the only ones who remain from your Father's board. They hired Jason shortly after his death and the others were added as members resigned or retired over the years. They work for you now. Don't forget."

The secretary lifted her head from the stack of paperwork in front of her. "You can go in now, Ms. Rompart, Mr. Goodman." She directed them toward a closed door to their left as she stood to lead the way.

Christine studied the sleek dress as the fabric swayed provocatively around her legs. *I might need to update my wardrobe.* The large oak door opened with a whoosh. The woman who escorted them became the epitome of a business associate as she allowed Christine and Barkley to go ahead into the room. She spoke to one of the men waiting. "Shall I bring the coffee service in?"

"Yes, please." An older gentleman stepped forward, his hand outstretched in a welcoming gesture. "Ms. Rompart, I am Richard Belcher, CEO of Rompart Industries." He clasped her hand in a firm handshake. "Would this be okay?" He pointed to the head of a large conference table. "Barkley. Good to see you again."

"Good morning Richard, gentlemen." The lawyer perused the faces of the executives seated around the table. "For Melissa's benefit, why don't you state your name and your position with the company?"

"I'll begin." Richard Belcher spoke first. "I was friends with your father and enjoyed the short time I worked with him. He acted in this capacity until his death when I took over. The firm, as you will find out, continues to be profitable." He turned toward the man seated next to him. "Brian."

"Good morning Melissa. I'm Brian Carruthers, the chairman of the board. Your dad and I operated closely together as well. We are pleased you decided to step into his shoes. At least that's why we assume you're here. I cleared my calendar for the rest of the day so we can help you become familiar with the workings of the company."

Melissa nodded, her smile tentative. *These men seem pleasant enough but an undercurrent of something more exists, I think.* She looked toward the man sitting beside Carruthers who seemed to be a lot younger than the other two.

His demeanor, all business, held no sign of friendliness as he introduced himself. "I'm Jason Mitchell, the firm's attorney since 2009. I handle any and all legal matters and act in an advisory capacity during board meetings and for new acquisitions." He reached across the table to shake Melissa's hand, their fingers hardly touching from such a distance.

"I'm pleased to meet all of you. Mr. Mitchell, did you know my father?" She leaned her elbows on the table as she waited for his answer to her question.

"Only what I've learned since joining the firm. I finished high school the year he died." He chuckled. "I understand the term shrewd businessman was appropriate. Do you take after him, I wonder."

"I guess we'll find out." She looked at the next man who seemed to shrink under her gaze. A phone buzzed from somewhere in the room. Melissa glanced toward Jason. The man stood as he placed his cell against his right ear. His frown told everyone he never enjoyed being interrupted.

"Mitchell here." Melissa listened to the words before he turned his back to the room. "I told you ..." The rest he mumbled but Mitchell's body language spoke volumes. He turned toward the room, staring in Richard's direction. His eyes gleamed and his free hand pressed over his heart. "Good." The sign of relief seemed too obvious. Melissa wondered about the cause.

Her gaze shifted once again to the man who was next in line for an introduction. She studied his demeanor as he ran a hand through His blond hair. "I'm Jerry, Jerry Dingham. I'm new to this company but worked for years in purchases and acquisitions for Firestone." His blue eyes sparkled in an attempt to gain her attention. "I look for new companies that need an influx of cash, firms which fit our profile. My department does the research and I present the data for the board's consideration." He licked his lips before continuing. "I ..."

"Yes, Jerry. We'll let Melissa absorb a little at a time, if you don't mind." Richard turned his body toward another man seated near the end of the table. From Melissa's vantage point, he seemed to slouch farther into his seat as the others swiveled to look in his direction.

"I work in human resources. We hire only the best and manage to retain our personnel longer than most companies, even with the economic downturn of late." He sat forward with his hands clasped on the table top. "Oh. I'm Bert Mason. I was hired two years ago."

Melissa smiled in his direction but picked up on the intimate conversation going on between Jason Mitchell and Richard Belcher. Whatever was said, Belcher didn't appear pleased. She forced herself to concentrate on the words spoken by Bert. *I hope I can remember all their names. Getting to figure out these men will take time.* "Thank You Bert."

Tom Golden and Dean Mathews looked at each other as if deciding who would go next. Melissa glanced at Barkley who gave her a nod of encouragement. She shifted her gaze to the one near her. "What is your position?"

"Tom handles the crews who renovate the companies we acquire while I look after liquidating assets we decide aren't worth refurbishing." He reached to shake her hand. "I'm Dean Matthews. This company's been my home for ten years. Nice to meet you."

"Right. Dean and I supervise several construction gangs who have the expertise to dismantle a non-profitable company or to resurrect a business with potential. We work closely with a team of architects from Matthews and Matthews." He leaned back in his chair. "Oh, right. I'm Tom Golden."

"Matthews and Matthews." Melissa looked toward Dean. "Any connection?"

His eyes linked with those of Richard Belcher as he returned to his seat. Belcher cleared his throat as if swallowing something less palatable. His smile in her direction seemed insincere. "Sounds strange, but we hired Dean away from his father and uncle who run Matthews and Matthews. We wanted someone with the skills to work closely with architects, who knew how to draw out of them what we needed. Anyway, you've met the board. Any questions?"

Melissa shifted in her seat so she could peruse the facial expressions of each man seated around the table. *I hope my penchant for reading people won't desert me.* "If I understand what you've told me, this company buys up smaller ones to either put them out of business or add them to the list of what we already own. Am I correct?"

All eyes turned toward Richard who spoke with some defensiveness this time. "It's more complicated actually. We also manage several properties for other companies and we own three large apartment complexes."

Melissa sat forward again and then leaned back. "Barkley told me some of what you do but I'd no idea the company had grown this big. How many employees?"

Bert Mason stood to his feet. "I can provide all the files for everyone but we employ 300 office staff which includes office administrators. We also work with construction crews."

"About 500 men and some women use their talents in that department. Some of them do the interior design of our restorations." Tom stood to his feet. "I need to move on the Anderson project." He looked toward Richard, "so if you'll excuse me." He walked toward the door on the opposite end of the room from the one Melissa and Barkley entered through.

Richard looked toward Melissa. "Are you up for a tour of this building?"

Chapter Thirteen

Christine walked through the door leading to the street right behind Barkley Goodman. Conversation was impossible. *I suppose that's for the best for now.* She took comfort in the straight back and purposeful stride of her lawyer. He looked down toward his right side and removed the phone from its holster as he walked toward the parking lot.

Christine skipped a step or two to keep up. "We need to pick up Chief from Jeremy. I miss him when he's not by my side."

She spoke more to herself, but Barkley chuckled while looking at the face of his cell. "Jeremy?"

"Ha, Ha. Very funny. My dog, of course." She reached the side of the large Lincoln MKS he had recently purchased. Looking across the hood, she caught sight of the frown as the creases appeared on the lawyer's face.

"What?" Barkley pounded his fist on the front of his pride and joy but careful not to leave a dent, Christine noted.

"What's wrong?" She hissed.

Barkley waved his hand for silence. "I'll ... we'll be right there." He pressed the button to end the call. "Someone stabbed

Edward Fine in the neck. He bled to death before anyone rescued him."

Christine pushed her hand to her chest. She felt nothing but relief that Nathan Brent would not be forced to testify but ... "Fine was connected to the other pedophiles in the area, I'll bet. Now ..."

"Yeah, I agree. I told the PC to expect us. Do you still want to go back for Chief?" Barkley slid into the driver's seat.

"You looked forward to the man's prosecution as much as I." Christine shook her head. "I'm glad for Nathan and Teresa but how many other kids are being subjected to these creeps. I hoped ..."

"God will provide another way. I cling to the thought." Barkley laid his head on the steering wheel for a full second before lifting his tired eyes and turning his key in the ignition. "What about Chief?"

"I'm having a hard time deciding. What if ... never mind. My car is at Jeremy's office too. You can drop me off later. Let's go find out what the PC can tell us."

Christine let her body relax against the soft, buttery leather seat as she looked out the window. Silence filled the car as each dealt with their own disappointment. Edward Fine deserved to be confined for the rest of his life. Maybe someone found out about his propensity toward little boys. But they placed him in solitary to keep him safe. "Barkley, did the caller tell you how someone gained access to him?"

He stopped his car for a red light, looked right and left and proceeded to make a right hand turn. "No. He said Fine died. Nothing more. I'm hoping we find out more from Chief Matthews."

"He doesn't like me. Every time our paths cross, when I stop by to visit Sergeant Irving, Matthews frowns at me." Christine spied a black car stopped at the intersection they pulled through.

"What did you think about your board of directors? They are working for you, whether they are warming to the idea or not." Barkley kept his eyes on the road but glanced in her direction every once in a while.

She forgot the black car. "I'm not making any judgments yet. I suspect more is going on than what they told me today. How ruthless are those guys when acquiring a new business or property? Do your dealings with them tell you anything?"

"No - but if they follow your Father's ethics, they'll only go after firms already on the edge of bankruptcy. How scrupulous they are is anyone's guess. Jeremy didn't uncover anything questionable ... not yet anyway." He flicked his eyes in her direction. "I wonder if they found out we investigated them before this visit."

"I don't particularly care if they do. What kind of a business owner would I be if I didn't gather every piece of information available about my staff? They haven't put Christine Smith and me together yet. So they might assume I hired Christine and you engaged Jeremy as you always do when you need an investigator." She paused in her assessment for a few seconds. "I intend to spend a lot of time going over the books and working alongside them to really discover a clear picture. I don't own the kind of time I need for a thorough investigation right now though."

"Giving up your investigator's license may be a necessity if you plan to work at Rompart. I don't see how you'd be able to do both."

"I've thought about that ... a lot." She paused again and swiveled in her seat to observe his face more clearly. "What do you think about the idea of selling the business?"

Barkley's head snapped in her direction. "Are you serious? That thought never crossed my mind. But ..."

"It's too much to think about. A huge decision, that's for sure"

Barkley glanced at her face intently but shifted his gaze to focus on the road again. "The company would be worth a lot of money, if their books are clean now. When your Father died, the scandal of drugs and laundering assets from criminals made the business far less valuable for a time."

"I won't do anything until I clear his name. The man I remember does not fit the profile of someone involved with drug lords." She pursed her lips. "The thought of selling is a moot point until ... well, until this is all settled. In the meantime, a little girl is missing."

"Now the ball is rolling with Rompart, we should keep in contact, though. How about I set up a meeting twice a week until your case is solved? Afterwards you'd be able to take a break from investigations for a while until you complete your search into company files back when your Dad was in control." Barkley pulled into the parking lot at the office building that housed the top cop in Winnipeg.

Christine unbuckled her seat belt. "Putting my investigation business on hold for a while may be a good idea. Arrange one week at a time for now. I'll work my case around their schedule but I hope, definitely, to find her before seven days is up. Any longer and I may never locate this kid."

Chapter Fourteen

Jeremy swiveled his chair sideways and leaned his elbow on the desk dominating his office space. Chief sat beside him, staring intently toward his face. "She'll be back soon, boy." He reached forward to rub the dog's left ear and ran his hand under the animal's belly for a scratch. "You like this, huh Boy?"

The canine closed his eyes for a few seconds, his enjoyment evident as he lifted the front of one leg to scratch where Jeremy's hand tickled his fur. His seated posture made the effort far greater than if he stood. Jeremy chuckled. "I kinda like having you here to talk to."

He turned to his desk again. One of his lawyer contacts hired him yesterday to locate a man who would receive a sizable inheritance. So far the recipient eluded him, a least in Winnipeg. "I guess I'll go back to school records and find out if he left the alumni any information about how to find him." Jeremy clicked his mouse over the search engine of his computer. Apparently the man graduated from the University of Manitoba. "A good place to start."

He chuckled again. *I'm talking to myself. Must be the presence of the dog.* He glanced at Chief again and the animal cocked his head as if understanding every word spoken. "Christine talks to you all the time, doesn't she?"

He stared toward the curtain-less window to the left side of his desk. *Wonder how the meeting went with Rompart.* He leaned back in his chair as the computer screen flowed with sites pertaining to the university. He ignored the information as he reflected on the status of Christine's finances. *She's got enough money to do anything she wants in life and yet she spends her time searching for missing kids who tear at her heart something fierce. Hmmmm.*

He thought about the few times she smiled at him. *Her countenance is usually so serious but once in a while, the real Christine sneaks through. Or should I say Melissa. Now that the man who murdered her parents is dead, maybe she'll revert to her given name. Of course, until they find out who killed him, she's probably better off keeping her two identities separate.* "She lives a complicated life, huh Boy?"

If only ... *Lord, you remember how close she came to dying at that pervert's place. She actually considered You might be real. I hate to ask for more disasters to happen in her life, but ... no forget I said that. I'll allow you to use me to reach her some other way. Keep her safe, please. Amen.*

He scrolled down to the web address for the alumni department at U of M. Spotting the phone number; he picked up his cell and punched in the appropriate digits. He pressed the extensions to gain access to a real person. *Computers are great tools sometimes and there are times they can be a pain.*

Finally a voice responded. Jeremy sat up straighter. "Hello. I'm looking for the whereabouts of one of your former students. Do you keep records on all your graduates in case you need to communicate with them?"

The woman on the other end of the call hesitated at first and asked why he wanted to find this person. "Coleman and Coleman hired me to locate him. My name is Jeremy Goodman. I'm a private investigator."

The woman asked for the man's name. "Joseph Dryden or at least that's the name his relative listed in the will. I'm hoping he's in your files." The woman hesitated again but asked him to wait while she looked. A minute or two crept by. *Seems like this name should be easy to locate if they keep accurate records.*

Jeremy reached beside him to pat Chief again while he waited. The woman came back on the line with the address she found to be ten years old. He smiled. "Thanks for looking." He wrote the information on a notepad and thanked her again before saying good-bye. He glanced at the intelligent animal next to him and spoke as if the dog understood. "The man lives in Regina if this is accurate. I'll search through the white pages to obtain a phone number."

Concentrating on his computer screen, Jeremy missed the swish of her pants and the click of her heels as she stepped over the threshold into his office. Her soft voice caused his eyes to snap upward. "Christine."

"Hi. I appreciate you looking after Chief." The animal pranced toward her, his tail lashing the air around him. She rubbed his head subconsciously. "Are you busy?"

"Nothing that can't wait." He stood. "Let's sit where we'll be more comfortable. Jenna's in today. Want some coffee?"

"That would be great. The day seems long already." She took the nearest chair in the seating area surrounding a square table. "I miss Chief when he and I are separated for any length of time."

"He's been good company. I can understand why you like having him around. Just a moment." He punched the button on the intercom. "Jenna, would you mind bringing in two cups of coffee? Christine ... cream and sugar?" Her nod gave Jeremy his answer. Completing his instructions to Jenna, he moved away from his desk to sit across from his office mate. "What's up?"

"The meeting at Rompart went well but as we got up to leave, your dad got a call from the top cop. Someone murdered Edward Fine in his cell. They put him in solitary and still someone got to him." Christine leaned forward to loosen the buttons on her suit jacket. She reached to pat Chief again.

"I understand you went to visit the PC afterwards. What's his take on this?"

"He's as baffled as we are. He agreed with me. I guess there's a first time for everything. Fine probably belonged to a larger ring of perverts in the city who wanted him silenced but how they got to him ..."

"Did you call Teresa Brent to tell her? She'll be relieved Nathan won't need to testify." Jeremy glanced at his door as his office assistant walked through with a tray and the coffee. "Thanks Jenna."

Christine smiled toward the other woman. "Hi Jenna. I didn't notice you when I arrived so I came on back. How are you feeling today?"

"Oh, not as bad as yesterday. I think I'm getting my strength back quicker this time. Thank God, I'm finished with Chemo." She turned to leave and looked back at Christine. "How did your meeting go?"

"Short but I got to meet all the board members. It's going to take a lot of work for me to understand the full extent of what Rompart does and how many companies they own. This was a good beginning, anyway." Christine glanced at Jeremy as she added the cream and sugar to her coffee. She took a sip.

"Thanks again, Jenna." He studied the woman, a friend as well as a co-worker, as she walked back through his door. "She doesn't complain much but I can see she's tired already and she just got here an hour ago. The cot idea may be a good one. If the woman would use the thing. She is stubborn."

Christine chuckled. "And that's how she's managed to survive each horrendous round of Chemo. Stubbornness." She took another sip. "This is just what I need."

"Anyway, I assume you called the Brent family." Jeremy took a gulp of his coffee. No messing with the black brew he liked.

"I did. After I warned them someone broke into my home and only touched my address book. Teresa and her sister took the kids to a cottage where they spent some of their childhood, a place not connected to them in any way. She uses a cell so I was able to still reach them. I told them not to phone anyone except when I called or for an emergency." She crossed her legs at the ankles. "Their sigh of relief came across loud and clear but Teresa said she was sorry the authorities couldn't glean more information out of Fine."

"Yeah. I'd like to find out how he and Devine were connected. Did the PC tell you if he had any visitors? Maybe someone who had contact with the other pedophiles in the area."

Her expression changed. Christine glanced toward Chief and back to her male counterpart. "That's the odd part. His lawyer met with him twice but no one else. Jason Mitchell is the same man who looks after all legal transactions for Rompart."

"You're kidding." Jeremy flopped back against the cushions on his chair. "Why would your company's attorney defend a pervert like Fine? Maybe he only acted as Fine's lawyer for the coin shop."

"I suppose. The Police Chief said one of the guards over-heard them arguing a number of times. He also said the sus-pected pedophile pranced around all cocky the last time Mitch-ell came to visit him. This is definitely something I intend to talk to Jason about the next time we meet. I don't want a shady lawyer working for my Dad's company."

"Your business now."

"Yeah, I guess. The idea hasn't sunk in yet." Christine stood. "Thanks again for looking after Chief. My appointment with a Dr. Steven Lombart is in a few minutes. He's the family doctor for the Anderson's. I want to find out if he suspected any abuse." She buttoned her suit jacket. "Jeans would feel more comfortable but I don't want to take the time to go home."

"The outfit looks great on you. So professional. Doesn't go with the dog, though." Jeremy chuckled. "I hate suits and ties, too."

She took a couple of steps toward the door. "My ranch upbringing didn't prepare me to be an office type person. One more reason to sell Rompart one day."

He escorted her through his door and to the main ex-it. "Are you thinking about selling the company?"

Christine waved toward Jenna. She glanced back at Jeremy and studied his expression. "You don't think unloading the company is a good idea?"

"How you handle your firm is really none of my business but ..." He swallowed uncomfortably. "I mean, I thought carry-ing on your Father's legacy was important to you." He opened the outer door.

"Maybe, maybe not." She shrugged. "Selling is only one option. I won't be able to do both ... look for missing kids and manage the company. So time will tell." She turned to step out-side and swiveled her head toward Jeremy again. "I don't plan on making any decisions until I find out who really killed my parents."

Jeremy nodded at her back and closed the door behind her. *Interesting.* He grimaced. *Her life is complicated.*

Chapter Fifteen

Christine opened the door to her Grand Cherokee. Chief jumped in forcing her to take an extra step backwards for balance. "Making sure I don't leave you behind again, eh?" She chuckled, slid into her seat, and buckled her seatbelt. She twisted her head to look at her canine as he settled in the back and put the car in gear for the trek to Dr. Lombart's office.

By this time of day fewer cars traveled toward the city center. Vehicles honked their horns; pedestrians strolled to appointments or spent their time window shopping. "We missed going to Denny's this week. Maybe tomorrow. Okay, Chief?" The dog woofed his approval.

Christine pondered her relationship with Denny Larson. *The man would make someone a wonderful husband. His ranch is a great place to raise kids and he's filled patience with them.* She recalled how Jimmy relaxed at Larson Kennels, a young boy so abused strangers scared him to death. Denny won his heart though, especially when he gave the boy one of his puppies.

Christine glanced in the mirror. Denny sparked a few smiles and today's recollection was no exception *but ... there's no chemistry between us. He's a friend, nothing more.*

She stopped the car for a red light. A few people crossed the street in front of her. Red changed to green and she accelerated through the intersection. At the next intersection, she made a left hand turn and pulled into the closest parking space at the clinic. "Chief, the weather is not too hot today so you can stay here. This won't take long."

She quickly stepped down to the pavement, locked the door behind her and entered the main door. Approaching the receptionist, she asked to meet with Dr. Lombard and handed the woman her license. She sat in the chair nearby to wait. No one else occupied the large room.

Christine glanced around. Three walls were painted a cheerful hue of green with a bright yellow on the last one. Several landscapes hung strategically with seating near tables containing a variety of reading choices. *I hope the doctor doesn't keep me waiting too long.*

Seconds later, the click clack of high heels warned of the receptionist's return. Christine followed her to the doctor's private office. Dr. Lombart appeared younger than she expected. His sandy colored hair flowed down to his collar where a few curls wrapped themselves over the fabric. His eyes locked with hers. "What can I do for you, Ms. Smith?"

Christine sat forward in her seat. "Sylvia Anderson hired me to find her daughter. I wondered ..."

"Samantha is missing? When did she disappear? She's been my patient since she arrived in this world. I ..." The doctor's face turned a slight pink. His voice shook.

Christine decided directness was in order. "Dr. Lombart. Did you suspect any abuse at any time?" His neck began to seep red.

He sputtered. "May I remind you Ms. Smith, that I am obligated to report such? Since I have not ..." He paused. The doctor leaned back against the chair he occupied. "No, no abuse. If anything, Sylvia has always been over protective of the girl but never a mark she didn't obtain from falling off a bicycle or playing on the school playground. Why are you asking about abuse?"

"Research shows children who are abused at home tend to run away. Mrs. Anderson refutes the idea of Samantha running away but I need to cover all bases. Right now, the search is at a standstill so I am checking out any and all possibilities." Christine stood and held out her hand to shake the doctor's. "Thank you for your time, Dr. Lombart." She turned to leave the small room.

"Wait." The doctor wiped his hands on his pants. "I suggested to Sylvia she allow her daughter some freedom. The girl is twelve after all and Mrs. Anderson walked her to and from school every day." He hung his head. "This is my fault."

"Dr. Lombart, you are assuming someone abducted Samantha. No evidence supports anything like that yet. However, it's my next thread to investigate. Your suggestion to her mother didn't cause a kidnapping." The doctor's eyes fill with unshed tears.

"I - I will never forgive myself if something happens to the child." He hung his head.

Christine cleared her throat to settle the lump threatening to spill into her own watershed. "Over the past few months, we've uncovered a string of missing children trafficked to pedophiles so we are knowledgeable about human traffickers in the area. They target kids for any number of reasons. Walking to school alone is only one opportunity but I understand Samantha always walked with friends."

Now the medical professional cleared the emotion from his voice. "Her mother indicated as much to me when she said the child's peer group always invited Samantha to go with them. Find her, Ms. Smith. Please."

"Um-m. Doctor, do you always form such a strong attachment to the kids you look after?" Christine tilted her head to soften her words.

"No. I mean, yes. Sometimes. But I deal with whole families and when Mrs. Anderson's husband walked away from the marriage ...."

"When did all this happen? She never elaborated when she and I met." The investigator stood straighter. Her hand left the doorknob.

Dr. Lombart paused. "I probably shouldn't say anything, but a year ago, the man disappeared for a few days. When he came home, he packed and moved out. Last month, Sylvia and I went out to dinner together. I care about her and the kids."

"So your involvement is not strictly professional?" Christine shifted her weight from one leg to the other.

Steven Lombart had the decency to look a little sheepish. "Not anymore. I gave her the name of another family practitioner and she planned to call him for any further medical visits. I've only seen her socially once more. We decided to take our relationship one step at a time."

"Maybe Samantha was distraught about her father leaving and your friendship with her mother."

"Sylvia wanted to wait a little longer to tell her although I wanted her to let the kids get used to the idea. I hate sneaking around." He moved toward the office door. "I have a patient waiting. Anything else?"

"No. Not for now. Thank you for your time. I'll be talking to Mrs. Anderson when anything comes to light, to keep her informed. She may need your support." Christine turned to leave, opened the door and walked through. She glanced at the doctor once more over her shoulder. His look of distress tugged at her heart strings. *If he discovers what I found out about human trafficking, he'd be even more upset.*

She strode briskly toward her parked vehicle. Chief danced in the front driver's seat. She pressed the unlock button on her key fob, opened the door and pushed the dog toward the far side of the car. "Okay, boy, settle down. I want to go visit with the coroner next. You can come with me even though he doesn't like dogs. He doesn't like humans either. The man causes one to disregard what he wants."

She inserted the key into the ignition and drew in a deep breathe at the same time. *The last time I met with John Belmont was anything but pleasant but I need to cross the possibility off my list.* She pulled into traffic.

The drive to the Provincial Coroner's Office took very little time. Located right next to the main police station in the center of Winnipeg, the large gray structure dominated the cityscape. Parking on the street this time, she grabbed Chief's leash and headed inside.

The short stature of the receptionist forced the woman to look up at her, as Christine approached the desk. "You can't bring that animal in here." The woman pointed toward the door.

"Chief goes where I go. He's a service dog. I need to meet with Dr. Belmont." Christine straightened her spine. She stifled the laughter trying to erupt at the woman's attempt to stop her.

"This oughta be good. I'll go find him right away. He'll send you packing along with the animal." She stood. Her march down the hallway sounded louder than usual as she stomped her heels on the floor with each step.

Now that's professional. She decided to follow. Belmont never sees anyone out here. She walked down the familiar corridor toward the coroner's private domain. The receptionist smirked in her direction but kept walking after leaving her boss's office.

Christine crossed the threshold into the dim recesses of Dr. Belmont's private domain. The man sat behind his oversized desk. "Ms. Smith. I might have known." His growl sounded ominous. "Keep the animal on his leash."

Christine decided to ignore his comments. "I need to find out if the body of a young girl, twelve years old, was admitted here in the last few days."

"What are you snooping into now?" He slapped his hand on his desktop. "Leave the police work to the police."

"John. May I call you John? After all we are neighbors." Christine smiled tentatively, hoping to soften the medical examiner a bit.

"No. You may not." He leaned back in his chair and crossed his arms before looking at her with his usual glare. "Why are you looking for a twelve year old?"

"She's missing, of course. That's what I do ... find kids who have disappeared." Her face muscles began to tighten. "Are you storing someone her age?"

"No. I'm not sure I'd tell you if I did." He rose from his seat so abruptly the chair moved backwards and hit a file cabinet. "I have work to do."

"Will you call me ..." She placed one of her cards on his desk. "... if someone about twelve comes in?"

"I suppose. Now, leave me alone." He shuffled toward the door leading to the room where the bulk of his activity took place. "The morgue is busy today and, since the city hired an incompetent to assist me, my job is more tedious."

His complaint sounded like the same one he'd uttered the last time Christine visited. "Maybe if you ... Oh, never mind." She stalked down the hall toward the exit without a backward glance. *The man is infuriating to say the least.* She dropped her head as she approached the outer door. *But he is brilliant.*

Chapter Sixteen

As soon as she settled herself in the driver's seat of her vehicle, Christine grabbed her cell phone and punched in the number for the former prostitute. The ring tone filled the silence as she reached behind to scratch Chief on his head. She smiled at the dog. "You probably want a short walk, eh ..." She focused on the voice responding to her call. "Hello. I'm looking for a woman by the name of Shonney Barrett. Is she available?"

With a noted hesitancy, the woman asked, "What do you want with her?"

"Sergeant Irving thought she might help in a case I'm conducting. I'm a private investigator searching for a missing twelve year old. I wanted to meet with her in person if she's not too busy." Christine waited patiently, afraid she'd told the woman too much.

"I-I'm Shonney. McDonald's is located near my house. I'll feed my two boys and come see what you want ... say ... in half an hour. You okay with that?"

The woman sounds too young to be mother to a couple of kids. Christine pondered the implication of the children whom this woman birthed in such horrendous conditions. "I'm sorry. I thought ... well ... never mind. I can be at the restaurant in 30 minutes. Will that be enough time?"

"Yeah, lunch don't take too long. Once the boys head back to school, I'll be free." She hung up and Christine listened to the buzz signifying the end of the call. She slid her key into the ignition and calculated the time needed to arrive for the interview. "Do you want to run in the park?"

Chief hopped into the front seat, no small task for a dog his size. His tail propelled itself in circles hitting the window on the passenger door with every wag. Christine chuckled. "I guess that's a 'Yes'." She grabbed her keys again and the dog's leash. Clipping the latch to his collar, she opened her door and let him jump to the pavement. Chief tugged her toward the green grass nearby.

She sidestepped a grease spot on the cement as her canine led her to the small enclosed park across the street from the ME's office. A wrought iron fence, short enough for her to step over and for Chief to bound across, circumvented the area, adding some charm to the space. Wood benches trimmed with the same scrolled pattern as the fence sat strategically along the walking path. Three people dressed in jogging attire ran, huffing past them.

Chief sniffed the grass in different spots, seeking a choice place to leave his mark, Christine walked with him, keeping pace with his purposeful strides. She took a deep breath of the cool air. "Won't be long." Chief ignored her.

She glanced around. The three joggers made their way to the other side of the park so she released the catch on Chief's leash. "Only a few minutes, boy. Then we skedaddle." She sat down on the nearest bench and leaned back. The wood cooled her backbone. *Soon this peaceful setting and the sidewalks will be covered in snow and ice. I hate for summer to end.*

Chief relieved himself against a tree and sniffed the area for the scent of other dogs. *He's a good tracker but a much better tension breaker for these kids.* She remembered Jimmy's reaction to the animal versus his fear of the men rescuing him.

Christine lifted her arm to read the time on her wristwatch. "Chief, come." She stood, waiting as her partner bounded toward her, his leap telling her how much he enjoyed the short respite. She reattached his leash and strolled, the dog right beside her, to the Jeep.

Chapter Seventeen

The man peered through the windshield. He drove the beat up pickup parked a block away from the Grand Cherokee. He'd been hired to follow the owner. He studied the woman who walked her dog across the street. It looked like she planned to release her canine to roam the park. *Some people don't care about their animals and the waste they leave for others to tread through.*

He snatched his notebook and journaled some details. *I'll bet the guy doesn't understand anything about this dame. He wanted me to tail her after the meeting but he didn't say she owned a dog.* He decided to contact the number of his client.

The cell phone in his hand vibrated as he picked the device up. He flipped it open. "Yeah?" The voice on the other end sounded curt. "I'm watching her now. She's giving the dog some exercise in the green space across from the Coroner's office." He listened to the increased volume. "How should I know?"

He sat up straighter as the woman bent down to the dog and attached his leash again. "I gotta go. She's moving again." He rolled his eyes. "Yeah, later. I'm friends with someone at the morgue. He might have some information for me."

His ear hurt when the caller barked additional orders through the phone line. "Yeah. Yeah. I'll keep outta sight. You think I never done this before?" He ended the call and slipped his vehicle into drive as Christine pulled away from the curb.

Chapter Eighteen

Chief sat quietly at her feet, as Christine kept her eyes on a young black woman who walked into the restaurant. The woman appeared a little older than she'd imagined. She ordered a coffee, and turned to gaze around the room. The moment the woman spied the canine, a smile lit her face. She turned back to pick up the beverage the hostess placed on the counter.

Dog and mistress stood as one to greet their new contact. Shorter by a couple of inches, she held out her hand. "Hi. I'm Shonney Barrett. I called Sergeant Irving and he corroborated your story."

Christine returned to her seat and Shonney took the one across from her. "He seems to respect you."

"Yeah. He looks out for me sometimes. I like your dog. Is he friendly?"

Christine placed a notepad on the table and glanced at Chief. "He is but he's a service animal so I don't encourage people to come too close. Except the kids. He comforts them until they are reunited with their parents." She flipped the pad open to a clean page. "The mother hired me to find a missing girl, about twelve years old. What can you tell me about the prostitution business in this city?"

"Boy, you don't beat around the bush. What did Irving say

about me?" A few crinkles appeared near the woman's eyes but her alabaster skin seemed flawless. Her dark brown eyes seemed concerned.

Christine checked where the other patrons sat. No one else was in the restaurant at the moment. "The sergeant told me you used to be a working girl. I believe that's the current term for prostitutes, right?"

Shonney flinched. "True and I was also a meth addict ten years ago. Since I left, a lot changed in the trade and on the streets. The girls are getting younger although my eleventh birthday only just happened before I partied for the first time."

"Eleven." Christine lowered her voice. "Eleven. What about your parents?"

Shonney grimaced and smiled. "I don't like talking about this much but Irving said to tell you everything so here goes. I ran away after an uncle molested me for the tenth time. I told my mother but she never believed me so I took off. I hitched a ride to Vancouver where I met Justice."

"A complete stranger picks up an eleven year old girl without trying to talk her into going home. How does that happen?" Christine scribbled some notes and looked the woman across from her right in the eyes. *Is she for real?*

"By the time I left for Vancouver, I learned how to dress and put on make-up to make me appear more mature. The trip took a few days. I made friends with some of the older kids on the street as soon as I arrived." Shonney held Christine's gaze before taking a sip of her coffee.
"So your parents never searched for you?"

"They might have but not to my knowledge. I believed at the time they wanted me gone." She took a quick gulp and glanced at the band on her wrist. "I can't be away from home too long. A neighbor keeps her eyes peeled for my boys but ..."

Christine sensed Shonney's unease as she used her boys as an excuse. "I understand. What does the culture look like here, in this city? Are you still in contact with the girls in the trade?" Christine reached down to pat Chief as if she needed the comfort of knowing something wholesome right then.

"A person not involved with the life won't get it. When I got to Vancouver, an older teenager acted all friendly and stuff. She introduced me to drugs, anything I wanted. Life was one big party after another for a while. One night I was high, I let this man ... he seemed old to me, probably about thirty or so ... do what he wanted. He ... well anyway, you can imagine, I'm sure. The next day, he owned me and put me out on the street to pay for my habit. I was hooked so ..." Shonney's voice held no emotion as if she spoke about another person.

Christine jotted down the sequence of events. "But this is Winnipeg, not Vancouver. Are the same things going on here?"

"You bet they are. They sold me to another pimp who transported me here. They trade women like pieces of meat ... boys too. If a big sporting event like the Grey Cup comes to the city bringing lots of men, they fill the streets and bars with girls to accommodate the traffic." Shonney took a gulp of the cooler liquid.

"So you maintain your connections on the street, still, after ten years?"

"I do. I want to help those girls escape the lifestyle like I did. I met a woman years ago who loved me without judging me. She introduced me to my Saviour. He helped me turn my life around and regain custody of two of my three boys as well as earn an education. I want the women still in bondage to meet Him too." Shonney smiled as if her life was anything but what it was.

Christine marveled at the glow of peace surrounding her. "What's this person's name? Can I visit with him ... or her? I need to find out how they extricate someone from life on the streets."

"Well, meeting him isn't an issue but an interview ... I don't think so. His name is Jesus and He is my constant companion."

Oh, for crying out loud. She threw up her hands. "That's it. You got religion?" Christine worked hard to not sound too disparaging. "I thought you talked about a person."

"I am. He's the most important one in my life. He helped me get clean, and stay sober. Without Him ..." Shonney's eyes filled with unshed tears. "I'd be dead."

"But didn't anyone help you besides some religious Icon? I mean ... a genuine person." Christine's frown flitted across her face but quickly vanished in hopes of securing the information to find Samantha.

Shonney continued. "Jesus is a person. He's as real as you

and I. He used Cherie Dubois in the beginning but she's moved to another city now. People come and go but the Lord is always here for me and my boys. I think you need to meet Him if you ever plan to locate this kid." She looked at her watch. "I gotta go."

Frustration laced Christine's next words. "That's wonderful ... for you. But, wait. I want to speak to someone who lives the life now. What methods would a pimp use to enslave an unsuspecting twelve year old?"

Before the reformed woman was able to stand, Christine grabbed her arm. "Introduce me to one of the girls still working the streets? I could go undercover for a few nights." *What? Where did that ridiculous idea come from?*

Shonney laughed. "You kiddin' me. They'd peg you as soon as you hit the pavement. You're too clean." Her black heritage began to reveal itself. "I'm sure not gonna bring you to that part of the city after working hard to maintain the trust of those girls."

Christine removed her hand. She lifted pleading eyes in Shonney's direction. "This child needs to be found before she's hooked on something or whatever they do. Jesus can't help me. Only you."

"No, not me. You can call but I ain't getting involved. My boys are all I think about now and I'm almost ready to graduate with my Bachelor's degree in social work. I ..." She took a deep breath and emitted a sigh of resignation. Putting her hand into her pocket, she pulled out a card. "Call me. I'll think about it. That's the best I can do."

Christine glanced at her as the woman stood. She grimaced and nodded her head. "I understand. Thank you for talking to me." She placed the card in her purse as Shonney exited the restaurant and quickly walked across the street. *What a story.* Christine shook her head.

She thought about where this brave woman came from. *She's a survivor, that's for sure and with two boys. I wonder why the third one doesn't live with her. Oh, right. Someone adopted him.* She reached for Chief's leash. "Come on, boy." She remained seated for another few minutes. Her face crinkled around the edges of her mouth in a grimace. *I can't believe I suggested I go undercover. I'm glad she didn't laugh her head off. I'm also relieved she didn't think the idea would work. That's not happening. No way.*

She led Chief out to the parking lot. Once he settled in the backseat, she took her place behind the wheel. She paused for a moment with her hand on the key. She glanced at the time. Five o'clock. *Enough for today. I need to call Sylvia and fill her in, though. Not much to tell her ... really. Speculation, nothing more.*

She turned on the ignition. *I wonder if Jeremy is at the office. He might be a great sounding board. He could provide some idea of what the next step is.* Her vehicle rumbled as she slipped the transmission into drive.

Chapter Nineteen

Jeremy checked the time on his computer. He pressed the intercom. "Jenna. Your work day is over. I'll lock up when I leave."

"How long you gonna be, boss? I can wait." Her voice revealed more than she wanted to let on.

Jeremy detected her fatigue. "Don't push yourself, Jenna. There's always tomorrow. Go home." He returned to the research he'd begun. His fingers were positioned to copy down the phone numbers he located for three different Joseph Dryden's. The creak of the exterior door signaled someone either coming or going. Dismissing the sound as Jenna leaving for the day, he wrote the first number on his scratch pad. Voices interrupted him.

Slipping his feet back into his shoes, he stood, walked around his desk and headed toward the door. Before his hand grabbed the handle, the door appeared to open by itself.

Christine poked her head around the frame. "Got a minute?"

"Uh, sure." He raised his voice so Jenna heard loud and clear. "Good night, my friend."

"Night, boss." The outer door opened and closed a second time.

"She's pushing herself too hard so I suggested she leave early." Jeremy motioned for Christine to sit on the sofa.

She looked at her wristwatch and then held the delicate bracelet out for him to check the time. "It's not exactly the middle of the afternoon ... almost six o'clock." She chuckled. "I suspect she, like you, gets caught up in her work and you both lose track of time. Chief is outside in my Jeep but we're hungry. Wanta eat somewhere and we can talk? I need to run something by you ... pick your brain."

"Let's go to my house. I can grill a mean steak." Jeremy walked over to his desk. He scribbled the other two phone numbers on his pad of paper and shut down his computer. "I can finish this stuff tomorrow."

"Sounds good. A steak dinner is a rare treat." She grinned and listened as her stomach growled for the third time. "Chief can wait till we're home."

"No way. A dog deserves to be pampered once in a while too. He's a working canine and needs his protein. Besides, he and I bonded. We understand each other." He grabbed his jacket and led the way toward the front door. "Do you know my address? I don't think you've ever been to my home."

"I'll follow you. You live in a duplex, right?" She jangled her keys as she strode toward her Grand Cherokee.

"Not for long. I visited with a real estate ... we'll talk later." Jeremy slid into his truck cab and turned the key. *This'll be fun. I'll enjoy some company for a change.*

Chapter Twenty

Her head jerked. Her eyes flashed open. She couldn't go to sleep. Her eyes focused on the dank interior of the well. Water dripped somewhere but their fruitless search ended as soon as dark descended once again. Her dry throat craved water. According to the other girl, her stay had been a long one. *How long* she wondered.

She ran a hand through her matted hair. Dirt caked her fingers. She and the older girl worked hard to dig through without success to the place where the dripping beckoned them. She stood. Standing on tiptoes, she tried to gain a handhold. The roughhewn, slimy walls contained no crevice to place even a finger.

She leaned back against the wall and then stepped away. She looked toward the sky. A few stars shone overhead, at least the few she saw through the narrow opening above her head.

Her eyes still held some tears it seemed. They slid unchecked down her cheek. "Why?" She screamed. But no one answered her. She thought about the soft bed, decorated in pink and blue, sitting in the corner of her room at home. She thought about the restroom adjoining her room. Another tear escaped

her lower eyelid. Her throat hurt but she screeched anyway. "Let me out of here."

A head appeared over the top of the well. "Hello dar-
lin. You ready to do what you're told?"

She hesitated, only a second. Her voice
squeaked. "Yes. Anything. Pull me up. Please."

The person above her dropped the lifeline. The corded
strands hit her on the head. She grabbed the course threads to
tie around her waist as she'd seen the older girl do. She used her
hands to hold onto the rope over her head. "I'm ready."

Her feet lifted off the ground as the red eyes of the rodent
sharing the well slipped closer. She pulled her legs higher. Her
body swayed in mid-air.

"Keep still." The man's voice sounded angry.

She stopped struggling as the rope lifted her slowly toward
the rim of the well. Her hands hurt from the rough braiding she
clung to. She grasped it tighter. Her head peeked over the edge.

She remembered the van, the one this man drove along the
sidewalk before the side door opened. She fought the course
hands as they yanked her inside. A bag was slipped over her
head. Now, however, she saw the man clearly in the moon-
light.

"You ready to obey?" He spoke quietly. He left her hanging.

The rope cut into her waist. "I want to go home." She
blinked another tear away. "I want my mother."

"You want. You want. I'll tell you what you want. You
wantta get outta the well, doncha?" His harsh voice almost
growled,

She cringed. *Can't make him angry.* "I'm sorry. Yes
I .... Please."

"I'll ask you again. You gonna obey me?" He snarled and
grabbed for her. "Otherwise I throw you back."

She shrieked, "No, please. I'll be good. I'll do what you
want."

The man lifted her over the rim. He untied the rope. His
hand scratched her arm as he pulled her toward his vehicle. "Climb in. Don't give me no trouble. We'll come back here
if you do."

She slid into the front seat and buckled her seatbelt. Folding her hands in her lap, she looked down. The vehicle swayed as the man filled the bench beside her. "Where are
you taking me?"

"No questions. Do as you're told." He started the van and
idled slowly forward. "Remember the well. Next time, you
won't be rescued."

Chapter Twenty-One

The dark sedan seemed to slither along the street. He drove a few car lengths behind Christine's Jeep. While the driver kept an eye on the crimson taillights, he punched in the phone number for the man most interested in the woman's whereabouts. He paired the cell with the car's Bluetooth system for hands free calling. He placed his hand back on the steering console. *Don't need a cop interrupting this call.*

"Hey, it's me. You guessed right. The girl works from Jeremy Goodman's office. He's an investigator too. His dad hires him from time to time. He does business with other lawyers, too." He listened as the man cursed angrily. "I figure she's a snoop too."

He waited for the renewed outburst on the other end to subside. The Jeep pulled up to a curb in front of a duplex. Goodman parked his truck in the driveway. *So this must be where the dude lives. I wonder if he and the woman have something going on.* A calm hesitation finally sounded in his ear. "This makes our job a little clearer, I think. We need to eliminate her. She comes by the snooping naturally and she'll hurt us."

The intensity of the man's reaction flowed like liquid asphalt through the air waves and into the caller's ears. "Yeah but..." The voice cut him off. "I guess. She's the dame who put Fine behind bars. I'm not going to jail for anyone. Even you." He pounded the steering wheel to punctuate his intentions. "Okay, I'll keep watching. Maybe a scare will stop her."

His disgruntled boss chortled sarcastically. The course voice added, "If she's the same woman who got Fine for kidnapping, his henchmen manhandled her a few times already. She keeps coming back for more. No, we've gotta be smarter than her. We found out she's the Rompart dame so we can keep an eye on her more closely. We'll take care of her if there's no choice. Maybe she wants to sell the company and won't give us another headache. Follow her. Watch what she does over the next couple of days. Afterwards we'll decide if she needs to be taken out of the picture."

The stalker spotted Jeremy and Christine, with Chief at her side, as they climbed the steps to the front porch and enter his home. "She's gone inside. This situation might be personal but they could also be talking business. I need to get closer. Maybe ..." His eyes roved along the side of the house. Another light flooded the back yard. "I gotta go. I'll stay back. Keep my eyes open ... for now."

He pressed the 'end call' button, dropped the phone on the seat and turned off the ignition. He waited in case someone else roamed the street this time of night. *I don't need any witnesses.* The area appeared quiet. The city lights came on. *The skies are still too light, though. I'll wait for about thirty minutes. I'll creep closer to listen, find out what they're up to.*

He leaned back and closed his eyes. The day seemed to go on forever. The woman led him all over town where she made one stop after another. *Maybe if I'd followed her inside the coroner's office, I might have some idea what she's up to by now.* His back relaxed against the cushion for the first time all day.

The sound of an approaching engine grew louder. He slouched deeper into his seat. The car drove slowly by. He scanned the landscape as the vehicle turned into the driveway in front of Goodman's house. *At least, I assume the snoop's lives there. Good thing I waited.* He sucked in a deep breath of air and shut his eyes again. *It'd be dark soon.*

Chapter Twenty-Two

A flood of light replaced the darkness inside the interior as soon as Jeremy flipped the switch near his front door. Christine stepped over the threshold. Her eyes investigated this man cave. Dark brown leather dominated the room but a few softer touches added warmth. "Looks like some woman gave you her two cents worth."

Jeremy chuckled. "My mother had a way with a room. Come on. Join me in the kitchen." He led the way through the large open space to a section separated by a bar. "Hang your jacket over the back of the sofa. Chief, you want some water?"

Jeremy grabbed a plastic ice cream pail from his pantry and filled the container half full with water from the tap. "Are you thirsty, Christine?"

"I am. Water would be fine for me too." She slid onto a stool and hooked her feet on the rung a third of the way from the floor.

Jeremy opened the fridge door and peered inside. "I have this bottle of wine ..."

"Great." She looked around the well-appointed kitchen

area. "You like to cook?"

"I do." Jeremy popped the cork from the bottle. He poured a generous amount of red wine into each of the two goblets sitting on the island in his kitchen. Jeremy slid the glass closer to her. "I hope you like a Merlot, the only red wine available at the moment."

"I'm not a wine connoisseur. I only enjoyed a couple of glasses in my life. Uncle Conrad and Aunt Connie never drank much and never allowed me to indulge since I was too young, according to them." She chuckled. "They always treated me as a kid. I complained about it often enough, anyway."

"I remember, when Mom still lived, I made the same assumption. They never let me grow up. A few years of running my own agency and Dad finally started to treat me as an adult. Even now, I catch him biting his tongue when we talk, working hard at not adding his two cents." He took a sip of the red liquid, cooled to the right temperature. Setting the glass back on the counter, he opened the freezer at the bottom of his refrigerator. "T-bones okay?"

"Are you kidding? They raised me as a rancher's kid, remember. I ate steaks from our own cattle three or four times a week, but not since moving to the city. I never learned how to properly cook one. Aunt Connie spoiled me." She took a tentative sip of her wine and a second. "This is good."

"Friends and I attended a few tastings and learned a little about what I like and how to serve wine. Some are best at room temperature but I like Merlot chilled." He grabbed two steaks and another package of round steak for Chief. "No T-bone for the animal." He shook the parcel at his canine friend and grinned. "Probably doesn't matter to you anyway."

"Chief will think he's died and gone to heaven. All I give him is dog food because Denny said a balanced diet is the best for him." She stroked the dog's fur. "But once in a while won't hurt, huh Chief."

"Speaking of Denny, you talk to him lately?" Jeremy placed the steaks in the microwave to thaw and reached into his refrigerator for a basket of mushrooms and some onions. "These'll go good with the steak. I sauté them in butter."

Christine took another long sip of the richly flavored red liquid. "Chief and I are looking forward to a workout at his place again. But no, we've not talked to him since he brought in the pup for Jimmy two weeks ago."

Jeremy decided to fish. "How long have you known him?"

"I contacted him from Texas before I ever moved up here." She leaned over to pet Chief on the head again. "I always wanted to find little kids. I pictured a service dog as a necessary part of the plan. Larson Kennels built a good reputation from what I gleaned from my research. Since the facility is near enough, we're able to continue to update Chief's skills without having to travel halfway across country."

"He seems to think of you as more than a client." Jeremy decided to dig a little deeper. "I mean, when we looked for you, he seemed really scared about what might happen to you. He's very protective."

"And as I told you, he's a friend, nothing more. I think he wants more. He's asked me out a few times but I try to maintain a business relationship as much as possible. He's a nice guy and I don't want to hurt him." She sighed. "I almost wish our friendship was different. I think he's great husband material but ..."

"...not for you." Jeremy set the chopped onions and mushrooms aside and reached under his counter for a stainless steel skillet. "Do you like onions?"

"Not unless you're going to eat them too," She pretended to check her breathe by breathing into her hand.

He chuckled. "We've both been too occupied to talk much since we returned Jimmy to his parents." He opened the fridge again and selected a bag of lettuce, some tomatoes and a cucumber. Tossing them gently on the counter adjacent to the bar, he handed Christine a knife. "Want to cut and chop while we talk?"

"Sure. I wanted to pass some theories by you - about this missing kid." She dumped half the lettuce into the bowl Jeremy placed in front of her. "The research and interviews are done. The girl is gone. No one has any information as to where or how or why. I also found out from Sergeant Irving that some human traffickers are in the area. I interviewed a former prostitute and ..."

"You didn't think human trafficking happened in this city? The blight is everywhere." He placed three good sized steaks in a plastic tray and proceeded to add several spices to a dish he commandeered from another cupboard.

"I guess I haven't given the whole culture a lot of thought. Pedophiles, yes, but ..." She gave the tomato in her hand a slight squeeze.

"That's human trafficking too. These vices are all tied together. The traffickers supply whatever the johns want, girls or guys and little kids too. The business is consumer driven. I hope the new bill passes in parliament that goes after the Johns and the pimps." He began to rub the spices all over the steaks.

Christine dumped a couple of chopped tomatoes into the bowl of lettuce. "There's no apparent reason for her to run away other than her parents got divorced about a year ago and her mother is building a relationship with a new boyfriend. But apparently she hasn't been told yet - about the boyfriend, I mean."

"Did your interview at the school give you any indication she's unhappy?"

"No, and that's what's puzzling. She seems well adjusted with lots of friends and not one of them said anything about a plan to run. They all, everyone, said the girl would never do that so ..."

"You think someone took her." Jeremy left the steaks to marinate and added some more wine to their glasses. He took another gulp. "So where do you start looking?"

"I'm thinking I need to infiltrate the prostitution trade downtown."

"Not a good idea." He shook his head from side to side. "Christine, you're too emotional. Your life would be in the hands of traffickers." Jeremy glared in her direction hoping his words penetrated her stubborn brain.

She chose to ignore his response. "Shonney, the woman I interviewed who used to prostitute herself, doesn't want to be involved but I think, with a little persuasion, she'll help." Christine finished slicing the cucumber, added the vegetable to the salad and stood. She walked behind the counter to clean the cutting board.

Jeremy placed his hands on her shoulders and turned her body to face him. "Listen to me. You have no idea what those men will do to you."

"Yes, I do. I can read. Shonney told me how they got her hooked on Methamphetamine and turned her out. I want to find the child before ..." She turned pleading eyes on Jeremy. "The kid will never be the same after they're done with her." A lone tear made tracks down her once dry cheek.

He wrapped his arms around her. "I told you." A shudder escaped her body. He watched her stiffen against the feeling of helplessness. "You're already emotionally involved. We need to come up with another plan." He looked toward the ceiling. His heart reached with confidence for the only one who could help.

Silently, he asked the Father for some insight. Christine stirred and pushed but he held her tightly. Before he realized he spoke out loud, he asked, "Father, help this woman in her attempt to find this child. Protect her. Look after Samantha, Thank you, Lord."

He opened his eyes to find her staring up at him from her place against his chest. "You really believe God, all the way from heaven, cares about us, don't you?" Her question held no sarcasm or distain this time.

Jeremy stepped back from Christine. He waited a second or two before answering. *How shall I say this, Lord?* "Yes, Christine. I know He's intimately involved in all we do if we let Him. He wants to help. He waits to be asked. He loves you."

Christine turned back toward the counter. Her back remained rigid but the words she spoke softened her response. "I accept God does exist. He helped me when that maniac held me captive, but intimately? Why? That doesn't make sense."

"Sure does. If you got to actually converse with Him ..."

Christine looked at him, her mouth slightly open. "Relationship? How am I supposed to build a friendship with someone who exists in outer space, a million miles from here? I can't even see him. I can't touch Him. I can't write him a letter." She slapped her hands on her hips in a gesture, Jeremy surmised, to accent the impossibility of his statement.

"It begins with trust. You flew in an airplane to get here, didn't you?" He looked over her head at the clock above his refrigerator. *I need to cook these steaks.* He noticed her positive response to his question. He grabbed the meat and headed toward the door leading to his small patio. "Come, watch a chef in action."

Christine pursed her lips and followed him outside. "What does flying have to do with anything?"

Jeremy turned the knob for his grill to the 'on' position and cranked the starter to ignite the gas. "How do you believe something so big will be able to float around in midair and not drop to the ground at any given time during the flight?"

"Well ..." Christine sputtered. "I-I guess I-I ..." She seemed to be hunting for the right words. "It just happens, that's all. The law of ... well ... aerodynamics or something." She looked toward him as if hoping she'd gotten the answer right.

"But, when you step onto an airplane, you trust everything is going to work, don't you? The process takes trust in the pilot, whom you never meet, trust in the maintenance crew who check out the plane to make sure all is working as it should, and trust in the mechanics of flying. Trust is needed to fly. In order to know God, trust is involved as well. That's the starting point. You need to trust He exists even when you can't look at Him." Jeremy lifted the lid of the hot grill and flopped each of the steaks down in the wire grate.

Christine remained silent. He envisioned wheels turning in her head as thoughts floated from one brain cell to another. *She's already accepted the possibility of God. Would she take the next step from possibility to probability?*

Jeremy decided to stay quiet, to give her time to digest the seeds he planted. He used the grilling fork to turn the steaks. *I never asked her how she like her meat cooked.*

"Jeremy, I understand, for you, God is real. I wrestled with the fact your father also believes and I believe he's an intelligent man. When Dixson ... or Caputo grabbed me, I thought my life was over. But that little boy exhibited the strength to survive under such horrid circumstances. Some higher power kept him alive, especially his mind. And when we ran, when the creep caught up with us, you arrived in the nick of time, in the middle of nowhere. I believe God brought you to us. However, He let someone kill my parents' and the killer almost killed me too. I'll never forget the panic, the horror of having a man chase me. Where was He then?" She folded her arms across her chest, the cool evening air making goose bumps. "I need a jacket."

Jeremy glanced at the woman as she turned to go back inside. "Bad things happen to good people, Christine. That's the world we live in. God walks us through them if we let Him but He likes to be asked. Besides, he did protect you. You ran right into a cop who believed a little five year old girl."

She smiled as she placed her foot on the floor inside Jeremy's kitchen. She bowed her head and looked toward him from the corner of her eye. "Yeah, He did." She slipped through the door.

"Hey, Christine. How do you like your steak?" A large lump commandeered his vocal cords. His heart floated a little *higher. The light bulb may not be all the way lit but a glow is beginning.* He smiled. *It's a start.*

Chapter Twenty-Three

The watcher made his way stealthily past the first shrubs. He tried to appear as if he belonged. He glanced across the street. *No one out walking.* He inched around the corner of the building. A fence crowded him somewhat but he slid sideways toward the backyard. Voices flowed toward him.

He pulled the collar of his suit jacket up around his neck. *Need a coat.* His imagination gave his breath visibility. He let his eyes rove over the small space near the house for a few seconds. He caught only a word or two. *Gotta move closer.*

He eased his body behind the row of shrubs bordering the structure. He took one step snagging his pants on a lower branch. He yanked free. The twig snapped. He ducked. He peered through the bush in the direction of the place where the voices came from. The disembodied words floated more clearly across the space. He started to breathe again.

Why am I hired for all the dirty jobs? Mitchell better appreciate what I do for him. With money. He inched forward again. One footstep at a time. A branch scratched the back of his hand. A curse filtered through his mind but he held his tongue. The words coming from his targets seemed more distinguishable now.

The woman spoke first. "I'm going to get my jacket." *I still can't see her or the Goodman character.* He stood as quietly as possible. The sound of a door sliding open and closed overshadowed his frustration. He waited a few seconds and inched closer still. *There.* The aroma of grilled meat floated in his direction. His stomach rumbled. *This better be worth the price I'll be paid.* His inner grumblings left a sour film in his mouth.

The door opened and closed again. He kept an eye on the man while the woman stepped to his side. He held his breath, listening.

The man spoke now. "Ever been on a motorcycle?"

Her voice grew a little louder, the pitch telling the watcher it was not a consideration. "No. Too dangerous." *Ha. The tart doesn't know what danger is.*

Goodman seemed intent on persuasion. "Not with the right rider. An easy ride through some of the countryside with the trees changing color is what we need."

The steak sizzled. The watcher's insides rumbled. His hunger pangs sounded loud to his ears. His abdomen growled again. *Can they hear?* He leaned a little closer.

The woman screamed, her hand covering her mouth instantaneously. Goodman turned. He backed up, tripped but regained his balance. He rounded the corner of the house. Footsteps sounded on the grassy area close behind the watcher.

He raced. He crossed the street. The handle of the car gave his hand a cold welcome. He slid into the interior of his late model car. Goodman pounded on his window as he yanked the gearshift into drive. He stomped the gas pedal, not daring to glance sideways. *Where is the investigator?* He stole a glimpse in his rearview mirror. The large man stood in the middle of the road. He cursed loudly and pounded the steering wheel. *Mitchell won't like this.*

Chapter Twenty Four

Christine ran to Jeremy's side. "Did you write down the plate number?"

"I did." He slipped the pad of paper he always carried into his pocket. "I wonder if the guy followed you or me."

She placed her hand over the left side of her chest. "My heart is racing. That creep scared the beegeebers out of me." She walked slowly back across the lawn beside Jeremy. "I thought, since Fine died, they'd forget about me."

"He may be spying on me, though. Some weird twists surfaced in this recent case. The man I'm looking for will be very wealthy when the lawyers deliver his inheritance. Someone in the family might think they deserve the estate more." Jeremy increased his stride. "Those steaks will be overcooked if we don't hurry."

"How can you think of eating at a time like this?" Christine skipped to catch up. "He might have been sent to shoot one of us."

"Not likely. He had lots of chances to do use his gun and didn't. He listened for information, nothing more. And I'll bet someone else hired him." Jeremy grabbed the tongs to flip the meat again. "The steaks are done. Let's eat. We can talk over food."

"Don't you want to check out the spot where he stood to find clues?" Christine's heart rhythm returned to normal. Now she gained speed on some anger. "I wish I'd brought my gun."

Jeremy chuckled. "You're a regular Annie Oakley." His voice grew serious as he plated the steaks and headed toward the door. "I don't think his tracks will go away before morning. In the daylight, we'll be able to locate anything out of the ordinary."

Christine reached her hand toward her agitated animal as soon as the door opened. "Everything is okay, Chief." She looked toward Jeremy who placed the platter of meat on the counter next to the salad. "He thinks we're ignoring him." Her stomach rumbled. "The aroma of those steaks is sure appetizing."

"I'm hungry too. Danger does that to me. Want some water as well?" He refilled both their glasses with wine.

"I think one glass of wine is good for me. I'll pour the water. Do you want some?" She made her way toward the sink.

"Goblets are on the right. The water is in a jug in the fridge." He took the stool beside the one Christine occupied earlier. He stood again. "I almost forgot Chief." He walked to another cupboard and retrieved a large stainless steel bowl. "Will this do?"

She looked toward him as she set two glasses of cold frosty water on the counter. "Perfect."

Jeremy placed the bowl with some of the steak cut up on the floor. "Will he eat any of the salad?"

"Fraid not. Chief is strictly a carnivore when he eats anything other than dog food. He'll love the meat." She laughed as the canine gobbled two more pieces.

Jeremy chuckled as well as he returned to his own dinner. "I'll say grace, okay."

Christine put down her fork full of steak. "Oh right." She bowed her head. She listened to Jeremy's entreaty for safety for the remainder of the evening before he asked God to bless the food. Christine pondered his words and lifted her eyes as Jeremy switched his gaze to her face. She blinked. His scrutiny seemed more than businesslike. She cleared her throat and decided to ignore the look. "I wonder who hired the creep. And why?"

He chewed his first bite. "Not bad even if my steak is a little overdone." He hesitated before continuing. "Have you considered you might have talked to someone with a vested interest in your search for Samantha, like the abductor maybe? I mean, the perpetrator probably doesn't want her found and you're jeopardizing a lucrative deal for him. Young girls must go for a premium."

Christine shuddered. "I can't visualize the type of person who would sell another human being in this day and age. I thought we'd learned something since the days of slavery."

"Apparently not the right things. Trafficking is on the rise." He stuck his fork into another piece of meat.

Christine followed suit. She chewed mindlessly, savoring the flavor but not fully enjoying the meal as anticipated. "This is good, Jeremy. My appetite is not what it was before I spotted our intruder, though. I have a lot to learn before infiltrating those working girls. Do they still call them that? I read the term somewhere."

"What did Shon ... er ... the recovered pro say people called them?" He sipped a little from his almost empty glass of wine. He gazed at Christine over the rim.

She stared back for a second but quickly lowered her eyelids. "Shonney referred to them as girls. Would you act as my pimp or whatever? Can you take the time?"

Jeremy choked on the mouthful of food he not been able to swallow in time. "Do I look like one of those sleezeballs to you? You don't look like a prostitute either."

"Make-up and the right clothing will fix that. Shonney might help us look the part. What do you think? I want to infiltrate the culture, to find anyone who may have seen a new girl - someone Samantha's age. Surely there can't be many who fit the description." Christine shoved another forkful of salad into her mouth. She studied Jeremy's face for any sign he might agree to her plan.

Jeremy scowled. "You do realize this guy tonight might send a photo of you to the very person who took the girl."

"My disguise will keep them confused." Christine hoped her confidence level grew as the evening progressed.

"Until we figure out why he spied on us ...."

"Which makes it all the more imperative for us to walk those streets. The sooner we find the kid, the better. They probably plan to ship her somewhere where we'll never find her." She munched on another bite of meat.

"I don't think this is a good idea. Dad will throw a fit if he finds out what you're contemplating. This is dangerous, Christine."

"And going after little boys in the hands of pedophiles isn't?" She smirked at him, trying to lighten the mood. "You saved me before and you can keep me safe this time. Come on, Jeremy. Work with me, for a night or two. You can use your days to look for your missing heir."

"Oh, right, after roaming the streets all night." He stopped chewing for a full minute and looked toward her with an intensity she'd not seen before. "Are you willing to pray with me about this? Maybe God has a better plan."

Christine sighed. "If that idea makes you feel more comfortable. So far, I don't see His plans working for the good of anyone involved. But we'll try your prayer." She bowed her head for the second time during the meal.

Jeremy began. "Father, you already know where Samantha is, who abducted her and how we can find her. Please direct our paths. Lead us to the perfect plan to free her from the people who captured her. In the meantime, please protect her. Amen." He looked up at the woman who sat beside him.

Christine blinked. Tears flowed freely down her cheeks. Jeremy's prayer touched her as none had before. *What's with that?* She swiped the water from her face. She glared at the man who seemed to have a smile on his face. "You find pleasure in a woman's tears?"

"No, Christine. Just a softened heart." He closed his eyes and glanced toward the ceiling.

"Quit that. You give the impression you and God are in cahoots or something." She angrily ran her sleeve over her mouth before draining her wine glass. She swung around on the stool. "I'm full. Chief and I will be on our way. I want an early start tomorrow. Tell me when you decide to help." She stalked toward the front door.

"Christine. Come on. Don't be embarrassed. I won't tease, I

promise. Let's talk about the plan some more." Jeremy strode after her.

She tugged her arm into one of the sleeves of her jacket. Chief stood expectantly waiting by the door. "The day has been incessantly long. Besides, don't you need time to listen for God to communicate with you? We'll talk tomorrow." She began to button up.

"Fine. But don't do anything or go anywhere without consulting me first. I'll take the time, if God wants me to. We'll sleep on it. Okay?" He opened the door for her and checked the street to make sure no one idled outside. The neighbourhood remained silently empty.

"See ya." Christine waved and walked slowly toward her Grand Cherokee. "God, I hope you know what you're doing. Please keep Samantha safe." She looked upwards hoping to see a benevolent God looking back. The sky held only stars.

Chapter Twenty Five

The crisp coldness of a late fall morning greeted Christine when she and Chief stepped outside the next morning. Her chest expanded as she took a deep breath appreciating the air quality in this country. The morning news reiterated the problem in China; with smog so thick the sun was invisible most days.

Her partner sniffed the leaves blown along the path leading to the parking area. A squirrel chattered at him from the trunk of a nearby tree but the dog ignored him. Christine opened the door of her vehicle for the animal to hop in before she strolled around to the driver's door. Grabbing a glove from her coat pocket she slipped the warm fabric on before touching the cold metal of the handle.

The leather seat made a crunching sound as she slid inside and turned on the ignition. "Br-r-r." She shivered. "Denny will probably let us use the arena for a work-out." She glanced at her friend in the backseat. "The air is too frosty for even you, this morning, Chief." She turned on the heat and shifted into reverse.

Before she backed to the street, her phone buzzed from the seat beside her. She placed her Grand Cherokee in park again and reached for the device. "Hello."

Jeremy's voice, annoyingly cheerful for so early in the day, answered her greeting. She grimaced. "Chief and I are going to Denny's for a workout. Shouldn't be too long. Wanta come along?"

Jeremy surprised her by accepting her invitation. He said he looked forward to another visit with Denny. Christine decided to ignore his next remark about the dog trainer being her boyfriend. "We can talk about our plans for tonight while we drive out there. I'll pick you up in ten minutes. I'm already in the car."

Jeremy said he'd be ready so she ended the call. She backed onto the street and retraced the route from the night before. She grinned. *He's agreed to my plan. I wonder if that means God approves.* Her head filled with the picture of Jeremy praying the night before. *We've become comfortable around each other. He's not bossy.*

Chief barked at a dog strolling with his master down the sidewalk. His nose left prints on the window as Christine turned down the street toward Jeremy's house. He stepped out on his porch as she pulled into the driveway. Her dog jumped into the front seat. "No you don't. You're not messing up more windows. Jump in the back, boy."

Jeremy opened the door as Chief hopped between the seats toward the back. "Good morning." He slid in.

"Good morning to you too. This morning is a cold one for a drive in the country." Christine backed toward the street, and with her attention slightly focused on the man at her side, she headed toward Larson Kennels.

Jeremy seemed content to scan the scenery as trees and houses slipped by for a few minutes. As if they'd already been talking for a long time, he broke the silence. "I received something rather interesting from your Uncle Conrad in the mail this morning."

"Oh. I thought you stopped working for him since the body of the killer was found." She thought about the last time she'd talked to her former guardians. *I need to call them more often.*

"Remember I asked him for a picture of the man he hired before you went to live with them. Well, he finally sent one. Said he went through a whole box of photos." He reached into the inside pocket of his jacket. "Do you recognize this man?"

Christine glanced at the photo. "Sure. His name is Rusty. He taught me how to ride a horse but otherwise, I had nothing to do with him. He worked out of a range cabin most of the time. Are you saying he's complicit in my parent's death?"

"No. But we need to think about the possibility that where you lived all this time was no secret to the killer. He took his time, waiting to find out if you might recognize him. This man disappeared after the break-in and murder at the Finder's ranch. Conrad said he never said anything about leaving." Jeremy reached behind to stroke the dog that seemed to listen intently.

"But you've found no proof he's involved."

"No, not yet. But your uncle asked the state police in Texas to find him as a person of interest. His sudden disappearance is suspicious with all that went on at the time." Jeremy wriggled into a more comfortable position. "Each thread of information will help determine if the intruder was after you and who he works for ... hopefully."

"I want to clear my Dad's name. The father I remember couldn't do ... well ... my memories of him are of a good person. Rusty seemed nice, too. He kept to himself. I never heard of a girlfriend or even a male friend. The other ranch hands were all married and had their own lives except when Uncle Conrad and Aunt Connie threw a party. Rusty never attended those shindigs." Christine eyes were glued to the road. "Did you really say you'd help me out tonight?"

"I did. I think, with the right disguises, we could pull this off and blend in. Why couldn't we dress the part but tell the girls why we're really roaming the neighbourhood ... to find a young girl? Did the woman say they would be sympathetic at least?"

"I'll call her and ask. She seemed determined not to become involved so I was led me to believe the others wouldn't either. But maybe they would help us out." Christine reviewed her conversation with Shonney. "The woman seemed insulated, as if her current life was all she cared about."

"Didn't you say she became a believer, a Christian?"

"That's what she told me. Said Jesus saved her." Christine's use of the name seemed natural. Jeremy studied her for a few minutes. She glanced at him before focusing on the road again. "What?"

Jeremy shifted his gaze forward. He grinned. "Nothing." He cleared his throat and decided to answer her question. "If she is a Christian, it seems strange she would ignore your plea to help find this kid. Surely she must abhor the idea of anyone, never mind a twelve year old, getting involved in the trade."

Christine nodded. "She says she does but she also said she is working to build a trust relationship with some of the girls and I think she doesn't want to jeopardize the inroads she's made so far. She's raising two of her boys and they're only seven and nine. She has her hands full." Christine turned down the lane toward the stable at Larson Kennels. "I'll call her while Denny puts my friend here through his paces."

Christine parked the vehicle in the usual spot and quickly opened the door for her rambunctious animal. Chief raced toward his trainer who approached from the direction of his large arena. She glanced at the tall man as he stroked her canine behind his ears. "Hello Denny."

"Hi Christine." He nodded toward Jeremy. Denny paused as he looked from one to the other. "You guys working on another case together?" His tone sounded a little agitated to Christine.

"Sort of. Jeremy is assisting with my new search for a missing girl. We decided to iron out some of the logistics in the car on the way here. Besides," She glanced at Jeremy. "He said he wanted to visit again."

Denny's face softened a little. "Wanta watch me put Chief through his paces, Jeremy?" He turned back toward the large stable. Jeremy matched his stride step for step as they moved away from Christine. Denny's next question invited further conversation between the two men. "You been busy?"

Christine listened as Jeremy mentioned his latest case. She reached for her cell phone. *The sooner I pull Shonney into our plan, the better.* She scrolled to recent calls and pressed send when she highlighted Shonney's number. As soon as the voice identified itself as Shonney, Christine outlined their plan of action. "I think we can entice the girls to our side. What do you think, Shonney?"

"Crack heads only care about one thing - the next fix. These girls work hard to earn enough money to score. The crack makes them smell bad and their looks deteriorate. They do what they can to attract a John. Finding a missing kid is not a priority but ... "

"They can tell us if anyone new moved into the neighbourhood."

"You think that man bring her here? They gotta initiate her first. Get her hooked. That happens somewhere else, I think. I only worked the streets in Winnipeg for a few weeks before I got out." The woman seemed more interested than before.

"Shonney, how would you feel if someone abducted your nine year old son, or even your seven year old? Samantha Anderson's mother is beside herself with worry. She wants her daughter back and she will do anything to make that happen. If we need to pay someone for an hour of their time to obtain this information, we will. Will you help us?"

"I can't go down there. Not any more. Too many bad memories. But ..." The hesitation in her voice gave an almost ethereal quality. Just above a whisper. "I'll help you dress the part. When you wanta do this?"

"Tonight. The sooner, the better. What time is the best time to infiltrate the street?" Christine's heart leapt in her chest both from excitement and from fear. Things might go wrong and they'd never find the child.

"The girls are turned out around nine o'clock. If you and your man are out by then, you'll have a better chance of finding someone to talk to you. Come over around 7 and we'll fix you up. You and I about the same size, right? A three?"

"Yeah, that'll work. What about Jeremy?"

"Who?"

"Jeremy. He's the man I will be working with." Christine allowed exasperation to tinge her voice.

"He a cop?" Shonney sounded more skeptical than in the beginning of the conversation.

Christine swallowed. *I guess he is ... sort of.* "No, not a policeman. How should he dress?"

"Tight jeans, black shirt and tell him to bring lots of chains." Shonney giggled. "We deck him out good."

"Chains? What for?" Christine took the phone away from her ear to stare at the device as if she'd misunderstood. "I won't let him chain me to anything."

"Girl, you so green. Chains ... to wear around his neck ... jewelry. Man." Shonney snickered. "You need to think about a different plan."

"Fine. Jewelry. We're doing this. We'll be at your house around seven." She hung up before the former prostitute laughed any more. She stalked toward the arena, her cheeks a little warmer than the weather outside. *I may be naive but I care about these kids. I can do this.*

Chapter Twenty Six

Jeremy's eyes followed Chief's progress through the complicated course Denny organized in the large arena where he regularly trained dogs for police work and for special needs service canines. Hoops, barrels, and fences dotted the landscape and Chief performed impeccably at each obstacle. He kept his eyes on the trainer as Denny hid an object while the animal worked on obstacles at the other end of the arena.

Denny sauntered to Jeremy's side. "Now check this out." He whistled for Chief and the dog answered by bounding closer to them. He sat as if at attention.

"Chief has the routine down pat, doesn't he?" Jeremy grinned in the animal's direction.

"He does but I change the course each time." Denny gave a hand signal. Chief turned his body away from them in one motion as soon as he stood. Jeremy admired the dog's fluid lines as he raced from one end of the track to the other until, with nose in the air; he caught the scent he looked for. A few seconds later Chief, with his trophy in his mouth, returned to the two men.

"Good boy." The trainer reached toward the dog with a treat in his fingers. Chief dropped the stuffed sock and gently accepted his reward. Denny turned to the younger man. "What did Christine mean about the two of you going out tonight? You think you'll find the kid better at night?"

"No, not so much but that's where we're going to start the search. Statistics indicate someone her age is a target for traffickers and ..." Jeremy hesitated. *How much does Christine reveal to this man about her procedures?* "Nighttime is the best time to begin our search, is all."

Denny hung his head. "I guess I'm kinda glad you'll be with her. I wish I had the skills to help. I liked the sense of doing something worthwhile when we found Jimmy. Rescuing kids from the criminals who abduct them is a good thing to do but ..."

"You're a great asset to Christine. Chief protects her as well as acting as a buffer for children who distrust adults. Your training made him the perfect partner for her job." Jeremy's left hand reached toward the phone hanging from his belt. "Excuse me."

Denny moved a few feet away as if providing the privacy he thought an investigator needed. Jeremy turned his attention to the caller on the other end of the line. "Who did you say you are?"

The gruff voice spoke loud enough that Jeremy removed the phone from direct contact with his right ear. "A lawyer, representing the estate, hired me to ..." The man interrupted him. "No. No one's coming after you. By the way, where do you live?"

Jeremy listened as the man calmed down a little although his voice still hurt his ears. "Okay. Listen, Mr. Dryden. You are Joseph Dryden, aren't you?"

The man confirmed his identity. "Your uncle Marcus Devine recently passed away and his lawyers want me to contact you so they can execute your uncle's desires according to his will. Are you available to come to Winnipeg and meet with them?" Jeremy listened to the man's affirmative response. "How soon?"

Joseph Dryden said he would be in the city by the weekend. He asked if the time worked. "Yes, I think so. Phone my number when you settle in and I'll take you to the lawyer's office." He ended the call. *I wonder what his connection is to Tommy Devine. The scumbag is also one of the beneficiaries so this meeting should be interesting.*

Jeremy replaced his phone and looked around to locate

Denny. His search found Christine standing near the other man at the entrance to the arena. Her body language seemed friendly enough but, by the way she held Chief's leash, he surmised she wanted to leave.

Jeremy strode quietly toward the couple. Christine's cheeks were flushed from the cold and her hair seemed a little mussed as if a breeze played hide and seek through her tresses. While her thumb and forefinger wrapped around the dog's collar, her other fingers caressed his fur letting the dog understand he was important to her.

She leaned down and threw her arms around the dog's neck as Jeremy approached. "Ready to go?" Denny looked none too pleased at the suggestion but he quickly hid his displeasure.

"I am." Christine straightened. She held out her hand to her friend. "Thanks again, Denny, for giving Chief a workout."

"Is he going to be with you when you search for that kid tonight?" Denny dropped his gaze to the dog.

She looked sharply toward Jeremy. She frowned before glancing back at Denny. "Probably. Why?"

"Oh. Just wondering." He turned to face the other man in Christine's life. "Take care. I'll see you again sometime, I'm sure." He led the way to the smaller door inserted in the big overhead door that opened the whole end of the barn. Denny grabbed the handle and pulled inward. He stepped outside and waited for the others to follow. "When do you think you'll be back again, Christine?"

"That's anyone's guess. Some free time depends on how this case goes. I'll call." She directed Chief toward her vehicle. "Thanks again Denny." She waved her hand in the air as she strode toward her Grand Cherokee. Jeremy followed close behind after shaking Denny's hand.

They reached either side of the Jeep at the same time, Jeremy slipping into his seat as Christine helped her dog jump inside and into the back. She slid to the driver's chair and started the ignition. "This trip was well worth it, don't you think?"

They pulled onto the road leading toward the highway. "What did Shonney say about our plan for tonight? She in or out?"

Christine filled him in. "The one thing she won't do, is go

with us. She wants no part of the scene, she says and yet she plans to -" She took her hands off the wheel long enough to make quotation marks with her fingers, "- minister to the women caught up in this trade. I don't understand. Why is preaching at them so important when they obviously want nothing to do with her?"

"What makes you think they want nothing to do with her? She's been out of the business for how long?" Jeremy finished fastening his seat belt and turned toward her.

"She's been drug free and out of prostitution for about five years. I find it strange that she wants to turn them all into religious people before they even show a desire to leave the streets. Anyway, none of my business. She thinks they'll be so fixated on getting a John to make money for their habit they won't waste time on us. But she doesn't think they'll interfere either." Christine turned her attention back to the road. "She suggests you wear black jeans, a black shirt with lots of gold chains as jewelry. That getup should make quite a sight."

"Certainly not my usual attire. What about you?"

"We'll go to her house at 7. She says the girls appear on the streets about nine." Christine snickered. "I'm almost looking forward to seeing how I will look after she gets done with me. My disguise should be even more unusual than your costume. I hardly ever wear a dress and she alluded to boots of some kind."

Jeremy chuckled. "I can't wait. But we need to strengthen our cover story. Are you up for lunch so we can go over a few ideas? By the way, my man called. He lives in Regina and not too enthusiastic about having someone look for him. I never told you. The uncle who died had the last name Devine, related apparently to Tommy. I can't wait to find out the connections in all this."

"Do you think your case ties into the pedophilia ring? I mean that scumbag sold Nathan to Fine and ..."

"Yeah. I know. I want to do some research on the uncle's background, find out what his contacts in the city are. But for now, let's concentrate on the task at hand. How about lunch?"

"That works. The air is cold enough Chief will do okay in the car while we eat. I'll feed him when we return to the office. Or do you want me to drive you home first?"

"No, the office is fine. I don't need to be anywhere this

afternoon. How about you?" Jeremy relaxed against the seat back as they traveled in a companionable silence for a few miles. Christine seemed to be thinking and didn't answer his last question. He decided to let his thoughts rove a little as well.

Chapter Twenty Seven

Christine leaned her forearms on the top of her desk. Peeking over the edge, she studied the slight rise of Chief's rib cage as he lay on his side near the door leading to the hall. *He's really tired after the workout this morning.* She pursed her lips as thoughts drifted toward the animal her parents purchased when she turned four years old. The Shih-Tzu seemed so out of his element on the ranch in Texas when the Conrad's took her in. Pokey acted skittish around so many large animals. Their hooves became a daily obstacle course. She died before her thirteenth birthday. She thought of the pain his death caused and wondered how long Chief would be by her side.

Her thoughts turned to Rompart Industries. She'd been too young to understand what her father did. He loved her and seemed to be home every night. She couldn't remember being neglected by him or her mother who remained at home with her all day. Her mom taught her to read and to sing in preparation for a private school they planned to enroll her in that fall. But life changed and she attended the public one with the other children from the ranch hand's families when the time came. *I need to clear his name. The police think he used to be involved in something criminal.*

Christine pulled up the file on her computer where she kept all the information she gleaned about Rompart and its employees. Richard Belcher, as CEO, worked for the company when her dad ran the firm. *I wonder whether he was implicit in the money laundering my father stands accused of. Maybe he was involved but not Daddy.* Rebuilding her family home brought back some good memories as she'd spent more time reminiscing about the Mommy and Daddy she missed so much. Her parents' residence overflowed with love and she purposed one day she'd duplicate that atmosphere in her own home.

Christine thought for a moment before picking up the phone. She punched in the numbers for Jeremy's direct line. When he answered, she invited him to her office. "I want to show you something on my computer."

Not even a minute later, his soft rap on the door gave Chief an excuse to raise his head. His lack of concern allowed him to close his eyes once more. Christine chuckled and said, "Come in. Don't step on the dog."

Jeremy stuck his head around the corner of the door. "Wow. Some protection he is. What did you want to show me?" He stepped into the room down the hall from his own office.

"I'm perusing these files I created about Rompart. How do we obtain a thorough background check on all the principles at the firm, police records if any, and financial records? I don't believe my father laundered money even if that might be the reason they killed him. Richard Belcher worked for Dad back then as did Brian Carruthers. Jason Mitchell came on afterward but why would he represent a scumbag like Edward Fine?"

"Well, my father could obtain a court order for those records but Carruthers, Mitchell and Belcher will find out you're checking up on them. If they are criminals, and they hired that man to kill your father, they'll come after you. It would be in their best interest to eliminate you so they can carry on at Rompart as is their practice. We should check a little more discretely ourselves first. I've developed connections and so have you ... now." Jeremy pulled the only other chair in the room close to her desk.

"Time is the problem. As long as you and I need to make a living doing our investigative work, there aren't large enough blocks of time available to do this properly." Christine pointed toward the coffee pot when she stood to refill her own cup.

"No thanks. You'd be surprised how much information we can secure with an hour here and a half hour there. Sometimes when I'm running three or four cases at the same time, that's all I can do. Right now, for instance ..."

"Yeah. That's kinda why I opened this file again. I'm free until seven. Would you take Richard Belcher and find everything you can on him and I'll deal with the other two?" Christine took a cautious sip from her coffee mug.

Jeremy stood. He glanced at Chief as he headed toward the door. "I've already got a head start. Dad asked me to check these guys out before your meeting with them. Nothing sent out a red flag then but I can be more thorough. Didn't you also do some checking into their job description at Rompart?"

"I did. But, like you, the search was only cursory. We might need to use each other's contacts as well.
Will that work?" She pulled a scratch pad close to her fingertips. "I like to find which websites I can access for free first and then, if I find I need to pay for a deeper background check, I'll know where to look for those too. You have some police contacts, right?" She poised her pen ready to take down the information.

"I'll contact them for all three. Their curiosity is aroused when too many people start pulling in favours all at once. Dad compiled some info too." He placed his hand on the door handle. "We can also ask Jenna if she'd help. She does a great job with research."

"Good. That's a plan then. Oh, Jeremy. When are you going to change into your pimp costume?" She giggled. "I can't wait."

He scowled in her direction. "Not till I absolutely need to. You'd better not razz me too much. You're going to look like a prostitute. That should be cute. Hey, that rhymes."

Christine listened to his laughter all the way back to his office. *You never mind, Jeremy Goodman.* She shrugged her shoulders and focused on the internet site she accessed. *Let's discover what we can on Jason Mitchell and Brian Carruthers.*

Chapter Twenty Eight

Christine stared at the computer screen. Her eyes burned. Her shoulders ached as if someone beat her with a steel rod. She raised her hands above her head to stretch some of the kinks out. Chief waited patiently to be taken outside. "Okay, boy. A walk will do the both of us some good." She stood, grabbed her jacket from the hook near the door, and slipped out the door toward the exit. Standing on the front walkway, she took a deep breath of fresh air and began to direct the animal down the sidewalk. The dog strained at being tethered for his walk. "I can't let you lose in this neighbourhood, Chief. Too many cars. Here I'll let the leash out all the way."

She proceeded to extend the lead tying Chief to her side. Her canine explored this tree and another. He needed only a few seconds to find the perfect one. She perused the quiet setting while she waited. A light dusting of snow covered some of the shrubs but most had melted already

The canine bounded toward her so she continued down the sidewalk to the first cross street. As her foot stepped off the curb, a car flew through. With no one else in sight, the gunfire from the open window went unnoticed but not by Christine. One bullet found its mark. She landed in a heap at the edge of the pedestrian corridor. The next car passed by without spotting her body lying in front of a parked vehicle.

Chief pulled himself free from her relaxed grip on his leash. He moved beside her and licked her face. Christine's eyes remained closed. The canine growled deeply; the sound appeared to come from his very soul. He looked around. No one walked close by. No one to help. Immediately his protective instincts sent him back the way they'd come. Facing the Goodman building, he howled, pain for his mistress evident. The distraught animal kept the racket up until Jeremy opened the door to investigate. Chief rushed to his side. The dog turned back to the street and ran, checking once in a while to make sure Jeremy followed.

****

Jeremy sprinted right behind Chief. As soon as he recognized the familiar jacket and the woman lying on the ground, he jogged to her side. His heart beat accelerated. "Christine, Christine." He assessed her condition as her coat flapped open. A crimson flow marked the spot near her left shoulder. He called 911.

"Operator. Someone's been shot. I'm at the corner of Williams and Hargrave. Send an ambulance. Please hurry." He proceeded to respond to the voice on the other end of the call with the details of whom, when, and how. Some of the answers to her questions seemed redundant at the moment. Information about who tried to kill her and how long ago eluded him. "Can't you speed them up?"

Jeremy cradled Christine's head while still holding his cellphone to his ear. Chief paced on the other side. *He'll need to be secured before the EMTs arrive. He won't let them near her.* Sirens sounded closer.

Precious seconds ticked by too slowly. The operator's calm voice worked to assure him. The Emergency Rescue Vehicle from the nearest fire station arrived in a matter of minutes. Jeremy gently laid Christine's head back on the cold pavement and disconnected his call. He reached for the dog's leash and pulled Chief to one side while the EMTs stabilized Christine for the journey to the hospital. An ambulance skidded to a stop next to them as they finished their job.

His eyes scrutinized the streets, houses, and empty yards in both directions. *Her assailants might be nearby? Did they study the proceedings to see if they'd succeeded?* He tugged on Chief's leash when the animal tried to move closer to his mistress. One EMT kept his eye on the dog but they proceeded to prepare their victim for transport. "Which hospital?"

"Are you a relative?"

"No, a friend. My father is her lawyer. She has no family in this city." Jeremy's voice sounded impatient, even to him. "I need to go with her."

"Health Sciences. You can come but not him." The man pointed to Chief before he shuffled the gurney into position. With the help of his partner, he lifted Christine tenderly onto the stretcher. The ambulance lights flashed through the neighbourhood as bystanders gathered on front walkways to gawk.

Jeremy's sense of unease increased. *Too many people.* "I'll take my car. This is her service dog so he'll be permitted into the hospital, I think. If not I'll leave him in the car." The man blinked as he moved toward the emergency vehicle with Christine. *I'm jabbering.*

He waited until the back doors of the ambulance were shut. Jeremy raced back toward his office to lock up after retrieving his jacket. He used his cell to phone his dad. "Christine's been shot. Meet me at Health Sciences. I'll fill you in when you arrive."

He opened the door to Christine's Grand Cherokee. *I wish I had my truck.* He checked the console. *No keys.* He walked briskly to the building, unlocked the door again and strode quickly inside. Her door stood ajar. *Thank Goodness.* He spied her handbag sitting on the top of her desk. *Hate rummaging through these things.* He finally found what he searched for at the bottom of the clutter. *Why do women put so much stuff into their purses?*

He covered the distance to the car in record time, but remembered he forgot to lock up. Jeremy secured Chief in the backseat, returned to the entrance, locked his door, and huffed toward the vehicle again. He slipped the key into the ignition. The Jeep roared to life. "We'll be with Christine soon." He patted the dog's muzzle.

Police. He pressed the speed dial for Sergeant Irving. "Bill. Christine's been shot." He listened to the policeman explain that a call about a shooting had come in but after the fact. Irving explained the scene was secure even if the victim had already been transported before the cops arrived. Jeremy interrupted. "Yeah, she lost a lot of blood. Someone tried to kill her. Didn't succeed but a policeman should be posted at her door in the hospital till we figure this out? I mean ..."

"I know what you mean. It's done. A uniformed officer is waiting until the docs finish with her. He'll stand guard outside the room she's assigned to. I'll tell him to look for you and Chief. I assume the dog goes too." The Sergeant dealt with distraught family members all the time.

"Thanks Sarg." Jeremy hung up, threw his cell phone on the right seat, and floored the accelerator. His heart pounded. Fear for Christine seeped from every pore, an emotion new to him, as if the shot sliced through his own body. Wheels screeched as he rounded the next corner. Fortunately, the intersection was deserted. *Please Lord. Keep her safe. Guide the doctors.* He spoke out loud with eyes open and scanned the horizon for nearby vehicles. He needed to be with Christine.

Chapter Twenty Nine

Jeremy paced the sterile waiting room. He stopped each time he heard footsteps outside the door hoping the doctor would come with some good news. The steps took whoever was walking by in a different direction. He slammed his fist against his leg. *What could be taking so long? The wait is worse ...* He sat down, his heavy heart transferring itself to the rest of his body. He hung his head and started to pray. *Lord, she's so close to accepting that you are real. Please don't take her yet. Keep her safe and help the doctors. Guide their hands. Amen.*

A noise by the door jarred his attention. "Hi Dad. Christine's still in surgery."

Barkley Goodman sat down and stretched his long legs in front of him. He patted his son's hand resting on the younger man's leg. "Do you know where she was hit? Where did the bullet enter her body?"

"I'm not sure but blood poured from her left shoulder. Before I examined her myself, the EMTs arrived on the scene. They didn't say much." Jeremy glanced at the doorway as someone in surgical garb walked past. "How long can it take to remove a bullet?"

Barkley stood. "Why don't I go to the nurse's desk and make an inquiry. They'll tell me her status since I represent her." He looked for confirmation from his son.

Jeremy rubbed his hands together as if trying to wash some stains away. He nodded at his father silently. Words failed to alleviate his distress. He remained silent. He studied his Dad's usual sense of purpose as he walked toward the hallway leading to emergency. *Father, please.* He took his fear to the only one who controlled the situation.

The sound of a chair scrapping across the floor filtered into the room but otherwise, silence floated around him like a shroud. Footsteps grew louder until Barkley filled the doorway again. "I couldn't find out any information from them either. I'm her lawyer, for goodness sake." He plunked himself down in a most uncharacteristic motion.

"Dad, something's wrong. My instincts are on overload." Jeremy's eyes glistened.

The older man shook his head. "No use borrowing trouble. God is in control. This is His call." He lowered his head.

Jeremy allowed his father a few minutes of silence. Surely the Father listened to his prayers and would answer quickly. *I don't want to pray for Your will to be done, Lord. I'm afraid You might take her and she's not ready to meet You face to face.* "Dad, are they at least guarding her?"

"Too soon to tell. The officer may be up in the operating suite waiting for the surgery to be over. The nurse never said anything about the police aside from wanting to speak to Christine after she comes out of recovery. Did they question you yet?"

"When I arrived. They asked me to describe the scene but by the time I got to her nothing stirred nearby. Christine walks Chief every now and again. She never informed me of her plans to go outside so I assumed she was glued to her computer until ... this dog loves his mistress and he acted some upset. I left him in Christine's car but things are taking so long ... he must be beside himself. Maybe ..." Jeremy gazed into this father's eyes for permission.

"Go. No sense in both of us warming these seats. You should be able to bring Chief inside since he's an official service dog." Barkley stared toward his son and nodded.

Jeremy left and walked with purpose toward the emergency entrance and the parking lot. He sucked in a breath of fresh air as soon as he stepped outside. His steps slowed but he picked up speed again as he neared the large SUV. Chief's nose seemed to be part of the window by the driver's seat. Jeremy opened the door cautiously, reaching for the leash still attached to the dog's collar. "Hi Boy. Let's go."

He guided Chief to the pavement and led him along a patch of grass. The canine sniffed the air and strained his tether to enter the building where his instincts told him he'd find Christine.

Jeremy walked swiftly, his footsteps working hard to keep up with the anxious animal. They strode through the door into the sterile environment. The nurse at the triage desk glanced up. Her frown became very readable. A security guard rushed toward them.

"Sir. You can't bring a dog in here." The man placed his hand on the revolver positioned at his side as if he would use the gun should this disturbed individual give him any trouble.

Jeremy pointed to the insignia on Chief's collar letting everyone understand his special status. "His mistress is in surgery. We'll remain with her lawyer in the waiting room, out of the way." He continued toward the small room separated from the main triage area by only a short distance.

He stepped inside. His father was nowhere around. Jeremy stopped for a moment. *I'll take Chief to the nurse's desk.* He retraced his steps.

As he approached the woman who appeared to be in charge, the one who frowned when he walked in with Chief in the first place, she scowled at him again. "That dog should be kept out of the way." She indicated the far corner of the room. "Sick people inhabit these rooms and the germs those animals carry ..."

Jeremy decided to ignore her. "I want an update on Christine Smith ... now."

The nurse gazed toward Chief and back again. "You can't take a dog in the room. Are you family?"

Jeremy glared toward the woman. "I'm her business partner and friend. I found her and called 911. My father is her lawyer. Where is he?"

"Mr. Goodman was escorted to Miss Smith in recovery by the doctor who operated on her." Her eyes glanced briefly in the general direction for the appropriate part of the hospital.

"Point the way." Jeremy placed his free hand on the counter in front of her. His eyes scanned the room for a supervisor. He hoped he pled his case sufficiently. "Please. She'll be worried about Chief. He brought me to her, for goodness sake, when she lay on the pavement. We need ... he needs to make sure she's alright. I'll keep him on the leash. Promise."

The nurse gave Jeremy directions to the second floor operating wing. He stepped off the elevator and headed straight for that nurse's desk. A no nonsense woman dressed in hospital scrubs eyed him curiously. Her friendly smile invited him to speak. "We're here to visit with Christine Smith." He nodded at the dog at his side.

The nurse sauntered around the counter and studied the animal. "He seems clean, well taken care of." She hesitated, giving Jeremy the impression she planned to do them a favour. "Okay, but only for a minute. You're lucky I love dogs."

"Thank You." He spotted Barkley talking to the guard at Christine's door. He walked toward them with the nurse's final words ringing in his ears. "Just five minutes all together."

"Officer." He inclined his head toward the uniformed man standing rigidly by the door. "Dad, the nurse said she'd allow Chief a short visit. Will you take him until Christine and I talk?"

"Sure but you won't be able to converse much with her. She's pretty sedated. That bullet came close to penetrating her heart but only grazed a vein which they repaired during surgery. The projectile went right through so another piece of evidence is still out there some-where. I hope the police find it. She's one lucky woman." He hung his head. "Thank you Lord." He watched the play of emotions cross Jere-my's face. "She's lost a lot of blood the doc says."

"Okay then I'll take Chief to Christine to set both their minds at ease. Be right back." Jeremy pushed the door open. His lips re-leased an involuntary gasp when he scanned the slight form beneath thin white sheets. Christine's face appeared a little blue next to the pristine hospital linens. An IV line hung from a bag of fluids. Her eyes fluttered.

"Christine."

"Chief." The word, almost a whisper, floated across the room. The anxious animal's tail wagged furiously in response. He laid his head on the side of the bed close to her hand. Even in her weak-ened state she caressed his muzzle. The tail beat the air a little hard-er. "G - good boy. Barkley told me ... you saved my life." She nuzzled him again with her fingers.

"The nurse let me bring him in but only for a minute. Dad will take him while we talk." He tugged Chief toward the door. The dog's legs stiffened and he remained rigidly near Christine's hand. "Come on, Chief. Gotta go. Let Christine sleep." He pulled again but the dog only moved an inch or two.

"Go. With. Jeremy, Chief. Good boy." Her eyes opened for a second and then closed. Her breathing raised her ribcage slightly and she moaned softly. "Hurt."

"Do you want some pain meds?" He wrung helpless hands. *What can I do?* He took another step nearer the door. This time the animal went willingly.

"No. Too dopey already." She forced her eyes to focus in his direction.

"Be right back." He pushed the door open and handed the end of the leash to Barkley. "I won't be long, Dad."

"Take your time. Chief and I will be outside the door." The older man's smile appeared more as a grimace. "Don't tire her out."

"She's already tired." He turned his body and went back to Christine's bedside. Jeremy grabbed the lone chair in the room and pulled the seat closer so she didn't have to strain her voice. "Christine, you awake?"

"No. C-can't you tell?" Her words held little volume so he tilted his head near her mouth to hear.

"At least your sense of humour is intact. Want me to bring you anything tomorrow?" He relaxed against the back of the chair and reached for her hand. He wanted to but didn't touch her fingers. "I need to cancel Shonney. Is her number in your phone?"

Christine's eyes opened at half-mast. "Cell ... in my purse. Last call, I think. I can't remember." She closed her eyes again. "Hard to keep eyes open."

"You just came out of surgery. The anesthetic is making you sleepy. Do you need some items from home?" Jeremy took a notepad from his pocket with a pen to write down her requests.

She took a shallow breath this time. "Slippers, robe, tooth-brush, and my handbag, I think. Probably other stuff but can't think." She inhaled again, the sound reminiscent of someone in a deep sleep. The catch in her breathing indicated the stab of pain the breaths caused.

"I'll bring them. You do what the doctor says. A uniformed officer is outside your door. No visitors allowed except dad or I." He glanced toward the ceiling. *Who wanted her dead?* "I'll visit in the morning." He turned to leave.

"Jeremy. Thank You."

He stepped through the door into the hall. Barkley waited with Chief. He faced the cop who returned to his position in front of the door. "Are you on duty all night?"

"No. My replacement should be here around five." The man acted as if guarding a gunshot victim happened every day.

Maybe for him, Jeremy thought. "Make sure the other officer understands no one is to be allowed in the room except medical per-sonnel. Someone tried to eliminate her and until we gather more infor-mation, everyone is suspect. I'll be back tomorrow."

"Yes sir. Sergeant Irving filled me in."

He turned toward his dad. "Let's go. I need to do a few things before I can turn my brain off and sleep.

Barkley led the way, Chief in tow, to the elevator. He de-pressed the button for the first floor and turned to face his son. "Did she say anything about the shooter?"

"No, I didn't even ask. In her words, she's too dopey. Tomorrow will be soon enough for all the questions needing answers. This was too close." Jeremy shuddered, a movement not lost to his father.

"The doc said the bullet went right through but barely missed her heart. Whoever shot her intended to kill, not wound." The lawyer stepped inside and the door closed.

Jeremy shifted his gaze toward his Father. "I've never been so scared. When I came to her ..."

Barkley chose to finish his train of thought before commenting on his son's last statement. "I want to visit with Irving when I leave here, check if they found anything at the scene. I hope they locate the bullet. We might be able to link it to a gun from a former shooting." He hesitated. "You're getting close to Christine, closer than you should I think. She's not a believer, remember."

"I know." Jeremy hung his head. "I'm trying to keep some distance between us but when her body lay so still ... I'll be careful dad. Jesus is pulling her, though. I can sense a softening when we talk. She's not as hostile as she used to be. I prayed God wouldn't take her yet and he answered." They walked across the lobby toward the exit. "Right now, I just want to discover who tried to kill her." A man with a camera around his neck barged through the door from outside as Jeremy followed his Dad through the same door.

Barkley spoke as he made a beeline for the parking lot. "She's working on that missing kid case and the traffickers may not like her searching into their business. What about the hostility from the Rompart executives? Of course, they don't relate to her as Christine Smith. I wonder who found out she moved her office to your place?"

Jeremy shrugged his shoulders. "The perp's in the sex thing are in the dark about her search for the kid. We planned to start tonight. We did some digging into Rompart's principles, too, but just this afternoon." He veered toward the Grand Cherokee while Barkley turned in the direction of his vehicle. "We'll talk tomorrow." He waved toward his mentor and led Chief to Christine's car.

Chapter Thirty

Christine's eyes opened slowly. The light from the window sent a stab of pain straight to her brain. She clamped them shut again. Someone had placed a blanket over her but she couldn't remember when. She pulled the sheet over her head and peeked through one eye. Then the other. *That worked*, she thought. Keeping the covers in place she lay still for a moment. The left side of her chest ached.

Right. Barkley told me. Someone shot me. She forced herself to think about the activities the day before. *I think it was yesterday.* She recalled the trip to Larson Kennels ... with Jeremy. *Why'd he come? Oh right. We needed to talk about ... Shonney. We were supposed to meet with her last night.* She tried to sit up but the effort exhausted her.

Jeremy. She vaguely remembered his presence the night before. *He'll look after Shonney. Oh-h-h.* The ache near her shoulder increased. The door swished open. Christine closed her eyes again wishing for pain-deadened sleep.

"Miss Smith. Good. You're awake. Want me to close the blinds?"

The voice sounded right beside her. "Please. Bright light makes my head hurt."

"I can fix that." Christine identified the sound of verticals being closed. She slowly lowered the sheet. "Why does my head ache so badly?"

The petite blond stood next to her and placed her hand on Christine's wrist. "You hit your head pretty hard when you fell after being shot." The uniformed attendant stayed quiet for a minute as she stared at her watch. She released her patent's arm and reached into her pocket for a thermometer.

"My chest hur ..."

The nurse stuck the instrument in her mouth before she finished. "Lay still and I'll increase the pain meds." She turned toward the IV pole located beside Christine's bed. "The doctor said you could have a higher dose for the first day if it was needed." She made the adjustment, removed the thermometer and made a notation on the chart at the bottom of the bed on her way to the door. She walked briskly through letting the portal swing shut behind her.

Christine looked around the room. She had the room to herself, no other beds beside hers. Her arm was hooked up to an IV. *I wonder what they're pumping into me besides pain medicine.* She spotted the raised side rails on the bed. She splayed her fingers across the sheet and remembered the cold nose nudging her hand. *Chief was here.*

She smiled when the nurse returned. "That's a good sign. Smiles first thing in the morning." She reached for the water glass perched on a bedside table. "I'll bet your mouth is a little dry." She held the water container for Christine to sip a little moisture. "Good Now, are you hungry for some breakfast?"

Christine thought for a moment. *Am I hungry?* She looked at her attendant. "Yes. Thank you. I don't remember eating yesterday."

The caretaker chuckled. "I guess that's not funny. You probably are a bit concussed and ... well ... getting shot will do that to you. Everything will come back in a day or two." She headed toward the door after making a note of Christine's temperature on the chart hanging at the bottom of the bed. "I'll be right back with some warm water to help you clean up before your food arrives."

Christine kept her eyes on her back as the nurse efficiently opened the door again and stepped through. A dark blue pant leg relaxed beside the door frame. She closed her eyes again but forced them to reopen. *Enough sleep for now, I think. I'm so tired, though.* She placed her hand tenderly over the left side of her chest. The thick surgical dressing under her thin hospital gown added a lot of padding. A picture of a dark sedan flashed across her brain. The window had been open.

She remembered walking Chief. She'd inhaled the aroma of someone barbecuing. *Or was that from the night before at Jeremy's?* Her mouth watered. *I hope breakfast gets here soon.* The door swished into the room.

"Here's some nice warm water. A clean face and hands will perk you right up." The little nurse set the basin on a rolling table she located near the far wall. She rolled the flat surface toward Christine. Stopping at the bottom of the bed, she bent at the waist. "Tell me when we're high enough." She pressed the button on the end of the bed.

Christine's head began to swirl from the motion as she was propelled upward. The nurse looked at her and continued to twist the handle more until Christine sat at a forty five degree angle.

"I think that's enough. My name is Miss Miller, Jennifer Miller. Call me Jennifer." She bustled around to the side where the basin and table were located. "Let's wipe the sleep away." She dipped a freshly laundered washcloth into the water and proceeded to apply the cloth to Christine's cheeks.

"I can do that." Christine reached out and Nurse Miller relinquished the warm fabric. The patient dabbed at her face again, digging into the corners of her eyes to wash the nighttime residue from them. *This feels so good.* Next she swiped the front and backs of her hands and wipe around her neck as best she could from her position on the bed.

Nurse Jennifer handed her a towel. "You did good for the first day out of surgery. Tomorrow, after you've been up a while, we'll do a more thorough job."

Christine relaxed back against the pillow, exhausted. "I'm still so sleepy. When can I go home?"

"That's up to your doctor. I think he plans on you being here a little longer than a couple of hours, though. You had a pretty close call." Nurse Miller gathered up the wash supplies and headed toward the door. "Your food should be here any minute. I'll bring you a toothbrush after breakfast, and some mouth rinse."

"Thanks." Christine closed her eyes again. She began to drift. At first she heard the clanging of pans or trays but soon silence prevailed.

"Miss Smith, Breakfast is here." This voice seemed loud with a nasal quality. This wasn't the former nurse.

Christine opened her eyes. The dark haired older woman presented a no nonsense attitude. She studied the woman who set the tray of food on the rolling cart situated where Jennifer left it. She angled the table to make it easier for her patient to feed herself from her raised position. "Thank You."

"I'll be back to collect the leftovers when you're done." The woman exited the room as the door swished close behind her.

Christine picked up the cover revealing a bowl of oatmeal and some toast. She put the spoon in the cereal but her attempt to fill her mouth failed. *This won't work.* She searched for the customary button to ring for a nurse. Finding it, she depressed the black center and Jennifer Miller rushed through the door. "What's wrong?"

Christine grimaced. "No emergency. Sorry to bother you. Could you raise the head of the bed more so I can feed myself?"

"Oh-h. Certainly. Give me a head's up when you're sitting tall enough." She bent at the waist and started to turn the crank.

Her body sat straighter and closer to the table. "That'll work." The little nurse smiled and headed back toward the door. A knock sounded. Before Nurse Miller answered, a head of black hair with bright shiny blue eyes appeared around the threshold. "Can I visit a minute?"

****

"Who? Me?" The nurse pushed him back out the door.

"No. The patient." He flashed his press card. "I understand she's a shooting victim."

"You can't go in. Where's the police officer who stood here?" She straightened her spine as tall as her short stature allowed. She placed her hands on her hips.

"Oh, you mean Officer Miles. I sent him for a cup of coffee." The man splayed his feet a few inches apart. "The people deserve to know if a killer is on the loose. I need to talk to your patient."

"No you don't." She spotted the errant policeman walking toward them from the small hospitality room. She glared at the man in uniform who had the job of protecting her patient. "Why did you leave your post? There are to be no visitors for this woman."

The reporter straightened his body and scowled. "Why?" Jennifer ignored him.

The uniformed officer returned to his position in front of the door. His embarrassed grimace went from the face of the nurse in charge to the interloper. "Connelly, you can't go in without prior permission. I thought you were trustworthy. You led me to believe you arrived here to interview someone else."

"Yeah, well. He barged into the room unannounced. It's lucky I was nearby. I'm going to report your neglect to the Chief." Nurse Miller grabbed the reporter's arm and steered him away from Christine's door.

"You're only making me all the more curious. What's so special about this patient?" Connolly reefed his elbow out of the nurse's grasp. "I'll go. But I'll be back. Freedom of the press and citizens right's, you know." He walked slowly toward the elevator.

Nurse Miller turned to the officer again. Her eyes blazed. "Someone tried to kill her once and you give a stranger access to her room?" She strode purposefully toward her station. "I'm having you replaced."

Chapter Thirty One

Jeremy stepped from the elevator as soon as the large door slid open. He walked casually toward the nurse's desk. "How is Christine Smith this morning?"

The young blond nurse looked toward him and grabbed a chart near her elbow. "You are?"

"I'm her friend and business partner. I'm one of only two people permitted to visit." He looked the woman in the eye waiting for her to ask for some ID. She didn't but he handed her his PI license anyway. "Can I go in now?"

"Sure, Mr. Goodman." She glanced at the chart. "The other person allowed in the room is also Mr. Goodman. Any relation?"

"My father, her lawyer." He shifted the bag he carried from one hand to the other. "Is she awake this morning?"

"Oh, yes. She's eaten a good breakfast but she's resting now. She's determined to leave here as soon as possible." The young woman chuckled. "She's tired of us already."

"Thanks." Jeremy turned toward the door leading to Christine.

"Oh, Mr. Goodman. I stopped a reporter from bothering

her this morning. We arranged for a replacement for the officer on duty at the time, too. He just let the man walk right in. Went for coffee, Can you imagine?" The woman huffed, her heightened colour indicating the depth of her feelings.

"What? How'd they find out?" Jeremy placed his free hand on his hip. His glare landed on the current man in uniform and in the direction of the nurse.

"I didn't tell anyone. Maybe the guard spilled the beans." The blond moved from behind the desk. "The snoop said he planned to be back. He kept asking why she was isolated from visitors."

"I'll speak to this officer."

"Two detectives called after I complained, said they'll be here shortly. They confirmed no one was to be allowed into her room. Except you two." She nodded toward Christine's door. "That young lady is lucky to be alive."

"Yes, she is. Did they tell you their names?" Jeremy took a step toward the room.

"No, they didn't. Do you want me to find out for you?"

He stood still for a second. He turned toward the nurse again. "No. I'll call and find out. Thanks for your diligence." He walked the last few steps to Christine's door. The officer standing guard asked for his ID so Jeremy fumbled with his wallet and produced his license again.

He tapped gently on the door. "Hi Christine."

Christine's voice sounded stronger when she asked him to come in. He stepped into the room, and let out the breath he held. "You look much better today. Wow, you gave us a scare."

"Sorry." She smiled but she left her head on the pillow. "I'm lying here trying to figure out who shot me but the picture of the man holding the gun out the car window is blurry. Who called 911?"

Jeremy filled her on the proceedings the day before. He handed her the bag he'd brought. "You asked for a toothbrush, your purse ..."

"I did. I don't remember you even being here. Was your dad here too?"

"Of course. You're his favorite client. By the way, two detectives are coming this morning. I need to call Irving and confirm their identities." He pulled his cell phone from the holster on his belt.

"I won't be much help to them. I wonder if they found anything at the scene." Christine straightened the blanket covering her. She reached for the glass of water from the table beside her bed.

Jeremy punched in the speed dial for Sergeant Irving. He lifted the phone to his ear and gave the person answering on the other end his name and who he wanted to speak to. "Hi, Bill. Are two detectives coming in this morning to talk to Christine? The nurse at the desk said they gave her a heads up when she called to complain about last night's security failure." He listened as the officer confirmed their assignment and their names. "Thanks." He ended the call and stored his phone.

"Sergeant Irving said Reagan and Costello will be here shortly. They're handling the investigation. Just a minute." He walked to the door and opened it a crack. "Officer. Be sure to check the ID of those two detectives before letting them in." He closed the door again. "Can't be too careful."

He looked at Christine whose eyes quietly followed him across the room. "I understand a reporter tried to gain access to you."

"Yeah. Before breakfast. He barged in but thankfully Nurse Miller can be a Momma Bear when she needs to be. Surprised the heck out of me. She seemed so timid and mild one minute and fierce the next. He never got all the way in. It won't be hard for him to figure out who I am from the glimpse he caught of me."

"We have to keep this out of the press but how? Reporters snoop around the precinct all the time and the police constantly have to control what gets reported and what doesn't. Those newshounds think people need all the details. Whoever tried to kill you might try again if they find out they failed the first time." He pulled a chair close. Jeremy took a seat after placing the bag of supplies on Christine's bed.

She dug through the contents. "Oh, good. A brush. I'll call Nurse Miller to help me with this bathrobe before those detectives arrive. Thanks Jeremy." She looked toward him with grateful eyes. "I'm glad you found me before I bled to death."

"You can thank Chief. I'm sure the whole neighbourhood was alerted by his frantic howl." He chuckled. "He wouldn't settle down at all last night until I brought him to you. He calmed down after making sure you're in a good place. He willingly waited outside with Dad afterwards."

"Speaking of Chief. Where is he?"

"With Jenna. She came in early so I left to gather the things you asked for. You acted kinda doped up when we talked so if I missed something, tell me and I'll visit your home again." Jeremy leaned back in the chair, raising the front legs off the floor. Christine pressed the button for the nurse.

Nurse Miller answered the call, her petite form slipping soundlessly around the door frame. She bustled over to Christine's bedside totally ignoring the presence of a man in the room. "What can I do for you?" She smiled toward her patient and shifted her gaze to Jeremy as if to ask why couldn't you assist her? *I don't think she likes me.*

Christine's eyes ping-ponged from one to the other. She smirked. "I need help getting this robe on before those detectives come by." She considered her friend for a minute. "Jeremy, please excuse us for a second?"

"Oh. Oh, sure." He jumped to his feet and moved around the end of the bed. "I'll talk with the officer outside." He opened the door, slipped through, and made sure it closed all the way behind him.

He looked at the man sitting on a chair next to the door. "When do you go off duty? Did they tell you who's going to replace you?"

"I leave at five, like yesterday. Say, why'd they pull Holloway?" The young man seemed intelligent enough but obviously his superiors kept upsetting situations to themselves.

Jeremy leaned against the wall. "You spot any reporters hanging around?"

"Naw. Just some guy sitting in the waiting room. He looks like he's expecting something but I don't think he's a reporter. Why?" He folded one leg over the knee of the other and laid his forearms across them.

Jeremy thought for a moment. *I wonder what the reason is for keeping this officer in the dark.* He decided to answer the officer's question. "Early this morning, the officer you replaced let a reporter into Miss Smith's room. No one is permitted to access her except necessary hospital staff, her lawyer, or me. So you be sure you don't make the same mistake."

"Oh, I will. I mean, no sir. No one. Why'd he want to interview her anyways?"

Boy, this guy must be a rookie. "He's looking for a story. She's a gunshot victim. I suppose somebody from the hospital leaked the information. Anyway, journalists usually don't take 'no' for an answer so keep an eye out. No reporters at any time under any circumstances. Understood?"

"No one gets by me. I brought my lunch so I don't need to go anywhere except for a bathroom break. Say, maybe I'll take advantage of you being here now to take a trip to the biffy. What da ya think?"

"Sure. Go ahead." Jeremy sat in the chair as soon as the officer stood. He leaned back against the wall and let his eyes rove past the nurse's desk to the man standing in the doorway to the small visitor's room. The man seemed to be looking elsewhere and, if he believed the worried look on his face, waiting for a doctor. *I wonder what his story is.*

The door beside him opened. Nurse Miller stepped through. "Miss Smith asked for you. I thought ... Never mind. Anyway, she said you'd stick around until the detectives left. Right?"

"Yeah, I guess. If she needs me." Jeremy slowly lowered the front legs of the chair and stood to his feet. He towered over the little nurse but he understood who was boss. "I'll wait till the officer comes back."

The words no sooner escaped his mouth when he spotted the tall officer walking down the hall toward him. Jeremy made note of the absence of the man in the waiting room doorway. He nodded a greeting to the uniformed guard. "That was quick. I'll be inside. Tell us before you allow the detectives to come in."

"Yes, sir." He sat down in the empty seat. He crossed his arms over his chest and planted his size twelves firmly in front of him, all business. Jeremy was thankful the police department took the attack on Christine seriously. He rapped lightly on the door.

A quiet invitation bid him enter so he opened the door again. The portal appeared large enough for a gurney to maneuver easily through. *You'd think the thickness would make the thing soundproof.* That was not the case, though. *We'll keep our voices down if we don't want some snoopy reporter to listen to*

*our conversation. If he's gutsy enough to return, that
is.* "Hi." Christine sat on the large chair in the corner.

"I thought this would be a better way to converse with
those detectives when they come. Did Sergeant Irving tell you
when they'd be here?" A pillow rested on her knee where the
arm attached to the IV lay.

She crushed the cushioned softness to her chest every now
and then. "You're hurting. Maybe you should stay in bed."

"No. I'll be fine. When are those guys going to be
here?" She winced when she took her next breath. "I'll be okay
till they leave and afterwards you can help me back to bed. I'll
probably be tuckered out by then anyway."

"Tuckered out, eh? That must be one of your Texas
phrases." He chuckled. "Irving said they should be here any
time this morning. So likely not too long from now. I called
Shonney last night. She sends you her condolences but understood you wouldn't be walking the streets any time soon."

"As soon as I'm released. I need to find the girl before they
do some permanent damage to her. She said they usually get
the young ones hooked on some drug or other and then turn
them out." She shook her head but before she uttered another
word, a rapid beat on the door interrupted their conversation.

Jeremy stood, walked to the threshold and peered outside. Two men in casual attire with badges hanging from their
necks waited patiently, one tapping his foot to some inner
rhythm in his head. Officer Demster introduced them. "This is
Detectives Reagen and Costello. I checked their ID."

"Thanks. Come in gentlemen. Miss Smith is ready for
you." The new-comers stepped inside the room filling the
cramped space. Jeremy decided to play host. "I'll go find a couple more chairs."

"No need." The one named Reagan replied. "Since the bed
is empty, we'll sit on it." Before doing so he sauntered over toward Christine. "Miss Smith. I'm Detective Reagan and this is
my partner Detective Costello. We'd like to ask you a few questions about yesterday if you don't mind." He reached out to
shake her hand gingerly, obviously aware of her inju-
ries. Costello did the same.

The detectives sat on the edge of the bed before they
opened their notebooks.

Reagan began. "Can you tell us what happened?"

Both officers took notes as Christine told her side of the story. She mentioned a dark blue sedan. Then she looked toward Jeremy. "I didn't tell you. The shooter stuck his gun out the window of a dark blue car." She looked back at two men. "Before I reacted, they shot me. At least that's what I think occurred. I can't remember anything after seeing the pistol."

"Can you describe the man who held the gun?" Detective Costello poised his pen to record her answer.

Christine frowned. "My memories are all fuddled. The whole thing happened so fast." She closed her eyes and rested her head against the back of the chair. She straightened. Her eyes popped open. "He had a tattoo. On his gun hand."

Reagan scribbled a little and looked back at her. "Can you describe it? Take your time."

Christine shut her eyes again. Jeremy sensed her effort to concentrate. *Lucky she's an experienced investigator. She has good recall.* He waited as did the two officers. No one spoke, afraid to mess up her train of thought. Costello glanced at his watch.

Christine slowly opened her eyes. "No. I can't remember anything else. Just the eagle." Her eyes opened wider. "An eagle. In the center. The eagle seemed to wrap around his arm."

The detectives looked at each other. Neither said a word, though. Jeremy didn't miss their facial expressions. "You familiar with the person who owns something like that?"

Costello spoke first. "If this is the same guy, he's a gun for hire. No connections in the community and doesn't stay in one place too long. We'll check it out." He looked toward Christine. "Now who wants you dead Miss Smith? Who did you p*** ... er ... excuse me, make angry of late?"

She glanced at Jeremy and back at the detectives. "I've been wracking my brain. But I can't imagine who. The case I'm working on is new so the perpetrator hasn't figured out I'm looking yet. I worked a couple of pedophile cases but ..." She turned toward her friend again. "Maybe the boss ... the one who got away ... the man who visited little Jimmy so often ... maybe he's worried we'll find out who he is."

Reagan looked baffled. "What are you talking about?"

"Two weeks ago, I found a missing boy, abused by this man who came at least once a week to molest him. We almost caught him. I've been too busy with my current case to even think about him again. All we can identify is his car." She swiveled her upper body, grimacing when the motion caused her added pain. "Jeremy, if he's coming after me, you're in danger too."

"How do we discover if he's the man? Two weeks is a long time if the creep is nervous. We've done nothing to spook him." Jeremy shrugged his shoulders. "That's one avenue to look at though."

"Who is he?" Reagan and Costello almost tripped over themselves trying to voice their questions.

Jeremy's gaze took in the slightly yellow walls of the room before settling on their faces. "That's the problem; we haven't figured it out yet. We can identify the face but no name. Nothing except ... he drives a black car. The shooter's car was blue, not black."

Detective Reagan glanced at his notes and closed the notebook. "I don't want to tire you. He probably hired this guy. You both need to come to headquarters and look at some mug shots. If this creep is part of the pedophile ring we've been trying to stop for two years, we want the information you've uncovered." He stern gaze fell on Christine. "As soon as you've recovered enough, Miss Smith. You too, Goodman."

Costello stood and pocketed his notebook. "Keep in touch. The sooner we ID this perp the better." Buttoning his jacket as he strode to the door, Reagan gave her a thumbs up. The door swished close behind them.

Jeremy sat back in the chair and looked toward Christine. "Interesting. I never even thought about that guy but the detectives are right. He is the most logical suspect. He obviously knows where our offices are." He dropped his eyes to the floor. *I wonder if he's been stalking Christine.*

"I think this killer and Caputo are one and the same, too. Makes sense. I need to go over to my former office building to try and find out who this pervert visited when I talked to him in the parking lot." She leaned her head back on the chair. "Help me to bed, will ya. I'll leave my robe on."

Jeremy helped her ease out of her seat and move cautiously toward her bed. She hung on to the IV pole Nurse Miller provided so she was able to be more mobile. Her body shook; the effort to stand upright too great for her at the moment. "Christine, you need to put this stuff on hold. Forget about everything until you're stronger. I can make some inquiries ..."

"The security guard at my old office building won't tell you anything. Even if I almost got him fired, he may just let the information about who Caputo visited slip if I use my feminine wiles on him." She chuckled. A large sigh escaped her lips as she lay back against the pillows. She allowed herself to relax completely, exhaustion displayed on her features.

Jeremy studied her for a moment. "Do you want more pain meds?"

Her eyebrows turned down at the corners giving away the frown she tried to hide. "I'm trying to wean off them but I hurt right now. So, yes. Just this once. Maybe a nap will work wonders too." She reached for the call button tethered to the side of her bed by a safety pin.

"I'm going to leave for now. I'll be back later this afternoon. Today is Wednesday. My client is meeting with Joseph Dryden on Saturday so there's time. I'll phone Shonney and find out if she will meet with me. Maybe I can talk her into going on the streets for a couple of hours with me. She'd pick up on something different before we would anyway." Jeremy pushed his arm into the sleeve of his jacket.

"M-m-m. You're right, of course but Shonney made it clear she would not become involved." Christine reached into her purse. "Here. Take this with you. Show the photo to her and try to help her identify this girl with her kids." She handed Jeremy the picture of Samantha Anderson. "I need to escape this place as soon as possible so I can do my job."

Her impatience was interrupted by the sound of the door opening again. Nurse Miller walked. "Mr. Goodman, you have to let this woman rest."

"I'm leaving." He glanced at Christine as she swallowed the medicine. "I'll see you later. You have my phone num ... Oh. I forgot to give you this. This device is an extra cell phone I use from time to time. Until you can replace or find yours. Dad went to meet with Irving last night after we left here but I haven't talked to him to discover what he found out. Your phone may be at police headquarters. I'll check."

Christine nodded, grasping the cellphone like a lifeline. "I'll make some calls and see what I can find out about Caputo, if he is the man we think is connected to those pedophiles."

Jeremy reached for the phone again. "No you don't. If you aren't going to sleep, let your body heal, I'll take this thing back." He softened his tone a little. "Rest, at least for today."

Christine sighed. "All right. Fine. But tomorrow I'm on the case." Nurse Miller gave him a high five and left, her chuckle following in her wake. Christine smiled. "I think she planned to say the same thing."

Jeremy walked toward the door. "That phone is for emergencies. Call me only if you need me to bring you something. Nothing more. Besides, the cell plan has a limited number of minutes." He opened the door. "Close your eyes. The officer will keep you safe from would-be intruders."

"Aye, aye sir." She saluted Jeremy's back.

Chapter Thirty-Two

Christine closed her eyes. She willed her body to relax. Thoughts traipsed around her brain cells, however, making
sleep almost impossible. *Maybe if I call Barkley, find out what
the police found at the crime scene, I'll be able to rest.* She
punched in the phone number for her lawyer. A busy signal
sounded. *Great.* She laid the device on the bedside table and
glanced at the clock situated over the door. *Lunchtime soon.*

Christine looked out the window. The sun shone brightly
today. *I'll bet the weather is frosty, though.* She grabbed the
phone again and pressed redial. This time the cell rang just once
before she answered the familiar voice. "Hi Barkley."

The man who understood her so well surmised she should
be resting and told her so. "I talked to Jeremy already."

"So tell me what you told him about where I was
found. My brain won't shut off but at least my body is relaxed. I
need some answers so I can proceed with my life. That missing
girl needs me to find her. How is Chief? Oh right, Jenna is
looking after him. Anyway, about the crime scene?" Christine
tapped her fingers on the bed.

Barkley informed her about the bullet found lodged in a

nearby tree. "Only one. He must be a good shot." He reminded her that standing still waiting to cross the street made her an easy target. "I get it but one bullet while speeding by in a car. Either lucky or skilled."

Christine winced when she shifted the device to her other hand. "What about my cell phone? Did they find that? All my numbers ... wait a minute. I remember telling Jeremy it should be in my purse. I left my handbag at the office. The scoundrel. He's commandeered my phone. He gave me a prepaid, said mine might turn up later."

Christine's frown hurt her head again. She reached for her purse to make sure. *Why would he do that?* Barkley spoke around his chuckle on the other end of the line. "He may be trying to keep you from making all sorts of calls."

"He's no right to take my phone. Did he tell you? That's one sneaky son you raised."

Her lawyer didn't see the harm apparently. He instructed Christine, as had Jeremy, to take the rest of the day and recuperate. "It's not every day someone shoots you. He may be back to finish the job so lay low. For a while anyway."

She harrumphed, letting Barkley experience her displeasure. "Mr. Goodman. Tell that son of yours to ... oh, I'll tell him myself when he comes back this afternoon. He's meddlesome." She sighed. "The painkiller is finally working. I can sleep now. Talk later. Oh, what caliber was the bullet?"

Barkley told her the 9mm was probably an automatic. "They really wanted to make sure I died." He reminded her she lived and if the shooter had been such a good shot, she'd have been dead for sure. His goodbye allowed Christine to lay the phone down on the table again. *I guess I was lucky.* She looked toward the ceiling. *Why do I seem to think about You at the oddest times? What do You know about this?* The thought about divine protection floated unbidden across her brain. She huffed. *Maybe.* Her eyes closed.

Chapter Thirty-Three

Jeremy pulled into the parking space in front of his office. *I'll bet Jenna is ready to relinquish the extra responsibility of caring for a dog.* He walked slowly up the walk and the four steps leading to the door. As soon as he entered, Chief stood to block his path as if asking about Christine. He patted the dog's head. "She's doing better." He spoke loud enough his voice carried toward Jenna as well.

The older woman strolled around her desk. "He's such a good dog, so well- behaved all morning. He started pacing by the door about ten minutes ago. He has good instincts."

Jeremy grabbed the canine's leash from the top of her counter. "I'm going to take him with me. He might soften the response of the woman I'm going to visit."

"Are you working on another case, Boss?" Jenna folded her arms across her chest.

He spotted the bruises. "You still bruise real easy these days. How long, now the treatments are over, before the bruising stops?" *She lost so much weight.*

She shrugged her shoulders. "They don't hurt ... just look awful. Anyway, do I need to be filled in on anything?" She moved back behind her desk.

"No. I'm helping Christine out a little. Going to meet with a former prostitute who might be persuaded to help me find the kid she's is looking for. She's a believer so I think I can build a better rapport with her than Christine. Are you okay to hold down the fort? I'm not expecting anyone to call or anything. I called Gibbons to tell him Dryden will be at his office on Saturday at 10 am. Otherwise ..." He took the remaining steps toward the front door.

Jenna waved. "I'll keep the home fires burning. I'll phone if someone needs you." She resumed the task keeping her busy before he arrived.

Jeremy closed the door behind them as he led Chief to his truck. This wasn't the first time the dog occupied his vehicle. He caught the animal placing his nose on the cold glass of the passenger door as soon as he jumped in. *More prints to clean up. Oh, well.*

The short distance to the ex-pro's neighbourhood took only a few minutes. Jeremy parked close to the address. He glanced at the canine, the dog's body turned toward the driver's door as soon as he stopped the truck. "I get ya, Chief. You wanta come too. Keep on looking as lovable as you do right now and you'll be doing me a big favour." He ran his fingers over the animal's silky fur. "Come on." He grabbed the leash.

Shrubs lined the walkway to Shonney's front door with vibrant colours. They sure broke the monotony of the dull late fall landscape. The door complimented the colour and led one to believe a welcome waited on the other side. Jeremy knocked and rang the doorbell.

Chief sat on his haunches. Footsteps announced the occupant's arrival at the door. He rehearsed in his mind what he wanted to say to persuade this woman to help.

The door remained closed but a voice from inside asked his name. Jeremy held his PI license so whoever used the peephole saw it and him. "I'm Jeremy Goodman. I'm here to speak to Shonney Barrett."

The door opened. The slim brunette standing in front of him peered at him with large brown eyes. Her complexion was clear, the dark skin scrubbed clean of any make-up. She wore fluffy slippers on her feet, with jeans and a t-shirt covering her slender frame. Jeremy blinked. *She doesn't appear the hard-*

ened ex-hooker I expected. He held out his hand. "Hi. Are you Shonney? I'm Christine Smith's friend and business associate."

"I guess you better come in den." The woman ignored his hand. "My boys'll be home for lunch soon. You gotta be gone. I don't talk about this stuff with them in the room." She led the way inside.

Jeremy followed. The dog snaked around his legs as they walked into the room. Chief stared at the woman they came to visit. He took a hesitant step forward.

"You bring Chief wit you." She bent toward the animal. "Come, boy." She reached out a hand soon immersed in the dog's luxurious fur. "Christine must spend hours brushing this animal." She rubbed Chief's coat and took a seat in the area of the room set aside for conversation. "Sit." She motioned to the sofa opposite her.

Jeremy obeyed, crossed his legs and tried to appear relaxed in her presence. *For some reason she intimidates me. I wonder why?* He decided to come straight to the point. "Christine is doing okay in the hospital but she's worried about the little girl. She tells me you're a Christian. You probably guessed she isn't."

Shonney chuckled. "She is surely obvious. She stiffen right up when I mention my Jesus." Her penetrating stare assessed the man across from her. At least that's how Jeremy's instincts reacted to her gaze.

He rolled his eyes heavenward and back down as if he prayed. He gazed discretely in her direction. "I've been a believer all my life. Christine seemed more hostile about my faith when we first met but lately she appears to be softening. Her heart is involved when she investigates the things hurting little kids. She can't understand, or refuses to accept the evil man does is not something God condones but allows. Her hostility has changed to confusion and searching, though." He dropped his gaze and glanced back up. "What's your story?"

Shonney told about the woman who helped her break the sin cycle in her life. "Cherie been out of the business for a lot of years but she keeps going back to try to bring one more tortured soul to Jesus. She showed me how to regain custody of my kids and put me on the right track to earning my degree in social work. Now I want to join her but the Lord placed me in a waiting pattern. Like them planes up in the sky before they come in for a landing." She pointed toward the ceiling.

"If you want to help, why are you refusing to go with Christine to the neighbourhood?" He uncrossed his legs and leaned forward, his forearms resting on them.

Shonney dug her fists into her hips at her waist. "I told you, man. God don't want me to go down to that place yet. I don't want to step ahead of Him."

Jeremy struggled with his next words. He believed she was capable of finding the girl. "Look. I don't think you should ever go anywhere without God going first. Why don't we pray specifically for His answer to this issue? He knows where the kid is and the best way to find her." He waited for Shonney's nod of approval and bowed his own head. "Father God, we believe you are omniscient and omnipresent. Please show us how to help this young girl. Give us direction, the right place to go, and the appropriate time to do this. Protect us, especially Shonney, as we search, Lord, and while we follow the trail, place a hedge of angels around Christine in the hospital. Point us to the man who shot her. Amen." He raised his head.

Tears streaked down Shonney's face. "I never thought He might need me to locate a missing kid, to go on the street yet. I am fearful of the place and my habits coming back but if'n He'll protect me, as you asked, I'll go. I've been thinking a lot about where she might be. I remember a house in one of them rich neighbourhoods where they bring the young ones, to break 'em in."

Jeremy sat up straighter. *I wonder why she never mentioned this place to Christine.* "Can you take me to the address - show me where the house is?"

"How we gonna get in there in the daytime? Too many people looking out dey windows." Her shoulders slumped. "No one still alive ever come up against the man before. Besides, my boys be home soon - like I said." She started shaking her head.

Jeremy leaned forward and took one of her hands in his. She snatched it back and placed her trembling appendage on her lap. "Do you understand where our power comes from, how majestic the God we serve is? The 'man' is no match for the Lord, if the Father wants the child rescued. Now is he?" He smiled, his confidence in the Father flowing into the room. "We'll go when the boys go back to school and be back here before they come home for the day. Promise."

Shonney's eyes seemed to grow bigger as she contemplated his words. "We'll be like warriors. Like the Bible says, right?" She stood. "I'm fearful somethin' awful but we do ... what them cop shows on TV say ... we do reconnaissance." She waited while Jeremy stood, leaned down to pat Chief, and led the way to the door. "I'll be ready." Her backbone stiffened.

"I'll be back at one. The dog might be able to help us. We'll pretend we're walking him and follow where he goes. I think Christine was given a scent bag for the kid. I'll check with her. Anyway, thanks Shonney." He grabbed the door handle before the woman took hold. "I'll be back later." He led Chief back to the truck. *Thank you, Lord.*

Chapter Thirty Four

Christine opened her eyes. She glanced at the clock over the door of her hospital room and sighed. She'd been asleep for over an hour. *I'll never accomplish anything if I sleep all the time.* She took a few deep breaths to clear the cobwebs before she reached for the glass of water by her bedside. *I guess I slept with my mouth open. Yuck.* She swallowed a lubricating gulp. Oh, this is almost warm. *Double yuck.*

Her purse lay on the right side of her bed beside her knee. *Good thing the rail was up. Who put that up? I don't remember anyone being in here.* She grabbed her handbag. *My phone should be in here. Oh, right. Jeremy stole the thing. Well, I'll use the one he left. Dang. The memory has none of my numbers. I gotta escape from here.*

Nurse Miller swished her way through the door, a cheery smile on her face. "I hoped you were awake. Lunch will be here soon. Want some help going to the restroom?" She lowered the bed rails.

Before Christine swung her legs over the side of the bed, Jeremy marched through the door. His grin lit his face giving him a boyish appearance. His eyes shone. "Guess what?"

"Your news can wait. My patient needs some priva-
cy ... for a moment, if you don't mind." The petite blond placed
her hands on her hips as if punctuating her request.

Jeremy's smile faded. "I'll be outside the door. Call me
when you're ready. In a few minutes, I have to go again. Come
on, Chief."

Christine immediately spotted the dog. Jeremy held his
leash tightly wound around his hand. "Hey, boy." She bent
slowly at the waist but only enough to reach her pet ... her partner. "You getting along okay without me?"

Chief whined and nuzzled her hand. He angled his body so
he leaned against her leg. Christine stroked his fur and tried to
stand straight without causing more discomfort to her shoulder. "I gotta go." She looked at Jeremy apologetically.

"Oh, sure. I'll ... we'll be outside." He backed through the
door, pulling a reluctant dog with him. "We'll come right back,
Chief."

Christine placed her left hand on her IV pole and her right
one on the nurse's shoulder. "How long before my strength
comes back?" She took the few steps to the little bathroom inside her room. She turned toward the nurse indicating her intentions to handle the rest by herself. But she waited for a response
to her question.

Jennifer Miller worked for four years in the surgical
ward. She shook her head. "You can't speed these things
up. Each person recuperates differently. You're already doing
better than most. Takes time. I'll be right here if you need me."

Christine sighed and closed the door behind her. She
glanced at her reflection in the mirror. A white face peered back
at her. Her hair conveyed a bad case of bedhead. She brushed
the fingers of her right hand through her tresses in an attempt to
straighten them. *I need a comb. I think Jeremy brought me a
brush. That should work.* Once she'd completed her task and
washed her hands, she stepped out into the cooler air of the
larger room.

Nurse Miller stood at the end of the bed. "All finished? Great. Now walk without any help."

Christine wobbled a little but she made her trek back with
no incidences. She collapsed against the pillows as the bed began to rise. "I can't believe how much a little bathroom break
takes out of me." She ran her hand over her forehead. "I'm even

sweating and I never sweat."

"Be patient. You had major surgery late yesterday. In a couple of days, you'll feel almost as good as new. Shall I call your friend in? He seemed chomping at the bit to tell you something."

"Yes. Please. And thanks." Christine took another sip of water as her eyes followed Nurse Miller to the door. "Oh, could you bring some cold water. This is a little warm."

"Sure. Be right back." She opened the door. "Mr. Goodman. You and the dog can go in now."

He strode past her and Chief bounded toward the bed. He placed his paws on the side but Jeremy stopped him before he jumped all the way up. The animal grumbled deep in his throat.

Christine giggled as she drew the brush she snagged from her purse through her hair. "He's never had his access to me blocked before. Be careful. He might bite you." She stuck her locks behind her right ear.

Jeremy ruffled the dog's fur as the canine looked in his direction. "Not me. We're pals. Speaking of pals, Shonney is going to help me this afternoon. Being a fellow believer can work in this game. She remembered a house where they take the girls to indoctrinate them. We're going when her boys go back to school after lunch."

"That's great. Darn. I'm stuck here. I want to go too." She pushed out her bottom lip in an exaggerated pout.

Jeremy pulled up the chair he sat in a few hours ago. "Quit complaining. It is what it is."

"Where is this house? Why didn't she tell me about the place right away?" Christine took a deep breath.

He folded his arms over his chest. "I wondered the same thing. Can we trust this woman?"

She thought for a moment. Her brow furrowed. "Irving gave me her name. She seems legit."

"Yeah, she does. Maybe she was so spooked by your request, she forgot. Maybe she's been talking to someone. I think her faith is genuine so I hope we can trust her all the way. Anyway, she and I will scope out the house this afternoon and decide how we can access the inside to find out what's going on. Other young kids might be imprisoned in those rooms as well." Jeremy stood to leave. "Chief, say good-bye."

Christine brushed her hand across the dog's head between his ears. She let her fingers stroke behind one of them. By the moan of ecstasy erupting from Chief's throat, she knew she found his sensitive spots. "Where are you taking my dog for the afternoon?"

"He's coming with us. Oh, Right. Did you receive a scent item for the Anderson kid?" Jeremy attached the leash again. "We're going to take him for a walk right by the house. If he catches her scent, Shonney's suspicions will be confirmed."

Christine thought hard for a moment. "If my memory serves me, the brown bag with one of her clothing items is in my office. Or did I forget to take the thing with me when I went inside? I can't remember. I didn't really think I would use a scent this time."

"Well. The scent might not help but, it might too. I'll stop by the office after I pick up Shonney. Your Grand Cherokee is parked where you left it, by the way." Jeremy walked toward the door. "I'll be back to fill you in later. In the mean-time ... rest. Build up your strength."

"Yeah. Like I can do anything else. You're pretty sneaky, you know. Leaving me a useless phone when you absconded with mine. I can't remember the numbers in my contact list."

"Exactly. Rest. The calls can wait." He opened the door.

Christine sputtered. "You don't play fair."

"See ya." He turned just in time to avoid a collision with another nurse carrying a tray of food. "Lunch time," He waved and headed toward the elevator, the officer from the morning nibbling on a sandwich at his post beside her door.

Chapter Thirty Five

Shonney reached inside her handbag for the can she carried everywhere she went. Canadians were not allowed to defend themselves but the authorities never said anything about bear spray. Her hand almost fit around the can.

"What are you going to do with that?" Jeremy chuckled as he attached the leash to Chief's collar before stepping out of his truck.

Shonney's large brown eyes looked like dark saucers of fear. "I'll disable anyone who tries to mess with me is what. At least long enough for me to run away and find help if I need to. I never walk the streets without being able to defend myself. I earned a black belt in Taekwondo. No one is going to take me prisoner ever again."

"Shonney, I'm not going to let anything happen to you. Which house is the one you think the man brings his victims to?" Jeremy scanned the neighbourhood as he locked the doors on his truck. The scared woman stood on the sidewalk. She wore boots, jeans and jacket, the attire of teens all over the city. A cap over her thick hair made her head larger in appearance.

She pointed across the street about three houses down to a large two story structure with a wrought iron fence surrounding the perimeter. "There were rumors about the place, but the girls I talked to described that particular house to a tee." She slipped her can holding hand back into her jacket pocket.

Jeremy wondered how drugged and brutalized girls kept their mind clear enough to notice what their prison looked like. *Survival instinct, I guess.* "Let's stroll past the house. I'll take some pics with my phone." A protest was about to erupt from the woman's mouth. "I'll be discrete."

Shonney whispered. "Someone's watching us even now. Oh man. I think I'm gonna be sick."

"Do you want to stay in the truck?"

"No way, Jose. I go where you go." She took a deep breath. "I'll be fine. Let's walk." She took a step closer to Jeremy.

Letting Chief's leash out all the way, he took the scent package out of his jacket pocket. He opened the top of the bag just enough for Chief to stick his nose inside. The dog sniffed for a few seconds and raised his head to sniff again. Jeremy patted his neckline. "Find her, Chief."

The animal walked slowly back and forth on the sidewalk. He whined, sniffed the air again and stopped. He gazed up at Jeremy. "No luck, huh Boy. Well, it was a long shot." He glanced at the woman, motioned for her to follow and the trio set off down the street. "He may pick something up closer to the house."

Shonney casually let her eyes roam toward the house. "No movement. But I guess we didn't think there would be. What would happen if Chief got loose and just happened to wander into the yard? Wouldn't you need to go after him? Maybe you would be able to move real close."

"Woman, you are born for this lifestyle. Good thinking. Lord, protect us." He kneeled beside Chief. The front of the house was only a few paces away with a driveway to the right of their target. Jeremy unhooked Chief's leash just enough so a good tug by the dog would release the catch. He patted the animal on the head. Remembering the commands Denny used when training, he spoke quietly but firmly, "Find, Chief. Find."

The search dog bounded ahead of them on the sidewalk. His leash detached from his collar and the canine recognized his freedom to go where any scent took him. He ran past the yard but turned back and headed straight up the driveway. The wrought iron gate stood open so the dog gained access to the back of the house right away.

As soon as he was out of sight, Jeremy called to him using a different name. "Come on Butch. Where'd you go, boy?" He took one step toward the open gate. He called again. "Butch, come boy."

Shonney pretended to be fearful they might lose the animal in that neighbourhood. "You gotta go find him before he escapes to the next street. Please." The panic in her voice spoke loud enough for any listeners on either side.

Jeremy played along. "Just calm down, honey. We'll find him. I'll go look for him. I'm sure they won't mind." He stepped gingerly onto the property and proceeded to follow the route Chief took to the back yard.

Shonney hesitated at first but then scampered after him. She called for the dog 'Butch' as well. "Come on baby. Come to Momma."

Jeremy sprinted past the side door of the house, and entered the back between the garage and the house. He spotted Chief playing with a young boy and a girl about the age of Samantha Anderson. "I found you." He sauntered slowly toward the trio, mindful someone was probably watching their every movement from inside. "Hi. I hope Butch hasn't hurt you or anything. He can be pretty rambunctious."

The boy stared. His lips moved a little but no sound came out. The girl stepped in front of him, shielding him with her body. "He can't talk." She dropped her eyes to the brownish grass at her feet. Her foot made a backwards and forwards motion in the dirt.

Jeremy let his eyes roam freely over the kid's appearance. They seemed clean enough but they definitely didn't trust him. The girl laid her hand along the dog's back. His gaze took in the unkempt yard, an old toolshed, and a well right in the center.

The girl took a step back from the animal and motioned to the boy. "We gotta go. Bye Butch."

Her hair seemed shorter. She sported brown locks while Samantha Anderson's blond tresses flowed over her shoulders. Her slender body seemed almost emaciated compared to the picture Jeremy remembered of her. Would a kid lose that much weight in a matter of days? He tried to memorize details as the children walked slowly toward the back door.

"Thanks for taking care of my dog." He attached Chief's leash. Jeremy sauntered back toward the street but not before noticing the man who opened the back door for the kids. They had been watched.

From where she stood Shonney's view was limited. "That's her, right?"

"Sh-h-h." Jeremy hastened around the corner after Shonney. "Those children sure had a good time with Butch," he said loud enough for anyone listening inside. "Don't you ever run off again?"

With instincts telling them to beat a hasty retreat, the couple kept their footsteps as casual as possible down the drive toward the street. They whispered. "I can't be sure she's the girl. This one is skinnier with brown hair."

Shonney spoke in a normal voice. "Let's take Butch to the dog park. He can run free." She lowered her voice to a whisper as they reached the sidewalk. "At first the drugs make you sick. You don't want to eat anything. And they probably dyed her hair."

"A man stood by the back door. The kid's faces showed fear, I think. He might be a mean stepfather or dad. Maybe those kids thought they were in trouble so had reason to be afraid. We can't go barging in with no proof something illegal is going on."

"I didn't see anyone else. How do we find out what's going on?" Shonney walked swiftly toward the passenger side of the truck. She shivered. "My skin is crawling. We're being watched."

Jeremy started the engine. "Yeah. They'd be able to run these license plates if they have connections. I should have thought to switch them with another set that goes nowhere." He made sure Chief was secure and put the gearshift into drive. "I think we need to access that house tonight. The sooner the better."

Her voice raised a decibel higher. "There's no we. I'm done. I'll bet I got three more gray hairs in my head. If you still need me to go with you downtown when Christine is ready to play hooker, I'll go but not back to that house." Shonney buckled her seatbelt. "Where's the picture of the girl?"

Jeremy reached toward his glove compartment. He opened the latch and pulled the photo out. When he handed it to the woman, the resemblance was noticeable. "That's her."

Shonney studied the picture. She shook her head. "From what I seen, she's a dead ringer. Tonight may be too late. They'll move her. That's what they do."

Jeremy thought for a moment. "They have no reason to think we are anything other than what we appeared to be ... two people looking for their dog. But, yes. Tonight is a must. If I can find where she is in the house, I'll bring her out and then call the cops."

"Why not get them involved first. Our missing kid is being held in that house. Maybe more. That's kidnapping."

"Yes but the girl may be long gone by the time we prove to the police she's who we think she is." Jeremy stepped a little harder on the gas pedal. Silence reigned inside the cab of the truck for the next few minutes

Shonney looked out the window. Jeremy glanced at her and shook his head. Her body trembled as, he suspected, she remembered her own life on the streets. The woman wrung her hands and massaged her wrists as she studied the pedestrian traffic along the now busier part of town. Shop windows flashed by. Car horns blared but pain filled her eyes. Most people had no idea what went on behind closed doors in some parts of this city.

Chapter Thirty Six

Christine slowly opened her eyes. *I seem to be doing nothing but sleeping, yet my body acts as if I've not slept in days.* Her mind began to think of all sorts of things she'd rather occupy her time with. *That young girl must be so frightened. They might have tried to kill me to keep me from finding her. How wide spread is this infection of human trafficking in our city?* She remembered the research explaining how drugs and prostitution caused so many other crimes.

She used the controls on the side rail to raise herself to a sitting position. The she pressed the black button for a nurse. A large sigh escaped as the door swooshed open.

"Hi. You're awake. Lots of rest helps the healing process." The overworked nurse bustled about straightening Christine's pillows, and checking her water supply. Her glass had been replaced by an insulated mug with a straw. "You need more water. Do you want to sit in the chair while I change your bed?"

Christine smirked. The young woman read her mind. "Great. I'm not used to lying around so much. My energy levels won't allow much else."

"That's not unusual. Sitting up will give you a break and you'll find you'll be able to stay out of bed longer each day. Been for a walk down the hall yet?" She grabbed the chart hanging on the end of the bed. "Not according to the notes here so ... let's help you up and into your bathrobe. You sit for a while so I can refresh your bed, and we'll go for a stroll. How does that sound?"

Christine stifled a stray yawn leftover from her nap. "Sounds really good. I'm thinking the sooner I start getting mobile, the sooner the doc will let me go home. Right?" She eased her legs over the side.

The energetic woman handed the patient her robe from the bottom of the bed. "That's about right, although your incision should be healed a little too. They don't want you back in here with an infection. Most of your sutures are inside."

Christine slipped her arms into the sleeves of her favorite bathrobe. She tied the belt to secure the opening and walked slowly, one step at a time toward the comfortable chair from the morning. "Did those detectives come back again?"

"No. And the cop outside is keeping everyone away. The reporter is persistent, though." She stripped the bottom sheet from the bed, replaced it with the top one and added a clean, freshly laundered top sheet. She switched the pillows around without changing the linen case.

Christine studied the efficient way she worked. *She doesn't waste any energy, that's for sure.* As soon as the nurse finished her task, Christine stood, eager to show the medical staff her improved strength.

"I'm Christine Clairmont, by the way. Should be easy for you to remember since our first names are the same. Take my arm and let's take a stroll." She held hers toward her patient.

"Hi Christine. I ..." The door banged against the wall. A flash illuminated the dark corners of the room and deepened the frown already visible on Christine's features from her exerted efforts to walk.

A man appeared once the remnants of the bright light dissipated. "Miss Smith. I'm Connolly Butler, a reporter with the Winnipeg Free Press. I understand you're the victim of a drive-by shooting. Can you tell me who wants you dead?" He thrust a tape recorder at her.

Christine sputtered. Nurse Clairmont quickly released

Christine's arm and barreled toward the unwanted intruder. "You can't come in here. Where is the officer?" She pushed the man backwards through the door.

His voice carried over the nurse's head. "I'm going to print the story with or without your cooperation. You might as well let me interview you." He brazenly tried again to nudge past the nurse. By that time, the returning guard grabbed the camera-bearing culprit by the collar and marched him toward the elevators. The commotion brought several people to the door of their rooms.

Clairmont shut the door. "I guess a walk down the hall right now is not a good idea. I'm going to find out how this happened. I'm so sorry." The distraught woman behaved as if the sneak attack targeted her.

Christine eased her body back down on the chair. "This is not your fault. I - He took a picture. I don't want my face all over the newspaper. I can't ... can you stop him?" She sent her stony gaze toward the other woman.

Clairmont pulled the door toward her. "I'll try. Relax. He'll remove the picture or else."

She rushed through the door. Through the opening she watched the woman grab the phone at the nurse's desk. Her head hurt. She tried unsuccessfully not to think of the implications of having her picture in the newspaper. *If the killer discovers I'm still alive ... what about Dad's company? They know Melissa Rompart, not Christine Smith.*

She stood, wobbled over toward the bed and grabbed the cell phone Jeremy left her. Thankfully she'd memorized Barkley's number. She tapped in her lawyer's office number and waited. As soon as his voice resonated in her ear, the words tumbled out of her mouth. "Barkley. My Picture. He plans to plaster it all over the newspaper."

She listened as the lawyer asked her to clarify. "The reporter Jeremy said hung around the precincts and hospitals is from the Winnipeg Free Press. He's Connolly something or other ... er ... Butler. That's the name. Butler." She took a deep breath. "Can you stop him?"

Barkley said he had contacts at the Free press Building and he'd try to reason with them. If he failed, a law suit would be the next course of action since no one gave them permission to publish the photo. Christine relaxed once again. "Thanks Barkley." Before she disengaged the call he asked how she felt this morning. "I seem to be doing as well as the nurse expected, anyway, but I want to leave here and find the kid. Energy is a problem. The snoop squashed the idea of a walk down the hall today."

Barkley suggested she take a stroll around her bed. "Yeah, good plan but not much room. I suppose anything's better than lying in bed all day. Talk to you later Barkley."

Christine stood again and took a few hesitant steps around the end of her bed. She walked slowly into the bathroom and turned around to go back. By the time she returned to the chair, her forehead glistened with perspiration. She pushed herself to remain on her feet and walk the short circuit again. *I can't believe how hard this is. I run almost every day, for Pete's sake.*

Christine finally gave into the tremble coursing through her limbs. She remained upright, though, instead of heading to bed. *I might be tempted to fall asleep again.* She breathed deeply. *This wasn't a marathon. Harrumph. This is disgusting.*

The door whooshed open again. Jeremy stood inside, his eyes taking in the shiny brow and labored breathing pattern of his friend. "You look as if ..."

"Yeah, I know. It doesn't take much to make me wither and fade." She stared back at him as he sat his tall, lanky frame on the edge of her clean bed. "How'd things go with Shonney? Find anything?"

Jeremy grinned. "I think we found her. She seems unharmed physically but ..."

"Were you able to move close to her? How did she react when she saw you? I mean, you couldn't lure her away?" Christine sat on the edge of her chair. "Are you sure the girl is Samantha?"

"Her hair is different but Shonney said the first thing they do is change their appearance. But otherwise, she looks the same as her picture ... a little thinner. She played in the backyard with a little boy. She said he couldn't talk." Jeremy crossed his feet at the ankles.

"You spoke to her?"

Jeremy smiled. He folded his hands in his lap and looked directly at her. "We walked Chief by the house but pretended he got loose. Boy, that dog of yours can sure improvise. He took off like a shot toward the back yard. He understood exactly what we wanted from him. I implemented the command Denny used yesterday morning."

"Of course. He's trained for search and rescue. Lately with all the kids we're finding, he's developed an affinity for them, seems to sense where they are. So he led you to Samantha. But someone had his eyes on her I'll bet." Christine leaned back again. She wiped her brow and ran her hand down the side of her bathrobe to remove the moisture.

Jeremy didn't miss a thing. "You sure you're supposed to be sitting up this long?"

She hushed him with her hand. "I'll go lie down again in a minute." She sat a little straighter to accent her ability to stay upright. "Was she being watched?"

"Yes. Our encounter with the kids lasted only a short time before a man came to the door and ordered them inside. No smiles or at least they tried not to show any. They seemed scared. Shonney thinks they'll move them now someone saw them. I'm going back tonight. In fact, I'm going over to the house right after I leave here. I'll keep an eye peeled to make sure no one leaves but when all is quiet, I'll find a way in and take her. We can't wait until you're out of the hospital."

Chapter Thirty Seven

The wind howled like a pack of wolves traipsing through the forest looking for easy prey. The frosty breath whipped around corners, lashing at any exposed skin. Jeremy huddled inside the car borrowed from his father. Barkley's attitude about the plan his son proposed for rescuing the little girl was less than enthusiastic. Jeremy usually kept his lawyer father in the dark when it came to some of the shortcuts he took. Bending the law was necessary sometimes to achieve his objectives.

A few splatters of rain hit the windshield. *Great. Just what I need.* He looked toward the house he spied on. So far no showed their face. He hoped another exit off the property was non-existent. *Christine is counting on me. Not to mention the kid.*

He took a sip from the travel mug of coffee he'd been savouring for the last two hours. *Even it's cooling off.* He shivered. Some heat may be necessary. The trees bent to the force of the wind outside. Shrubs, short and tall, surrounded the house. *That'll make getting close without anyone seeing me easier.* He planned to wait for sleep to overcome everyone in the house. Then he'd find a way in. *A floor plan would be nice.*

He leaned his head back against the car seat twisting his

gaze toward the house again. Nothing moved except the trees. No moon tonight. *That helps me but anyone wanting to move those kids would find the darkness helpful too.*

Jeremy glanced in his rearview mirror. A dog barked nearby. The person walked the animal along the line of vehicles parked beside the sidewalk. He crouched down on the seat. *Wouldn't do me any good to be reported as a suspicious stalker.* The dog howled again right beside his car. His body was tense. When the dog moved away, he relaxed again

He peered above the dash. The man and his canine companion walked a long way down the street now. *It's time. I'll sneak closer to the house. Things are quiet.* He stuck his head out the door. *Good. Not raining hard.* He carefully closed and locked the door. A short sprint across the pavement, through the wrought iron fence and down the driveway toward the dark, silent house took only a few seconds.

The bedrooms were probably on the south end of the house. If everyone slept, the tools in his pocket would make his break and enter easy. He patted his jacket to reassure himself. Jeremy slithered past one tree and hid in the branches of another. He saw a window within arm's reach. He studied the frame and determined it wasn't one of those new triple pane types.

If I use my knife to jimmy the lock, then raise the sash ... he went over the steps in order to gain access. A face appeared. Jeremy almost gasped out loud. The man looked toward the street. *Did he hear me?* He tried to control his breathing. He plastered his body against the wall of the house. Careful not to step on a twig, he inched back into the tree.

Now, is that the kid's room or does the room belong to the kidnapper. The pervert might be checking on the girl or he's getting ready for bed. Lord, only You know at this point who sleeps where. Give me knowledge, Father, and Your peace.

Jeremy took a few seconds to calm down. He decided to move toward the next glass filled opening, the only other one on this end of the house. He skulked along the wall as soon as the man disappeared inside. He stuck to the trees as if part of them. Inching to the second window, he spotted a tiny crack between the sill and the frame. He listened. *Nothing.* He moved closer.

The open space at the bottom of the window seemed large

enough for his fingers to squeeze through. He tried to peek inside. Total darkness enveloped the room. He couldn't make out the shape of any furniture. His heart rate increased again which made quiet breathing more difficult.

Jeremy willed himself to relax. He took a deep breathe. He carefully pushed the bottom of the window. The opening widened a mere inch. He shoved up again, using more of his hand for leverage. The sash raised about six inches this time, making a slight scraping sound. He stopped.

Jeremy leaned back against the wall of the house giving his hand a chance to recuperate from the pressure needed to lift the window. He shook them. He rotated his body to face the glass again. He crouched down. Using his palms, he pushed up with every bit of strength he owned. The gap increased slowly.

Grabbing hold of the inside of the frame, he hoisted himself through the space. He paused to listen. Soft breathing came from somewhere nearby. He slowed his own intake of air. Jeremy eased his tall body over the ledge. He squatted under the soon-to-be escape hatch. He hoped.

Lying prone, he inched across the space between the window and the bed as soon as his eyes adjusted to the dark room. A slender lump lay under thin covers. An arm splayed over the edge of the mattress, a child's arm. Jeremy grinned. *Good. I picked the right room.*

He rose to a crouch. He tried to see the face but the blanket covered most of it. He eased to a standing position. He was afraid his joints might creak and give him away. He stood still, hardly breathing and listened. The house appeared uncommonly quiet. He looked toward the child again and reached forward. His hand brushed the covering away from the thin face. He bent closer to get a better look in the dark. The eyes opened,

Alarm raced across the features of the little girl he stared at. She prepared to scream. Jeremy clamped his hand over her lips just in time as a muffled screech erupted around his fingers. "Sh-h-h-h. Are you Samantha Anderson? Your mother sent me." He whispered but even then he feared the kidnapper would come into the room at any minute. "Let's go. Now."

The frightened eyes looked back at him. The child began to struggle, her legs kicking out, and her arms hitting his legs. He eased his body down on the bed to cover her appendages, to calm her but she fought all the harder. She bit his hand. "Kid, listen. I won't hurt you but you need to be quiet."

The slight body under his lay still. He glanced down as large tears formed around the edges of her eyes. "Are you Samantha?" She nodded. "Will you stay still so we can talk?"

The girl sniffed. He lifted his body a little to one side but remained on the bed. "Your mother hired my friend to find you. I'm the man with the dog. Remember?

She nodded. Her eyes closed again as she swiped at the tears accumulating on her lower lids. Her head glanced toward the door.

Jeremy became aware of the sound at the same time. Footsteps. He gazed frantically for hiding place. "Pretend you're sleeping." He rolled off the bed and, in one motion, slid underneath using her blanket draped over the edge to shield his location. The door opened.

Light shone across the threadbare carpet. Jeremy's gaze fixated on the unlaced black boots. They took a step into the room. Soft breaths evaporated into the night time darkness. The boots backed up. The door closed behind them. Jeremy let out the breath he held.

The child whimpered. Jeremy eased himself out of the bed. The girl's eyes never left his. They traveled the length of him. He lay quiet giving her the opportunity to study him. Would she call the boots back? How badly had her trust been destroyed by that monster? Jeremy smiled, trying to earn the right to speak.

The girl shoved her covers aside. She swung her legs to the floor. Tears streamed down her thin face. "Who are you?"

Jeremy remembered the photo. Slowly he reached into his pocket. He pulled out the picture Christine gave him. He handed it to the girl. "Your mother gave this to my friend. She's written your name on the back."

The girl looked at the photo but didn't reach for it. Jeremy turned the snapshot over. Samantha stared. Tears raced down her cheeks as soon as she recognized the handwriting. "My mom wrote those words. Where is she?" She hiccoughed. Her small hand clamped over her own mouth. "He'll come back."

"Will you come with me?" Jeremy moved slowly to a sitting position. "We need to hurry before the man comes back. You can tell your mom what happened to you, okay?"

Her body language told him she'd take a chance on him. She grabbed the photo and clutched it in shaky hands. Her tiny voice whispered again. "Bring Travis too."

Jeremy stood. "Who's Travis?"

Samantha took a step closer, her thin dress the same garment she wore earlier in the backyard. "He's the little boy I played with. He doesn't speak. But they hurt him. He screamed when the other men came."

Jeremy's heart wrenched as his imagination filled in the blanks. "Which room is Travis in?"

Samantha stepped toward the bedroom door. "He's in the next room."

"You're not going with me to find him, little girl. I want you to climb out the window and hide until we come out. I'll go, I promise." Jeremy placed his hand tentatively on her shoulder. He gave her a slight push in the right direction.

"He won't come with you. You could be one of the bad men. He trusts me. I-I g-gotta b-be there when you w-wake him." She sobbed her last words. Samantha looked toward the window.

Jeremy recognized the war raging inside her. Those creeps haven't taken away her compassion for someone younger. *She is one brave girl.* "Samantha, I tell you what. When does the man with the boots come for you again? Will he let you sleep all night?"

She nodded her head. "He said my training begins tomorrow. He brought me here this morning from the well he put me in. He doesn't touch me much. But ..." Another tear slid down her face.

Jeremy bent at the waist to peer into her eyes. "Any other men here?"

"No. Just him." She trembled.

"Okay, then let's go. You lead the way so when Travis sees us, it's you he spots first." Jeremy walked stealthily toward the door. The girl followed, her footsteps silent as her slender form eased itself through the crack he allowed. They moved as ghosts to the door of the room he guessed to be the one he'd seen first.

They listened. Jeremy placed his forefinger over his lips

reminding Samantha to be absolutely quiet. He grabbed the doorknob. It held tightly. The door was locked.

Chapter Thirty Eight

Samantha's breathing accelerated beside him. Jeremy paused for a scant few seconds, thinking about his next move. The longer they lingered at this door, the more apt to be discovered. He placed his finger over his lips when he glanced at Samantha. He patted his pocket and slowly drew out the tools nestled inside. Samantha's eyes grew larger.

Jeremy unsheathed the lock picks and inserted them into the doorknob. He listened for the latch to release with a minimum amount of noise. He checked over his shoulder anyway. The house remained cloaked in darkness. *Sometimes good things happen when in the dark, Lord.* He thought about their ability to sneak to safety because the dark hid them. Not always. The words flowed through his soul as if spoken aloud. *I see you.*

Jeremy quickly turned the knob on the door, eased the wood barrier open enough to allow his and Samantha's body to enter. He shut the portal cautiously. He stood still and listened. *Did the kid remain asleep?*

Samantha crept closer to the prone child. Jeremy remained quiet, amazed only a day had passed since she arrived at this house. Already a connection was forged with someone who also didn't belong here. He gazed at her gentleness as she reached a hand to caress the boy's shoulder. He stirred. His body jerked and moved away from the hand.

"Sh-h-h-h." Samantha whispered from her side of the bed. "We've come to help you escape."

The boy turned his head toward her. An involuntary groan escaped his lips. She placed her fingers over her own mouth to still his fear. He rolled toward the side of the mattress. He swung his bare legs over the edge. Not a stitch of clothes covered his thin little body.

Jeremy grabbed the t-shirt thrown on the floor. He extended some shorts to the kid as well. The child dressed himself, his movements telling the story of an earlier torture.

Samantha looked toward the door. Jeremy followed her gaze. *Did something attract her attention?* He placed a hand on the boy to still any motion. They listened, scarcely daring to breathe. The house creaked in the midnight gloom. No footsteps sounded outside. Jeremy let out an exasperated breath. "Let's go."

The frightened stare from the child said his whispered words scared him. Jeremy waved his hands at him to spur him to action. Samantha bent to help. The boy rebuffed her attentions as he pulled his shorts over his bruised body under the sheet. Jeremy sent a brief thank you in God's direction for the boy's continued modesty.

The boy stood. His body trembled. Dried blood was visible on his leg below his pants but Jeremy couldn't take the time to address the situation right now. They needed to go. He led the way to the door, listened first, and grabbed the knob. He opened it a crack.

He peered down the hall. The air seeping through the space definitely seemed fresher than the atmosphere in the room. He breathed deeply and allowed Samantha, her hand encapsulated by that of the boy, to go ahead. They stepped into the passageway, Jeremy followed, and he turned the knob gently to close the door in silence.

Their sparse movements made their trek completely soundless. They slipped along the wall to the room next door. The trio eased their bodies inside once they opened the door. The crisp air in the room reminded him the window remained in its elevated position. He motioned the kids toward their avenue of escape.

He lifted Samantha out first, then the boy. They stood in the shivering cold safely out of the house. He placed his leg over the sill. He eased his frame past the edge. Jeremy's body relaxed a little as soon as his feet hit the dirt.

He led the way against the siding, keeping them hidden as much as possible in the trees and shrubs. Samantha seemed to understand instinctively they wouldn't be safe until they reached his vehicle. She never made a sound but encouraged Travis with her motions. *I wonder if that's his real name.*

Just as Jeremy stepped away from the last sheltering shrub, a man's voice called to him from the darkness. "What do you think you're doing?"

He motioned for the kids to remain hidden. He stumbled a little and his words tripped over themselves as he slurred his response. "Ma skey wone fit. Who're you anyway? Ma wifey invite you in?"

The man hesitated. "You're drunk. This isn't your house. Go home. Get lost."

Jeremy listened as the door slammed shut. He staggered to the street in case the man still scanned the area. Minutes ticked by before he waved his hand for the kids to run toward the pavement. They scooted from the trees. Samantha raced as fast as her young legs allowed through the wrought iron gate with Travis close behind. Jeremy followed. A shot whizzed past his right ear. He never stopped. The children came to an abrupt stop almost tripping him. "The blue car." They walked swiftly forward, ducking their heads instinctively.

Another gunshot, closer this time, interrupted the peace and quiet of the neighbourhood. Samantha screamed but Travis never uttered a peep. Jeremy wondered if the child would ever speak again. They stopped beside the borrowed vehicle. He unlocked the door with the key fob but another shot tore into the front tire. The girl screeched again as she scooted inside. The boy followed, both laying prone on the backseat.

An involuntary expletive erupted from Jeremy's mouth. He glanced toward the wheel as he, too, slid into the driver's seat. *Sorry, Dad.* He fit the key into the ignition his first try. He turned the engine on, and stepped on the gas pedal. The disabled car roared to life and moved down the street. The last shot shattered the back window. Jeremy kept going.

Chapter Thirty Nine

"You're lucky that creep couldn't shoot straight." Jeremy leaned back in the chair beside Christine's bed. Two kids, bedraggled and fearful, huddled on the floor against a wall. Tears glistened along the lower edges of Christine's eyes when she looked at the rescued children. They already called Mrs. Anderson and Sergeant Irving.

Christine motioned for Samantha to come stand beside her bed. The girl stood up slowly, her fatigue making all movement an effort. She cautiously placed one foot in front of the other. "Where's my Mom?"

Christine smiled after swiping the telltale moisture from her eyes. "She's on her way. Your mother's been frantic. She hired me three days ago to find you. Jeremy told me you met my dog, Chief. He'll be very excited when he sees you again." She glanced at their rescuer. "What did your father say about the condition of his car?"

Jeremy smirked. "He acted a little peeved but happy for the outcome." He ran his hand down Samantha's arm. "I'm sure you didn't sleep too well last night, little lady, but tonight you'll be back home, in your own bed, with your mother."

The girl's eyes filled, her tears dripping down emaciated cheeks. "He'll find me. He'll put me in the well again. The walls hide spiders and rats. The blackness makes them invisible but I listen to their scratching and I imagine them slithering all over me." Fright caused streams of water to flow faster. She wrapped her arms around her thin body. "We had no food, only a little water until he took the other girl out. He left me with nothing ... all alone."

Christine reached toward the child. She hugged her a little awkwardly given the fact she was laying on her side. "The police will want you to tell them what happened but they will talk to you only with your mother in the room. Maybe they can prevent another little girl from going through what you did." She nodded toward the little boy who dozed sitting up against the wall. "What has Travis told you? How do you communicate if he doesn't speak?"

Samantha glanced over her shoulder toward the boy. Her eyes filled with empathy. "He's been in that place for a long time, I think. He wrote his name down for me, I think he's learned how to write some words but not everything. He held up five fingers when I asked how old he was. We needed to be careful because of the man."

Jeremy looked at Christine. "The police will search the data base for kids who've been reported missing. I hope they get results quickly. His healing will take a lifetime, I suspect."

Christine dropped her head. A lone tear hit the sheet leaving a wet spot. "I wish the authorities had the evidence to round up all these ... "Her hands clenched into fists as she looked toward the kids. "Enough said."

Jeremy patted her hand. "I agree." He looked toward the children. "I wonder if I should let Travis sleep. Samantha, do you want to come with me to the cafeteria for some breakfast? We can bring something back for the boy."

The twelve year old looked from one adult to the other. "He'll be scared if he wakes up and I'm not here."

"Okay, let's wake him. Food can be a comfort." The girl walked over to Travis. Her footsteps hardly made a sound.

She crouched in front of the boy and gently shook his arm. The child startled awake and stared intently at the girl's face. "We're going for some breakfast. Wanna come?"

Travis glanced around the room a few seconds more and stood, not saying a word. He walked with Samantha to Jeremy's side. The boy looked up at the man who never touched him, even to place a hand on his shoulder. He blinked.

Jeremy smiled toward him. "Hungry. You can choose anything you want. The cafeteria is on the first floor so we'll take the elevator again." He glanced at Christine. "When Irving and the mother arrive, tell them we'll be right back."

She answered his smile. "Mrs. Anderson won't wait. Eat a good breakfast you guys. Think about me chained to this IV pole." Her effort at lite humor appeared lost on the kids.

The door closed behind the rescued and their rescuer. *Jeremy is amazing. God did you have something to do with his character?* She leaned back against the pillows, her energy level waning as the adrenaline rush left her. *What a way to start the day.* She marveled that the search for Samantha had ended. *The pervert shot at them. I wonder if he was the one who put me in here.*

She decided to use the restroom to tidy up a little in the few minutes before Sergeant Irving and Sylvia Anderson arrived. She slid her legs out from under the sheet and over the edge of the bed. Sitting quietly for a few seconds to allow the dizziness to pass, she stood, grabbed the IV pole and walked slowly toward the little bathroom. *Today this comes out. I can't wait.*

Christine ran a brush through her hair, brushed her teeth, and put some moisturizer on her face for the second time that day. *The air is so dry in here.* She applied lotion to her arms, but when she bent to reach her lower limbs a wave of dizziness just about toppled her over. *That's another thing I can hardly wait to recover from.*

She sauntered slowly back to bed but decided to make a detour around the end to the chair Jeremy vacated. She took a deep breath as soon as she lowered her body. *Standing takes too much energy.*

The door whooshed open and a short man in a white lab coat walked in. He held out his hand. "Hi Christine. I'm Dr. Benson. I'll be the one looking after you until you're ready to go home. Your surgery went well according to Dr. Matheson. Now your recovery depends on gaining back some strength. Let's listen to your chest." He placed his stethoscope right near her incision sight. The nurse replaced the dressing on her wound before breakfast, a smaller one than the one directly after surgery.

Christine took a few deep breathes, each causing a sharp

pain but not as bad as the day before. *A good sign I hope.* She waited for the doctor's instructions.

He checked her pulse rate and strode to the chart at the end of the bed where the nurses wrote her vital signs regularly. "Looks as if you're well on the road to recovery. Another day or two should be all you need. Now let's remove the IV." He picked up the call button and pressed the center.

Nurse Miller bustled through the door as if waiting for his signal. She brought a tray of instruments with her. "Yes, doctor?" She obviously didn't want to assume anything.

"The IV can go. Christine is doing well. Maybe even better than expected." He smiled toward his patient.

She grinned back and held her hand toward the nurse. "What about this dizziness?"

He chuckled. "That's from lying around all day. Done any walking down the hall at all?"

Nurse Miller pointed to the newspaper sitting on the bedside table. "A reporter has been nosing around. Fortunately, Christine's lawyer managed to stop the photo he planned to run with this piece he wrote about her in this morning's paper. If she leaves the security of this room, he'll waylay her again. The officer guarding the door is keeping him out for now."

Dr. Benson pursed his lips thoughtfully for a moment. "Well walking in the room will suffice for now. Once you're up and about at home, the dizziness will disappear, I'm sure. Continue to rest, walk when you can, and eat everything on your tray. The best medicine encompasses all three. We've done our job, now it's up to you." He walked toward the door. "You're expecting visitors. Don't overdo, all right?"

"Yes doctor." Christine waved, happy to sever her connection with the IV pole. She patted her hand. The soreness from the needle remained. She leaned back again the seat cushions, as the nurse straightened up her bed, folded the blanket to lie over the end, and raised the bed to a full sitting position again. "You do a good job, Jennifer."

"No problem. Do you need anything else?"

"Some ice water, please." Christine smiled and shut her eyes. *Rest. Harrumph. That's all I've done. But at least Samantha's been found. Thanks to Jeremy.* The door opened and closed, behind Nurse Miller she supposed, until she heard a man clear his throat. Her eyes popped open.

Bill Irving spoke first although Christine surmised, by the disappointed look on Sylvia Anderson's face, the mother wondered where they'd taken her daughter. "We can come back later if ..."

"No, we can't. Where's Samantha?" Mrs. Anderson looked in the direction of the tiny restroom.

Christine smiled her assurance. "Your little girl is down at the cafeteria having some breakfast, Sylvia. She'll be right back. Why don't we talk while we wait for them?"

Sergeant Irving motioned for the woman to take a seat on the bed. She pulled the extra chair close to Christine instead. She sat but soon bounced back up again. "I need to hold my daughter." She took a step toward the door.

"She's with my associate, Jeremy Goodman. He's the one who actually found her. I'm a little incapacitated right now." Christine let her head drop for a second, hoping to keep her emotions in check. "You can join them if you want. I thought some preparation was needed so you don't scare her and the boy."

"Boy. What boy?" The woman wrung her hands and returned to her seat. "What happened to my baby?"

Sergeant Irving took out a pad of paper from the inside of his jacket. He poised a pencil to begin taking notes. She glanced back at Samantha Anderson's mother. "They held your daughter in a well for the last three days, maybe more. She thinks he put her down the hole as soon as he took her. She hasn't eaten much since she's been gone. She's lost weight and some scratches and bruises from her ordeal are in evidence but otherwise, she seems untouched physically."

"Oh, My poor baby." Tears welled in Sylvia's eyes. "Why would he drop her in a well?" She shook her head.

"They apparently kept another girl with her for the first couple of days." Christine stared at the distraught woman. "Samantha needs to tell what happened to her to the Sergeant and she needs to be checked out by the doctor to assess what, if anything, was done to her. You're here as support. The calmer you can be the better for her. Do you understand?"

Irving added his recommendation. "Kids clam up if they think what they're saying is hurting their parents. We need her story to catch this guy."

The woman nodded her head. "I'll be okay. Who's this boy?"

Christine looked toward Irving. "They held him captive at the house where they kept Samantha. She wouldn't leave last night without him. She said he screamed before Jeremy found her."

Sylvia Anderson's eyes glistened, her unshed tears kept in check. She glanced at the policeman. "Will you be able to find his parents?"

"If a missing child report is filed, we'll find them. If they didn't ..." He left the rest of the sentence unspoken.

Sylvia looked from the sergeant to Christine. "Why wouldn't someone tell the authorities their kid is lost? What happens to him if they aren't found?"

The patient rubbed her hand over her eyes. A burning sensation gave credence to the emotional roller coaster she experienced since Jeremy arrived with the two kids. "Child Protective Services will place him in a safe environment until the court declares him a ward of the province. Right, Sergeant Irving?"

The man cleared his throat before answering. "Neither of you want to hear this but it's the best we can do in these situations. Right now, let's concentrate on finding his family. Thankfully, Samantha is taken care of or will be as soon as the doctor releases her. If she can identify this pervert, we'll be closer to putting one more deviant away for good."

The sound of the door opening interrupted the flow of the conversation. Jeremy used his hand to hold the door ajar while the much shorter figure of the preteen walked through. Her hesitation ended when as she caught sight of her mother.

Those who witnessed the change in the girl's facial expression drew an exaggerated breath of relief. Samantha ran to her mother, arms outstretched. She nestled into the familiar, safe place. Her sobs flowed nonstop. "Momma, Momma."

Christine swiped at the stray trail of moisture escaping her eyelid. The men in the room did likewise. Almost forgotten, Travis leaned his body past Jeremy's to study his friend. His face remained as stoic as before. Christine frowned in the man's direction.

Jeremy placed his hand on Travis's shoulder. "The mac

and cheese was really good, right Travis?"

The boy swiveled his head to look up at the tall man at his side. He inched from under the hand, obviously uncomfortable with any touch at this point. He remained silent.

Samantha's tears subsided as soon as she remembered Travis needed her. She sniffed, ran her hand across her nose and cheeks, and sniffed again. Her mother reached into the handbag she carried and produced a clean tissue. Samantha walked toward the little boy while drying her wet cheeks. "Mom, this is Travis. They stole him before me. He can't speak but I understand what he wants."

"She sure does. Travis told her exactly what he wanted to eat and how much." Jeremy grinned, relishing the girl's take charge attitude with the boy. "Samantha, you will let the doctor look at Travis, though." He glanced at Christine. "I'm going to find a female to check him out."

"Good idea." She searched the face of the police officer. "Sergeant, can the report wait, at least until the doctors determine how they fared physically?"

"Sure. As long as our interview happens today. I need to rally my detectives on this in case ..." He cleared his throat. "... in case he tries to replace what he lost."

Samantha glanced from one face to the other. She wrapped her arm around Travis. "The man said ..."

Sylvia placed her fingers over the girl's mouth. "Sh-h-h. Honey. Not now. You're safe and so is he but Christine's right. We need the doctor to make sure you're both okay."

The girl led Travis by the hand toward her mother. "Mom, can you come with us?"

Travis stared toward Christine and shifted his gaze to study the older woman sitting on the edge of the bed. The anguish of uncertainty left his face. He reached toward Sylvia Anderson.

The smile on Jeremy's face grew broader. He eased himself past the door jamb and let the heavy wood structure close behind him.

Christine glanced at Sergeant Irving. "You can wait here. When the kids check-up is over, they can come back to tell you their story. Will that work?"

The seasoned veteran stood to his feet. He shook his

head. "I'll come back here in about an hour. That should give the doc all the time she needs. I need to make some phone calls." He cleared his throat once again.

Sylvia looked in Christine's direction. "I think you should rest and we'll ..." She nodded toward the children. "... come back as soon as we can." She took a step toward the door.

Christine's shoulders drooped. "I'm so happy Jeremy found her. I don't really need the whole story, I guess. The cops can take over now." She slowly inched her way to her feet. "Oh-h-h Man. my body thinks its old."

Sylvia Anderson grinned before she turned to the door. "We'll come back here to talk to the sergeant. You didn't find Samantha but if you hadn't taken the case, Jeremy wouldn't be involved. So ... we'll be back. Rest."

The police officer held the door open for the mother and daughter, watching as Travis clung to the woman's hand. He glanced at Christine before following the trio through the portal.

Christine shuffled toward the bed. Her room seemed larger now she was alone. Quieter, too. She yawned. *A nap is in order.*

Chapter Forty

White coated attendants, women in colourful hospital uniforms, and men with stethoscopes around their necks walked up and down the hall. *A lot of people here this time of day,* he thought. He strode swiftly toward the door where the woman and little girl exited moments before.

The cop standing guard earlier was gone. *Hopefully, he's gone down the elevator with the other one.* He harrumphed. *They think the chick is important or something.*

He thought about the orders he received as soon as the paper came out that morning. *The guy acted all hostile. I wonder why they want her dead.* He shrugged his shoulders. *No never mind to me. Long as he pays me.*

He approached the door. Glancing carefully from right to left, he shoved - slowly. He stepped inside, one foot in front of the other, listening for any sounds indicating the woman's location. He hoped she slept. *Make the job easier.*

He stuck his head around the door frame as he eased his body through the doorway. His eyes adjusted to the dim light. He checked the restroom as he moved past. *No nurse hanging around. Good.* The woman lay with her back to him. *This is going to be easy.*

The man reached inside the pocket of the lab coat stolen from the doctor's lounge. He retrieved a thin wire, coiled but easily unwound. He also took the gloves stashed in his pants pocket and slipped his hands into the leather. The coil fell through his fingers and landed at his feet.

He bent at the waist, picked the metal coil off the tiled floor, and began to uncoil it. He wrapped the ends securely around his index fingers, stretching the wire taught. He moved closer to the side of the bed. He'd acquired the habit of moving soundlessly in prison.

Soft breathing wafted through the room. But the woman stirred. She rolled to her back. Her eyes stared at him for a few seconds. She looked from him to the wire. Her mouth opened. He couldn't let her scream. He leaned his body closer. Too late. She let out a screech sure to bring half the hospital into the room.

The man reversed his movements. He took a couple of quick steps to the door, dropped his head to avoid being seen by any security cameras in the hallway, and scurried through.

"Hey. Stop." The cop was back. He rushed toward the stairwell. Heavy footsteps sounded close behind. *Gotta find another way.* His contract was irrevocable. Like a rat, he scampered down one flight to the next. He ran faster. One more floor and he'd reach the parking garage. *Home free.* A gunshot hit the cement wall near his right ear. *I need to clear the doorway as soon as possible.*

"Stop. Police." *Right. Like that's gonna happen.* He raced through the final door, made his way past three parked cars and ducked between. He rolled under the vehicle with the best clearance and lay still. He slowed his breathing, taking short silent puffs of air into his overworked lungs.

Footsteps pounded the pavement. Black boots stopped right in front of where he hid. The odour from the grease spots on the pavement wafted toward him. His nose itched. He couldn't sneeze. He placed his hand to block the unpleasant scent.

The footsteps grew faint. The large boot encased feet disappeared from sight. He took a deeper breath. Then another. *A few more minutes and I'm gone. I wonder if she got a look at me long enough to give my description to the cops. Oh, well.* He pulled off the wig he wore and the thick mustache that went with it. *She'd be wrong.*

Chapter Forty One

Christine screamed again. *The thug left but ... a wire was wrapped around his hands. He planned to kill me, right here, right now.* She placed her hand over her racing heart. *This is getting ridiculous. Where is the police officer who is supposed to be guarding my door?*

The door slammed open. Jeremy raced toward her. "What happened?"

"You t-tell m-me. A guard should be outside. Where is he?" Her accelerated breathing almost made the words shoot out of her mouth as if from a shotgun at close range.

Jeremy blinked. "You screamed and I came running. The officer escorted Mrs. Anderson and the kids to the emergency department for their check-up. We got sloppy. "

Christine forced her body to relax against the mattress. "Would you push the button to raise me up? I'll never be able to sleep now." She lifted her upper torso slightly to make the bed lift easier. *I couldn't do that yesterday*, she thought.

Jeremy complied but she still hadn't told him what happened. "I woke up to a man standing over me with a wire, a very thin wire. He was poised to wrap the thing around my neck, I think. Anyway, when I screamed he fled."

"Too bad you didn't have your gun here. I think the police officer chased him down the stairwell. His pant leg disappeared through the door. Gunshots sounded soon afterwards. Did the intruder have a pistol?" Jeremy sat one hip on the end of the bed.

Christine moved her feet to accommodate his large frame. "I didn't spot a gun, just the wire. I think I surprised him. I wonder if he's the same guy who shot me."

"Was there anything familiar about the man?" Jeremy laid his hand on her leg. He patted the sheet. "I'm so sorry, Christine. I guess we forgot why you're here for a second. Those kids'll break your heart."

"Yeah, I lost track of my own situation for a little while too." She blinked. "Those kids hurt so much more than I do but we need to find out who wants me dead. He's not going to stop, is he?" She pulled the blanket closer to her throat. "I want to go home but ..."

Jeremy frowned. "Not anytime soon, you're not. Not until we figure this out, anyway."

Christine huffed. "I can't stay here indefinitely. Besides, he got into my room here. I'm no safer here than I would be at home."

"Christine." Jeremy's exasperation surfaced. "People roam these halls twenty-four hours a day. At home, you're a sitting duck."

"Not with Chief." Her eyes lit up. "Say, why not seek permission to let him guard me until they let me go home? He'd certainly be more reliable than the two officers who've been assigned the job."

"And who's going to take him for a walk several times a day? Christine, what made you wake up when you did?" Jeremy glanced toward the door. He shifted his gaze back to her ashen face again.

"I dreamed someone called my name. At first, the voice annoyed me. The dream was peaceful enough, I think. Can't remember. Anyway, I surfaced from a deep sleep to find out what he wanted." She inhaled slowly. "I thought the person standing over me was you for a second."

"Not me. But I think God woke you up in time." Jeremy

couldn't help the smile spreading over his face. "He protected you."

Christine blinked. "Oh, that's preposterous. Someone else called me. The voice was as clear as you and I talking. Not some distant ..."

"Christine, our Lord is not distant from us. The Bible says where two or three are gathered in His name, He is with them. He's a personal, relational God, who wants nothing more than to be the one you turn to when trouble strikes." He smirked in her direction. "With you, that's just about every day. Besides, I'll bet if you ask the nurses, no one else entered the room. A male nurse hasn't done any of your care, has he? Face facts, God is coming after you. He wants you for His own and He doesn't plan to let anything happen before His time."

"So once I capitulate, He'll leave me to my own devices? Sounds inviting." Christine grimaced as she said the words thinking the description didn't fit the God she was beginning to realize had her best in mind. "I will ask around but ... does God really speak so noticeably? I mean, like you can hear His voice?"

"He does. Christine, your heart is softening to the Father. Do you want to commit your life to Him, to doing things His way? We can pray right here, right now, if you'd like."

Jeremy's cheeks reflected his heightened colour. Her heart quickened with peace and capitulation. Did God care that much about her? Did he wake her? *Are You here now? Father, can you hear my thoughts.* She swallowed. The idea seemed daunting. She pulled the sheet closer to her face. She never understood Jeremy's self-confidence before. *I thought he acted arrogant but ...* "Okay, I give. Doing anything, finding missing people, seems to need divine guidance. I can't ignore Him any longer, I guess. Where do I start?"

Jeremy's eyes glistened, although he seemed not aware of the moisture. "Do you believe sin or bad choices, whatever you want to call them, are part of who you are? Do you admit, you're not perfect, based on God's standard of perfection?"

"Oh, for crying out loud, who is? No, I am certainly not perfect by anyone's standards but definitely not by God's." Christine sat straighter.

Jeremy chuckled. "The first step in admitting you need a Saviour is understanding your imperfections. Do you believe

Jesus died on the cross because He loved you when you didn't deserve His love?"

"I'm beginning to but I imagine I'll understand a lot more as time goes by. I want God to be the one I count on, the one I'm accountable to. He's already done so much and that's just the stuff I recognize. My eyes and ears are probably missing a bunch." Christine teared up as she realized the truth of her statement. "He really does love me."

Jeremy angled his body so he was able to examine her facial expressions more clearly. "Christine, God tells us in His Word He created us for a relationship with Him. He wants to communicate with us every day, to visit with us over the things happening in our lives, and the issues we're dealing with. He loves each of us as if we are the only friend He has in the world."

Christine blinked. Her eyes glistened. "I've lived my whole life as if alone. Oh, I grew up with Uncle Conrad and Aunt Connie but they're not my parents. I don't have any siblings either so ... I like that about God. He can be my family, right?"

Jeremy lowered his gaze for a few seconds as if praying for the right words. He cleared his throat. "The Father, our Creator is waiting, Christine. All you have to do is believe, acknowledge you aren't perfect, that you've made some poor choices, ask His forgiveness, and give Him full control over your life. Do you want to pray?"

She bowed her head. "Lord, I do understand. I've botched some things in my life a time or two. I need You and since I know you're real now, thank You for saving me today. Thank You also for dying on the cross for me when I didn't even believe You existed and when I certainly didn't deserve the gift. Please take control of my life whatever that looks like. I'll be teachable, I promise. Thank You, Amen." Her heart beat calmly in her chest. A sense of peace and being cared for flowed through her limbs. She shyly glanced at Jeremy. "I don't talk to God as good as you."

He chuckled. "You'll learn and ..." He reached across the bed and opened the drawer next to her. "Here's a Bible for you to begin. Reading His Word will help you build a relationship with Him. This book contains a lot of good life lessons. Some of us call the Bible our instruction manual. Start with the Gospel of John." He handed the paperback to her. "Do you own one?"

"No, why would I? I thought only weaklings needed all this religious stuff, remember? But you're certainly no weakling and neither is your dad. Where do I buy one for home?" She flipped through some of the pages. "This one doesn't look as if it's been opened." She clutched the book to her chest.

"Sad but true in many cases. But, now you can remedy that." He grasped her free hand. "Welcome to the family, Christine."

"I - I think ..."

Before she finished her train of thought, the door burst open and Sergeant Irving rushed into the room. "Christine, are you all right? They told me what happened. He got away but ... you can identify him, right? Was he the same guy who took a shot at you?"

Jeremy stood to his feet. His indignation added creases to his forehead. "He didn't just take a shot, he shot her and no, Christine said this assassin looked different."

Christine laid the Bible beside her on the bed. "I can certainly describe him but this guy wore a mustache. The drive-by shooter was clean shaven."

"I wish I had more to go on than a flimsy description." Irving placed his hands on his hips and shifted his weight to his left leg. "What's the motive here?"

"Nothing we can come up with anyway." Christine looked toward Jeremy. "We'll keep praying."

His eyebrows raised, the sergeant said nothing. He shook his head. "I'll be back with the detective you worked with before to put a sketch together. Maybe a drawing will trigger something in someone's memory." He stared at her. "For a young woman, you seem to attract a lot of bad guys. Why is that, do you think?"

Christine shrugged her shoulders. "I thought the cases I've been working on might make someone nervous but ... now I'm not so sure." She glanced at Jeremy again. *I'm always checking him out lately.* "I need my phone." He raised his hand to point toward the one sitting on her bedside table. "Not that one. Mine." She threw him a fierce grimace.

The door opening again interrupted Jeremy's sigh of resignation. Sylvia Anderson walked through with two very quiet children. She nodded in their direction as soon as the door closed again. "The doctors were very thorough. I don't think the kids liked all the poking and prodding. The blood work was met with some resistance, at least on Travis' part." She steered her charges toward a corner of the room. "They're ready for your questions now, Sergeant."

Bill Irving pulled a chair close to the young pre-teen and the little five-year-old. A notebook materialized from his pocket. "Good. Would you kids like a pop or something before we begin?"

The interaction between the robust police officer and the children was fascinating to watch. Samantha seemed quite relaxed around him but Travis, his head hanging almost in his lap, would not make eye contact. *Getting some information out of that little boy is going to be difficult.* Christine closed her eyes. *Father, calm his heart. If he is able but just won't speak, please give him the incentive to do so. Help his comfort level, Jesus. Thank you. M-m-m. So that's how life is going to be from now on. I can ask you anything, right Lord?* She smiled.

When Christine opened her eyes, she caught Jeremy smirking in her direction. "What?" She made another face at him.

"Nothing." His grin grew wider. He leaned closer to her side.

His whispered words brought shivers crawling up her spine. "Together we're going to be a force to contend with, I think." Christine swallowed, sending a plea to the Father for a right perspective concerning Jeremy.

She blinked. "We're not together. Remember, no partnership. Just colleagues sharing office space."

Her words forced a look of consternation to replace Jeremy's grin. "We should reconsider. We work well together and ..."

She shrugged. "Let's think about it."

Chapter Forty One

Anger charged the smoke-filled air. Sparks flew as exple-
tives filtered down on the head of the man sitting calmly at the
end of the long table. Three men, clad in designer suits,
marched from one side of the room to the other. "She's as good
as dead. I need to wait until they release her. The hospital is too
crowded."

The youngest of the three professionals spoke first.
"You're an idiot. Incompetent. It may be too late by the time
she gets out. She's got a big mouth and her lawyer will make
big trouble for us. A simple job, you said. You handled worse,
you said." The words were pitched into the room.

Another man stepped in front of him, blocking his vision.
He stuck his face right in the seated would-be assassin's face.
"Kill the woman or you're a dead man." His cold, lifeless eyes
held the man's attention. "Three days. No more."

His voice took on the timbre of a whine. "What if she ain't
out by then?"

The third suit picked up a book from the coffee table near
a seating arrangement and threw the heavy tome at the killer.
He missed hitting him by mere inches. "We don't need to hear

the details. Complete your contract. Understand?" He glanced toward the other two. "Who decided to hire this - this ..." He waved his hand in the would-be killer's direction. "No more mistakes." He stalked to the door leading to the outer office. "Get him outta here before somebody stumbles across him."

The door closed behind him and the gun-for-hire rose to his feet. He braced himself for more recriminations but straightened his spine. "I don't take kindly to threats." His words sounded from the depths. "I've never failed to deliver. The job is as good as done." He strode to the same door. "I won't be back until then."

The two remaining men threw their arms in the air. Exasperation passed between them knowing choices had evaporated. They turned their bodies away from the hired killer as he exited the room, dismissing him with their posture.

The younger one spoke cautiously. "What do we do if he fails and she figures things out?"

Hands on hips, neither wanted the answer, but the other man said the words anyway. "We'll leave the country."

Both dropped their gaze to the floor. Thoughts of what that implied ran through their minds, separately yet connected, their fates intertwined. *Life is so good for us right now. Three days he said. Hardly seems enough time.* His heart rate accelerated a little.

The youngest collaborator walked toward the door. "It is what it is." He slid through the portal leaving the remaining man staring into space. The door closed behind him and he stalked toward his office, his computer, and his top coat. *I need some fresh air.*

Chapter Forty Two

Christine leaned back in the bed. Sylvia Anderson took both kids with her when she exited the hospital room for the second time that day. The sergeant gave the Andersons permission to take the boy home since he seemed so comfortable with Samantha. With the girl's help, he found his voice. A gruesome story of abuse and neglect tumbled out. The memory of his parents was lost apparently.

"Jeremy, the depravity of people never ceases to amaze me. You told me about sin but these things seem so much worse. These perverts kill the minds of their victims as well as their bodies. You want to cut the creeps into pieces, and feed them to the dogs. They don't deserve to live." Tears flowed down her cheeks, unchecked now the children were safely on their way home.

Jeremy walked closer and placed his hand on her shoulder. His eyes glistened as well but he controlled his emotions better than Christine. "I want to forget I'm a Christian when stories like this surface." He stepped back from her bed. "You probably should sleep. Why don't I come back this evening and we can talk some more about your new faith."

She grinned in his direction. "Gonna play teacher, are ya?"

"Do you mind? You might want to give my dad a call before you nod off. He's been praying for you for a number of years." Jeremy headed toward the door. "I'll make sure the guard is where he's supposed to be, although I think after the chewing out he got from Irving, he won't be going too far. Later, Christine." He made sure the door closed softly behind him.

Christine looked toward the Bible lying beside her. The hunger like urge to read the little book pulled at her but the need for some restful slumber won the battle. *I'll call Barkley after I wake up.* She shut her eyes. *Lord, please guard me and anyone else who might step in the way of this person who's trying to kill me.* Her breathing settled into a regular rhythm before she was finished talking to God. Sleep descended quickly.

****

Jeremy glanced up and down the hallway. Nothing seemed out of place but, he reminded himself, he didn't recognize all the faces of the staff who worked here. He looked around for another chair to accompany the one occupied by the police officer on duty. Stepping into the small waiting room at the end of the hall, he found what he searched for.

Jeremy glared at the man guarding Christine's door. Then his gaze softened. *The recent breach is as much my fault as his. We both forgot.* "When are you being replaced?"

The officer's eyes studied his face for a few seconds. "I volunteered for a second shift. I screwed up. Won't happen again."

The man's look of contrition gave credence to his words, fostering compassion in Jeremy's heart. "My name is Jeremy Goodman, by the way." He held out his hand.

"Sergeant Irving told me you are only one of two people allowed in her room. With so much coming and going today ... Mrs. Anderson needed some help, I - well - sounds like another excuse. I'm Justin. In my two years on the force, guarding someone was not assigned to me." He leaned his chair back against the wall bringing the two front legs off the floor by an inch or two.

Jeremy studied the faces of the nurses at the desk. "I wish

the same people worked here every day. I don't remember any of these people." He glanced at the young officer. "How old are you?"

"I'm twenty-three, sir. Why?"

"Well, I'm thirty and been asked to protect people many times. I messed up today too so it's not about being experienced or not. We simply do our job the best we can, with the Lord's help." Jeremy let out a long breath of exasperation. *I guess I'm still a little on edge*. He sighed. "We'll both make sure she gets some uninterrupted rest, okay?"

"No one will sneak past me again. You can come back later if you want, make a coffee run or something." He dropped the front legs of the chair to the floor.

Jeremy paused before he spoke again. He didn't want to leave the impression he didn't trust the guy but trust was an issue anyway. *I need to be here*. "It's okay. I'm not needed anywhere else at the moment. I left the room to let her rest."

"Oh." He glanced away but then turned his gaze back to Jeremy again. "Sergeant Irving told me you're an investigator. How do you find a job like that? I mean, how did you become a licensed PI?"

Jeremy leaned back in his chair, keeping the legs firmly planted on the floor like his mother taught him. He organized his thoughts before speaking. "I always wanted to be a cop, right from the time I learned to express myself. Dad wanted me to be a lawyer, like him, and mom thought an accountant would be a nice, safe career choice. I went to the police academy after graduation instead, took the training and graduated but the life wasn't what I thought. I worked as a beat cop for about six months. On my days off, my Father asked me to do some investigating for a case he had. I did and loved following the clues to find the evidence needed. The rest is history. I work for several lawyers and I sometimes work for him as well, so we're both happy. Mom died a couple years ago so my being an accountant is not an issue." He looked at the young cop. "How about you? What made you want to become a police officer?"

The cop's eyes dropped to the floor and back up again. He seemed to study Jeremy a little before responding. "My dad's a policeman, my grandfather as well and two uncles. I guess I joined the family business. Working as a PI when I retire from the force sounds like a plan, though. I love solving mysteries."

Before Jeremy said anything further, a bright flash invaded his peripheral vision. His eyes jerked toward the light as a man, rather slight in stature, rounded the corner of the waiting room. He jumped to his feet as the intruder sauntered toward them.

"Hey man. You guarding the woman who got shot?" The intruder's voice carried louder than the voices of anyone else nearby. His swagger gave away his sense of confidence in the job he did.

Jeremy wasn't fooled by his tone. "Why are you interested? Why did you take our picture?" He placed his hands on his hips as he barred any access to Christine's room. The young officer stood shoulder to shoulder with him.

The man held a card out to them. "Come on. I want an interview, that's all. I work for ... well, read this."

Jeremy snatched the information out of the man's fingers. "So, you're with the Sun." He looked toward the cop. "His name is Benny Kingerski. Remember the face and the name. He's not allowed anywhere near her." He nodded toward the closed door. His gaze shifted toward the reporter. "Understand?"

"Hey man. It's the right of the people to read all the facts. Freedom of the press and all that." He stood his ground, his eyes drifting toward the room where he suspected his next story lay. "Who're you anyway?"

Jeremy looked at him with his most fearsome gaze. "None of your business. Now give me your camera so I can erase the picture. Or my father, who happens to be her lawyer, will call the Sun to exercise his client's right to sue your sorry self. Understand?" He asked for the second time.

The man seemed to shrivel a little. "I'm just doing my job. My boss acted all hostile when the Free Press scooped us on this story. How come you let him cover it? My sources ..."

Jeremy heart almost stopped. *Sources. I should use mine.* "Thanks buddy. Now move along. You print the photo and your career will be history, I can guarantee that fact." He walked a few steps past the desk keeping the reporter in his sights. The small man grunted his disapproval but sauntered toward the elevator. Officer Justin crossed his arms as if pleased he'd done his job.

Jeremy punched in some numbers he used from time to

time when he wanted information from the streets. A couple of rings later, a sleepy voice answered the phone. Jeremy made sure the man he phoned listened attentively before he made his request. "I want you to spread the word. I'm looking for the scuttlebutt on a hit. It happened two days ago to a woman in White Ridge."

The person on the other end provided his usual complaints about police interference. "Yeah, she's the one. Find out who and why. Find the guy and cultivate an acquaintance. I want this information ASAP, understand?" He said that a lot these days.

Jeremy hung up and turned back to the cop standing beside his chair. The reporter had vanished. "That should generate some buzz and maybe some answers ... if we're lucky."

"We work with CI's on the street too. I wonder if the detectives checked their sources." The man in uniform sat down again. "Reporters. I hate those guys."

"They're just doing their job." He smirked. "Yeah, I don't like them either."

Chapter Forty Three

Christine slowly opened one eye and then the other. *I slept.* She smiled. She flexed her arm and leg muscles. *Good as new ... almost.* She glanced at the clock. *Almost time for dinner.* She threw the sheet backwards away from her body, swung her legs toward the floor, and sat on the edge of the bed for a few moments. *The dizziness is not as bad as this morning. Sitting in the chair most of the day seems to help.*

She stood hesitantly, grabbed the bathrobe she'd discarded at the foot of the bed, and slipped her arms into the sleeves. The hospital provided some disposable slippers so she slid her feet into those for the trek to the bathroom. Purposefully, she straightened her spine. The pain reminded her the shoulder still needed healing but the discomfort was manageable. *I'm getting better.*

The few minutes in the restroom refreshed her. She completed her tasks and decided to check if the guard remained at his post. Christine grabbed the handle for the heavy door. Before she pulled the weight toward her, however, it opened from the other side.

Nurse Miller bustled inside. "Good, you're awake. Your dinner is here. I took the privilege of ordering a tray for your friend too so he can eat with you." She straightened the sheets, smoothed the blanket toward the pillow and pressed the button to raise the bed.

Christine stopped her. "Can I sit in the chair for my dinner?"

The nurse chuckled. "You can. You must be getting better. They told me you experienced some intrusions earlier ... in fact a lot of excitement by the sounds of it. Tuckered you right out, I'll bet."

"This hospitalization hasn't been boring that's for sure." She thought about her faith and a smile involuntarily warmed her cheeks. "I made a decision today. When someone is watching out for you ..."

"Yes, Mr. Goodman ..."

"No, I don't mean him." She paused. "You said you ordered a meal for someone. Who? The Guard?"

"No, Mr. Goodman. He's been sitting outside your room all afternoon. I guess he doesn't want any more intrusions ... er ... attempts on your life." Her frown turned quickly to a smile again. "Anyhow, I assumed ... well ..."

"He's a friend, nothing more. What about the usual guard, the one the police department sent? Where did he go?" Christine moved closer to the chair, turned her body around, and sat.

Nurse Miller giggled. "Two knights in shining armour protect you." She stopped talking for a minute. "I guess I shouldn't make light of what happened. The intruder almost killed you ... again. Those things don't happen around here." Her sober expression relaxed again. "Now, I'll find your trays and tell Mr. Goodman he can join you, okay?'

Christine smiled as the nurse allowed the door to close behind her. She let herself relax completely. The chair cushioned her shoulder through each movement. The door opened again, a large hand holding it while her caregiver entered, arms laden with two filled trays.

Jeremy followed the woman inside. "Did you sleep?" He nodded in Christine's direction as he took one tray from Nurse Miller and laid the food on the rolling table.

"Hello to you, too." Christine snickered. "I did. Now I'm ravenous." She patted her stomach.

He wheeled the table close to her and cranked the handle to the proper height. The nurse added the second tray gently. "That works. Enjoy your supper, you two. I'll be back later to gather the trays and bring you some medication the doctor ordered for tonight. Sleep is the best medicine."

Christine glanced toward the small framed woman as she hustled back out the door. Her hands folded in her lap; she waited for Jeremy to pray for their meal. The warmth of knowing this about him spread through her as he asked the Lord to bless the meal. *I'm no longer on the outside looking in.* Hastily she focused on the prayer and added her own thanks.

Jeremy searched her face. "Angels dance in heaven when one of us accepts Jesus' gift of Grace. Did you know that?" He removed the lid from his plate.

Christine did the same. "M-m-m looks good." She picked up her fork and filled her mouth with some of the mashed potatoes. Swallowing quickly, she responded. "Angels dancing. Now that's a neat concept. This room would be full with what I haven't learned yet. I read the Bible for a few minutes before I dozed off but that's all I managed." She added some meat to her empty mouth.

Jeremy chewed his food slowly before taking a sip from the glass of milk on his tray. "I still haven't discovered all God's Word has to teach me. My reading and studying the Bible began in high school. Dad will also admit getting to understand our instruction manual takes a lifetime."

Christine's movements stopped. "Do you think your church would accept me? Does your Father attend the same one?"

"He does and they certainly would. A group of ladies get together weekly for Bible study during the day and another one meets in the evenings. We men meet on Thursday mornings usually but this week, we'll gather on Saturday. Anyway ..." He shoveled some more food into his mouth and proceeded to talk around the tasty morsels. "... the worship on Sunday prepares us to handle life as it comes. The pastor is always right on with what we need to learn, too."

Christine nodded as she leaned back against the cushion again. "I'd like to go with you one time. Afterwards, I can attend on my own but the idea of church seems a little daunting for the first time."

Jeremy chuckled. "You'll do fine. By the way, Dad is bringing Chief by this evening."

Christine grinned. "Oh, great. I miss him." She sat closer to the table and filled her mouth again. "I didn't call Barkley so telling him in person about Jesus will be fun." She almost hummed as her Lord's name rolled off her tongue. "It's funny. I can't remember why I was so opposed in the beginning. It seems as if I've always belonged to Him."

Jeremy smiled as he looked at her face. His smile sobered. "Christine we should go over the attempts on your life. The muggings and break-ins happened because your searches for missing kids brought you undue attention from the wrong people but this time ... well ... these people are seriously after you. I may find out something tonight yet. I phoned a person I use as an informant from time to time. He's going to keep his ears to the ground, listen to the buzz around town."

Christine lifted her head from the dessert she ogled. "I never thought of that. I'll bet the police ..."

"Yeah, the officer outside said he called Irving and suggested the same thing. So their CI's will be keeping their eyes open too. Somebody will spill the beans, we hope. In the meantime, we need to figure out where to take you when you leave here."

"I told you. Chief will warn me, give me enough time to either vacate my house or use my gun. I am licensed to carry, remember."

"Just make sure you shoot when he's coming toward you. If the police think he ran from you, they'll charge you with attempted murder or they'll throw the book at you if he dies. Canadian laws are different from American." Jeremy set his fork and knife across his empty plate.

"Your country's rules are ridiculous. I can't defend myself?" She harrumphed, her indignation apparent by the stiff posture she displayed. "Anyway, the alarm company wired my place for any contingency, I think."

Jeremy leaned back in his chair. "I think you should stay somewhere else. Some place unfamiliar and where whoever this is can't find you."

"We'll never find this guy if no one comes after me again."

Jeremy pounded his fist on the table top making the trays

jump an inch or two. "You're not going to be the bait in a trap. The whole idea is preposterous. It's also dangerous. Out of the question." He shook his head. "Not gonna happen."

The woman grinned. "Don't you think God is strong enough to protect me?"

"Christine." Jeremy barked at her. "The Bible says not to test God and that's exactly what you would be doing. Forget it."

"Fine." Christine decided to change the subject. *I'm not sure how the conversation went in that direction anyway. I'll give the idea more thought, though.* "What time is your dad coming with Chief?"

He frowned. Glancing at his wristwatch, he replied, "I think he'll be here in about ten minutes. He wanted to stop by on his way home." He paused. "Ask him and I'm sure you'll find I'm right about this."

Christine chose to let the thought of her acting as a decoy drop. *How would I pull something like this off, anyway?* She pushed the table to one side. "I'll tidy up before he gets here." She walked slowly toward the bathroom. Jeremy examined every move.

Chapter Forty Four

The room buzzed. Sergeant Irving gazed toward the front entrance where a large, tattooed man stood leaning against the desk. *I wonder why he's giving Crandall a hard time.* He shrugged. *Not my problem.*

He shifted the stack of paper beside his right elbow. *I need a break, a cup of coffee, fresh stuff, not the syrup served around here.* He pushed his chair back. *I think I'll go buy a Timmies.* His mouth watered. *Tim Horton's is the best.*

He grabbed his uniform jacket from the hook near his cubicle. Slipping his arm into the sleeve, he snatched car keys from his desktop and strode toward the front door. Before escape was possible, however, Police Officer Crandall stepped in his path. "Sergeant, this guy says his information is for you alone. He'll only speak to you."

Irving rolled his eyes. *So much for my coffee.* He studied the man before him. "Who're you? You look familiar."

"Yeah, well, you arrested me three years ago for fighting." His cheek twitched. "Name's Belcher. Jerry Belcher."

Irving's eyes opened wide. "You're the guy who beat up a woman, almost killed her."

Belcher's voice erupted in a growl. "Woman. That wasn't no woman. When he put the moves on me, I belted him. He deserved a beating." His nostrils flared. "Men shouldn't oughta go around calling themselves dames and dressing like one."

"I remember." Irving pointed toward his cubicle and the chair located to the side. Once Jerry Belcher sat down, he returned to his own seat. "What do you want?"

The street thug leaned back, crossed his legs at the ankles, and rested his left elbow on the desk. "The word is you was asking about the girl who got shot. What'll ya give me if I tell ya who I think might be involved?"

Irving frowned. "How can I trust anything you say?"

"Because I'm related to the creep but he does what he can to forget I exist." He pounded the desk with his meaty right fist. "The guy's as crooked as they come."

"So you have a beef with him and decided to get him into hot water. Right? Anything to even the score even if the truth is absent?"

"Oh, it's true all right. I overheard him. I ..."

Irving sat forward, his face staring at the larger man. "I thought you said you had no contact with him. How's he related to you?"

"He's my older brother. Thinks he's smarter than I am. He may be rich but I would be too if I had a gig like he does. We don't talk ... much. But I was coming to visit him ... anyway, what's in it for me?" Jerry clamped his mouth shut.

"If your information checks out, you'll receive the usual fifty bucks. But we always check the facts out first." Bill Irving smirked. "A lot of you guys looking for your next fix offer to give us some tidbit or other. We like to work with the informers we're familiar with rather than the rats we don't know." He chuckled at his use of rat.

"I ain't no rat. I wanted ta help. That's all. Anyway, my brother's name is Richard Belcher. He's been the big cheese at Rompart Industries for over twenty years. I went ..."

"You telling me that Rompart is part of this? Why?"

"Do I look like an encyclopedia? He told someone on the phone to finish the job. He said the woman was a liability. She stuck her nose in something that was none of her business by the sounds of it. A woman detective or something?" He glanced around the room. "Can we trust those guys? They can listen in on our conversation." He nodded toward the policeman sitting at the next desk talking to another officer.

"Unlike the world you live in ..." Irving looked at Belcher's tattoos and his straggly beard for emphasis. "We can trust the people who work here." He relaxed against the back of his chair. "Tell me more about this brother of yours."

Jerry lowered his voice. "During my younger days, my brother lived alone. He worked for Rompart way back but not as the boss or anything. Anyway, the owner got hisself wacked and Richard took over."

"What made you tie his comments the other night with the girl? Maybe he talked about someone else." Irving took a clean sheet of paper and began to scribble some notes.

"He said the newspapers ran a story on her in the morning edition. I looked. The reporter told about the broad getting shot." Jerry's lack of eye contact was troubling. "Richard didn't know I was in his house. Now you gotta not hold that against me, okay. I sometimes take things to hawk them for some dough."

"Man. Some witness you'd make. The lawyers will eat you up and spit you out. You better show us concrete proof your brother is involved or ..." Irving scowled at the man.

"I heard what I heard." He smacked one fist into the palm of his other hand. "The clock said three o'clock, yesterday afternoon, okay. Not night. Can't you place a bug on his phone or something; check all his incoming calls around that time? Maybe find the device he called from. He's put out a contract on the woman and he won't stop till she's dead. I thought you cared about women."

Irving sighed. "Tell me exactly what he said, word for word." He poised his pencil to begin writing.

Jerry made invisible quote marks. "You idiot. I thought you was a professional." He paused, rolled his eyes toward the ceiling, and continued. "You got three days. Do it or you're a dead man. That girl already is a liability." He looked into Irving's eyes. "Word for word what he said. Honest."

"So. Why come to me?"

"Well, like I said. I heard on the street you was looking. Besides, it's time that high and mighty brother of mine got what he deserved." Jerry sat forward in his chair. "When can I expect my money?"

Irving sent a look of sheer disgust in the thug's direction. "I told you. When we check this out. We'll need to be cautious. Rompart owns a whole firm of lawyers. The mayor is a personal friend I think."

"Yeah, well." Jerry Belcher stood to his feet. "Don't make me wait too long. I'll keep my ears peeled and if I find out more, I'll get in touch." He turned toward the door. "Oh, sounded to me like the guy Richard talked to was not too bright. He stopped to explain a word every now and again."

"I said word for word and now you're telling me he explained some words. What else did you miss?"

Jerry scowled right back. "I told ya everything. I'm outta here." He sauntered to the front door as if he owned the place.

Irving studied the man's back. *What do I do with this little tidbit? I can't obtain a warrant for a supposed conversation someone, an addict no less, said he heard. Maybe I need to confirm they're related first.* He shouted toward Officer Crandall. "Bring that guy back here."

"Sure, Sergeant." The officer jumped up from his seat, rounded the corner of his desk and raced toward the exit.

Irving perused the notes in front of him. *If this Richard Belcher is really part of Rompart ... I'll call Barkley Goodman. He'll be able to tell me.* He reached for the phone. Before he punched in the numbers for Goodman and Son, Crandall returned with a frustrated man in tow.

"What you want now?" The thug glared at Irving as the younger officer quietly slipped back to his work station near the front.

Bill Irving pointed to the chair Jerry Belcher warmed a few minutes ago. "Take a seat. I need some information to connect the dots." He positioned his pencil for more note-taking. "Who are your parents? You were born when and where? How old are you and how old is Richard? We'll check out your story after we make sure you are who you say you are."

"You got that already." He glared toward the sergeant as if his antics intimidated anyone. "You arrested me, remember. My file contains all the information. About my parents anyway. And date of birth. As for my brother, he's sixteen years older than me. Do the math." He stood again. "Don't bother me again until you are prepared to pay me some cash." He patted his open palm and turned back toward the front door.

Irving shook his head and made a note to check Jerry Belcher's record. He picked up the phone again. *Let's discover what Barkley can tell me.* He waited while the device rang a couple of times.

The soft lilt of a woman's voice interrupted the next ring. He responded to her request to help. "I'd like to speak with Mr. Goodman."

The woman introduced herself as Clare, Mr. Goodman's assistant. She informed Irving her boss was away from the office at the moment. He left a message for Barkley to call and hung up. *Well so much for that.* He woke his computer up. *Let's find out what Belcher's been up to.*

Chapter Forty Five

Christine moved slowly from the restroom toward the center of the room. Jeremy stood. "You want to sit here?" He pointed to the comfortable arm-chair near the window, the place she spent most of the morning.

She smiled at her spiritual brother. *This new relationship sounds kinda nice.* "If you don't mind. The other one is too hard." She completed the steps to reach the chair in question. "We're spiritually related now, aren't we? I read something about that somewhere." She frowned as if trying to remember where.

Jeremy grinned. "Yes, you probably did." He kept his eyes on her as he sat down on the bed. "The Bible refers to us often as brothers, sisters, or children of God. Through Christ, we become God's offspring. In that regard, we are related." He quickly hid the frown the statement invoked. "In our case, we're also colleagues and maybe partners, if you want. I mean ..."

Before he continued with his train of thought, a soft knock announced a visitor. The door opened a crack but a wet nose pushed all the way. Chief's furry body crashed through the portal and raced toward Christine. He poised himself to jump into her lap when Barkley Goodman yanked on his leash. "Not yet, boy."

A feminine giggle erupted as she leaned down to bury her face in the animal's fur. "Oh, I've missed you so much." She grabbed handfuls of doggy fur and ran her fingers through the thickness. She glanced at her lawyer. "Thanks, Barkley."

The older man chuckled. He reached toward his son to shake hands. "Quite all right. I enjoyed having a dog around again and Clare ... well, she thinks she died and went to heaven. I didn't realize she loved animals until she looked after Chief. I think when we marry, I'll buy ..."

Christine's face blazed with the man's confession. "You're getting married? How awesome! I am so happy for you, Barkley. When?"

Jeremy interjected. "I tried to find that out, too, but he claims they still need to set a date." He looked at his dad. "If you guys sneak off and elope, I'll be some upset."

Christine grinned in her lawyer's direction.
"Right. Eloping isn't an option. We gotta make a big deal out of this. All your friends and colleagues. And us." Christine began to tick off her list on her fingers.

Barkley chuckled. "You forget this is my wedding. And Clare's. We'll do the inviting. When the time comes. We want to enjoy the engagement a little, not rush into anything before we catch our breath. Time is in abundance." He pulled the hard backed chair closer. "How are you doing, Christine?"

She looked at him with a grin. She glanced at her friend, before shifting her gaze back to Barkley. "Jeremy tells me you prayed for me."

Barkley studied the younger man. He shifted his eyes back to his client. "I guess the secret's out. If truth be told, we pray ..." He pointed from himself to his son. "... for all our clients. God asks this of us. Why? Are you offended?'

"Oh, heavens no." Happiness floated around her heart, her smile a visible response. "Jeremy helped me pray to accept Jesus today. Your prayers were answered." The warmth from her cheeks spread down her neck.

Barkley eyes quickly filled. "Oh, Christine. Ever since your parent's death, I prayed God would reach out to draw you to Himself. WooHoo. Great news, better than anything you told me recently."

"Even more exciting than getting engaged?" She giggled.

"Well, besides that." He moved closer, leaned down and gave her a paternal peck on the cheek. "Welcome to the family."

"Jeremy explained the whole family thing to me before you arrived." She reached down and scratched Chief between the ears. "Everything is so new but ... I do believe God has my back. After the earlier incident."

The lawyer's face clouded. "What?"

"The Father woke Christine before her attacker wrapped a wire around her neck. We assume that's what he planned. The police are going to send a sketch artist over tomorrow morning so she can describe the man."

"Right here?" Barkley's voice raised an octave. "What happened to the guard? Sleeping on the job?"

Christine glanced at the door to make sure the young man was out of ear-shot. "He helped my client, Sylvia Anderson, take her two charges down to the emergency department for a full exam after their ordeal." Her cheeks grew a little pink when she thought about Jeremy's response. "Now your son won't go home."

Barkley chanced a quick glance at Jeremy. "I think you can understand his concern, can't you? After all, you work out of the same office."

Jeremy forced his gaze to remain placid. He reminded Christine they did complete an assignment together recently. "We haven't worked a joint operation a lot but I made the suggestion we become official partners at Goodman Investigations."

Barkley cleared his throat. "Something to think about for sure but like my wedding, take things slow. Once a partnership agreement is drawn up, the contract is not so easy to dissolve if something goes wrong."

Jeremy opened his mouth to protest but closed it almost as quickly. "I guess we don't need to rush into anything, right Christine? Our first priority is to find the person who tried to kill you."

Christine glanced at his face. *He's hiding something. Maybe he wants to partner with someone else. Maybe I'm not reliable enough. He doesn't trust me.* She remained silent as

she studied the father and son before her. A tinge of disappointment crept into her chest. *Why does that bother me?*

Chapter Forty Six

Barkley Goodman walked slowly across the parking lot. The crisp air reminded him of the days when he and his late wife strolled along city streets after dinner. The practice became their way to unwind after a busy schedule. He drew in a deep breathe. *So many things still remind me of her.*

He looked back over his shoulder toward the hospital entrance. Christine healed faster than he expected. *She's certainly a handful ... like her father. His independent streak caused me, as his lawyer, some massive complications. He kept making decisions without consulting me. His daughter is exactly the same. I can't believe she thinks playing decoy to trap her killer is a good idea. I'm glad she's isn't getting out yet.*

He inserted his key into the ignition of his town car as soon as he sat on the plush leather seat. *Jeremy is going to have his hands full.* He chuckled. *The last obstacle is removed. Now he can pursue a personal relationship with the girl. I hope he gives her some time to grow as a Christian before he distracts her.*

His large car crept through the parking lot to the nearest exit. Barkley reached for the knob for his stereo system and turned on the music station he loved to listen to most. Soft jazz floated in the once quiet interior. *I wonder if Clare would like to go out for coffee.* He picked up his phone but placed the device on the passenger seat. Noticing a break in the traffic, he pulled over toward the curb to make the call.

The short conversation confirmed dinner was a more appropriate choice since neither had eaten yet. The early evening would ensure no crowds barred their way for a quiet meal. Barkley told Clare to be ready in twenty minutes. Before he dropped his phone on the seat again, the cell emitted the ring tone indicating an incoming call from the police station. "Hello;"

Sergeant Irving seemed excited about something. Over the years, he and Bill exchanged information about different people. The officer understood Barkley acted as Christine's lawyer and he'd also been told her real identity. "Bill, you still at work?"

The sergeant came directly to the point. "You can't be serious. They were a little reluctant to meet with Melissa but murder. Why? What did he say their, or I should say, his brother's motive was?"

Irving proceeded to fill Barkley in on the interview with Jerry Belcher. The lawyer shook his head. "No, Bill. I can't think of anything to make them want Christine ... er ... Melissa out of the way. In fact, I don't see how they found out they are one and the same. We've kept her picture out of the paper. Unless they hired someone to tail her."

The conversation got really quiet as both men spent some time in thought. "Bill, I'm picking Clare up for dinner. Call me tomorrow and tell me what you find out about this Belcher character. He's probably giving you a load of bull." He cleared his throat as a stronger expletive wafted its way through his brain cells. "If this is the case, Christine is in a lot more trouble than we first thought."

Sergeant Irving reiterated the brother's description of Rompart's ruthless CEO who delved into criminal activities and had been for a long time. He voiced Barkley's thoughts. Maybe Richard Belcher ordered Xavier Rompart and his wife killed. Maybe Belcher and not Rompart laundered money. Maybe Christine was right.

Barkley ended the call, dropped his phone onto the passenger seat and wrapped his hands around the steering wheel of his car. He laid his forehead between his fists. *What a mess.* He lifted his head, checked his mirrors, and pulled back into traffic. *Just when you think things are going to smooth themselves out, something else crops up.*

He did the one thing that always put the right perspective on situations of this nature. *Lord, protect Christine and Jeremy, too. His heart especially. She needs to find out if her father is an innocent bystander. Help the authorities catch whoever is behind the attacks on her. She's a new believer, Father. Keep her safe. Direct me toward my life with Clare, too. Thanks, Father. Amen.*

Chapter Forty Seven

Jeremy turned his back as Christine removed her bath-robe. The bed rustled as she slid between the sheets. "Can I turn around again?"

"You can. I'm decent. Why don't you go home for some sleep? You've been up a long time." She lay on her side to face him.

He settled his frame into the comfortable chair recently vacated. "I'm okay. I might nap right here."

"Jeremy, don't be silly. Besides, they won't let Chief stay here all night." She patted the bed beside her. The canine walked toward his mistress, laid his head on the sheet and wait-ed. Her hand came to rest on his scalp, almost of its own voli-tion. Her fingers flexed back and forth as she demonstrated her love for the animal.

Jeremy studied her silently at first. *She seems more content with Chief by her side, that's for sure. Maybe if I leave him here overnight, she'll sleep better. I'll take him out before I head home and come back first thing tomorrow to take him for a walk again.* "He's a service dog. You keep him with you to-night. I'll walk him tomorrow morning." He paused. "Christine, you dropped the idea of drawing the killer out, right? Dad seemed pretty adamant about your importance to Rompart."

"Yeah. Right. They've been running the company all these years without me. I look forward to understanding what exactly my Father accomplished in his short life, though. I also want to clear his name. But I won't be held prisoner here while some maniac wants to kill me. I want to be proactive, not reactive."

Jeremy sighed. "You're impossible. Let the cops look after this." He stood and began pacing around the end of her bed. Chief's eyes followed his movements. "Sergeant Irving put some feelers out on the street and so did I. Information will come in soon, I hope. Then we can go after this guy. For right now, you concentrate on getting well."

Christine lowered her gaze. She paused as if in deep thought before uttering her next words. "You're probably right. I still need to rest a lot. I'll wait for a few days before tackling anything on my own."

Jeremy studied her expression. "Can I trust you? You look sincere."

"Oh, come on. When have I ever lied to you?"

"My discernment capabilities are not honed to a fine tune with you yet." He chuckled. "I'll give you the benefit of the doubt, for now. Want some fresh water before you close your eyes?"

Christine smiled in his direction. "No. I've got plenty here. Can you find a bowl for Chief, though? Maybe the nurses have something useful."

Jeremy stood to do her bidding. He strode through the door, making sure the uniformed cop sat nearby and sauntered to the nurse's desk. "Is there something we'd be able to use to give Christine Smith's service dog a drink? I'm leaving him with her tonight."

The nurse thought for a moment, smiled, and walked the short distance to the supply closet. She returned with a large, metal bed-pan in her hand. "This'll work, I'm sure. You'll be here first thing in the morning, though, to take the animal outside. We don't need any canine messes to clean up. How's she doing?"

Jeremy grinned. "She's getting her feistiness back. We'll need to keep track of her activity level so she doesn't overdo. That's her nature."

The nurse chuckled. She pointed toward a small paper cup. "This'll do the trick. At least for tonight." A tiny white pill sat in the bottom.

"Sleeping medicine?"

"Ordered by her doctor since he's ended her IV treatment." The nurse resumed the paperwork she had dealt with before Jeremy interrupted her.

He walked toward Christine's door. He stopped to acknowledge the police officer and proceeded to enter her room again. "Here's all they came up with. It'll do, I guess."

Christine chuckled. Chief's gaze drifted from one to the other and toward the metal container. Jeremy emptied her water jug into the bowl and placed the receptacle before the dog. Chief lapped as if he'd come in after a long, hard run.

"I'll go fill your container. I think the nurse plans to be here soon with your night time meds." He retraced his steps to the door and returned a few minutes later with a dripping container of ice cold water. He set the water on her bedside table. "I'm going to visit with the officer for a little while and then I'll come take Chief for a walk before I leave for the night. Okay?"

"Sure." She lay back as if settling in for a good night's sleep. Jeremy left through the door again.

Chapter Forty Eight

Christine closed her eyes. She thought her way up her body. She wriggled her legs, her arms, and moved her torso from right to left. *I actually feel pretty good. Considering the surgery two days ago. I wonder if I have the stamina.*

She rolled over on her side. Her legs swung to the floor as she slid off the bed. Placing one foot in front of the other, she assessed her capacity to work around the remaining pain level. Christine stood by the small locker. Her fingers gingerly grasped the handle and pulled. Inside, she discovered the clothes and the jacket she wore when she was admitted. She retraced her steps to the bed and lay down again. *Jeremy will be back soon with my dog. I'd better look as if I'm down for the night.*

She covered herself with a sheet and yanked the blanket over her frame. She sipped from her water jug as her friend opened the door. Chief led the way toward her. "Hi boy. Did you enjoy your walk?" She glanced at Jeremy. "Thanks for taking him."

"My pleasure." He patted the dog on his head. "I'll be here by seven to repeat the exercise."

Christine dropped her gaze, using Chief as an excuse to not look at him. She stretched and yawned. "I guess I'm more tired than I thought." She pointed to the empty paper cup the nurse gave her with the sleeping pill inside. "They made sure I'll sleep like a log tonight."

Jeremy nodded, his expression revealed concern. "I hope you didn't overdo today. This guard will be diligent all night so you don't worry about any intruders. By the way, did you request a bottle of water for him? Very thoughtful."

"I figured he might be thirsty. I've been so self-absorbed. I've not given any thought to his comfort or lack thereof. After all, he's guarding me. Keeping me safe." She cleared her throat. "I'll be fine, Jeremy. Go."

He headed toward the door. "I'll be back." He gave his best Arnold Schwarzenegger impression.

Christine chuckled. "See you tomorrow, bright and early." She waved and turned on her side away from the door. The heavy wood closed behind him.

Turning on her back, she glanced at the clock. *A couple of hours to kill.* She decided to buzz the nurse again since she wasn't allowed out the door. An older woman in purple nurse's clothing walked in. "Can I help you with anything? You're supposed to be asleep."

Christine yawned. "I will be soon. I wanted to make sure the guard drank lots of water tonight."

"He might like some coffee as well to enable him to stay awake. I'll see that he gets some. Sleep well." She retraced her steps.

Christine kept her eyes glued on the nurse's retreating form. She glanced toward Chief curled up near the side of her bed. "Rest boy. We're going to need our strength."

Christine bent her body into a fetal position and relaxed into the mattress. She ached for sleep although not because some medicine enhanced her ability. The round white pill lay under her pillow. She closed her eyes. *A couple of hours won't hurt.*

Before long, soft whispers of breath escaped her lips. Chief accompanied her with louder snores. The room's dim light made checking on her nearly impossible when a nurse made her rounds an hour or two later. The dog didn't miss the woman's visit as he opened one eye when the door closed.

Christine jumped. She straightened her body, wincing as the pain in her shoulder reminded her she laid in a hospital. *I really nodded off.* She rolled toward the side of the bed where Chief lay when sleep overtook her. *He doesn't look too comfortable. He's used to sleeping on his bed.*

She pushed against the bed rail on the right side of the bed as she swung her legs toward the floor on the left side. Sitting upright for a few minutes, she thought about what she planned to do. *Something needs to be resolved. Waiting is over.*

She crept quietly to the locker. Taking her pants, shirt, and undergarments from the hooks inside, she laid them on the bed and began to remove the hospital gown. *I won't miss this thing.* Chief stood beside her looking up as if asking, "Where are you going?"

Christine decided to whisper an answer. "If the killer is outside waiting, we'll smoke him out." The dog cocked his head to one side. Are you sure? His eyes always were more expressive than any animal she'd played with at the ranch.

Cab. Right. I need to call one. She searched for the cell phone Jeremy left her. Finding the device in the bottom of her handbag, she picked it up but stopped. *No address book.* She plopped the phone back in her bag. *I hope I find one at the main entrance of this place when I leave.*

She reached for the shirt she wore when a bullet tore a hole through the left shoulder. She stuck a finger into the blood -stained tear. *I was lucky. No, I'm blessed. I think that's how Jeremy would describe events. God looks out for me, obviously. Otherwise ...*

Lord, do you fathom what I don't? Where is this guy? A small arrow of doubt skittered through her body. *Is that you God? I need to do this. As long as I'm in here with a guard at the door, the killer will be waiting. I want to flush him out; end this.*

Who's going to protect my back, you ask. She quickly tied up her runners. *Jeremy, of course. Once he understands I mean business, he'll come around to my way of thinking. He'll look after me.* She gazed heavenward as if answers might float down from the sky. Then she thought about her colleague again. *What if he gets hurt?*

The idea sent a wave of pain rippling through her chest as if someone hit her sore shoulder. She winced. *Can't happen.* She plunked down on the bed again. Puffing, as if finishing a five-kilometer run, she looked heavenward again. The God of the Universe looked down on her, nudging her toward the right thing to do.

She shook her head. *I'm imagining stuff.* Her head refused to give up on an active God, however. She remembered Jeremy telling her the Father conversed with him many times. In his heart. *Is that how we talk to you Lord? I didn't even think before I spoke to Him but ...* She slipped her arms into the sleeves of her jacket, the hole on the left shoulder as blood encrusted as her shirt.

I wonder why they didn't cut these off me when the EMTs brought me in. Isn't this what they usually do? Did you plan that, too, God? So I could escape from here? She wrapped the strap of her handbag over her right shoulder and attached Chief's leash to his collar. The question of a plan filtered into her thinking. *I don't have one. Yet. Once I'm home ...*

She took a step toward the door. Stopping mid-step, she turned back toward the bed. *I need them to think I'm still here.* Using her pillows, she constructed a form covered with her sheet and blanket. Christine glanced at the door and back at the bed. *They may not even check. But if they do, this'll work.*

She retrieved Chief's leash again and walked back to the

door. *I hope all the water is working on the officer.* A sliver of light penetrated the darkness in the room as soon as Christine opened the door. The police officer checked the time. She closed the door until only a thin slit remained, enough to spy on him without being seen.

She waited. The guard nodded at the nurse who walked by on silent feet. He glanced at his watch again and twisted his head to look toward the door. Christine quickly shut the gap hoping he hadn't noticed. All seemed quiet. She reopened the door a tiny crack. He stood. She pulled the door a little wider. He sauntered toward the empty nurse's desk. He shook his head and strode purposefully down the hall in the direction of the men's room, Christine assumed.

She stuck her head around the frame of the door. Chief did the same but at knee level. They simultaneously swept their gaze up and down the space outside the door. The emptiness beckoned. "Now's the time, Boy." She spoke softly, the dog peering toward her face. They stepped out into the shadowed hallway, the lights dimmed for a peaceful sleep.

Chief walked farther into the corridor, Christine close behind. *Where's the stairwell?* She decided to move left. A large window indicated the end of the hall. *I hope the staircase is this direction.* She tip-toed as quickly as her new found strength would allow. Adrenaline coursed through her veins. Her heart pumped; the fear of discovery foremost in her mind.

She spotted the doorway before Chief did. Reaching for the handle, she pulled inward and escaped into the damp, cement encased stairwell. The canine gingerly stepped down but he stopped to look behind to make sure she followed. Christine reassured him by taking two steps at a time.

She paused. *That hurt. I need to be careful or I'll rip my incision open.* She grabbed the handrail and placed her foot on the next step down. Chief took two to her one. He stopped at the next landing waiting for her to catch up. *Good thing I only need to go down two floors. Otherwise ...*

At the bottom of the second staircase, Christine decided to

get her bearings. She motioned for the animal to stand behind her as she slowly opened the door. She stepped out into the brightly lit hallway leading to the emergency department. Unlike the floor upstairs, this place bustled. A few people sat crumpled in plastic chairs waiting to be seen she surmised. Others held coffee cups in hand or read a book as they waited to find out the fate of a friend or relative. Christine nonchalantly walked through their midst as if everyone strolled through hospital corridors with their dogs.

She spotted a cab outside the door. Her footsteps quickened. She pushed the door open, stepped back to allow Chief to exit first and followed him toward the taxi driver. He waited patiently, leaning on the side of his vehicle. "Where to, lady?"

Christine gave him the address to the office she shared with Jeremy. She hustled her dog into the back seat and carefully lowered her frame in after him. The driver scooted around the hood of the cab, slid through the driver's door. He flipped the lever to begin calculating the price of the ride.

Christine let out a soft breath. Her body relaxed as she glanced backwards once to make sure no one followed her out the door. She leaned against the seat cushion and placed her hand on Chief's collar. "Good boy." She caressed his fur and scratched between his ears. The dog turned his head to look at her as if to say, "I hope you know what you're doing."

Chapter Forty Nine

Three days. *Harrumph. I'd like to see the bas**** do a more professional job.* He rested his forehead against the steering wheel of the no-frills rental. He hoped the dents and scratches made the vehicle blend in. *My information better be correct. The orderly is a dead man if he's not telling me the truth.*

He pushed his back into the seat cushion. His throat burned from the sip of coffee he gulped too quickly. Squinty eyes roamed down the street toward the nearest intersection. He scanned the darkness. Which way would she approach her office?

He thought about how he would spend his money once he completed this job. Working overseas most of his life, building his rep, quickly grew boring so his return to Canada about a year ago added to his connections. He hooked up with Teresa soon after arriving in Winnipeg. The wait for a lucrative contract paid off. He'd be rich when this ended.

His vision took in the trees bordering this quiet neighbourhood. *I wonder why these private type detectives always choose a residential area. Must not need the signage or walk-in traffic.*

He leaned his head against the rest and closed his eyes. *I could use some sleep.* Too many things messed this job up. *This time, I won't make any mistakes.* Glaring headlights announced the arrival of the vehicle as soon as the cab turned onto the street. His body tensed as the public transport drove closer.

He'd not be seen from his vantage point. Chosen with great care, he hoped from this spot no one would pick out a stranger lurking about. *Nosey types always resided in these quiet neighbourhoods. Don't need someone calling the police about a prowler. Damn.* He sat up straighter. *Two heads. She's got the dog with her.*

He studied the car as the driver pulled up in front of the detective agency. He watched the interior lights of the woman's Jeep flash, lighting up the inside of her vehicle before she exited the taxi. She stepped from one vehicle and moved toward the other. The animal followed. The dog's eyes roved from left to right, searching. *Better not be me.* The watcher remained still, hardly daring to take a breath.

He glared at his target. *You should be dead already. I don't miss.* He scowled. *Now, what do I do? The dog'll warn her. I'll follow. See where she's going. Probably home. I can take her down at her place.* He listened to the sound as she started her engine. *I'll wait till she turns off the street. Then the mutt won't hear my car start.*

He slunk lower in the seat as the jeep pulled away from the curb. She headed away from his vehicle. He turned the key in the ignition, dropped the gear shift into drive, and rolled slowly after his quarry. *Not much traffic. She'll be easy to tail.* He focused on the red lights ahead of him. *Tonight you die, lady.* He chuckled and then burst out laughing. *People are so predictable.*

Chapter Fifty

Christine released a sigh, relaxing in the interior of the car she'd abandoned three days before. She sniffed the familiar scent of a vehicle she kept meticulously tidy with a definite dog odour. She glanced toward Chief. *My friend.*

The traffic seemed sparse. *The time is not really late yet. I wonder where everyone is. I'll bet a football game is playing at the stadium. That always thins out the streetscape.* She raised her sore shoulder a few inches. The sharp pain reminded her the recent wound still needed healing.

Christine lifted her eyes to the rear view mirror. Headlights about ten car lengths behind her drew her attention. Tempted to ignore them, her senses prickled. *Let's confirm he's following me before I call Jeremy.*

She made a right-hand turn and sped up. *I obviously can't go home if that's who I think he is.* The glow in her mirror turned the corner as she turned left toward the city center. *I wish I could make out what type of car he's driving. And the license plate.* She reached for her handbag. Her cell lay on top.

She glanced at the phone, flipped the device open, and pressed speaker. *If only I had my IPhone.* She punched in the number for Jeremy Goodman from the short contact list. The cell buzzed once, then again. *Come on Jeremy. Answer.*

A sleepy voice spoke from some distance away. "Hello. Who's calling at this time of night?"

"Wow. You're grumpy when your sleep is disturbed in the middle of the night." Christine snickered nervously but quickly tempered the fear as she spotted the headlights in her rear view mirror again.

"Who's this? Christine?" Jeremy sounded wide awake now. "What's wrong? You okay?"

"I'm fine." She paused. "I'm being tailed and I thought ..."

"What do you mean you're being followed? Where are you?"

"I'm on Osborne, near Jubilee. I picked up my Jeep a few minutes ago and sure enough, someone is following me." She glanced toward Chief and shifted her gaze to the mirror.

Silence filled the car. Jeremy's next words left no doubt as to his frame of mind. "Damn, woman. I told you not to do this." His voice rose to the decibel of a shout. "You lied to me."

"I need to find out who wants me dead. I figured ..." She swallowed. "Well, I thought if you tailed the man or woman who's tailing me, we'd catch him, force some information out of him and turn him over to the police. Come on, Jeremy. Work with me on this."

"What other choice is there? Where are you now?" He growled. "I'm going to wring your neck for risking your life this way."

"I'm near St. Mary's Road. I thought I'd pull into St. Vital Center to walk Chief or, at least, appear to. I'll be careful until you arrive." She directed her Jeep down the usually busy main thoroughfare. Tonight, only a car or two occupied the traffic lanes.

"Don't stop when you get there. Has he ever run beside you for exercise? That way you remain a moving target instead of a sitting duck. I'll be at your location in about twenty minutes. Christine, I'll kill you myself if someone shoots you again." Dead air told her he hung up.

She glanced at Chief. He jumped into the front seat as soon as she began talking to Jeremy. "He is one angry man right now. I hope I don't cause his death." She made a left turn into the parking area of the city's largest shopping mall. "You wanta run, boy?"

Chief barked once as Christine stopped in the center of the lot. She reached across him to open the passenger door and let him jump to the pavement. "I won't go fast but stay away from the car, okay?"

Chief bounded away as he spotted a shrub close by. He sniffed his way around the plant and raised his leg as she idled slowly away to circle the building. A pair of headlights pulled into the entrance to the mall. His high beams flashed once and turned off. *I can't tell if he's the shooter.* The scratches and dents of the aged vehicle spoke volumes.

She scrunched herself lower in the seat. *No need to make myself too big a target.* She checked to make sure Chief ran safely beside her Jeep and glanced back at the other car. *He's not moving. He's probably wondering what I'm doing. If I can keep his attention, Jeremy will be able to sneak up on him.*

Christine turned a corner around the JC Penney store. She drove slowly waiting for her animal to catch up with her. She circled back. The car still sat in the same spot. She decided to stop. She figured her distance from him was twice what it was when he first shot her. *Here's hoping he needs to get closer.* She stepped out of the Jeep, called Chief to her side, and ushered him back inside. That creep will certainly be able to see me clearly anyway. She returned to the safety of her car.

About to make her way through the parking lot again, she spotted the man stepping out of the waiting vehicle. She resisted the urge to speed away as he leaned against the side door, light up a cigarette, and nonchalantly blow some smoke into the air. He appeared to be anything but interested in her.

Christine paused a little longer before shifting into drive. Her hand gripped the lever. *Maybe this isn't the person who tailed me from the office. Maybe* ... a shot rang out, shattering the windshield of her vehicle. Chief yelped as Christine's body fell face downward over the dog. The Jeep slowly rolled toward the curb as soon as her foot left the accelerator.

Chapter Fifty One

His hand touched the rough surface of the wall. Jeremy leaned closer to the protective cover of the JC Penney store. He stepped to the corner as the first shots rang out. He thrust his body around the sharp protrusion, his gaze resting on Christine's car as she disappeared from sight. *She's shot. Again.* His insides tumbled like the Super Roller Coaster Ride last summer that caused his last meal to vacate his stomach.

A gun flash snapped his attention to the only other vehicle in the parking lot. He scoured the landscape looking for a way to take the culprit by surprise. *Good thing I wore dark clothes. No moon either. Thank You, Lord.* He inched along the wall, covering the distance to the shooter's car in record time. He slipped silently behind the bumper.

The man still focused. His eyes never left the Jeep, its engine still running as the vehicle's tires butted up against a curb. He raised his gun a second time and rained several shots toward Christine's car.

Using his right hand, Jeremy eased his revolver from the holster at his side. He stepped closer, his feet as silent as if covered in padding. He steadied his gun-hand. In one swift action, the butt of his pistol connected with the soft tissue behind the assailant's ear. The limp body flopped against the side of his car.

Jeremy slapped handcuffs on one of the man's wrists. A groan and the ensuing struggle failed to stop the second cuff from surrounding the side mirror of the gunman's car. Jeremy's fist hit its mark when he slugged the still scowling face.

Shouts followed. Then curses, some unfamiliar to Jeremy. He ignored the verbiage as he raced for Christine's car. *She's got to be okay. She just has to be.*

Chapter Fifty Two

As another shot filled the silence of the late night hours. Christine glanced at her animal. Blood seeped from his left shoulder. The dog lay still as if mimicking her posture. "Chief." She laid her hand along his leg. "I'm so sorry boy. Jeremy will be here soon." Glass shards covered the upholstery and the dog's coat.

Christine held her breath. Night sounds and distance traffic noises swept over the interior of the vehicle. Her eyes lifted to the windshield. *Nothing but dark sky.* The low rumble of her Jeep reminded her the gearshift wasn't in park. *What's he waiting for?* Her body trembled. *Maybe this was a bad idea.* Silence dominated as she strained to listen for the killer's approach. Chief whimpered again.

Someone yanked open the driver's side door. Cold air floated inside the Jeep. Christine screamed. Chief's low pitched growl contradicted the flap, flap of his tail next to her. She glanced up. *Jeremy.* He reached a hand toward her to guide her to a sitting position. "He's handcuffed to the side mirror of his car. Did he hit you?"

"No, but Chief's been shot. I need to transport him to the emergency vet clinic twenty minutes from here. Did he tell you anything? Who is he? Where do you want me to meet you when Chief is looked after?" Christine brushed a stray lock of hair behind one of her ears and pressed her hand on her sore shoulder. "I'll be fine," she answered to Jeremy's look of concern.

"That guy planned to take another shot. He was so focused on you; he didn't see me drive up. I knocked him on the head with my gun." Jeremy's gentle touch ignored her words as he searched for any damage from the gunshots.

"I'm all right, okay?" She brushed some remaining shards from her clothing.

The irate man glowered at her. "Yeah. Well, that's because your guardian angel works overtime. I handcuffed the creep before he recovered from the blow to his head. This is his gun; looks like the same caliber as the slug they took out of your shoulder." He glanced once again toward Chief. His scowl told her his mood was as intense as when she spoke to him on the phone. "You go do what you need to for your dog. I'll meet you at your house after I turn this guy over to the cops." Jeremy gazed thoughtfully at the dog and back at Christine. "I'm not through with you yet. This worked but the results had the possibility of being so much worse. We'll talk later."

Relief seeped from every pore in Christine's body. "This is over, for now anyway. Once we find out why he wanted me dead and who hired him, if he is a contract, we'll do more investigating." Jeremy slowly walked back toward the assassin cuffed to his car. Shouts of anger filled the air, curses adding steam to the killer's indignation over being so easily caught.

She rushed around her car, opened the passenger door, and released the seat as far back as it would go. Chief whined, "Sorry, boy." She grabbed the hem of her shirt and tore a strip off. Tying the fabric around the dog's shoulder, she stemmed the flow of blood. "We'll take care of you right away, Boy. Don't worry."

Once she made her animal as comfortable as possible, Christine returned to the driver's seat. She paused before shifting into drive. She glanced in the direction of her assailant but she sat too far away to obtain a good look at the man. As soon as the Jeep started to roll forward, she steered toward Jeremy and the captured killer. She stared at the face as she came closer. *He looks about the same size as the intruder in my room.* His clean shaven head revealed a tattoo along the right side of his scalp. He lifted his head. His look of contempt sent shivers down her spine. She gasped. *Those eyes. That's Devine.*

She stomped on the brakes. Leaning her head out the window, she glared back at the man. Her voice squeaked a little. "His name is Tom Devine. His head is bald but I'd recognize those eyes anywhere. Remember. He's connected to Fine and the kidnapping of little Nathan. Why is he out of prison? I thought they charged him as an accomplice."

Chapter Fifty Three

Jeremy looked from one to the other. "So. Devine, eh?" He glanced at Christine. "I'll take care of this. You go. If Devine doesn't want the full weight of the law to come down on him, he'll give up the name of the man who hired him." He scowled toward the thug still handcuffed to the side of his vehicle. The captive glared right back, moving his shackled wrists in the hope of breaking free.

Christine waved as she slipped the Jeep into drive again. "I'll see you later." She gave the would-be killer her attention. "Someone isn't going to be too happy with you."

Devine opened his mouth. His disdainful sneer accompanied his response. "You're dead. One way or the other." He snapped his chin upward. "You're dead." His shout echoed off the surrounding buildings.

A play of emotions revealed a little fear but then resolve as they flit across Christine's face. *Inwardly seething*, he surmised. Instead, she smirked. "You're a loser." Devine growled in response before Christine pulled out of range and entered the thoroughfare toward the street.

Jeremy clapped his hand hard on Devine's shoulder cutting

off any further exchange of threats. "A charge of attempted murder is not one you'll escape so easy. We're both witnesses. But you have information we want. The courts may go easy ..."

He unhooked the handcuffs from the assassin's door post and re-cuffed his wrists behind his back. Jeremy ushered the man toward his vehicle, pushing once in a while to keep him off balance.

"We'll soon find out what Sergeant Irving can get out of you."

Chapter Fifty Four

Christine blinked. *Jeremy will handle everything.* She pressed the button to close the window and eased her car toward the exit of the parking lot and out into the street. *Chief needs me now. Devine can keep till later.* He clearly wanted to kill her and might be the man who shot at her two days ago. She shook her head. *He's sure changed his looks.*

The night traffic thinned even more. Stop lights blinked red, green, and yellow as if rush hour congested the streets with commuters heading home after a long day of decision-making. She kept her speed at the limit as she drove toward the city center again. The emergency clinic, near confusion corner, always had someone on duty. As she headed downtown, she expected more cars and trucks eventually.

She glanced at Chief again. The dog seemed to be sleeping. She hoped his still; quiet demeanor meant he was resting. "I love you, Boy." Her heart ached as she thought of losing him. "You'll be okay." Her words assured him, but were also for herself.

Christine focused on the drive. Traffic did thicken a little but she parked at the curb in front of the animal hospital in record time. Slipping out the driver's door as soon as she turned the ignition off, she strode to the closed clinic door. She pressed the buzzer and glanced back at her car. *Lord, heal him.*

Only seconds later, the door opened. A man dressed in scrubs looked toward her and then her vehicle. "Can I help you?"

"My dog's been shot." Christine pointed at her Jeep.

The man made sure the latch on the door sat in the unlock position, slipped through the door and walked briskly toward the car. "Let's have a look."

She opened the door. She stepped aside. The man leaned forward to examine Chief. "I'm Doctor Emmons." He lifted the makeshift bandage away from Chief's shoulder and slid his arms under the animal's carcass. "He's lost a lot of blood."

Dr. Emmons carried the dog in the direction of the building. Christine followed. She moved ahead of him to hold the door open. "Will he be all right?"

"I'll know as soon as I examine him. We'll remove the bullet at least. Right now, the outcome is anyone's guess." The doctor bustled through the reception area, ignored the examining rooms, and walked all the way back toward his operating room. Christine strode close behind expecting at any minute to be told she couldn't stay. Her insistence was a foregone conclusion. Chief needed her reassuring presence.

"You can hold this light." The doc surprised her. "Talk to him. Keep your voice calm to help him."

She did as he asked. "Good boy, Chief. Doctor Emmons is going to make you all better."

As soon as the physician removed the cloth covering the wounded shoulder, blood seeped down onto the table. The doc probed, pulled the hair away from the wound and sopped up the red seepage with some gauze. "I need to cut his hair for a more complete picture of what we're dealing with. I'm going to sedate him and place him on an IV of whole blood." He looked at Christine. "You can wait while I suture him up." He nodded toward the waiting room as he attached a plastic bag of thick red fluid to a hook hanging overhead.

Christine patted Chief's head. "Can I stay till he's asleep?" The dog lifted his head an inch off the table at the sound of her voice. "Okay, Boy." The animal settled down and closed his eyes again. "Fight, boy. Don't give up." Her eyes welled with unshed tears.

"That won't help him." The doctor groused at her. "He'll react if he thinks he's upset you."

Christine swiped at the wetness. "I can handle this."

Skepticism spread all over the man's face but he said no more about her leaving. He injected Chief behind the shoulder. Her hand over his heart revealed the minute his body relaxed in deep slumber. "I'll wait outside." She allowed her tears to flow freely as she moved to the doorway. "Please take good care of him. He's my service dog and my best friend. He took the bullet for me tonight,"

"I'll do all I can. You can be assured. He's a strong, healthy animal." Dr. Emmons turned his back to her as he resumed his task.

Christine let the door swing shut behind her as she sat on one of the hard plastic chairs in the medium sized room. Pictures of champion dogs of all breeds decorated the walls. She wiped her hand across her eyes. *God.* The thought came out of nowhere. *Does He care about animals?* She wondered. *I'm so new at this.*

Christine bowed her head. *Father, I don't know if you look after dogs too but Chief is special. Please help the doctor, steady his hands, and make my animal all healthy again. Thank you.* Tears coursed their way unchecked down her cheeks. Thankful to be sitting in an empty room, she whispered, "Please Lord. Please."

Chapter Fifty Five

Jeremy grabbed the assassin's arm as soon as he opened the passenger door of his Dodge Ram. All the way to the police station, Devine tried to coerce the investigator into letting him go. None too gently, he hauled Christine's stalker to the pavement.

"How about fifty thousand? I'll bet you owe almost as much on this here truck." Devine's voice took on a pleading tone.

Jeremy swung his arm backward as if intending to slug the man responsible for almost killing a friend. "Shut up, Devine. Just close your trap." He pushed the culprit toward the entrance to the cop shop. "I can't wait to hand you over to the cops and this time you'll be charged with attempted murder. You won't be released for a long time." He shoved again.

The soon-to-be inmate opened his mouth but then clamped the orifice shut just as quickly. He stumbled, his cuffed hands no use to him for balance. "Hey, watch it."

Jeremy pulled the large glass doors open, shoved Tom Devine through the portal, and marched up the stairs right behind him.

The desk sergeant raised his eyebrows as he took in the civilian directing a man in handcuffs through the door. "Who's this?"

"This man tried to kill Christine Smith tonight and I suspect he put her in the hospital three days ago. He made an attempt on her life while she recovered. Is Sergeant Irving ...?" He looked at the clock on the far wall. "No, I guess not. Well then, I'm making a citizen's arrest." He pulled his investigator's license from his pocket. "I'm Jeremy Goodman."

The uniformed officer in front of him yawned. He studied the card in his hand and looked back at the investigator. His glance included the would-be killer. "I reserved a nice cell all ready for him. Name?"

"He's Tom, or Tommie Devine, a recent guest of yours." Jeremy wrapped his hand around the culprit's forearm and squeezed. "I'm charging him with attempted murder on the life of Christine Smith. She'll come in tomorrow to identify him. He shot her service animal tonight as well, so animal cruelty can be added to his offenses. I'm sure once we investigate farther; we'll find a lot more. This guy is a bum."

Jeremy unlocked the handcuffs. Devine scowled as he rubbed his wrists. "This man is harassing me officer. I never did nothing to his girlfriend. Or her dog. I mind my own business."

The sergeant glowered at the criminal. "Shut up. You have the right to remain silent. If you give up that right, anything you say will be used against you in a court of law." He continued to repeat the Miranda rights. He glanced at Jeremy. "Wouldn't want him getting off on a technicality, now would we?"

He grabbed the man's upper arm. Looking around the large open space cluttered with desks in all states of disarray, he spotted the policeman he looked for. "Thompson, come over here and escort this thug to the holding pen."

"Sure thing, Sergeant." A younger version of the officer walked toward them. He wrapped his own cuffs on Devine's wrists and yanked him past the desk and toward the back of the room. The clang of a metal door opening and closing assured everyone the criminal was no longer a threat.

Jeremy looked at the cop at the reception counter. "When will Sergeant Irving be in?"

"His shift starts at eight. He's usually here a little before." The officer returned to his seat and the paperwork in front of him. "Bring your witness in so we can process this punk."

"We'll be here in a few hours. Finding out who hired this shooter is a top priority. He's got no reason we can think of to do this on his own. He's working for someone." Jeremy backed away from the policeman, turned around and headed toward the main entrance. He waved over his head and pushed the door open.

Once outside he stopped, inhaled the cool night air, and contemplated his next move. *Either Christine got too close to someone in the trafficking business or someone else wants her dead. Her parents' killer is already gone so no need to identify anyone. Someone probably hired him to do the job all those years ago but I can't imagine someone wanting to open that can of worms.* He gazed at the few stars he saw lit up in the city sky.

He took one step and another toward his truck parked at the curb. Sliding inside, he turned on the ignition. *I wonder if Christine is still at the vets. Maybe.* He performed a U-turn toward the center of town and the address of the emergency clinic. *I'll check.*

Traffic thinned drastically, especially the closer he got to the downtown area of Winnipeg. Things still erupted nonstop behind the scenes, of course. Drug dealers, pimps, prostitutes, and other forms of illegal activity always increased in the early hours before dawn. Empty streets did make his trek a speedy one, however.

The lights from the vet clinic and the Jeep shone brightly when he stopped behind the Grand Cherokee he recognized as Christine's. *She forgot to turn them off. Her battery will be dead.* He shut the engine off, stepped out and locked his truck before walking to the driver's door of the SUV. He tried the handle. The car opened without any effort. *She didn't lock the door, either. Can't blame her. The dog means the world to her.*

He reached inside, turned off the headlights, and checked the ignition. *Lucky no one wanted to hijack a vehicle.* He pulled her keys from the console and locked the Jeep. Moving toward the clinic door, he yanked the handle.

His eyes quickly adjusted to the bright office lighting as he spotted Christine sitting by herself on the hard plastic seat. "Hi."

Christine's head snapped up. "Hey. What are you doing here? I thought you planned to stay and pull some information out of the creep."

"Irving went home already so we caged him till tomorrow. They want you to come down and give a statement in the morning." He looked around the impersonal room. "How's your animal?"

"The doc sedated him to remove the bullet. He says Chief should be okay but ..." She hung her head. Then she stared at the ceiling. "I need him to be better. He shielded me with his body."

"Chief did what Denny trained him to do. He'll be fine if the vet says he will." A door opened and the two weary detectives looked at the man wearing green scrubs as he wiped the perspiration from his brow with a clean towel. "How is he doc?"

The veterinarian sat down opposite them. "He's a strong, well-cared-for animal. He'll be fine. The bullet didn't do any major damage. In time, he'll be as good as new. The blood we infused should be enough to help him heal rather quickly with some tender loving care. He'll be ready to go home in a day or two." He stood, shook hands with Jeremy and Christine, and walked toward the door. "I'll lock up after you leave."

"Oh. Can I say good-bye first?" Her eyes glazed over with tears of relief.

The doctor shifted his weight and looked at her with tired eyes. "For a few minutes. I need my rest, too." He motioned for her to follow and he led the way back through the door where he took the dog such a short time ago.

Christine's friend lay motionless on his side. She ran her hand over the fur between his ears. They moved. "Hi Chief. Good boy." She spoke in as soothing a voice doing her best to smother her emotions.

Her effort to remain calm impressed Jeremy. *Chief would not react well if Christine acted upset. They are a pair, no doubt about it.* He decided to speak his well wishes. "How are ya, Chief?" The dog's tail thumped the table as if beating a tune on his own drum.

"He always reacts so positively to you. Why." Christine lifted her head. "Thank you, Lord."

"He knows a friend when he sees one." Jeremy's eyebrows arched a little skyward. "You prayed, did you?" He stroked the dog below his bandaged shoulder.

She made a face, wrinkling her nose at him. "I did. I think God loves animals too. Doesn't He?"

Jeremy chuckled. "I'm sure He does. He made them as well as us and told us to take care of them. You did your job. But ... I didn't think you spoke to the Father much. Some people don't spend much time talking to Him at all."

"At first, after the doc told me to stay out in the waiting room, I felt all alone. But I sensed His presence right away." She grimaced. "I'm so new at this. The sense of peace seemed so real. So I talked to Him."

Jeremy blinked. *Crying would not be right.* "I'm glad." His voice softened so much she needed to listen intensely.

A cough behind them reminded the pair they were no longer alone. "I really need to find my bed."

"Sorry doc." Christine cleared her own throat. "Chief, I'll be back in the morning. Sleep well." The doctor wheeled him toward a kennel, a large one. He picked the dog up gently and set him inside the waist high enclosure. "Be back tomorrow, Boy." The animal whined and closed his eyes.

"The medication will wear off by morning but, in the meantime, he'll be out for the rest of the night." The vet snapped the kennel door shut. "Now, let me walk you out so I can lock up." He glanced at Jeremy but focused his attention on Christine. "I won't be here when you come tomorrow but the physician on duty will be up on Chief's care." He walked them toward the outer door. "Good night."

"Good night doctor, and thanks." Christine smiled tentatively. She ambled toward her vehicle.

Jeremy waved toward the vet as he closed the door. He reached into his pocket, pulled out Christine's keys and handed them to her. "Looking for these?"

"How ...?" She yanked them from his fingers. A look similar to shock traveled across her face. "How did you find these?" She rubbed her shoulder.

Jeremy explained how she left her vehicle. "You're in some pain yourself."

"Just a twinge once in a while."

"Yeah, right. Go home. Sleep. We'll talk in the morning. Phone me when you wake up and we'll schedule a visit with Chief as well as a trip to the police station. I can pick you up." He walked a few paces toward his truck.

Christine closed her eyes and rubbed her hand across her face. "I think I'm exhausted. I'll call tomorrow." She threw her hand in the air haphazardly and then used the fob to unlock the car. "Jeremy thanks."

He waved her appreciation aside and stepped into his vehicle. Turning the ignition on for the umpteenth time that night, he sat contemplatively as Christine drove away. "My life seemed pretty dull before you came along, girl." He chuckled tiredly and put his truck in gear. "Dull is okay, though." The rumble of the motor reminded him the drive home wasn't over yet.

Chapter Fifty Six

Christine yawned. She leaned her head from side to side. The pull of ligaments holding her neck in place screamed for relief. The last couple of tense hours didn't help. *Thank goodness traffic is sparse.* She turned a familiar corner. *Bed sounds so good.*

Although usually well lit, the light post near her house and the one lighting up the entrance to the park had burned out. She strained her eyes toward her driveway as she idled closer to the little house. *Not my home for much longer, though.* She planned to place the little home on the market as soon as the renovations to her parents' house were complete.

Shadows created by the full moon overhead filled her yard. The hair on her arms stood on end. She reminded herself the man who tried to kill her occupied a jail cell. *I forget how much I rely on Chief. I trust his instincts.*

A yawn escaped again as she put the Jeep in park and shut off the ignition. Christine's closed her eyes. She squeezed the bridge of her nose to ease an ache not yet full blown. *I need some sleep.*

She eased slowly to the sidewalk to stand on legs wanting

to crumble with tiredness. *Lord, please look after Chief.* The prayer reminded her He controlled the situation. Christine placed one weary foot ahead of the other as she stepped in the direction of her front door.

A movement. Out of the corner of her eye. *What?* A flicker of light appeared near her living room window. She crept toward that side of the house, trying hard not to step on the dry leaves dotting the landscape. Her body trembled. Her legs shook as badly as the hand holding her handbag. The odor of burning wood wafted toward her.

Kerosene. She moved closer and peered cautiously ahead. The flicker grew to a blaze. Fire outlined the contours of her home. Christine dropped to a crouch. Her eyes scanned the yard. Not a twig seemed out of place. She inched closer to the front wall facing the street. She grabbed her cell and dialed 911.

Keeping her eyes alert, she explained her dilemma to the dispatcher. The voice on the other end of the call assured her the police and fire vehicles headed her way. Christine hung onto the phone as if clinging to a lifeline. Taking a deep breath took a greater effort. The emergency operator spoke calmly assuring her the sound of the sirens would fill the night air any second.

An ear-splitting siren filled the otherwise still, black night. Screeching at a pitch intended to wake even the soundest sleeper, one truck and another pulled in front of the house. Christine thanked the operator and placed her cell back in her purse.

The brakes on the trucks locked into place at the same instant the men clad in fireproof gear scampered to the ground. One, she assumed to be the lead fire fighter, scurried toward the blaze now lighting up the entire side of her house. He quickly assessed the situation and began yelling orders. He stepped beside her. "Miss, move to the sidewalk. Let my men do their job. This fire will be out in no time."

Christine stood but never left the spot.

"Miss. Please." The man placed a hand on her arm as if to escort her.

She blinked. "Oh, of course." She stepped gingerly around the hose lying in her path. From her new vantage point, a large spray of water doused flames trying to eat her house. *So much for getting some sleep.*

The leader walked to her side once again. "The fire is under control. Can you tell me what happened? I need to make my way inside to access the damage and inspect for any residual embers waiting to reignite."

Christine nodded her head and led the way to her front door. "I just got home. Some of the street lights blacked out and I thought someone peeked around the corner. By the time I got closer, an obnoxious odour filled my nostrils and I spotted the fire. I called 911 right away." She inserted her key in the lock. "Thank you for not breaking in and doing more damage."

"The blaze remained small and controllable but any longer and your house would be fully engaged. Gas did you say?" He walked around Christine to enter her residence first. He swung his flashlight toward the side of the living room now exposed to the elements.

She remained rooted to the doorway. Smoke filled the room.

The fireman placed his mask over his nose. He poked and prodded and moved a couple of furniture pieces to the gaping hole in her house. "I'll take these outside and give them a decent amount of water. To make sure."

Christine stood still. A tickle rustled its way up her throat and escaped her mouth. Then another. She backed through the door and inhaled the fresh, clean air. Another cough tightened the soreness in her head. The pain threatened to erupt in full force.

She rubbed her temple. *I'm obviously not going to be able to stay here tonight. But where?* Her mind seemed cloudy. Thinking hurt.

The fire inspector left her house and approached as if some important information needed to be told. Instead, a question creased his brow. "You said something about gas."

Christine swiveled her head in his direction. She stared at his face for a second. "Oh. Yes. The scent of kerosene wafted toward me first before I spotted the flames." She blinked and ran her hand across her forehead.

The man frowned. "Are you telling me you think this might have been set deliberately?"

"I - I never gave the idea much thought but ..." She furrowed her brow causing the ache to increase enough to bring a tear to her eye. "I guess that would be the correct assumption since ... well ... someone already tried to kill me tonight. But I thought he resided in jail."

The fireman placed his hand on his hip. "Whoa. And you're out here all by yourself? Do you have a place to stay the rest of the night?"

Christine swiped at the tear before a drop escaped. "Not anyone I want to wake at this time of the night. I'll find a motel."

"Well, I suggest you call someone rather than be alone if someone wants you dead. Whoever you think you caught, either someone else is in cahoots with him or the wrong man is in custody. Anyway, the arson inspector arrives first thing in the morning. If arson is the cause the police as well as the fire marshal will be called in. Tell me where you're staying tonight so we can reach you."

Christine shook her head slightly, trying not to exacerbate her headache. "My lawyer is Barkley Goodman." She reached into her purse, found the card, and handed the information to the fireman. "I'll be in touch with him as well."

Even in the dim lights coming from the remaining floodlights the firemen dismantled, Kindness emanating from the man's facial features. "Are you sure you're going to be okay?"

Christine nodded. "I'll be fine."

"What if the culprit is outside watching all the action? He might follow you and ..."

"I'll go to a hotel with security. One large enough he won't find me easily. I own a permit to carry. If you wait, I'll grab my weapon from the lock-box."

"I'll go with you." He placed his hand as a comfort on her back as they walked back inside. "You'll need to lock this door as well. We'll find some plywood and cover the hole in your living room before we leave."

Christine's smiled tentatively. "Oh, right. The gun safe is in my bedroom." She led the way and using the light from the flashlight the fireman held, located her Smith and Wesson handgun and followed him back toward the door. She grabbed a box of shells as well. "Thanks for taking care of my house. I think I should be able to salvage most of my stuff before the repairs happen. I planned to move soon anyway." She worked at turning the corners of her mouth into a grin but failed. "I'll contact my lawyer first thing in the morning."

Christine stashed her gun into her purse planning to load it before leaving the driveway. She walked slowly back to her Jeep, slipped inside and heaved a huge sigh. Every bone in her body screamed for rest but she needed to find a safe place first. *After I arm myself.*

Chapter Fifty Seven

Jeremy rubbed the remaining sleep from his eyes. He glanced at the clock located on his large cedar lined dresser. *Eight Thirty! Whoa!* He rolled his weary body over the side of the bed and landed on his knees. *Thank goodness for carpeting.* He stayed that way for a few minutes. *My body is reacting like I just got to bed.*

Watery eyes blinked twice before comprehending the gray overcast outside his window. *My senses are as bleary as the sky.* Jeremy slowly stood to his feet. He swiped his hand across his eyes and grabbed the bridge of his nose with two fingers. *A shower will clear my head.* The ring tone assigned to his father interrupted his step toward the bathroom.

Now what? He reached for his IPhone, pressed the appropriate button and raised the device to his ear. "Good morning Dad."

"Christine's in trouble." The older man's voice seemed to tremble with emotion, an uncommon occurrence for him. He was used to his Father's sense of calm in any situation

Jeremy asked the obvious. "What now? I left her early this morning. We caught ..."

"Someone tried to burn her house down last night. Fortunately, she arrived in time to reach the firemen before the damage took the house down. A lot of smoke and one wall but ..."

"But we apprehended the man who attempted to kill her. Where is she now? Is she alright?" The news worked on Jeremy's system faster than any shower to wake him up. His heart also beat as if he'd run a race.

"As far as I can tell. From the sound of her voice, she didn't sleep much but she's safe. For now." Barkley Goodman emitted a seldom used profanity, for him anyway. "Some person is determined to take her out. And, since you caught one culprit last night, it appears more than one assassin is after her."

Jeremy sighed. "Guarding her is becoming a full time job. She's found a safe place, I presume?

"Son, catch whoever wants her dead. I don't mean the hires. Find out who's behind this." Barkley cleared his throat. "Sorry. I didn't intend to imply you weren't. She's at the Fairmont under the name Julie Parsons. I told her I'd call you."

"Dad, I'll do what I can. The woman doesn't always listen. I advised her against doing what she eventually did but ... well, we did catch Tom Devine. He shot Chief and ..."

"She went over all the details with me. Make arrangements to stick by her side until this is all cleared up. She took a suite for herself or you both might want to consider staying at my house, or even your house. She needs a bodyguard whether she agrees or not. When do you plan to go to the police station?"

Jeremy shifted the phone to his other ear. "I guess we'll decide after I talk to her. We need to find out any information Devine will tell us and who hired him. I think the Crown Attorney will offer him a plea if he gives us what we want. I'll make some calls and plan a course of action. Do you want me to call you later?"

Barkley seemed to hesitate before answering. "Son, I want you to keep alert. I wouldn't want anything to happen to you either. These people are ruthless. Tell me when you decide how to proceed." He hung up after a hasty good-bye.

Jeremy punched the end call button as he walked the few steps toward his bathroom. *First a shower.* He dropped the phone on the vanity, turned on the hot spray, and set out some toiletries to pack in case he stayed somewhere else tonight. *This place won't work. They found out we're connected and may come looking for her here. I'll make sure no one is following me when I leave here.* He stepped under the shower, closed the glass door, and let the water soak away the remaining cobwebs from a too-short night's sleep.

Chapter Fifty Eight

He slammed the phone down on the kitchen counter, hard enough the case cracked. *I hired someone who I was told was reliable. Time is running out.* He'd think of something else.

He sipped the hot liquid. The coffee burned as it traveled to his stomach. He placed the cup firmly on the island and stalked toward his tiny office. *I'll never earn the confidence of the big boys if this situation isn't remedied. I deserve better. Harumpff.* He ran a hand down the side of his silk suit.

He paced around his compact desk, and back toward the door. Turning, he walked to the chair and sat. He rubbed his hand over his eyes. *Now I gotta take care of this other bum, too. Devine's gonna talk if I don't.* He leaned his forearms on the desktop. *Who can take the creep out from the inside? I shoulda never let him lose the last time.*

He hit the desk with his closed fist. He wrapped his other hand over the sore spot. *I'll call the boss. He'll ... No I can't do that.* "Why didn't I wait until she walked through the door of her house?" His frustration bounced off the walls.

Only two days to make this go away. *The boss'll kill me like he did Casio. The guy worked for him a long time.* An idea flitted across his usually analytical mind. *A hostage. Someone to bring her to a place of my choosing. And this time, I'll handle the details and the execution.*

Chapter Fifty Nine

Christine replaced the hotel desk phone to its rightful place and sighed. *Jeremy is mad. Wow!* She'd never experienced his anger before. *I wouldn't want to be the person who's behind all this.* Then she frowned. *I don't need him to be incensed for me. I'm angry all by myself. I can deal with this bum.*

She walked into the bedroom and grabbed the jacket flung over the chair from the night before. She stopped. *I'll tell the desk clerk Jeremy is expected.*

She reached for the phone by the bed. "Hi. This is Julie Parsons." She paused for a short second as she realized her blunder. She forgot to tell Jeremy she used another name. "Yes, I checked in last night." She waited a minute while the man located her on their computer. "Yes. Room 2011. A friend, Jeremy Goodman, will stop by shortly. Send him right up." The clerk said he would. "Don't give my room number to anyone else, okay?"

She slammed down the receiver a little harder than she intended. *This clandestine life is not for me. Harrumph!* She wandered over to the window, peeked through the closed curtains from her twentieth floor perch and decided to open her drapes. The sunlight instantly warmed her skin. She scanned the street below. People the size of ants seemed to flow along the sidewalk as if standing on a conveyor belt.

Turning from her lofty view, she went over to the in-room coffee maker and prepared a pot for Jeremy's arrival. Christine glanced at the bedside clock. *I'll call the fire inspector. If they found anything conclusive, that'll prove I wasn't imagining things when I spotted that guy.* She sat down, placed her hand toward the phone but a knock on the door interrupted her. *Jeremy.*

"Coming?" Her step quickened as she approached the door. Her heart skipped a beat as soon as she observed the scowl that greeted her. "Not my fault." She glared right back at the man who had become more important to her than she wanted to admit.

Jeremy walked across the threshold, his usual cordial greeting absent. "You couldn't prevent the fire but I suspect if you'd remained in the hospital - as I suggested I might add - that event might not have happened. Someone wants you dead. Is that not clear to you, woman?"

Christine waved the full coffee pot at him and poured a cup in response to his nod. "I am fully aware my life was threatened. Twice ... no, I guess three times now. I want to catch this person. I suppose the right word is persons since we already caught one." She was jabbering.

Jeremy reached for the steaming beverage. "I think these guys are taking orders from someone."

"But why? What did I do to make so many people angry for crying out loud?"

"Oh, like stop a pedophile from selling children. Or how about recognizing the man behind the kidnapping of little Jimmy. And now you can access your parent's files where it's anyone guess what kind of information we might find. Your parents were murdered, remember, and the killer was likewise taken care of. You've made a lot of enemies, I think." He paused and looked back at her with a smirk on his face. "For someone so pretty."

Christine looked away from the man, her face a flaming mask, she surmised. "Quit teasing. I'm serious. Sure, I did interfere with a few child molesters but they needed to be stopped. They still need to be apprehended. Because I've managed to rescue a couple of kids ... that hasn't ended their evil plans, I'm sure. We have to catch them and put in jail where they belong."

"And that is why you have a target on your back. I suspect we will find all these cases are intertwined." Jeremy took a sip from his coffee cup. "This is not bad for hotel fare." He took another gulp.

"I need to make some calls and then I want to go visit Chief. When can we meet with Sergeant Irving to find out who hired Devine?" She slipped her arms into the sleeve of her jacket. "I want to gather some clothes as soon as I gain access to my house again."

Jeremy sighed. "Christine, take this threat seriously. You can't continue to carry on as if nothing happened." He looked toward the window. "We should decide where you will be the safest and I intend to stick like glue until we find the person or persons who want you dead."

Christine grimaced. "I can't sit around here and do nothing. Oh, by the way. I checked in here under the name Julie Parsons."

"Right. Dad told me. We have to move you to a safe place where no one can find you." Jeremy leaned his full weight on one leg with his hands plunked firmly on his hips. His body relaxed for a second before he sat down on the chair in front of the desk. "Make your calls. We'll figure this out."

Christine stared at the wall over his head for a few moments. He was right. Her back stiffened. *I can help find this creep. I know I can.*

Chapter Sixty

Christine's call to the fire inspector confirmed what she already knew, giving her the proof she needed. She described the crime scene from the night before to Jeremy. "Someone crept along the side of the house just before I turned off my headlights. Chief would have chased the guy down."

"Whoever started this discovered where you live." Jeremy's frown drew his eyebrows into a straight line. "Christine, God understands what's going on here. You're new to this but I pray for His guidance when I'm searching for someone. I believe He helps me find the answers I need. Do you want to ask Him about this before we head out?"

She shrugged her shoulders. "I remember He helped Jimmy and I escape that monster but I guess I forgot to include Him this time. He also pointed us to Samantha. By the way, maybe we need to talk to some of the working girls again to find out where more of those houses are, the ones where they break in these kids. We'd be able to put a big dent in their trafficking business if we keep on their tails."

Jeremy shook his hands toward the ceiling. "You've not listened to a thing I've said. You are to keep a low profile until we ferret out who wants you dead. Do I need to repeat that declarative statement again?"

Christine hung her head. "I know. I know. I want to stop these creeps once and for all so no more children go missing." She paused for a second as she marshaled the tears seeping into her lower eyelids. "God help us."

"Yes, Lord. Show us how to put an end to the threat on Christine's life. Place your hedge of angels around us as we go about the tasks before us today and Father, guide us to the perfect place to hide out in the meantime." Jeremy lifted his head.

Christine grabbed a tissue to blow her nose. "Do you really believe in angelic beings? We've talked about this before but ... angels, really?"

Jeremy's frustration with the woman in front of him dissipated. "You are so new to this walk of faith. Let's keep this conversation for another time. We need to check on Chief."

She nodded but the questions about the existence of angels kept rolling around in her head as they walked out the door and down the hallway toward the elevator. Christine pressed the down arrow. They conducted their trip to the main lobby in silence.

As the door opened, Jeremy asked, "Did you leave anything upstairs?"

"No. I only had the clothes on my back when I arrived last night. Why?" She took a step to the front door.

In full body guard mode, he placed a restraining hand on her arm. "Why don't you check out? We'll find a better place to keep you safe."

Christine thought about his suggestion for a few seconds. "My parents' house is almost ready for me to move into. I'll remove their furniture from storage instead of taking the things from my house right away. If they're watching the house ..."

Jeremy's gaze took in the entire lobby. She assumed he thought about her suggestion at the same time. Finally he spoke. "It's a consideration. Let's go check out first and think about this idea some more."

The pair walked to the reception desk, paid the bill for the night before in cash, and officially vacated the room upstairs. Jeremy led the way to the exit,

He apparently took his role as a body guard seriously, something Christine was unaccustomed to. He stopped before going outside. His head twisted right and left before he stepped aside to let her precede him through the doorway. I have no say in the matter, I *guess*. She sighed and strode purposefully toward the large black truck, her ride for the rest of the day, she supposed. Her Jeep remained, with permission, in the parkade.

Chapter Sixty One

As at the hotel, Jeremy led the way out of the vet clinic. He used his body to shield her as they walked quickly toward the truck. He almost pushed her into the passenger seat before he raced around to the other side. He slid in and started the engine before a word passed between them.

Christine looked out the window, making note of the cars parked nearby. She leaned back into the cushion and gazed across the cab at Jeremy's intense expression. "Jeremy, maybe we should hire a bodyguard. I mean, maybe we are too ... well .... involved. Er ... I ... we're friends after all and ..."

"Christine, I'm a professional, bodyguard or investigator, either one. Your Uncle Conrad hired me to protect you. I intend to do the job and our relationship, such as it is, won't interfere. I promise." He drove to the end of the street and turned in the direction of the police station.

"I'd feel bad if someone hurt you because of me. That's all." Christine looked out the window again. "Chief looked a lot better than he did last night. I sure miss having him attached to me."

Jeremy chuckled. "That description fits. Did you notice the

way he lifted his head when you spoke. Injured or not, he wanted to assure his mistress he was on the mend. The doc said your animal recovered from the surgery so well he'd probably be able to go home in a couple of days. More ears to listen if someone is around who shouldn't be."

The traffic seemed especially heavy for that time of the morning. Christine looked toward Jeremy again. "Is something going on downtown today that I've forgotten?"

"No, just the usual, I think. No matter how hard the cops work to stop the criminal element in this city, crime seems to escalate on a daily basis. We're close to police headquarters so some of this is probably due to lawyers, and offenders coming and going."

She glanced out the window again. "We have no idea what the lives of these people on the sidewalk are like. Some of them might be living a quiet life but others may be into all kinds of trouble. How many of them, as normal as they look, are pedophiles and human traffickers?"

Jeremy checked his rearview mirror. "Evil seems to be on the rise no matter where we go, what city we are in, or even if we are in an urban area. Peaceful country life is a thing of the past, I think." He angled the truck toward the curb in front of the cop shop. "Here we are. Now let's see if we can find some answers."

Chapter Sixty Two

Sergeant Irving ushered Jeremy and Christine to the empty room next to the cubicle where Tom Devine cooled his heels since Jeremy brought him in. "He's not said a word. He's also not asked for a defense lawyer."

Jeremy studied the sullen man on the other side of the one-way mirror. "I wonder why not. He certainly hollered for one when we arrested him for the Brent kid's abduction. The scum-bag got him off, too."

"His attorney and Find's were one and the same, right? Find had the misfortune of receiving jailhouse jus-tice." Christine clamped her mouth shut. She stared at the man who'd tried to kill her the night before. *Sure, a noxious pervert, but killer?* "Who's yanking his chain?"

"That's what we intend to find out. No matter how long it takes." Sergeant Irving headed for the door. "You guys can lis-ten as long as you like but this may take all day or longer." He opened the door and stepped into the hall.

"Thanks sergeant." Jeremy settled into the chair closest to the viewing window. Christine took another one. They glanced at each other and turned toward the view of the other room as

Irving and a plain clothes detective entered. The uniformed officer leaned against the wall in the corner while the detective took the metal seat across from the perpetrator. "Now Mr. Devine. Why don't you tell me what happened last night?"

The would-be assassin glared at the man in front of him. "You gotta get me into witness protection or something or I ain't talking."

Jeremy's head jerked toward Christine. "Whoa. We thought he'd put up a fight," he whispered.

"Maybe that's how he intends to get what he wants. They just began to question him." She focused on the degenerate, His hands shook. "He does seem nervous. I wonder if anyone visited him some time last night."

"You mean another inmate?"

"Or a cop. Someone got to him and made him pretty scared." Christine allowed herself to envision a dirty policeman. *What are the possibilities?*

Devine seemed to shrink in his chair. "You guys want me to name names but I ain't saying nothin' until you offer me a different identity. A new place to live, too. Far away from here."

The detective eyed the man across from him. "What can you tell us that would warrant protection? You're nothing but a creep, a pretty common one at that." He snickered. "You haven't got an original thought in your head. Why should we protect you?"

Devine's eyes bugged from his face even larger than when they caught him the night before. "The girly and her boyfriend told me they want the information I got. Go ask them." He thrust his jaw line toward the detective. "You'll find out."

The police investigator glanced toward Sergeant Irving who took a couple of steps to the table. The men conferred with their eyes before Irving sat in the other chair. "Goodman said he thought someone hired you to kill the Finder woman. Right?"

"Not before I'm assured of protection." Devine leaned back. His smug expression remained on his face as he turned toward the mirror. "Make me a deal and I'll talk," he shouted to the clear image of his own head and shoulders.

Jeremy stood and glanced at Christine. "We need to invite

the Crown Attorney in here. Only he can make such a bargain." His hand reached for the doorknob.

"Do you think he really has any information?"

"Devine may look stupid but he's cunning. All night he's remembered Find dying in his cell at the hands of an unknown. Maybe he thinks the lawyer arranged the hit and that's why he's not asking for one."

Christine's head snapped in Jeremy's direction. "Fine's attorney was Jason Mitchell, Rompart's attorney. What does Rompart have to do with men like Find and Devine?"

"Remember. When we asked Jason, he said he owned a practice besides his work for the company. He said he just did what lawyers do, defend his clients. I've never liked these types who will offer a defense for anyone for a few bucks."

"I think as soon as I begin to take over the reins at Rompart, I'm going to hire a new attorney for the firm. I don't like him, the little contact I've had with him and ..."

"So. You decided to take over your father's business." Jeremy wasn't sure why the idea bothered him. "We'll discuss this at another time, though. I need to talk to Irving." His hand turned the doorknob and he stepped out of the room.

Christine listened as a knock sounded on the other door. The sergeant opened the door a crack and walked through. *I wonder if Jeremy will succeed in getting the Crown Attorney involved.*

Chapter Sixty Three

Christine stood for a few minutes to stretch her muscles. The atmosphere in the small room had become too close for comfort. The air reeked of smoke. *I guess some residue remains on my clothes from the fire.* The doorknob turned just before Jeremy walked in, "Where did you go? I thought you planned to persuade the Crown Attorney to take an interest in this case."

"I did. I mean ... that's where I went. The man is a stickler for doing things the right way, though and he won't offer Tommy any protection until he listens to what Devine can tell us. So ..." He turned toward the window. "There he is now."

Christine walked slowly over to stand in front of the one way glass. A tall, lean man with slightly graying hair stood with his back to them. He leaned on the table where the perpetrator rested his head. "Well, Mr. Devine. What is your story? A witness will swear you shot at Miss Finder last night. She will also testify. You haven't anything to bargain with as far as I can tell."

Tommy sat back in his chair. "What about motive, eh? I ain't got one. So I musta been hired. I'll tell you who put out the contract if you protect me. The man has long fingers."

The lawyer straightened his shoulders. He placed his hands on his hips. "We'll consider it if your information warrants our protection. Who hired you and why?"

"Damned if I know why. He never said." Devine tried to rise but his hands were cuffed to the table, his feet bound with a chain. "I need the agreement in writing."

The Crown Attorney turned toward the door. Christine gasped. She sat heavily down on the seat located behind her legs. The familiar voice spoke before placing his hand on the doorknob. "I'm outa here."

Jeremy glanced at Christine's pale face. "What's wrong?"

Before she answered, Devine hollered at the retreating back of the Provincial Prosecutor. "Wait. Okay. I'll tell you." He swallowed as if a large lump blocked his airways. "Judge Collins. He paid me."

The Attorney heaved a sigh of disgust. "Sure and Irving here is Santa Claus."

"No. I told you the truth. Why, is anyone's guess, but before they released me the last time, the judge ordered me brought to his chambers. In order to get out, I had to make sure Finder didn't survive. He wouldn't say why." He looked toward each of the men in his interrogation room. "You gotta believe me. If I go to Remand, he'll arrange for my death just like Edward Fine."

Jeremy and Christine listened attentively. "I can't fathom ..." he began.

"I can." She pointed toward the lawyer. "That's Desmond Caputo or Dixson. He may be the Crown Attorney, Brian Fleming, but he's used those other names as well, a different one for all occasions, I guess."

"Christine, are you sure?" Jeremy stood closer to the window. "In that case he won't be giving Devine any witness protection, I'll bet. Do you think the judge is tied in with this pedophilia ring?"

Christine hesitated before she answered and then shrugged her shoulders. "We won't possess all the facts until we tie the judge to Caputo. How can we even prove Collins did in fact hire Devine? His word certainly holds a lot more weight than a killer's."

"I'll make sure I talk to Sergeant Irving alone when the

prosecutor leaves." Jeremy shook his head. "No wonder we've had a hard time stopping these perverts. I think someone in this police department is involved as well. Someone scared Devine last night or this morning before we arrived."

Christine stood. She walked past the window and back again. The Crown Attorney asked the perp if he had any proof.

"Whatda ya mean, proof? I never took his picture if that's what you want. He just told me ..."

"Did anyone witness you go into his office?" The detective, not a man to be left out of an important investigation, looked at Irving and back at Devine.

The criminal started to shake his head. Then he stopped. "Yeah, my lawyer, Jason Mitchell. He gave me the message."

Sergeant Irving frowned. "I guess we'll have a chat with Mitchell then. He was court appointed, right."

"I ain't got no money for lawyers." Devine relaxed in his chair. "He'll tell ya. You'll see."

The Crown Attorney shrugged his shoulders. "That still doesn't prove Judge Collins told you to kill the Finder woman. We need more than your word."

Sergeant Irving shifted his weight from one leg to another. "We can protect him, though, until we investigate his claims, right? This would be a big case with lots of tendrils reaching into the justice system. Gathering the facts will take time."

Fleming stared at the police officer a long time before answering. Christine thought he looked as if he tried to figure a way out of the mess he was in. *I plan to make sure you don't escape getting what you deserve, Caputo, Dixson, or whatever your real name is.*

The corrupt prosecutor cleared his throat. "Keep him in solitary for now. That should make him feel safe ..." He moved toward the door. "Keep me up to date on the investigation." He made a grandiose exit as if he was the most important man in the system.

While Irving and his detective made Devine ready for his trip to the Remand Center, Jeremy and Christine chose to stay behind the one way glassed in room. The sergeant would join them shortly. "How are we going to tie those two together? Jason Mitchell must be part of this as well. How my father's company executives trust the man is beyond me?" She grimaced. "I wonder what else is going on at Rompart."

Jeremy patted Christine's shoulder. "We started out this morning thinking this would be a simple act of some child molester's wanting you dead. But to find out our justice system contains some corrupt members, is disconcerting. How can such educated men be involved in sex trafficking of little boys? The whole idea is sick."

Christine walked back and forth a few times but then sat down as if the weight of the world resided on her shoulders. "Prosecuting guys like these seems like a hopeless situation. I mean, all their bases are covered, I'm sure. One will vouch for the other. If Jason's is one of this crew, he's not going to admit the judge wanted to meet with Devine. No way."

Jeremy leaned against the door. "I'll bet my father would help us. His fingers reach into a lot of different legal communities. Maybe he is familiar with someone we can trust who's outside the system. We'll call him as soon as we leave here. I want to listen to Irving's take on things."

Just as the man's name came from Jeremy's mouth, the door opened. "Boy that revelation I never expected. I always admired Judge Collins."

"That's not the half of it." Christine and Jeremy spoke simultaneously.

Irving closed the door. "What else?" He looked from one to the other.

Christine began. "I recognized Crown Attorney Fleming."

"Of course, everyone knows who he is," The sergeant jumped in.

"No, I mean as someone else. He's the man who tried to kill me and little Jimmy. He's Dixson or Caputo." Christine swallowed and looked toward the floor waiting for the police officer to absorb this latest piece if information.

His face spoke volumes. "Devine's not safe. We need to get him out of there." He hastily yanked the door open and strode to the squad room. "Did Vickers leave for the Remand Yet?" he hollered. Two officers pointed to the door leading to the parking garage. "Stop him."

Chapter Sixty Four

The two investigators waited beside Sergeant Irving's desk. Five minutes later the police officer returned, his head shaking in disgust. "I couldn't stop him. He was halfway down the street before I got out the door."

The sergeant grabbed the desk phone. He asked for the dispatcher. "Elena, call through to the policeman who took Devine to the Remand Center. Tell him to come back here ASAP." He listened while she repeated his instructions to her. "Right. Tell him to find me as soon as he gets here." He turned to look at Christine and Jeremy as he replaced the phone. "We'll find a safe house for him."

Jeremy nodded. "How," he continued, "are we going to keep the information from the prosecutor?" He took one of the two chairs arranged along the wall and moved it beside the sergeant's desk. He motioned for Christine to sit before he retraced his steps to locate another one for himself. "Let's talk about the attempts on Christine's life and the implications of Judge Collins' contract on her."

"Yeah, if we can believe Devine. I've been acquainted with Collins for a long time and he's always seemed above board, honest. Now ..." The sergeant took his seat. He glanced at the paperwork scattered on the top and leaned his forearms on the closest pile. "I guess we operate as if the allegation is true until we find out otherwise. Christine, how do you intend to handle this threat on your life?"

She gazed up at Jeremy and waved a hand in his direction. "I am to put up with a body guard, it seems, and we'll change where we live in the meantime. But I still need to look after Chief when he comes home from the veterinary hospital. That bullet hit too close for comfort."

Jeremy's eyes widened at her mention of her dog. "Christine, Chief can't come home with you. He makes you too conspicuous. Maybe Denny will keep him till we settle this."

"Jeremy, no. I count on him to warn me of danger or strangers. He's always been alert to things. I need him." Christine's pain radiated near her heart. The thought of not having Chief nearby hurt. "I can't be without him."

Jeremy placed his hand on her knee. "Christine, nothing can be the same for a while. We need to hide you in plain sight and we can't do so with the dog around. Denny takes good care of him, you know that." He patted her leg again.

"I know but ..." Tears filled her lower lids, one escaping to leave a trail down her right cheek. "I'm going to miss him so much." She straightened her back and swiped at the wetness on her face.

Sergeant Irving interjected, "Even if Devine lied and Collins didn't pay him, someone did. Some creep wants you dead and ..."

"It was Collins." She stared toward the wall behind the officer's head. "Tommy has no reason to lie."

"Maybe he thinks we won't give him protection if his boss is just some low life ..." Jeremy nodded in the sergeant's direction. "Let's look at this from all angles."

Christine crossed her hands on her side of the desk top. "If the Crown Attorney is involved in this pedophile ring, what's to say the judge isn't? No, I think Devine told the truth and ..."

Running footsteps interrupted business as usual in the squad room. Everyone looked up. The officer who drove the creep to the Remand Center ran into the room. "He's gone. Someone was waiting for us. They made me lie on the pavement while they took him out of the vehicle. They wore masks and didn't even bother to remove his cuffs. Sorry, Serge."

Sergeant Irving looked the young officer over from head to toe. "You hurt?'

"No. Just mad. I guess I never thought ... I mean ... the man did talk protection and all. He seemed scared and then he goes and does this." The policeman walked over to the water cooler.

"That does seem strange." The sergeant spoke so quietly no one heard him except the two at his desk. "I think we have a leak."

Jeremy glanced at the officer standing guzzling cups of water. "You don't really think Devine arranged this, do you?"

"When would he have the time?" Christine offered.

The sergeant gazed around the room, his eyes hooded. "I hate to think it but ... Vickers, get over here."

Chapter Sixty Five

Jeremy and Christine retreated to the waiting area at the front of the squad room. He made room for her to sit beside him on the bench and leaned closer to her ear. "Sergeant Irving looks determined. He'll work his way to the bottom of this, no matter how unpleasant things become."

"Not able to trust a colleague is hard, I'll bet. I can sure understand what he alluded to, though. How did Devine's rescuers find out the route they took? Devine didn't have access to a phone. How he notified anyone of his whereabouts is a mystery." Christine whispered her suspicions behind her hand so no one in the near vicinity could read her lips or overhear. "This is beginning to look like a mess for the legal system."

Jeremy glanced around the room. "Let's leave and check on your house. We can decide if the location is feasible as a safe house for us. You wanted to grab some things from your current residence too."

"Yes. I agree. I haven't inspected the renovations on my parent's house for a few days. A week actually. They may be finished." She stood, brushed her hands down the leg of her pants, and took a step to the door. "If my clothes don't all reek of smoke, I can hardly wait to change into some clean stuff. I'll call Denny on the way." She grimaced.

Jeremy nodded sympathetically. "You'll have to admit, leaving Chief with him is warranted. He's too visible." He placed his hand on her elbow. "Let me go first."

As before, Jeremy used his body to shield her as they stepped out the door and strode toward the street. They made their way quickly toward his truck. Christine spoke over her shoulder. "They might have already figured out you're protecting me. We may have to ditch your vehicle, too."

He directed her to the passenger side. He secured the door behind her as she buckled her seat belt. He walked rapidly to the driver's side. His speedy movements had the vehicle in gear and rolling out of the parking space in record time. "We'll drive around a bit in case someone is tailing us."

Jeremy pulled into the traffic on Portage Avenue a few seconds later. He glanced in his rearview mirror on a regular basis, keeping track of the vehicles around them.

Christine yanked her phone out of her handbag. "I'm going to call Denny." She punched in the numbers.

He shifted his gaze to her face. "Maybe this extra security won't be for long."

She grimaced before speaking into the device in her hand. "Hi Denny. I need a favour." She went on to explain the recent events leading up to her request to board Chief at his kennels. "Oh, good. Would you pick him up directly from the vets tomorrow?" She shifted her gaze in Jeremy's direction.

Jeremy nodded and smiled a silent encouraging message to her. He checked the mirror again. Cars of all types drove past, followed, or traveled ahead of them but none sent up red flags. Once he was satisfied that no one seemed overly interested in them, he turned toward the subdivision where Christine currently lived. He continued to scan the traffic, though.

Christine ended the call with a promise to stay safe. Denny's derogatory remark about Jeremy not able to secure her safety reminded her that his thoughts leaned to the personal sometimes. "I need to phone the vet to fill him in on the change in plans." She punched in those numbers this time.

Her male counterpart remained silent. He focused on the world around them, wanting to keep his wits about him. Someone might be watching her house. He scanned the street as soon as they pulled onto the familiar stretch of pavement. All seemed quiet.

Christine finished her call as they drove into her small parking space. Yellow crime scene tape flapped in the light breeze as Jeremy escorted her to the front entry. She glanced around her neighbourhood. *Dr. Belmont won't like all the traffic on his street.* She directed her gaze to the doctor's house. Everything appeared quiet.

He led the way around the house toward the side where the fire did the most damage. "I'm glad the firemen boarded this up."

"Yes. They said they would." Christine shrugged. "Once the carpenters finish on my other house, I'll send them over here to do these repairs. I'll have a quote from the insurance company by then." She turned to walk back to the main exit.

Jeremy followed this time, hoping to keep her back safe in case someone tried to take another shot at her. "We need to get inside."

Christine unlocked her door, stepped into the interior and sniffed. "Oh, the odour of smoke is everywhere. I may have to find a laundromat to wash all my clothes." She headed toward her bedroom.

"I'm going to take a look around. Check if anything is out of place." Jeremy walked down the hall to the kitchen. He took in a deep breathe. *Here the air is free of the smoky odour.* He glanced out the back door. A large bundle of twigs filled the space at the bottom of the door on the outside. *The creep planned to start a fire here as well. Good thing she came home when she did and not before. If she'd been sleeping ...* "Christine, come here," he hollered toward the living room.

A couple of minutes later, she crossed the threshold into the kitchen. "What's wrong?"

"Take a look." Jeremy pointed to the back door.

Christine checked outside. Her brown lawn had plenty of leaves to rake up but nothing caused her alarm. "What?"

"Check down by the door."

She glanced down. "Oh. My." Christine turned toward him. "He wasn't done yet."

"No. If you had arrived home earlier, the outcome might have been quite different." He smirked. "Guardian angels."

Christine grinned right back, her heart a little lighter at the thought of someone constantly protecting her. "You think?"

"I do. The Bible is clear about them serving mankind. There are no such things as coincidences. God loves you and sent his angels to protect you. God's Word says so." He made sure the lock engaged and turned in her direction. "Do your clothes give off a sooty scent?"

"Not something that a good airing couldn't take care. I'll pack enough for a few days and be right with you. Would you gather up my computer and everything in my desk?"

"Sure." Jeremy retraced his steps and ended up near her work space, an area close to where the fire happened the night before. "I hope you own an external backup system." He took note of the damage done to her once organized home office.

Christine appeared at his elbow. "Oh, no." She touched her laptop, tried to open the cover but the lump of plastic covered her hands in soot. "I did use a backup. Thank goodness."

"Take an inventory of all you lost in here before you submit a claim to your insurance. They should pay for the cost of replacement and the other furnishings in here as well." He looked around the room. "Everything is pretty much trash."

Christine sighed. "I guess I thought to purchase new furniture when I moved anyway. I'll move mom and dads out of storage in the meantime."

Jeremy glanced at the woman who already lost so much. "My relationship with my dad is such a close one, I can't imagine how you manage with both of yours gone. You must miss them a lot."

Christine's silent nod met his sympathetic inquiry. She chose to ignore her sense of loss. "I'll be back in a minute and we can leave."

Chapter Sixty Six

Jeremy decided, while he waited for Christine, to phone his father with an update about his client. He punched in the numbers and listened for the older Goodman to answer. "Hi, Dad. How's your day going?"

His father got right to the point asking how Christine sounded. "She's fine. Packing up some things to move. We're not really sure yet but we're thinking her parents' house might work if the renovations are done or close to being finished."

His father's agreeable response coincided with his assessment. "She's one tough cookie, all right. She's most distressed about leaving Chief at Denny's but otherwise as stoic as ever." His father reminded him she'd needed to be strong all her life. "I know. I'm glad you are in my life. I can't imagine what my life would be like if you died as well as mom. Speaking of ... how's Clare? You two set a date yet?"

His father chuckled at Jeremy's Segway into his private life. His sarcastic response left no doubt Jeremy would be told in due course but not before. "I hear you, Dad. Keep me posted is all. Love ya. Here's Christine. Gotta go."

He ended the call and reached to help his friend with the

heavy suitcase she rolled behind her. A duffle swung from her shoulder. "Here let me take that from you." Once he secured the suitcase handle, he stepped toward the door. "I'll take a look first."

Chapter Sixty Seven

Sergeant Irving finished grilling Officer Pete Vickers in one of the interrogation rooms. The man clammed up almost immediately and asked for his union rep. "You're going to need a lawyer young man. Your representative won't be able to help you with this. In fact he may even want to bust your nose himself."

"I didn't do anything wrong. You can't pin the creep's escape on me." The young officer's face remained sullen.

"No? Well I think you've run out of options." The sergeant walked back to the squad room, slamming the door so hard the windows nearby rattled. *I hate a turncoat.* He strode over to his desk, all eyes in the room plastered to his back. His senses were confirmed when he glanced around the room. *They can't believe Vickers is a dirty cop.*

Just then, a detective, his cell phone in his hand, headed toward the door passing Sergeant Irving on the way. The detective studied the man who had run the precinct for more than a few years now. He decided to fill the sergeant in one the recent events. "Got a call. Dead man found in vacant lot near the museum. Description sounds like Devine. Might be wrong." He shrugged his shoulders and kept on going to the exit.

Irving frowned. "Keep me posted." *Damn. Our one witness.* He stood clumsily, knocking his chair sideways. His heavy footsteps returned to the interrogation room where Vickers had been given time to think about his choices. He pushed the door sending the portal flying towards the adjacent wall with a loud bang. "Okay, you may be facing a murder charge now. You better start talking."

The officer's face grew even paler than before the Irving left the room. "What? No. Things were supposed to be ..."

"What? You thought your buddies would just rough him up a little? Think again. Now I want some names." The older man's face turned almost purple with rage. "The man was a witness against a Provincial judge and maybe more pedophiles besides. You're not dumb so give us what we want and you're going down as an accessory to murder. No names and you'll face the full charge of first degree murder."

The young man swallowed. His downcast eyes searched the table in front of him as if seeking a way out. Irving waited. Vickers gulped again. "I was never told a name. I received instructions in an envelope pushed through the side of the door in my locker. When I came to work the next day, another envelope contained the money for the information I provided."

"How did they approach you in the beginning?" Irving slammed his large fist down on the top right beside the boy's hand.

Vickers flinched. "They sent me a phone number in the mail. I called. The voice was altered. I never recognized who he was."

"Convenient." The sergeant thought for a minute. "What kind of things did they want you to do?"

A knock on the door interrupted Irving's questioning of the junior officer. He growled as he opened the portal. "What now?"

Another uniform handed him a note. A glance confirmed his worse fears. He looked toward Vickers. "Devine is identified, left in a vacant lot, thanks to you. Now answer my question." He slammed the door.

The young cop's face blended in with the stark white wall behind him. His eyes grew glassy. His fright was almost something touchable, "At first, they asked for little things. Who worked what shift and where. They seemed especially interested in the investigators, what case they covered. Things like that."

"And you gave them this information how?"

Vickers swallowed. He looked up at the large man hovering close enough to hit him. "I made a phone call every morning."

"Give me the number."

"It's untraceable. I tried. After a few weeks, I wanted out. I couldn't find out who the cell number belonged to. They threatened to kill my family if I stopped. All of them. Aunts, uncles, cousins, all of them."

Sergeant Irving calmed down a little. "What's the number?"

Vickers slid a hand into his pants pocket. He pulled out a piece of paper. "They change it every week or so."

The police sergeant reached for the scrap. "When did this one activate?"

"Three days ago." The disgraced cop placed his hands between his knees. His shoulders shook. "What's going to happen to me now?"

Irving decided to wait with his answer to the question. "Three days, eh? Enough time to trace this number if we can." He looked at Vickers. "You aren't the first police officer to be tempted by extra cash. But we can't allow you to tip these guys off. And while all I want to do is lock you up for accepting a bribe as an accessory to murder, I can't send you to the Remand, obviously."

He stepped to the door, opened it a crack and stared at Vickers. "I'll be back."

The sergeant strode purposefully to his desk and picked up his personal cell phone. He quickly tapped in a number only used twice in his life before. "Let me speak to Father Benedict."

Chapter Sixty Eight

Christine gazed out the window. The owners, of houses with high walls surrounding the properties, installed security systems at the gates. The neighbours kept to themselves. *I'll do some research to find out who lives where, I think.* "Jeremy, did you by any chance check out any of the people around here?"

"Well," He turned his truck toward the gate blocking access to her house. "When we found out Edward Fine owned a house in the area, I did a cursory investigation on a few of his neighbours but nothing of interest popped up. Why? What are you thinking?"

Christine stepped out of the Dodge Ram without answering, walked over to the keypad and punched in the code to open the large barrier. She strode swiftly back to the passenger side and slipped inside again. "A remote for this gate is in the house and I can access the intercom from the interior as well. The trade's people used the back gate but the security company is going to replace that system as soon as they're finished." She leaned back in the seat while Jeremy drove through. "I thought we should check out the neighbours who live close by, just in case."

He steered to the back of the house. The parking garage

doors were shut. Not another soul seemed to be around, no cars or trucks in sight. "I forgot to ask you which door you wanted to go through. I assume there are keys for all of them?"

"This entrance will become the second residence but we can enter the primary one from here as well." Christine led the way to the door. She inserted her key and the door opened with a whoosh. Everything appeared to be cleaned up. "I guess the carpenters are finished. I'll call Norland Securities after I confirm the job is done." She looked around. "I like how this turned out."

Jeremy silently sauntered around the room designed to serve as a living room. The windows had been enlarged and the kitchen was no longer visible from the entryway. The large foyer they passed through displayed several doors to other rooms. "Did they add a bedroom or two down here? Does your space include the upstairs?"

"It does. Come on, I'll show you." Christine proceeded to give him a tour of the house. "I couldn't divide this home into two apartments as such because of zoning regulations but the Residents Association approved an in-law suite. This one is larger than the usual home for elderly parents."

Jeremy appeared impressed. "This is well laid out and big enough for an entire family. Are you planning on renting to a single person or a family?"

She grinned. "One person or a couple wouldn't matter. I hoped one day to hire a housekeeper for my residence and she might want to live here. For now, we'll keep this space vacant. Come this way."

She led Jeremy to a door at the end of the hall leading to the kitchen and dining area. Built into a wall housing a pantry, Christine unlocked a door accessing her future living quarters. "This will be kept locked on my side all the time and the tenant can lock this side as well."

"You thought of everything. It didn't take the contractors very long to finish this redo." Jeremy strolled into the nearest room, surprised to discover the configuration of the original kitchen. "It's almost like they moved the entire room over a little." He waved his hand in a circle around the room.

Christine chuckled. "In effect, they did. We saved a bunch of money by taking everything apart and reinstalling the same cabinets and appliances here. Come check out the living room."

Jeremy followed her to the front of the house. The room they walked into seemed smaller than he remembered but still larger than anything he lived in previously. "Did they move the walls over?"

"A lot more than that but essentially, yes. Do you think this will work for a hideout, in the meantime?"

"Who's name is the property registered in?"

"Your Dad's. When I started to renovate, we changed the title from my parent's to his so he conferred with the contractors keeping my face out of it. I think its best we leave things that way for now. Caputo and his cohorts won't find any reason to tie me to your father, will they?" She slid the drape covering a large window aside for a quick peak.

Jeremy contemplated her question before answering. "Maybe we should talk to Dad for an answer. He'd know better than anyone if Christine Finder is connected to him in any public forum." He slipped his phone out of the holster. "He's Melissa Rompart's lawyer of record but I don't think any recorded legal dealings for you as Christine were ever needed, were they?" He dropped his gaze toward the floor to answer his Father's greeting. "Hi Dad. Christine and I are at her house. We're thinking of using this place since she's not known in this neighbourhood. She tells me your name is on the lease but we wondered if anyone will connect you to her as Christine Finder."

She studied Jeremy's face for insight into his dad's response. His relaxed facial expression told her what she hoped for. *Not connected.* She listened as Jeremy filled him in on the recent revelations.

A gasp flowed through the airspace as soon as he revealed Judge Collins put out the hit on Christine. "I understand Dad. That Justice carries an impeccable reputation or so we thought. Do you remember her telling us about Dixson, the pedophile, and Caputo, the man she encountered at her office building being one and the same? Well he goes by another name. Crown Prosecuting Attorney Brian Flemings." Barkley's incredulous exclamation bounced off the walls of the room. Jeremy lifted the phone from his ear.

Christine hung her head. Jeremy's expression took on a thunderous hue. "The corruption may go even farther. The word of a dead assassin but ... Yeah. Devine was killed. Some guys took him from the squad car transporting him to the Remand. They found his body a half hour later. Irving is questioning the officer who drove the police car."

Christine wandered toward the staircase while Jeremy finished his conversation with Barkley Goodman, his father, and her lawyer. She spun back around and motioned for him to speak with her a moment.

He asked his Father to hold on. "What's wrong?"

"Nothing. Just ... ask your Dad if he would arrange for my parent's furnishings to be delivered from the storage unit? At least some of them. Maybe a couple of beds, some living room chairs, a desk or two and dining set for the kitchen. We can make do with those few pieces, couldn't we? If he came to accept delivery, no one would find out we're in residence." She looked hopefully toward Jeremy.

"Good thinking. Yeah, that should do us." He turned back to his Dad.

Christine continued up the staircase and into the bedroom area. The large rooms made space a non-issue. Having her friend in one of the bedrooms might seem strange but ... *Oh for goodness sake,* she chided herself. *He's only going to be here as a body guard.*

She began to picture them spending more time together, twenty four seven in fact. A warm glow flowed through her core, causing an unusual amount of heat to travel up her neck to her face. *Lord, help me keep my mind on the situation at hand. Help us figure out how to prove the ties between all these creeps to end this trafficking business. Thank you for sending your angels to protect me. Even Jeremy.* She blushed again as an image of him with angel wings traveled across her brain.

Chapter Sixty Nine

Judge Raymond Collins sat behind his large mahogany desk. He absently grabbed one sheet of paper and another, tossing them back where they came from. His scowl, firmly in place, was a trademark when he presided over a case. Underneath, well hidden from prying eyes, a slight tremor existed. His hands shook. If crying was a habit, he'd have succumbed to his anguish.

The doctor gave him the worse possible news. He was diagnosed with Aids. He would die. He wrapped his fingers around a vase of flowers, something his office assistant insisted on placing on his desk every morning. He threw the arrangement across the room. The resounding crash against a mirror on the far wall would bring her to the door if she still sat at her work station. The day had grown late but he didn't want to go home.

He grabbed his cell but before he punched in the familiar numbers, the device vibrated in his hand. He checked the caller ID and answered. "I just picked up this thing to call you." His voice was little more than a growl.

He listened patiently to the person at the end of the call for a few minutes. Patience wearing thin, he interjected. "You took care of the liability, right? You have as much at stake as I do. Your reputation wouldn't fare so well if ..." The voice on the other end grew louder. "Fine. Make sure no one else can identify either one of us."

Collins paused for a second. "Where did the kid come from? The one you stashed out at your cabin?"

Collins waited while his partner in crime sputtered and gave an excuse why the boy was taken in the first place. "Yeah, he's gone but he can pick us out of a lineup, if they find him. Locate him. He needs to be eliminated. And so does that snoopy broad. They're problems for both of us."

Justice Collins stood with the device in his hand. He walked to the front of his ornate work table as he listened. He began to pace. "I want her dead. You understand. Call in your informants in the department. They'll tell you where she is. I don't care how the deed is done. Get rid of her."

He slammed the phone on his desk and then picked it up to slam it again. He wanted to hurt someone. Why him? *Grace will need to be tested.* He thought about the last time he and his wife of forty years made love. *She'll never understand. I needed more. I tried to stop. I should have ended this a long time ago. She doesn't satisfy me anymore. The scandal.*

The judge went back to his chair. He sat down heavily. A grunt erupted from his throat. He opened the drawer near his left knee. His Smith and Wesson stared at him. Temptation, relief, the weapon spoke of a way out.

He picked it up and caressed the barrel with his fingers. *What if?* He dropped the gun into the space allocated for five years. He'd become a little paranoid of late. *The snoopy woman's fault.* His anger toward the fear she instilled in him erupted in spittle dripping down his chin. *She's a dead woman. I'm surrounded by incompetents. Devine got what he deserved.*

I'm a respected member of this community. How dare the scum name me to the police. He stood and paced back and forth in front of his desk as was his practice. *No one will believe a known dirt-bag over me. Nothing to fear but fear ... I ...*

I need a warm body, someone new. That'll take the edge off this latest piece of news. Some aids victims live a long time. I can beat this. They're coming up with new medicines all the time. I'm a Federal Judge, after all.

His thoughts traveled all over the place. He could end it. He might survive. His brain hurt. How his dependence on the love little boys gave him escalated was a mystery. Life seemed as if ... *That's what I'll say. I'm addicted. I'm sick. This little dalliance is like a fix.* He placed a phone call and grabbed his coat off the rack beside his office door. He stalked out of the building, glancing ahead to make sure no one spotted him. He glanced behind checking that no one followed. He would feel better soon.

Chapter Seventy

Jeremy peered at the time piece attached to his wrist. He shifted his gaze toward the street and the large historic structure on the other side from his parked truck and then glanced at Christine. "I can't think what's keeping Judge Collins. Sergeant Irving assured me he left promptly each day at five thirty. My wristwatch says it's seven o'clock."

"Maybe he's ..." She leaned toward the windshield to scan the area more closely. "Isn't that him now?" Christine's sigh gave away how bone weary she was after her sleepless night. *So much happened since she left the hospital.* Jeremy perceived her discomfort as she rubbed a sore spot on her shoulder. *She's been sitting still too long. These seats aren't the most comfortable for this kind of surveillance.*

He stared at the figure walking swiftly to his car. "He's the judge all right. I hope he leads us to something we can use to put him and his buddies away for a long time." He turned the ignition on in readiness. "We'll stay far enough behind so he won't spot us but I don't think he'll recognize this truck. You, on the other hand ..."

"Yeah, I get the picture. If he's the person we think he is, he ordered my death. I guess I got too close for comfort, eh?" Christine curled her lip in a sneer directed at the car ahead. "I'd like nothing better than to terminate his sorry ... I mean, stop him."

Jeremy pulled the truck between two other vehicles as soon as Collins traveled about five car lengths down the street. People coming back downtown for an evening event and others heading home late like Justice Collins made traffic heavy. "Christine, did you look up his home address before we left your house?"

"I did. He lives on Shaftsbury in Tuxedo, near the west end. Why is he traveling east I wonder." She leaned her back into the cushion. "This side of your truck isn't used much, is it? The seat is stiff." Christine rubbed her shoulder again.

Jeremy chuckled. "A little sore are we? Think you left the hospital too soon?"

"Never mind with the 'I told you so'." She paused to find the tail-lights of the vehicle they followed. "He's not traveling as if he wants to get anywhere fast, is he?" She looked back at him. "I hope the furniture from the storage unit is in place so we'll at least be able to collapse on a bed when we return home. Your dad said he handled everything, right?"

Jeremy kept his eyes on the street and the car ahead. "He's not in a hurry but he is definitely going somewhere. Check it out ... he's turning up ahead." He steered the black vehicle closer to the intersection where Collins taillights glowed in the direction he turned. "Dad will take care of everything, don't worry. Chief is looked after, thanks to Denny, so we can devote our time to catching this scumbag." He turned around the corner slowly, hoping the creep had continued farther and not parked nearby.

"A provincial judge seems out of place in this part of town." Christine kept her eyes on the silver Porsche as it slowed near a larger house about halfway down the block. "He drove into that driveway.

"People in neighborhoods like this ask no questions so the creeps congregate and give the area a bad name." Jeremy slowly let the truck idle forward and caught the Porsche's taillights disappear as a garage door descended.

Christine pointed to the house. "The place is one of the more expensive looking residences but I wonder what Collins is doing here. Maybe he supports a mistress."

"Yeah, the house looks about five or six years old. We'll give him a few minutes to scurry inside, like the rat he is. We'll sneak closer for a better look-see." Jeremy unhooked his seatbelt. "As soon as we confirm the judge is up to no good, we'll call Irving. He's waiting."

Christine looked toward him. "Thanks for letting me come with you tonight. I would hate sitting at the house by myself."

Jeremy grimaced. "My better judgement told me to do just that ... leave you behind. This pervert wants your life, not mine. However I've made peace with your stubbornness and your passion about stopping the creeps is commendable. I probably couldn't stop you from coming anyway. Stay behind me, okay?"

Christine scowled at him and unlatched her seatbelt. "I'm not that hard to get along with." She opened her door and glanced back at Jeremy. "It's important, to me, that I follow this to the end. I rescued too many kids these creeps tried to destroy, not to mention all the young women who've been drugged into prostitution. Samantha would have ended up on the streets if we hadn't intervened. These guys are bad dudes." She slammed the truck door a little harder than she intended.

Jeremy walked around to her side. Ignoring her flushed cheeks, he began to lay out their plan. "I'll take one side of the house, you take the other. As soon as you witness anything, you come find me and I'll do the same. Collins can only be in one part of the house at a time." He looked at the sky. "Darkness is coming fast. We should be safe if we don't hustle too near the windows. Keep to the bushes, if you find any."

"Jeremy, I've done this before. I understand how to case a residence, remember."

Chapter Seventy One

Christine checked both sides of the street for activity that might give them away. Locked doors and darkened interior lights told of residents already turned in for the night. "We'll still need to keep our eyes peeled for late arrivals until we're hidden over by the house. I don't want those men to sneak away."

Jeremy ran quickly across to the other side and then eased himself into the driveway and the bushes bordering the house. Christine followed right behind but stayed to the right of the garage away from the house. She skirted the out building, slipped her body through a narrow opening in the fence and gained access to the back yard. Garbage was scattered everywhere. The space seemed totally neglected, a sharp contrast to the appearance in front.

She crept along the back wall where some unkempt bushes hid the peeling paint. Spider webs glistened from the single light shining from the back door. She calculated her chance of being discovered. Nothing grew by the house, not even some flowers. This area doesn't look like anyone spends time out here. She slithered toward the house, slowly at first and then more quickly, sticking to the shadows. Only one window lit the yard beyond on this side of the building.

Her cautious footsteps took her to the back of the house. A twig snapped and she shuddered. She clung to the crumbled siding. She waited. Did anyone overhear her approach?

Silence reigned. Christine eased her silhouette closer to the window directly above her head now. She looked around for something to stand on but found nothing. *I hope I can view the inside.*

She stood on her tiptoes. Her eyes peeked over the edge. The kitchen she peered into contained bottles of liquor on the counter. A couple of goblets rested beside them. *Voices.* A man materialized through the door frame, leading to the rest of the house, she supposed. She ducked but her ears remained fine tuned to the sounds inside. *Two men.*

"This'll take away the stress. A good stiff drink works every time." Ice tinkled into a glass and the sound of pouring liquid came next. "How long did the doctor give you before you're full blown? I mean, you're only HIV, right?"

A deeper voice, she assumed belonged to Judge Collins, spoke next. She lifted her head upward as the reprobate clarified his condition as aids already. "The doc says I must have been infected for over a year or so." Christine surveilled him taking a long gulp of fiery alcohol. His grimace confirmed the strength of the liquid. The man was Collins all right but she didn't recognize the other creep.

"I can't let you use this kid."

"Whadda ya mean?" The judge cleared his vocal cords and wrapped his hand around the man's throat. "I paid for him and I intend to grab my fix ... er ... want my pleasure satisfied." He shoved the smaller framed man away from him. "You can't tell me who or what I do."

"But judge ..."

The justice reached for him again. "Don't use my title here, you fool. What if the kid gets away, like Jimmy did? After all the time of preparing and conditioning him, he goes missing. That woman ..."

Christine listened to his rampage about her interference and what he wanted to do to her. She shivered. His hatred toward her seemed like a concrete brick headed in her direction. Her instincts told her to duck and run. *They've stashed a kid here somewhere. We need to rescue him.* She straightened her back. *That's what's important, that and getting proof this Federal Judge is a criminal.*

As she stood with her back against the house, footsteps broke the silence. Christine thought about dashing to the back of the garage but before she made her move, Jeremy appeared beside her. "I can't monitor anything from the windows at the front. The drapes are drawn tight. What about you? Detect anything?" Jeremy's low voice forced her to concentrate all her efforts to listen.

She quietly cleared her throat. "Collins is inside with another man. They've hidden a child who's been here awhile apparently and the creep is planning on raping him, not for the first time. He's infected with Aids."

"And he's decided to infect a child? These outwardly upright citizens possess a wicked disregard for human life ... other than their own." Jeremy's look of disgust gave a pronouncement to his words. "I'll bet the kid already has Aids."

"Shouldn't we call Irving? Right now. Before he drinks himself into a stupor and damages that little boy anymore." Silence followed Christine's whispered suggestion.

Jeremy scowled. "The sergeant wants us to catch him in the act. Otherwise the courts won't believe our word against his. He's a prominent judge, well-respected." He stopped speaking for a second.

"But ..." Christine experienced a frantic rumble in her abdomen.

"I stashed a camera in my glove compartment for the proof we'll need. Remember how I found a window open a little when I rescued Samantha. Why don't you go around front and look for a way in. I'll catch up with you." Jeremy strode into the shadows again before she was able to ask any more questions.

She followed. The street lit up the brickwork on the bottom half of the building and illuminated the siding above. However, shrubs, large enough to hide behind, decorated the landscape giving her some semblance of protection. She quickly scooted behind the first one.

Christine glanced back at the truck but Jeremy had parked his vehicle out of her line of sight. She turned to the task at hand.

She let her hand slide across the sill and her fingers walked toward the glass. This one remained firmly closed but maybe ... She tried to lift the sash. The window wouldn't budge. She pushed again in case the paint held tight. The portal wouldn't give an inch.

She listened and looked for the next opportunity to gain access to this building of horror. Her body fit nicely along the back of the shrubs keeping her protected until she made her way to the other glassed opening. This frame seemed stuck as well.

A third window appeared right beside the second within inches of each other. *Enough space to build a wall between,* she thought. She placed her hand on the sash but the rustle of bushes caused her to scoot down the siding and inch further into the plants.

"Find anything worthwhile?"

"Jeremy. You scared the daylights out of me ... again." She stood but remained hidden from the street. "I checked two of them but not this one." She reached up and grabbed hold of the sill. Her fingers clawed their way to the glass but ... wait. No glass. She looked up and found an open window. She pointed toward the open window for Jeremy's benefit and chuckled at the look of surprise on his face.

"I hoped but never thought we'd be graced by luck twice in a row." He smirked. "For evil dudes, these guys are either stupid or they think no one will ever catch them. I'll hoist you up first. I'll hand you the camera before I crawl through." He cupped his hands together.

"The opening is too small for me." Christine pushed the sill upward and, unlike the first two, the sash moved easily. The creak from the dry wood erupted as loud as a firecracker, though. She stopped pushing and the two investigators listened attentively. A whimper as soft as a cat's meow was all they detected.

The interior door slammed against the far wall. Christine crouched under the window while Jeremy dove for cover inside the nearest shrub. Someone turned the light switch on illuminating most of the room and shining on the shrubs beside the house.

Chapter Seventy Two

A soft gasp preceded the first words spoken by the man who entered the room. "Hi Billy my boy. Been waiting for me?"

The voice seemed softer than Christine had listened to before but she recognized the judge. She glanced toward Jeremy and nodded. He eased his body toward the sill, making sure he crouched below the pervert's line of sight. He raised the camera and inched up to the window.

Christine's mind understood waiting but her heart carried a tremendous amount of pain. Bile seeped into her throat at the thought of putting a child through this nightmare. They needed to catch him in the act. Then the police would be called in. She patted the revolver Jeremy insisted she carry.

"Quit whimpering. Don't you want to play with me?" Judge Collins allowed his impatience to creep into his speech but gentled his voice again. "Come sit with me."

Christine caught the creak of a chair, the furniture piece complaining about the weight settled into it. She lifted her head enough to detect where he was. A small boy with blond hair hanging over his eyes walked slowly toward the man. "I don't wanna." The boy's lips moved as tears leaked from eyes as wide as saucers and filled with terror.

"Oh, come on. I love little boys." *The creep sounds as if he truly believes what he's saying.* Christine wondered how many times he'd tortured this kid. The boy slowly mounted the man's knee. He swiped at the moisture but streaks of water kept coming. "Here let me wipe your eyes."

Christine's stomach lurched as if she'd be sick. Bile almost choked her but she swallowed quickly. *We can't let this creep escape and this evidence will put him away for a long time.* The reminder did nothing for her sense of well-being.

Jeremy raised his arm with the camera to the sill. Christine cautioned him as the judge sat in the center of the room, the pervert's profile attesting to his identity. They ducked as low as the bushes would allow. "Can you video this scene," she whispered.

"I can." He hesitated. "Why? Do you think that would be better than a quick picture?"

"A photo of any compromising situation can be explained. But a video ..." She kept her voice to a whisper as she tried to make her point. "Live action makes it more real, don't you think?"

He grinned his acknowledgement. "Glad you're thinking." He focused on the buttons on the top of the device. He found the correct one.

Christine inched her head over the window sill again. Collins held the child in a tight grip. He moved the frightened child back and forth across his lap. "Oh, that feels so good. You make me feel good, do you know that." Her stomach lurched again as the child's body acquiesce to the man's demands. *This boy has been through this before.*

She motioned for Jeremy to take her place. Her partner shifted his shoulder holster a little farther under his armpit. He patted the weapon for reassurance and settled his camera noiselessly on the wood window frame.

Christine slid down the wall. *I can't look.* She placed hands over her ears. *He'll gather the evidence. I'll call the police as soon as he filmed enough. Lord, why don't you protect these kids? How can you let this evil persist? Please help us record the information on video without the boy being traumatized any more than he already is. Please Lord.*

Tears streaked down her face. She sensed Jeremy's gaze on her and acknowledged his heart hurt as her's did. *If he could hide his eyes, he would.* She looked toward the street, the supposed normalcy. *People have no idea what goes on here. They think their home is safe but evil flows from this place and taints all who wander through the neighbourhood.*

One of Jeremy's first instructive lessons was about spiritual warfare. He explained how reading her Bible, meditating on the words she read and memorizing scripture would help her fight the battle she perceived she was in ... now. *I still don't understand enough. The enemy had the upper hand here. Where's Billy's guardian angel, Lord?*

Jeremy dropped to crouch beside her. "Got what we need. Let's go."

"We can't leave the child alone with that monster." Christine voice rose a little and then she whispered as quietly as before. "What if they kill him when the police arrive?"

Jeremy placed his fingers over his lips and motioned for her to join him back at the truck. "My plan will take care of that."

Chapter Seventy Three

The phone crashed into its cradle when Sergeant Irving
dropped the device and motioned for two other policemen
standing nearby. Placed on alert several hours before, trustworthy officers answered his summons. *A dirty cop in my squad
room is unthinkable*. He exercised extreme care now and would
until this gang of perverts resided behind bars.

The two uniforms moved silently behind him as they exited the building. "We've been given an address and probable
cause to execute a search warrant." He walked swiftly toward
an unmarked car. "Use caution since a child's involved."

His cell phone rang as soon as he sat in the passenger
seat. "Hello. Yes. Good." He refilled the cell holster. "A Judge
signed the paperwork. Let's go."

The car containing three officers raced out of the police
compound and down the street toward the nearest intersection. Light traffic made sirens unnecessary. Lights identified
them as cop cars so other vehicles moved easily out the way as
they sped by.

"You guys got kids?" He looked from one policeman to
the other. Both nodded, their faces grim. "Hard to imagine your

own kid in a situation like this." The sergeant let that thought permeate the silence in the vehicle.

The driver growled. "Jail is too good for these creeps. And to think he's a judge. Did they tell ya who the second guy is, Serge?"

"No but that doesn't matter. He's going to prison like Collins." He motioned toward an intersection up ahead. "That's the turn."

Officer Fletcher steered the unmarked car slowly around the corner. Irving pointed toward the right. "Goodman's truck." They pulled in behind.

Jeremy stepped to the side of the unmarked car. The sergeant opened his door as did the other two officers. "Some judge issued a warrant. Where's Christine?"

"She's waiting by the window. We're hoping Collins will leave the room but if he doesn't she's prepared to fire her weapon to protect the kid." Jeremy continued to describe the lay of the land. "A couple of us can take the back entrance and the rest can use the front door."

"That works." Sergeant Irving led the way across the street. He and Officer Fletcher ran covertly around to the back door after everyone synchronized their watches. Jeremy and the third policeman approached the main door.

Jeremy checked his time piece. "Okay. Here we go." He pounded on the door. "Open up. This is the police." All remained quiet so the officer hammered on the door more forcefully. "Let us in."

Lights flared throughout the neighbourhood at almost the same time as the flashing beams illuminated the entry of the house. Someone unlatched the door with a click. The wood structure opened slowly. "What's the problem, officers?"

"We're here to execute a search warrant." Jeremy stepped inside and around the man who tried to stop them.

The man sputtered. "But ... but ... you can't ...."

"Yes. We can." The policeman handed him a copy of the document.

Sergeant Irving's voice hollered from the back of the house. "Fletcher is posted at the back door. Goodman, you secure the front."

Footsteps scurried from different areas of the house and

Collins planted his body in such a way to block access to the bedrooms. "What's the meaning of this? I'm a Provincial Judge. This is my residence."

Sergeant Irving walked so close to the man his nose almost touched the judge's bulbous appendage. "This warrant is for the entire house and the surrounding property. The document is legal and we intend to execute it, judge or not. Now out of our way." He turned toward the officer guarding the back door. "Fletcher, cuff this man."

The sergeant continued down the hallway where he'd been told they held a small child. He opened one door, made a cursory inspection of the inside and went on to another room. *Thank goodness, Christine didn't need to use her gun.*

He placed his hand on the door knob. The cold metal turned in his palm and revealed a tiny crack between the frame and the door. Christine's water filled eyes peered up at him. "He ... he strangled the boy before I managed to stop him." Tears streamed down her face as she backed into the room. Irving slipped past her.

His eyes gave the room a momentary inspection before his gaze locked on the small body lying beside a large rocker. The child lay naked but the bruises caught the sergeant's eye first. "Christine, go find your friend. I'm bringing the Crime Scene guys here. With your statement, we've got this sleaze ball for murder now."

"I don't think he cares anymore. I overheard him tell the other one he is infected with Aids." She sniffed. "When I got back to the window, after Jeremy and I formed our plan to protect him, Collins had traumatized the child so much he was almost catatonic. The judge sat with this stupid look on his face." She swiped at the tears that continued to make their way toward her neck. Her body trembled. Christine placed her hands over her stomach. She placed her hand on her stomach as it heaved again and then escaped to the restroom.

Sergeant Irving let her go. *I'll obtain a full statement later.* He grabbed his cell phone. Punching in the numbers for the police department he asked for the officers who would secure the scene and go over the place with a fine tooth comb. Once he completed the call, he walked back to the kitchen.

Judge Collins tried to coerce the officer into letting him go when Irving stepped into the room. "You aren't going anywhere except to prison for the rest of your sorry, miserable life. You won't be able to escape now we obtained eye witness proof of your crimes including the murder of the kid."

The second man gasped. "You killed him. You had no right ... I owned him."

The sergeant glanced at the flushed features of the other pervert. "Who are you?"

"I need a lawyer." The man intended to exercise his rights as the judge taught him.

The senior cop walked toward him, using his size to intimidate. "Not until you tell us your name and how you're connected to this sleaze ball." He cuffed the magistrate on the back of the head.

"That's brutality." Collins blustered as his sense of self-importance surfaced again.

"Fletcher. Did you observe me hit him? What about you Goodman?" Irving swung around to include Christine. "I think this woman will also testify I didn't strike you."

Judge Collins took one look at her, lifted his cuffed hands to the air above his head and shook both fists. "So. You're in on this. I should've killed you myself instead of hiring incompetents. This is not over, not by a long shot." He screamed at her now. "You're gonna receive what you've got coming. Wait and see."

Jeremy stepped to her side. "By the time you're released from prison, you'll be ready for a nursing home." He raised his camera. "With this video, no one will question your guilt." Jeremy shook the instrument in the judge's face.

The man wilted. "I can't do time. So many of those guys are behind bars because I put them there. They'll come after me. I can offer you names. Make me a deal."

"Not if I can help it." Sergeant Irving glanced disdainfully at the investigator. He motioned his officers to cuff the other man. "Name?" He looked sternly toward the self-professed home owner.

"I am Pastor Archibald Friesen. I minister at the United Church on Young Street. This is a home for young boys, kids nobody wants. I run this place." He stood straight as if a rod fused his back bone. "I did nothing wrong. I ..."

"Shut up." The judge sneered at the meek individual the

man became. "I've got lawyers for both of us."

The front door opened and three men wearing protective gear over their shoes, and gloves on their hands walked into the house. "Hi John." The one in charge nodded in Sergeant Irving's direction. "What we got?"

Chapter Seventy Four

Christine inserted a key into the lock on her parents' former residence. *Once I make this place my own, my sense of
ownership will increase, I hope. Right now ...* She glanced at
Jeremy. *The man is incorrigible.* "This case is over. Collins put
the hit out on me and he's in jail where he belongs. I don't think
your guarding me is necessary."

He gave her a shove through the door. "Do we know for
sure that no one else placed a contract on you? No, we don't. So
until we can be sure, I'm sticking like glue. Besides the trial to
convict Collins will take a while. I can't wait till he's put away
for life. You are a material witness, one who will make the case
against him a lot harder to prove without your testimony." He
walked into the large living room and sat on the sofa his father
arranged to be delivered. "This room is huge. My place would
fit in here."

"Did you find another place to live, one to accommodate
all your assets?" She grinned. In a singsong voice, she teased
him about men and their toys.

Jeremy chuckled. "I like your smiling face. I missed those
dimples" He crossed one leg over the other. "No, not
yet. Nothing fits. As soon as I walk into a unit, I sense some-

thing is not right. Hey." They both spoke at once.

"You could rent the other side of this place." Christine clamped her hand over her mouth. *What am I thinking?* "I mean, the apartment is pretty small compared to this side and the back entrance would be yours all the time but ... maybe not a good idea."

"No. I think that's a great plan. How much you charging? Two bedrooms, right?"

She folded her legs under her as she sat on the love-seat matching the sofa. "Three. With two baths. Fifteen hundred a month."

"Whoa!" He grew pensive for a few moments.

Christine pursed her lips. "The real estate agent said that was the going rate for a place this size. The price is probably a little out of your range, right?"

Jeremy sat quietly thinking. "How about I trade some of the cost of renting space at my building for a reduction in rent here? Say about one thousand and you can use the office free of charge. How does that sound?"

The peel of the doorbell interrupted Christine's response. She unwound herself and walked quickly to the front door. Peering through the peep hole, she smiled. Her lawyer stood sideways perusing the landscape. She detached the chain, unlocked the deadbolt, and opened the door. "Hi Barkley. Come in."

Always impeccably dressed, her attorney and Jeremy's Dad entered the foyer. "I hope I rescued enough of your parent's furnishings to make you a little comfortable for the time being," He began. He waved toward Jeremy. "Hi son. Did you guys just arrive? From out there it doesn't appear as if anyone is home."

"That's the way we want things." The younger man stood and sauntered toward the older man. "What brings you out today?"

Barkley Goodman glanced at Christine. "I have a vested interest. Besides, I want all the scuttlebutt."

She placed her arms around his waist. "Thanks for taking these pieces out of storage. This way I can visualize whether I want to keep anything. I don't think my parent's style is mine."

Jeremy led the way back to the sofa. "Christine and I

hashed out the details of a more permanent living arrangement."

"Son! Marriage first." Barkley scowled. "Christians don't live together outside of wedlock. I thought I raised ..."

Christine burst out laughing, enjoying the sheer look of fright and consternation passing over Jeremy's countenance. She clapped her hands and spotted Barkley's quizzical expression. "Not in the same place. Jeremy is trying to talk me into letting him rent my second unit."

Barkley sent an apologetic glance in his son's direction. "Oh. By the way, speaking of marriage, Clare and I set a date. We thought since this is a late blooming relationship, December would be a good time to make our arrangement permanent. She's a huge fan of Christmas so ...."

Jeremy chuckled. He reached across to ruffle his Dad's almost white hair. "So you're going to dress like Mr. and Mrs. Claus ..."

"Very funny. The wedding will actually be very elegant with red and green accents, that's all." Barkley's grin appeared to be as wide as his face.

"Wonderful news, Barkley. I wish you and Clare every happiness." Christine gushed but she was authentically pleased. *I wonder when my turn will come.* The thought fractured her sense of peace. *Where did that come from? I'm not even dating anyone.* She glanced at Jeremy in time to notice him duck his head. Hm-m-m. "Maybe your Father would like to visit the other unit."

He cleared his throat. "Yeah, how about it Dad? Wanna check out where I might be living?'

Barkley shook his head. "I need to hurry. Clare and I are going to find a caterer. We've already booked the church."

Was that a streak of pink Christine perceived near his collar? He coughed. "I really came to fill you in on the news coming from the Law Courts Building. The Crown Attorney is under investigation and been taken into custody, thanks to Judge Collins. Apparently, he's one vindictive, angry man and plans to take whomever he can down with him. People are still reeling from the charges against a man they respected their entire career. But the names are beginning to come out."

Christine scowled. "I can't believe a pastor is involved in

all this nastiness. I'll bet his congregation thinks he preached to them under false pretenses. I mean, I don't understand much yet, but the Bible is certainly clear about the sin of adultery and doesn't the Word say somewhere Jesus likes kids?" She shook her head.

Jeremy's frown deepened. "I hate when someone in a leadership position in the church falls but those are the people the enemy goes after in a big way. Christine, don't let the fallibility of one man drive you away from your new found faith in Christ. Christians are forgiven, not perfect. Unfortunately."

Barkley decided to ignore the conversation about her spiritual growth as he stood to leave. "Keep me posted. I'll let you know of any new developments in the case. You keep safe, young lady. Oh, your board of directors is ready for a meeting to go over the workings of the company. Now may be as good a time as any to take over the reins of Rompart."

"Jeremy and I worked out a way to protect me and still live a normal lifestyle. I have some loose ends to tie up with the Anderson case and I need to contact Teresa Brent. Give me a few days and I'll set a time to meet with the board." She walked her lawyer toward the front door.

Barkley stopped and turned to face her. "You decide what you want to do about your other house?"

"Now the authorities ruled the fire as arson, they are still searching for some clues. Once that's complete, I'll hire the same construction company to repair the house. I plan to move out completely so the place can be sold. I always wanted to live here anyways." She opened the door. "Say hi to Clare for us."

He waved and gave his son a pointed glance. "A double wedding would be fun, don't you think?" He chuckled. "Later you guys. Take care." He let his hand add its farewell again and strode toward his car parked on the driveway.

Christine lifted her eyes toward Jeremy and lowered them again as she closed the door. She walked slowly back to the living room as he sauntered down the hall toward the connecting door leading to his future home. She sighed. *His dad is sure getting pushy. We may work together but nothing more. I mean ... we're friends and all but ... I do like him. He exhibited such anger toward me, though.* Her thoughts tumbled over themselves. *What has Barkley figured out that I haven't?*

Chapter Seventy Five

Sergeant Irving picked up the phone. Convinced Collins told him the truth this time, his beefy fingers punched in the number for Jeremy Goodman. As soon as the investigator's voice responded to the ring on the other end, the sergeant identified himself and continued. "The detectives questioned the judge ... ohhhh, I hate calling him that ... anyway, Collins all night. He's given us some more names, a few we haven't looked at before but it appears like he's on a first name basis with most of the ringleaders. The group has been operating in the area for five years or more. A lot of kid's lives are destroyed. The creep says they eliminate them once their usefulness wanes. They're sold to someone in another city, turned out on the street, or killed. He blamed Fleming, said he never murdered anyone."

Irving noted Jeremy's tone of disgust. "Yeah, I appreciate that. Till last night. Anyway, we got him and some of the principles so I thought you'd wanna have the facts. We'll be rounding them up all day." He glanced around the near empty squad room. *Boys are gonna be busy.*

Jeremy congratulated the police for doing such a good job. "No, thank you and Christine. I think this case shook her up a little. She gonna be okay?" He listened as the younger man explained a little about their plans. "Oh, by the way, Collins planned to take care of her himself this time. To quote the good judge 'no more incompetents'. So I guess she's safe enough to carry on as usual."

Sergeant Irving ended his conversation with a promise from Jeremy to bring Christine around for a full statement. As he hung up, he sat down heavily. *I need a bath with disinfectant.* His grimace gave away the ugly images taking up space in his brain. He shook his head. *Glad I don't need to listen to anymore. For today anyway.* He gathered his jacket from the back of his chair and aimed for the main door.

"Sergeant, you going home this early?" The officer who manned the information counter slapped him on the back as he strode past. "Must be nice."

"Yeah, well, I worked here all night. My eyes are so scratchy; I can hardly keep them open. See ya tomorra." Irving walked through the door into a warm, sunny day. He looked toward the sky and strode to his private vehicle. Once inside, he placed his hands on the steering wheel, lay his head down, and wept. He cried for the families destroyed because of the perverse nature of mankind. His heart broke for the kids who would never be the same again and for those who would never enjoy another birthday. He shed tears for the ones still missing and those children who can't remember what love is or a safe place to sleep at night.

He relaxed against the cushions and looked out the window to scan the area for someone who might be watching. Sergeant Irving sniffed. *I used to enjoy this job. I thought I made a difference. Now the crud keeps getting deeper. We wipe the mess off but more takes its place.* He put his car in gear. He leaned toward the driver's door again. Images of three smiling faces filled his troubled thoughts. His grandchildren. He loved them almost more than he did his own kids. He needed to visit with them. He backed out of his parking space and headed toward his daughter's home. *I need a hug.*

Epilogue

Christine leaned her chin on her hand, her elbow resting on the desk she managed to salvage from her former home. She allowed her eyes to travel over the furnishings in her new office space. She sighed. *Even though I owned the little house, that residence never seemed as comfortable as this place.*

She searched through the storage unit holding her parent's twenty year old belongings. She kept a few pieces but donated the rest to the Mennonite Central Committee for their thrift shop. Christine added what she saved from her house and purchased anything else she needed to complete the look. *This is home.*

A faint knock sounded on the door connecting her space to Jeremy's and then the doorbell. He moved in three days ago. Christine pushed herself to her feet, limping a little from the recent fall she experienced when she tripped over Chief. "Come on boy. Let's go find out what the neighbour wants."

The canine stood slowly. "The shoulder still giving you some issues?" She patted his head. "I'm so happy the injury wasn't more serious. This scared me enough." The dog measured his steps to hers as they approached the locked door. The Goodman investigator decided the apartment suited his needs for more room to house his toys.

She unlocked the door and pulled the obstruction open to his infuriatingly perfect blue eyes. "What can I do for you neighbour?" she asked.

Jeremy held a cup in his hand. "May I borrow some sugar?" He grinned and winked at her.

"Yeah, right. What do you really want?" She placed her hands on hips encased in the usual tight fitting jeans.

Jeremy's grin grew wider as his gaze traveled the length of her. "You're looking mighty spiffy today. But I really need some of the white stuff. I'm baking cookies."

Christine let a giggle escape, "Most men are not so at ease in a kitchen. What kind of cookies? I may need to come sample a few when you're done." She led the way to her own cooking area, a more simply furnished room without all the gadgets like Jeremy's work space.

Jeremy followed, after wrapping his large hand around Chief's head and scratching his ears. "He's acting his old self again. Good." He entered the sparsely equipped kitchen. "I'm making oatmeal raisin. When are you going to purchase some cookware to display on your pot rack?"

Christine stuck her tongue out at him. "When my schedule allows. I can't seem to clear my calendar for the meeting with Rompart never mind thinking about doing any cooking. They're never going to trust me to run the company if I can't pull my act together." She opened her pantry door, walked in and grabbed the container of sugar he needed. "Is one cup enough?"

Jeremy appeared at her door. "This is a wonderful space. One will do. I should stock my apartment with all the essentials now that I'm living here permanently." He glanced at the empty containers decorating the counter. "What are you planning on using those for?"

"I'll store doggie treats in one and ...."

Jeremy howled. "Figures." He stepped back to let her pass. She attempted to put him in his place with a glance but to no avail. He laughed all the harder. "I never met a woman so inept in the kitchen."

Christine harrumphed as she passed him. "The cook always took care of this room and what went on inside. I worked the cattle with the boys. I led a busy life outside."

Jeremy set the cup of sugar on the granite countertop and

followed as she steered him toward the coffee maker. "Want some?"

"No. I'm good." He continued on into the living room. "Did you talk to Teresa Brent?"

"I did. She's concerned about the trial. Since Tommy is dead and so is Fine, Nathan won't need to testify but the whole affair is already all over the news. Every time the child listens to anything, he gets so quiet, his attitude scares her. Otherwise, she said he's doing great with his therapist. She's still keeping the kids home though, so I suggested maybe she needs to visit with someone to help her security issues again." Christine curled her feet under her on the sofa; the new one she purchased to match a love-seat and some occasional chairs. She painted her room a light gray to compliment the dark sofa.

Jeremy glanced at the decor he inspected for the first time. "When did they deliver these?"

"Yesterday. Like?"

"I do." He sat in one of the blue and gray chairs that seemed big enough to fit a man with a larger frame. "Is Teresa going to find someone?"

Christine frowned. "That's anyone's guess. But she's sure keeping a tight rein on those kids. They'll never move past this if she doesn't relax a little. Samantha's mom managed to give her daughter some freedom but life has been hard." She took a sip of the coffee she made earlier. "Those perverts don't just ruin the life of the children. Their entire family is affected. You spoke truth when you described this thing wicked disregard. They don't care."

Jeremy nodded his head. "And the law isn't tough enough. If the authorities in some third world country caught these creeps, I'm sure the punishment would more aptly fit the crime and would be a tremendous deterrent from any further thoughts along those lines." He let his gaze land on her face again. "You'll be much happier working at Rompart away from all this filth."

Christine seemed contemplative for a second. "I hope so but someone needs to continue to go after these guys. Irving says for every one we take off the streets, two more take their place. That's hard to fathom."

Jeremy leaned back in his chair and crossed his legs. "Do you remember what Pastor Isaacs said two weeks ago in church? We're living in a time several Bible writers prophesied as the end times. A characteristic is the rise in evil and that certainly is the case these days. No one mentioned anything about sex trafficking five years ago and now the news is full of the details."

"I certainly never overheard the term human attached to trafficking talked about in Texas but Uncle Conrad and Aunt Connie kept me pretty isolated from the rest of the world. Looking back, what happened outside the ranch was outside my purview. I'm not sorry I grew up that way. Just the reason behind the need. The dream is back, by the way." Christine's face gave away the intense feelings her nightmare evoked. She dropped her gaze.

"Does that mean we still need to find out why someone murdered your parents'? We discovered who but they killed him. The police ... or at least Irving ... thinks the guy who paid him to kill your mom and dad is still alive and that's who ordered the assassin eliminated. Maybe I need ..."

"No, we need." Christine grimaced. "I keep dragging my heels at going to work at Rompart and I think this unfinished business is behind my reluctance. This thing is hanging over my head and has to be removed before I can fully trust my board." As the last word left her mouth, the phone rang in her office. She stood and headed to the closed door, Chief right beside her.

Jeremy's eyes seared a hole in her back as she walked through the opened glass door. She grabbed the cell before the caller hung up "Hello. Yes, I'm Christine Finder." She listened to the frantic voice on the other end of the call. "Let's meet for coffee and you can tell me all the details. Are there pictures?"

She glanced toward the doorway as the woman used an incongruous term. Jeremy lounged against the frame listening to her part of the conversation. "Wait a minute. I thought Mennonites subsisted as a religious sect, very devout. How could ... never mind. We'll talk about all this at Tim Horton's. Say about an hour from now. Is that okay?"

The woman sounded impatient but agreed to meet anyway. Christine said good-bye and looked toward Jeremy. "She said she escaped from somewhere in Mexico and abandoned her kids. She wants someone to rescue them but she's scared out of her mind. I'll visit with her but this sounds like something way over my head. You interested?"

He straightened. "I might be but I thought you wanted to stop rescuing boys and girls from perverts?"

"I do but this doesn't sound the same. She called them the Mennonite Mafia. I thought these folks were good people. I gave them all my parents' furniture. They help people. Anyway, the woman said she'd explain more when we got together."

"Christine, we need to pray about this before we meet her. Maybe God doesn't want you doing this stuff any-more." Jeremy planted his feet apart and clasped his hands in front of his lanky frame.

She bowed her head as she sat on the edge of her desk. She didn't wait for Jeremy to begin. "Lord, please give us your guidance. More than we do, You understand what this is all about. Bring peace if this is something I or we should be do-ing? Amen."

Her mentor added, "Father, we trust there's a plan for our lives. You used us in the past to help people. Is this another one of those times? Send clear direction, Lord. Amen." He raised his head and looked toward Christine. "The word mafia raises the hair on the back of my neck. This might be way over both our heads."

"I appreciate your caution. But I said we ... er ... I'd meet her. Let's find out what this is all about and then we can de-cide. She sounded scared but she really seemed to believe what she said. I need to change. I'll be at the garage in 30 minutes. Okay?"

Jeremy turned toward his own doorway. "Are we taking your Jeep or my truck?"

"I'll drive. I have the direction for the Tim's she talked about. Later."

****

Christine pulled her Grand Cherokee into the first parking space she came to after turning into the Tim Horton's lot. As soon as she exited her vehicle, she smelled the tempting aroma of fresh brewed coffee. She motioned toward the never ending line up for the drive through and grinned. "I've never passed one of these shops without a line-up."

Jeremy fell into step beside her. "Yeah. I love their brew." He reached for the door handle and allowed Christine to enter ahead of him.

She slowly perused the patrons seated at nearby tables. One lone woman sat as far as possible from the other coffee drinkers, her fingers wrapped around a steaming cup. Christine inched toward her, her smile meant to put the woman at ease. The woman raised her head making eye contact. "Hi, are you ...?"

"You must be Christine Finder. Please. Sit." The woman looked to be barely out of her teens.

Christine glanced at Jeremy who already stood in line for their coffee. He acknowledged her as she sat in one of the chairs nestled around the table. She pointed to her cohort. "Jeremy Goodman is an investigator I work with sometimes. If you don't mind he's going to join us."

The woman reached her hand forward to shake Christine's. "My name is Helen Rempel. I don't care who meets with us as long as they're willing to help." Her hands shook as she lifted her mug and took a sip. "As I said on the phone, my kids need rescuing. I - I left them in Mexico about six months ago and ..."

"Why don't we wait until he joins us? Then you won't need to tell us your story twice." She perused the restaurant as Jeremy placed his order. "He won't be long."

Helen took another drink of coffee. "Shops like this didn't exist where I came from. We were lucky if we got to eat in a restaurant once a year. My husband pretended to be too busy to take us out anywhere." Her eyes glanced up as the man who accompanied Christine approached and set two cups down.

He reached his hand toward Helen. "Hi. I'm Jeremy." He took his seat and leaned an elbow on the table.

"I'm Helen. Rempel." She looked from one investigator to the other as if waiting for their signal to continue her story. Hesitantly, she began. "I escaped from our village about six months ago. The trip was so dangerous I didn't want to place my kids in harm's way so I left them. Now I want to hire you to free them before they get any older."

Jeremy posed the first question. "Out of where? Are they with your husband?"

Christine waited for Helen to give him the information. "Sounds to me as if you're afraid of him. Am I right? Do your children fear him, too?"

"They aren't probably in any danger yet. They're only 3 and 4 years of age. My daughter is four but the men begin using the girls around five years old. I don't want her to be raped by them." Her eyes glistened with unshed tears but her tone sounded matter of fact.

Jeremy flinched. "You mean some of the guys sexually abuse the kids where you come from?"

Christine interjected. "Surely your husband would protect his daughter. And what about your son?"

"The boys become mules for the drugs they smuggle into the surrounding cities and countries." Her flat tone gave away the tight rein on her emotions. Christine surmised she tried hard not to cry in the busy restaurant. Mrs. Rempel leaned forward and looked intently into Jeremy's eyes. "Not some of the men. All of them."

Jeremy gasped. "What kind of place do you come from?"

Helen wrapped her hands around her coffee cup again. "The community is a Mennonite village in that location since the beginning of World War 1 when many of our sect left Canada to escape conscription into the army. They are pacifists, at least when they arrived, but over the generations, their corrupt belief system made slaves out of the women and criminals out of the men. They kill anyone who crosses them and the people lie to the police who try to bring them to justice. Behind their back they are called mafia ... the Mennonite Mafia. They are ruthless, drug dealing murderers and I want my children safe and out of there."

"Can you obtain legal custody of them?" She found the extent of this woman's fear hard to understand. "Why not take your husband to court? Did the authorities post any outstanding charges against him?"

Helen shifted her gaze from Jeremy to Christine. Keeping her voice low, she responded. "No law exists to protect the people in my village. Women become chattel, handed off from one man to another. The children are all but ignored until they can assist in the illegal activities or until some man decides he needs a fresh body. My husband left me no choice but to leave when he traded me to a big, fat boss man who loves to beat his women." She hung her head. "I either escaped or I'd be dead by now. And then where would my little girl and boy be?"

Christine looked toward Jeremy. She shook her head as her eyes stared into the hot, dark brown brew in front of her. "Helen we are Christians. We want to pray about this and do some research before we give you an answer. Will that be okay?"

"Oh, but I thought ... I mean. Can't you make arrangements to go find them right away? They need me. They deserve their freedom from that hell hole as soon as possible." Helen leaned forward, pleading with her eyes. "You help find lost kids so I thought ..."

"We do." Jeremy placed a hand on her folded ones. The frightened woman pulled them back to her lap so fast she almost spilled her coffee. He sighed. "Sorry." He continued, "We can't just go into a foreign country to kidnap two children. A careful plan will take time and information. Can you supply us with everything you can on this village, where it's located, and the names of some of the criminals living in the community? Then we'll decide. Okay."

The woman's face drained of any remaining colour. "You want me to rat out those guys? They'll kill me."

Christine reached across the table and took one of the trembling hands from Helen's lap. "Do you want us to succeed? Precautions are needed so your kids aren't hurt in the process. A clear understanding of everything about the place and the people will help us be successful in our mission. We'll contact you in a few days. Okay?"

Christine and Jeremy rose at the same time, leaving the warmth of their chairs for another patron. Helen followed their example. She handed them a piece of paper. "Here's my phone number. Please call me as soon as you've decided whether you're going to take my case or not. If you don't go, I need to find someone else." Her disappointment hung heavy in the air. Her face clouded. "I can't believe someone who finds missing kids would abandon mine." She stalked out the door and walked quickly away.

Christine looked at Jeremy as they, too, exited the coffee shop. "I thought we ... I was finished with all this." She sighed as she followed him back to the Jeep. "Now what are we going to do?"

Dear Reader

If you liked Wicked Disregard, I would appreciate it if you would help others enjoy this book, too, by recommending to friends, family, and book clubs, and/or by writing a positive review for Amazon, Barnes and Nobles, Goodreads, and Smashwords.

If you do write a review, please send me an email at barbarawrites14@gmail.com. I'd like to add you to my e-newsletter list so that you can get updates about upcoming new releases. Thank You.

Watch For
the fourth book in the
Finders Keepers Series
Coming 2017

Finder's Keepers Mystery Series

BOOK ONE

An ominous shadow hangs over her, as Christine Finder, alias Melissa Rompart, visits the brutal slaying of her parents most nights in a dream. The threat of discovery propels her to search for the whereabouts of the killer to see the man brought to justice. In the meantime, the killer stalks her mind while she operates Finder's Keepers, an agency that searches for the people her clients hire her to find. Nathan Brent is only four years old and missing. Will she find him in time or will the killer find her first?

http://amzn.to/1io0CKR

313

BOOK TWO

Evil pursues Christine, in this the second book of the Finders Keepers Mystery Series. Retreat is not an option but her move forward makes her vulnerable to the very evil that took her parents' lives. Faced with yet another missing child, she embarks on a search that takes her out of her comfort zone to question her chosen career, her abilities, and her belief system as she helps stricken parents find closure. Christine finds herself confused about her growing interest in Jeremy but she is distracted by the essence of evil that surrounds her.

http://http://amzn.to/1mdOQWa

More books by Barbara Ann Derksen
Wilton/Strait Murder Mystery series

Book 1

Vanished! That's what Andrea Wilton and Brian Strait discover when they come to visit their best friends one evening. Where could they be and does God answer prayers, two questions they find the answers to as they journey to another world of voodoo, murder, and more missing people. Andrea and Brian also discover each other as they learn to scuba, fight a common enemy, and search for the proverbial needle in a haystack.

http://amzn.to/VjW34a

Book 2

Andrea Wilton and Brian Strait, from *Shuster Detective Agency*, take on another case to find a missing person. This second book in the series introduces DJ Wiebe, a biker who rides with The Sons Riders, a Christian biker ministry. Another biker, a member of The Demons Raiders, is missing and presumed dead. DJ, his friend, hires *Shuster Detective Agency* to find him. He initiates Andrea and Brian into the biker culture, a world that encompasses motorcycles, leather, drugs and murder.

http://amzn.to/HO63y7;

Book 3

Brian Strait and Andrea Wilton discover that relationship and intrigue go together when they embark on their third adventure, back to the Caribbean. A visit cut short, the two sleuths uncover a plot that challenges their faith

when they search to clear a friend of murder. Their hunt for truth brings them head to head with the black market, human contraband, and culprits who will stop at nothing to line their pockets.

http://amzn.to/HHSfmB

Book 4

Brian Strait and Andrea Wilton leave behind a cruise ship at the Miami harbor for a short visit in the bustling metropolis. Their plans are to purchase wedding finery before flying to the Dominican Republic to marry.

A surprise awaits Andrea when she arrives at the bridal boutique. Trent and Diane Michner, best friends, are waiting to share their special day with them. Andrea believes everything is perfect.

Fate has other plans, however, when Diane and Andrea are kidnapped by Chechen mafia members who spirit women away to several other countries into slavery. Andrea fears for her friend's life when Diane is taken elsewhere. In captivity, she wonders if her wedding was just a pipe dream and where God is in all this. She also encounters a young girl who is hurting and in need of a Savior.

Brian, with the help of Trent and a young friend from the Dominican Republic, Troy, begins a frantic search for his bride-to-be, encountering drug addicts, dirty cops, and murder victims. His faith in God is stretched as he wonders why this has happened to them at this time in their life.

http://amzn.to/13WlYaW

More genres by
Barbara Ann Derksen

Children's Books
Shih-Tzu Puppy Adventures
Scruffles Finds a Home
Squirrels Are People, too

Devotionals
Straight Pipes
Two-Up, Riding with the Lord
Chrome, Shining Faith
Chaps
Road Trip
More Than Bells

Other
Dance With a Broom
Second to None, Warrior Voices

**All books can be purchased and shipped
directly to you from
www.barbaraannderksen.com or email:
barbarawrites14@gmail.com to find out more**

Acknowledgements

It takes a team to complete a book. I wish to thank my Lord for the gift of writing. Without it my imagination would remain tethered and frustrated. But above all, I thank Him for the ideas, the audience, and for the opportunity to learn new skills every day as I home my craft and interact with other writers.

 I wish to thank everyone who has ever read one of my books and for your diligence in placing a review where you purchased the book. Without you, my words would remain hidden and of no use to anyone.

I also wish to thank my husband for his patience. His input is important to the finished product as he helps me stay true to my male protagonist by making suggestions as he proofs the book.

Linda and LeRoy Collins are special friends who help me find missed typos, overworked words, and inconsistencies. I truly appreciate the time they expend on my behalf.

I also wish to thank Laura J Davis for doing a simple edit of this latest book. Her suggestions have been most helpful and I have learned a lot about writing and mine in particular.

I really do hope that you enjoy this latest attempt to give your imagination a workout as we delve into another world and step out of your comfort zone into Christian Suspense.